# ROBERT LOCK

# *Murmuration*

Legend Press Ltd, 107-111 Fleet Street, London, EC4A 2AB
info@legend-paperbooks.co.uk I www.legendpress.co.uk

Contents © Robert Lock 2018
The right of the above author to be identified as the author of this work has
been asserted in accordance with the Copyright, Designs and Patents Act
1988. British Library Cataloguing in Publication Data available.

Print ISBN 978-1-78-719824-1
Ebook ISBN 978-1-78719823-4
Set in Times. Printing managed by Jellyfish Solutions Ltd.
Cover design by Gudrun Jobst I www.yotedesign.com

**Robert Lock** began a degree in Applied Biology, but decided science wasn't for him. He worked in Paris and then as a tour director taking US students round Europe. He eventually became a professional photographer, writing three novels in his spare time before *Murmuration*.

The story is set in a seaside resort, its characters inspired by those he has met through his job on the local newspaper.

The title came to him while watching the starlings dance over and around North Pier.

*To Caroline, for always knowing when I needed to write*

# Yesterday

# Murmuration

"Roll up! Roll up!"

Look! There he stands, scarlet frock coat flapping in the breeze, a circus ringmaster balanced, improbably, on top of the promenade railing. In one white-gloved hand his top hat continues the line of his outstretched arm as he gesticulates towards the birds now gathering on the pier theatre roof, while with the other he beckons to his audience, drawing them in.

"Roll up!" he hollers again, moustache flexing. "See the artistry of nature displayed for your delectation and delight! Take your seats for the greatest show in town! Never the same performance two nights running! A miraculous demonstration of timing and synchronisation in such numbers as to take your breath away! Watch these masters of the air as they perform their mysterious dance only inches from disaster!"

But is this merely circus ballyhoo designed to lure the gullible? Indeed it is not. Not here, not as a mauve-coloured dusk settles on the resort, like the house lights dimming. The birds assemble in their hundreds, their thousands, and the wind quietens, for it feels something akin to love towards the starlings. There is something of the wind made visible in what the starlings do.

They come, until the theatre's white roof is black with them, drawn irresistibly to this priapic statement of Victorian engineering. But is it merely instinct that calls them? And why the pier? The town possesses any number of edifices that would suit their purpose just as well, so why do the starlings choose the pier? Perhaps it is simply easier to target from the air, a bold exclamation mark standing out from the resort's jumble of rooftops. Perhaps the clear air around the pier affords the birds a broader canvas on which to work. Or maybe it is simply that they recognise the resort's heart, its defining venue, and know their nightly show deserves top billing.

Then, as though on some secret signal, the birds take off. For a moment there seems only chaos, a dark explosion above the theatre, but within seconds the starlings settle into their shifting cloud: the murmuration. Could there be a more appropriate noun? What better word is there to describe the sound of an audience as the curtain rises on a much-anticipated performance? Whoever coined it had a poet's touch.

Up, down, back and forth, changes of direction and rhythm as perfectly orchestrated and paced as the finest symphony. Yet the display's most astonishing fact is that it weaves this magic from nothing more than thousands of birds flying wingtip to wingtip. Are there leaders amongst the flock, dictating its course? Maybe the movements are externally driven, either by subtle atmospheric changes or magnetic fields. And whatever their motivation, how do the birds on each manoeuvre's outer edge know that they must fly slightly faster than those in its centre? Because there is never a collision, or a moment's hesitation; the starlings dance, impeccably, for perhaps half an hour, before scattering to their roosts across the resort, returned to the individual scraps of black which no one deems worthy of a second glance. It is like the dismantling of some kinetic sculpture by its dissatisfied artist, who flings the fragments to their studio's furthest corners, where they will lie until tomorrow's twilight brings them together once again.

No one will squabble with the ringmaster now, demanding their money back. They have seen the greatest show in town, that much is certain. In fact they are slightly embarrassed by their former cynicism. Yes, they heeded his call, because humankind has a fondness for showmen which does not necessitate a belief in their claims, but, in all honesty, they were not expecting much. What can a few birds achieve, after all? And then, as the starlings began to shapeshift above them, a silence settled on the crowd which reflected a different form of disbelief, one born out of enchantment. There is little room for magic in this tumultuous modern world — it requires quiescence and humility — so when it does manifest itself the contemporary mind tends to over-analyse the spell being cast. You can see the questions in their upturned faces: how can so many thousands of individuals act in such concord, with such beauty? What allows them to subsume their own needs and desires for the sake of this hypnotic display? And to what purpose?

A small, dark-haired boy watches the birds and tries to visualise what they are seeing. He imagines it must be similar to the thrilling disorientation of a rollercoaster, all tilting horizons and surging undulations, but a child's imagination, for all its strengths, tends to the anthropomorphic. The starlings are born to fly, so their eyes are perfectly attuned to spatial freedom. If only the boy could glimpse, even for a moment, what the birds see. Because the murmuration is a collective not only in flight, but also in vision.

As individuals, starlings have good eyesight, but in their thousands they are able to see through the world's disguises and discern the beauty or horror that lies beneath. Mother Nature has need of a monitoring system with which to oversee the behaviour and wellbeing of the creatures living within her borders; what could be better to act as agent than the ubiquitous starling, the dowdy starling, the unremarkable starling? Their ancient eyes, calibrated to detect the smallest of details, when multiplied a thousand-fold become a truly awesome sense. Listen to them chatter as they fly! This is their ongoing visual narrative, a stream of information regarding the small field of view available to each one of them as it tilts and scrolls beneath their wings, passed on to every other starling in the flock. Each of these fractions, processed within the murmuration and converted into an astonishingly detailed picture, offers a true window on the world for an otherwise blind Gaia.

And, as the birds have danced above the pier for one hundred and fifty years, how many lives have passed beneath them, how many stories? Men and women, their children, their children's children; lives so brief and fragile when compared to the enduring strength of the pier, but possessing a depth of feeling that iron and timber would exchange their immutability for in an instant. Only the ephemeral can truly appreciate the infinite.

Who, then?

In 1880 the starlings see Georgie Parr, music hall comic, emerge from beneath the pier, walk for some distance across the sloping shingle and then sink slowly to his knees, fall forward onto his hands and vomit.

In 1941 the starlings see Mickey Braithwaite, proud member of the Observer Corps, sitting on the edge of his sandbagged look-out post as he watches their movements above him with sweet and imperfect eyes, imprinting on his mind a message which would turn him into a hero.

In 1965 the starlings see fortune-teller Bella Kaminska hurrying to close her booth. In her haste she drops her key — there, there it goes, falling through a gap between the decking's planks, caught like a dying ember in the last shard of sunset — and leaves the shutter unlocked, such is her need to be free of the pier.

In 1989 the starlings see Colin Draper, pier archivist and local historian, slumped in a deckchair where he has been all day, his soft, flabby body wrapped in a grey raincoat. He appears utterly amorphous, more discarded sack than man.

Today the starlings see comedian Sammy Samuels through the window of his dressing room above the pier theatre. He lights another cigarette with the glowing tip of his current one, grinds out the stub and picks up a copy of the local paper.

But is this the extent of their vision? Of course not.

As Georgie Parr steps out of the dark green shadows beneath the pier the starlings notice two small scratches on his jaw. His hair is dishevelled, and one sleeve of his coat has been ripped at the seam. There is a staccato quality to the way Georgie's limbs move, as though he keeps forgetting how to walk, and the starlings can tell that the tears running down his face are for others long dead.

They watch Mickey squint upwards. The birds know how much he is enjoying their display by the wonder in his tenaciously blue eyes; they also know that the extraordinary events of that night's blackout will fundamentally change him and leave this most guileless of men with an enduring appreciation of life's secret lyricism.

The starlings note a creamy wink from Bella's moonstone ring as her trembling hands attempt to guide the padlock through the shutter's hasp. The key falls and vanishes, to await its discovery in the twenty-first century by a metal detector enthusiast, who is disappointed by his corroded find and tosses it aside. Bella gestures her abandonment of the booth and hurries away, leaving the shutter to inch upwards, revealing some of the faded photographs depicting her more well-known clients. One has fallen from its original position and now lies on the windowsill, the bleached image of a popular singer standing next to Bella, his features reduced to a pale rictus. The fortune-teller heads towards the resort without a backward glance, so she never sees a starling flutter down from the onion-shaped dome of the booth to stand on the pier and watch her go. It fluffs the feathers on its back, a gesture that looks remarkably like a shrug.

With Colin the birds are quite able to discern the two sorrows that struggle for supremacy within his innocuous frame, and which have pinned him to the pier for hour after hour as he tries to reconcile them both. They also note the dandruff sprinkled on the upturned collar of his coat, the scuffed toes of his shoes, and an affinity for the pier so deeply felt that he is almost as much a part of its structure as the girders and planks.

The dressing room window affords a glimpse of Sammy Samuels' isolation, a detachment assiduously worked towards over his many years in showbusiness and which he now maintains with a seething, relentless dedication. They see a felt-tip circle round one of the 'escort' advertisements in the local newspaper. More than anything, though, the starlings recognise a coldness in the comedian's eye which shakes them to their core.

Each generation of birds can also sense a connection between all five people, like a slender and yet vital thread, though this conjugation of fates is at the very limit of even the starlings' vision. They see it, but not its details, nor the extraordinary parallels that reverberate backwards and forwards along the thread, giving it its strength as well as its calamitous ending. The starlings are content within their limitations, however; they defer to a superior vision, which observes Georgie, Mickey, Bella, Colin and Sammy in their naked whole, mindful that an untimely death will shiver along the thread from one to the next until it finds reconciliation. The starlings, knowing what they can see in these briefest of moments, are terrified by the concept of how much detail there is to be observed across a century and more. They know it would send their tiny bodies spiralling upwards into the darkest blue, until their beaks gaped in the vacuum of space and the swirling planet below was reflected in the smaller universe of their eyes.

Moments. That's all we can cope with. Fleeting moments, and yet they can be filled with the kind of detail and mystery that characterise so much of the pier's history. And if one second, seen through the right eyes, can hold within it the lives of five people, what else is a description of an hour, or a week, or a year, than an exercise in omission? Is this how the birds dance around what would otherwise be an overwhelming narrative? If only we could ask the starlings.

If only.

# 1865

# The New Frontier

The air vibrated with incessant hammering as labourers riveted together another section of the pier. Pairs of them were positioned along the wooden scaffolding, timing their blows in perfect synchronisation to drive home and spread the red-hot rivet, whilst a third wielding a large pair of tongs prepared to pluck the next from a brazier of coals. Further out, towards the low tide mark, a team of men laboured at a capstan, which was gradually screwing a pile deep into the sand. A sheen of sweat sparkled on their bare backs, and snatches of what sounded like a rhythmic sea shanty carried on the breeze to the resort's early visitors, who were taking the air on its new promenade.

George Parr guided his wife Katherine to the railing so that they could watch the work more closely. Their train had arrived the day before, carrying them to the coast on gleaming new railway lines and depositing them in a town where construction work seemed to be taking place on every street corner. Long terraces of bay-windowed homes, the ornate facades of impressive stucco or red-brick hotels, foundations covering an acre of ground where a winter gardens and theatre were to stand. The resort, blossoming at remarkable speed from its origins as a coastal farmstead and cocklers' cottages, was an incredibly dynamic and exciting place to be, particularly as George was attempting to build his reputation as a music hall entertainer. Here, he felt, was where his future lay; the resort possessed an almost tangible air of confidence, of unlimited potential. His career was choking on the squalid vapours of England's city theatres, but here was space, and light, and clarity. These were surely the perfect conditions in which to perform.

"They say it's to be longer than the pier in Margate, by all accounts," George informed his wife.

Katherine, whose hand was resting in the crook of her husband's arm, gave him a playful squeeze. "Why do men love iron and steam and noise so?"

"Do we?"

"Oh, yes. The only things that can bring a tear to a man's eye are engines or bridges or ships. I think you would all love to be engineers, hammering and banging away."

George grasped the wrought-iron railing in front of him, as though there were some answer to be found within the metal. "I suppose they are all attempts to impose our will on nature," he replied. George surprised himself at the rapidity and intuitiveness of his response, which he felt sure was down to his wife's bright and enquiring mind. Katherine loved to analyse and discuss any number of subjects, and even though it was not considered seemly for her to voice her opinion too rigorously across the dining table or in public, she often took the opportunity when they were alone to engage her husband in debate. He loved her all the more for her wit and reasoning, which he knew had sharpened his own mind in necessary response, but George Parr was still Victorian enough to occasionally feel uncomfortable with the suspicion that Katherine was his intellectual superior.

"Ah," she exclaimed, "so really these vessels and structures are for their creator's gratification and honour. Why else attach a maker's mark to them?"

"But," George countered, "doesn't any creator deserve recognition? Writers have their name on the front of their books... artists sign their paintings... is a bridge any less of an achievement?"

"Certainly not. It will probably endure for far longer than most books, *and* be of more use."

George turned to look at his wife. With the sun directly behind her parasol her profile was reduced to little more than sharp-edged shadow, giving a close approximation to the black paper silhouette that they had both posed for whilst at a fairground soon after their wedding. When the silhouette artist first showed Katherine her image she had argued that it was more caricature than portrait — 'You've made me look like Mr Punch' she had grumbled — but George could see how the set of her jaw grew bolder when she became absorbed in a discussion.

"I find it hard to determine on which side of the argument you stand," he complained. "Are you saying you agree with me, Kate?"

She smiled slightly. "A prudent wife will always agree with her husband, my darling."

"Is that so?"

"Indeed it is. However, you are a man, George Parr, and will always look at the world through a man's eyes. Certainly I would not want you to look at *me* through any other."

George was shocked. "Katherine!"

"But," she continued calmly, "you will necessarily observe things differently, and that is only right and proper. Take the pier, for example."

"The pier?"

"I think it illustrates my point perfectly. You, my darling, doubtless regard the pier as another example of our society's wonderful engineering skills. Its iron and wood have been tamed and turned into something useful. The sea and the beach have been conquered, the engineer's legacy assured. I, on the other hand, look at the pier as it emerges and wonder about all the hundreds of people who will one day walk along it, who will laugh, and cry, and do all the other things that make us unique. What will it see, George? What will the pier see?"

"I think you do men a disservice, Kate. We are not completely insensible to the..." he delved for the correct word, "*soul* of a structure, and what it might mean to the people who use it."

Katherine looked up at her husband and noticed for the first time that his dark sideburns now contained one or two flecks of grey in front of his ears. These minuscule signs of time's passage made her feel, for one horrible moment, immensely sad; was George Parr destined for disappointment in life? To be denied fulfillment in his greatest ambition?

"Do you see it?" She asked, pointing out to where the furthest pile was being driven.

"See what?"

"The pavilion! Our engineers love to finish their piers with a splendid pavilion, all domes and turrets like an Indian palace. And whose name is posted there, top of the bill? Why, Georgie Parr of course! The pier has made you famous, my love."

George strived to extrapolate the struts and latticework and beams already assembled and imagine the rest of the structure reaching out, forever to impose its form on the horizon's as yet unbroken parallels, but the resulting mirage, a translucent and flimsy construct that danced before his eyes like a trick of the light, could never have borne the weight of a pavilion or theatre. It lingered for a moment, little more than a spider's web, until a gull's harsh scream overhead broke the spell, and there was only sea, and sky.

"You can see further than me, Kate," he said, unable to disguise the self-reproach in his voice. "Finding a space in the halls for the following week taxes my mind to its limit."

"Then you must hire an agent," Katherine determined, "so that all your efforts are brought to bear on your act."

He laughed and shook his head. "If there is an agent to be had who does not require payment then I shall take him on immediately."

Katherine swivelled the parasol so that half of it was behind her husband's head and half hers, effectively shielding them from anyone on the promenade. They were enclosed in a diffusely lit microcosm, its only window facing out to the expectant sea. "George Parr," she began, all playfulness gone from her voice, "the man I married was determined and ambitious, a fighter to the last. If he has departed then I see no reason why I should remain either."

George was stunned. The railing beneath his hand felt suddenly red-hot, forcing him to relinquish his grip. "Are you saying—"

"George, look at me."

He focused on her eyes, and saw in them such love and belief that he came close to tears.

"We have no money," she stated, "and that is perfectly fine. Our home is a succession of small rented houses with peeling wallpaper and blocked chimneys, and that also is perfectly fine. My father has not spoken to me properly since I went against his express wishes and married what he described to me as a 'music hall clown', and that, too, is perfectly fine. What I cannot countenance is your surrender, my darling George. To abandon your dreams now, when I *know* they are within your reach, would be not only a huge loss to the theatre, but also a betrayal of my faith in you. You are *funny*, Georgie Parr. Do you not hear the laughter? Are you struck deaf on stage?"

He took a breath. There was a sharp edge to the air, the iodine clarity of seaweed, that caught in his throat, and in that moment George understood that his destiny lay here, in the resort, performing on the pier above the waves. "Do you know, I distinctly recall an encore at Clerkenwell last month, and I am almost sure it was for me!"

Katherine giggled. "Of course it was for you! I remember when you came home, you were so excited you couldn't sleep."

"Ah, a most unfortunate bout of dyspepsia, as I recall."

"That's better!"

"I think this sea air agrees with me," George said, taking another deep breath. "It has the same effect as a good wine."

A rhythmic squeak was approaching from their left. George and Katherine turned to see an old man being pushed along the promenade in a wicker bath chair. A thick rug of dark blue wool almost totally enveloped what was clearly a desperately thin body, but his hands, which were draped limply on the chair's tiller like two white gloves, seemingly retained strength enough to steer while his nurse pushed from behind. A tweed deerstalker hat, ear-flaps down, sat loosely on his head, which was as pale and mottled as his hands.

As the chair drew level with them George touched the brim of his bowler hat and Katherine smiled sweetly. The old man lifted the index finger of his right hand, indicating to the nurse that he wished to stop, a request she complied with immediately.

"A beautiful day, sir," George noted.

The old man's eyes moved slowly in their sockets, a cautious investigation of some visionary quadrant bounded by illness or weariness, as though to assess for himself the accuracy of George's observation. "A beautiful day," he confirmed, in a voice as thin and translucent as tissue paper.

"George Parr, sir, and this is my wife Katherine."

"Francis Delahay," the old man replied.

"We were just remarking on the quality of the air," Katherine said. "Are you visiting the resort as part of your recuperation, Mr Delahay?"

The old man's breathing, rapid and so shallow that it hardly moved the blanket on his chest, quickened slightly. "I fear… matters are somewhat… advanced… for even the… sweetest of air to… " The natural rhythm of pauses between breaths lengthened as he searched his mind for the right word. "… effect any… lasting… recuperation."

"Our apologies, sir," George said, embarrassed by Katherine's unwitting *faux pas*. "My wife did not intend any discourtesy."

Francis Delahay raised one hand slightly to dismiss the apology. "I have… been given… quite some time… to become accustomed… to my illness. It is as… familiar and aggravating as… a family member."

Katherine knelt down beside the bath chair and laid her hand lightly on top of the old man's bloodless appendages. The nurse was so astonished by this gesture of intimacy from a total stranger that she let out an audible gasp, but Francis himself seemed unperturbed. Indeed, the ghost of a smile flickered across his face.

"Your hand... is warm," he noted.

"And you, Mr Delahay, are a brave and kind man."

The nurse, somewhat mollified by her charge's reaction, made a show of arranging his blanket. "Mr Delahay was an officer under Lord Nelson," she informed them proudly in a broad West Country burr. "Fought at Trafalgar, he did."

"Trafalgar! Then you are indeed brave."

Again the dismissive lift of the hand. "I was... a terrified... midshipman... on the *Tonnant*." Francis' pale blue eyes, so absent they seemed to look out from another age, drew to some semblance of focus at his accurate French pronunciation of the ship's name. "The gunners... knew what to do...Captain Tyler... had drilled us... mercilessly. They had little need... of me."

Katherine looked up and addressed the nurse. "Have you looked after Mr. Delahay for long?"

"Nearly two months," the woman stated proudly. "Mr Delahay's family took me on as sick nurse from the Westminster Training School, and I'll be with him to the end, whenever the Good Lord deems it fit."

"In that case... " her patient remarked, "my dearest Miss... Winterbottom... pray do not... unpack... your summer clothes."

George, Katherine and the nurse exchanged the briefest of glances, which nonetheless communicated, in the fullest terms possible, their admiration for and sympathy with this man, still capable of self-deprecating humour even when fully aware of his impending fate. Perhaps it was simply a defence mechanism, a show of bravado in the face of death, but Francis Delahay's spirit shone from within the failing husk of his body and rendered every detail of the resort sharper and more precious. The sun glittering on a ruffled sea; the scarlet diamond of a child's kite weaving a pattern of delight on the blue sky; the salty tang carried on the wind from a whelk-seller's cart, all made beautiful by one man's valedictory excursion. Even the growing limb of the pier, which Francis Delahay would never see completed, appeared more solid, as though by acknowledging his own destruction the old sailor had granted the accretion of wood and metal a blessing. 'I take my leave,' he was, in effect, saying, 'but you must stay, and give many more people an afternoon like this.'

Katherine gave his hands the lightest of squeezes, imperceptible to anyone but its recipient, and stood up. "Enjoy the rest of your promenade," she said.

"Godspeed, sir," George added.

Mr Delahay closed his eyes and nodded, seemingly exhausted by their brief conversation.

"He tires so easily," Miss Winterbottom explained, tucking in the blanket so tightly it seemed as much restraint as comfort, "but thank you for your kind words." She glanced up at them. "Do you live here?"

George looked at his wife, who raised her eyebrows in an exaggerated expression of amusement. "We hope to," was his cautious reply.

"It *is* a lovely place," the nurse said, returning to her position behind the bath chair. "There's something about the seaside, isn't there?"

"Indeed there is," George concurred. But what? What was it behind the nurse's vague perception that created the resort's magic? Could it be bound up in the geography, the dynamism and uncertainty of the frontier? Did having your feet planted securely on good Victorian engineering allow one to better contemplate the stark mirror of an ungovernable ocean?

Miss Winterbottom set off with little more effort than that which would have been required had the bath chair been empty, and yet, despite the flimsy nature of its contents, the chair carried with it the ballast of a good life, a life played out as much on the sea as on land. Perhaps this was why former Midshipman Delahay could regard his imminent annihilation with such equanimity; a lifetime's intimacy with the sea, its benediction of safe passage over so many years, had given him a sense of perspective barely glimpsed by those who contemplated the waves from the promenade. Maybe the pier, which in many ways was a vessel of sorts, would offer those who stepped aboard some fraction of his insight.

George watched the bath chair and its attendant squeak grow smaller, quieter, until it was obscured entirely by a horse-drawn bathing carriage being guided towards the beach. "Trafalgar!" He exclaimed. "Imagine being able to say that you fought at the Battle of Trafalgar!"

Katherine returned her hand to the crook of her husband's arm. She was sure Francis Delahay thought of the battle in far less romantic terms than did George, but she realised that to point this out could easily jeopardise all her efforts to instill in him a more optimistic outlook. She decided instead to impart a piece of information that, for the past month, she had kept secret for fear of any celebrations proving premature. Now, however, Katherine was sure of both her condition and its relative stability. The flutterings of a waning life that she had felt through the veteran sailor's skin had somehow resonated with the stirrings of the new one within her, as though Francis had urged her to take George into her confidence.

"I'm pregnant, George," she said. "Shall we walk a little further?"

# Zlatka

Almost six months had elapsed since their trip to the seaside, and now George was back plying his trade on the stages of London. In Islington the Collins' Music Hall audience were being particularly raucous and unforgiving that evening. Those in the gallery, which traditionally housed members of the public with an inclination to voice their opinion about the turns, had concocted a series of put-downs and heckles that, though undeniably trenchant, were also offensive and cruel. Their latest victim was the girl currently on stage, a contortionist from the Far East who had burst into tears in the middle of her performance. George, watching from the wings as the next act on, felt some sympathy for her, though this was tempered by her obvious understanding of her tormentors' vivid anatomical references, making him question her claimed Siamese origins. But then, he admitted to himself, all of us who step on to these boards are, to some extent, a fiction, constructed to better clothe the bones of our act. If this young woman said goodbye in a broad East End accent to her Limehouse family as she left for work in the afternoon, and yet the moment she stepped through the stage door of a theatre she became the 'Silent Rubber-Limbed Disciple from the Golden Temple of Chiang Mai', then what did it matter? Music hall audiences were, by and large, all too familiar with the mundane; what they wanted… what they *demanded*, was to be transported to somewhere extraordinary, and if this required a degree of credulity that was unlikely to be countenanced in everyday life then they were more than willing to give it, if that act then repaid their trust with a few minutes of laughter, wonder or song.

To her credit, the contortionist wiped away her tears and carried on, hooking one leg round the back of her neck and then gradually raising herself on tiptoe whilst balanced on a small three-legged stool. Whether it was a gesture of support for her resolve, appreciation of the pose, or a combination of both, the contortionist received a generous round of applause. Even the gallery audience fell silent, a truce that disconcerted George somewhat as he imagined them re-grouping for another assault on the following act.

A hand landed on his shoulder and gripped him tightly. "Damn near see straight down Cock Lane when she does that, eh Mr Parr?"

George smiled. He did not have to turn to know who had whispered the lewd comment in his ear. "You have the morals of a sewer rat, Henry Dickinson," he replied.

"Ay," the stagehand conceded, "but still, a tumble with the likes of madam there'd be an experience, don't you think?"

The contortionist had replaced the stool with a velvet-covered block. This heralded her final and most extraordinary pose, meaning of course that George would soon be following her into the cold and unforgiving limelight. He felt his heart begin to beat more rapidly, and he fiddled nervously with the cheap satin of his cravat, which had unaccountably begun to scrape against his neck like sandpaper.

Settling herself stomach down on the block, the black-haired young woman began to arch her back, at the same time slowly raising both feet, curling her legs until she could reach backwards and catch hold of the ballet pumps, thus forming an almost perfect 'O' shape of body and limb. George found himself staring at the gently curving mound between her legs, pushing against her tight-fitting suit as she brought her feet lower and lower until they rested on the block on either side of her head. He tried to put the stage hand's comments from his mind, but there was a frankness about the contortionist's display, an eroticism that could not be denied. He imagined kneeling in front of her, ripping open the cloth of her suit to allow him access. How dark she would be, a coarse and vigorous blackness so unlike Katherine's soft pale brown. What would it be like to enter her while her body, both internally and externally, was so tautly coiled?

Satisfied with the positioning of her feet, the contortionist paused for dramatic effect, taking in several deep breaths as though preparing for one last supreme effort. The orchestra drummer began a slow crescendo on the snare, and from his position behind the curtain George could sense the audience draw closer, quieten, until the hiss of the limelight burners could be heard. The contortionist shifted slightly, manoeuvring her arm backwards, wincing as her shoulder-blade became more and more prominent until, with an audible crack, her right arm angled up behind her head and she grasped her left knee. There were gasps and several noises of sympathetic discomfort, but the girl was not finished. The drum grew more insistent. Gritting her teeth, the contortionist began the same process with her left arm, but this time when the pop of dislocation echoed round the theatre she let out a thin wail of pain. Breathing heavily now, and shutting her eyes for one last supreme effort, she inched her hand closer and closer, fingers trembling with the effort, until at last she clasped hold of her right knee. Tilting back her head triumphantly, her smile directed at the auditorium was the perfect combination of accomplishment tempered with the suffering required to achieve it. The orchestra gave her a climactic hit and the audience burst into vigorous applause, including a scattering of whistles and shouts.

As the applause continued the girl began to disentangle herself, resetting her arms with little more than a sort of rotational shrug, straightening her back and rising off the block until upright, banal, even, she gave a slow bow that did not stop at ninety degrees, or one hundred, or one hundred and twenty, but simply carried on, her body closing together like the victim of some invisible instrument of torture. When her forehead touched her shins the applause redoubled, but the contortionist knew not to hold the stage and risk losing the audience. In one graceful movement she straightened again, gave a final, more conventional bow and hurried into the wings. As she passed George the smell of her filled his nostrils, a potent combination of musky perfume and sweat that, to his alarm, aroused him in a far more guttural and brutish manner than ever his Katherine could have done. Her feral odour was like a physical affirmation of the stage-hand's coarse remarks. George felt intoxicated and ashamed, attracted and repelled in equal measure, but no matter how he tried to picture' Katherine's clear blue unswerving gaze all he could really think of was the contortionist's slightly hooded brown eyes as she glanced at him in passing. There had been little or no emotion in that glance, apart perhaps from the natural empathy of a fellow performer, and yet there was something quite beguiling in this absence. It spoke of simplicity and detachment, an unequivocal eroticism.

Sam Collins, owner of the theatre and a fine singer in his own right, strode to centre-stage. "Ladies and gentlemen… ladies and gentlemen, your appreciation again for Areva, the Rubber-Limbed Disciple from the Golden Temple of Chiang Mai!" He thrust one hand in the direction of the wings. "Quite remarkable. Quite remarkable." The applause died down. "And now, ladies and gentlemen, it is my very great pleasure to introduce a comedian who is no stranger to this stage… but I've asked him back again anyway!" The laughter was generous, because the people of Islington were grateful to Sam for providing them with a cheap source of entertainment. He held up his hands for quiet. "He's back to make you forget your troubles, so let's have a big Collins' Music Hall welcome for the Lord of Laughter, the Camden Clown, your very own… Georgie Parr!"

George bounded onto the stage, almost colliding with Sam,

who made a great show of avoiding him. Their accidental choreography was well-timed enough to appear part of the act and elicited a good deal of laughter, but what the audience could not see was the theatre owner's expression, which was so venomous and intimidating that George forgot his opening line. For several interminable seconds he stood there, staring out at the expectant faces. He could sense the audience's receptivity, its willingness to find him funny, but George knew that this warmth could evaporate in moments; he had to capture them now, or risk being heckled mercilessly for the rest of his act. And then Henry Dickinson's off-stage remark echoed in his mind like some vulgar prompt. To the stagehand it was little more than a throwaway remark, the sort of thing he might say to friends in a pub, but for George it was career-altering, one of those mysterious moments of inspiration that have the power to transform lives. Unfortunately for George it also, ultimately, destroyed his.

"Wasn't she truly a goddess?" he said. "You know, I had the pleasure of escorting her home the other evening after work, but all it took was one wrong turn and there I was taking her up Cock Lane!"

For the briefest of moments there was near silence, broken only by several audible gasps. George was terrified that he had gone too far, that his use of the unequivocal phrase had gone beyond what was acceptable in the halls, which already tolerated a level of innuendo far in excess of that allowed by society as a whole. How could he ever explain his disastrous opening line to Katherine?

And then the laughter began, tumbling down from the gallery and spreading across the tables in the stalls, accompanied by several ribald cheers from men who had obviously watched the contortionist with similar thoughts.

George, a seasoned enough performer to sense the mood and understand the need for momentum, racked his brains for another phrase to continue his ad-libbed adventure.

"A wonderful thoroughfare, to be sure," he said, a note of

nostalgia in his voice, "but not, alas, a route my wife lets me take with any degree of regularity."

"You and me both, mate!" Someone called from the gallery, to more cheers.

George nodded in sad solidarity. "The last time I drank from that particular fruitful vine Lord Stanley was living in Downing Street!"

Where was it all coming from? Even as he marched to the edge of the stage to begin his next pun there was a part of his consciousness, standing apart from the improvised storyline like a detached observer, that marvelled at the process. How many times had he listened to Henry Dickinson, or men like him, and unconsciously filed away the subtle and not-so-subtle phrases describing the methodology and machinery of sexual congress? And why had he done so? George had never regarded himself as particularly *risqué*; indeed, as he looked out at the flushed and smiling faces of the audience — *his* audience — the controversy that was sure to follow his performance terrified him, but there was also an undeniable thrill, an offering up of himself to the moment, that made his heart pound.

"You know how it is, though, ladies and gentlemen," he continued in a rather more sly and knowing tone. "Tell a girl you know the way and she'll follow you anywhere, even when it's wet and dark!" George turned to the side, showing himself in profile to the auditorium, and spoke in an exaggeratedly high-pitched, feminine voice. "Oh sir, I've gone and lost me way 'ome, and that copper's 'ad me for a dollymop…" At this he had to pause until the cheers and laughter died down. "… show a girl a bit o' kindness and get me 'ome to me own front door."

He then turned to face the opposite wings as a physical way of differentiating between the characters in his monologue. "Certainly, madam," he said, lowering his voice and adopting a grandiloquent tone. "How far do you want me to take you?"

He turned again. "Oh, all the way, sir!"

And again. "*All* the way?"

And again. "*All* the way!"

George could not help smiling. After all his analysing, all the post mortems and sleepless nights following yet another lukewarm reception for his act, he had finally found his own distinctive voice through a combination of happenstance and blind panic!

He turned and looked up to the gallery. These cheapest seats were the harshest of critics, ruthless in their denunciation of an act that failed to thrill or amuse, but they were also the most radical. If a performer showed them something new, which they could see was either physically dangerous or risked causing a scandal in polite society, then the gallery was ready to embrace it. George would not forget where the laughter had come from first, an endorsement that gave the rest of the audience the confidence to join in and seal his victory. Now he spoke directly to them and hoped that they would sense the gratitude within his words. "Well, we were there in a couple of winks, round the bend and up the back, because the girls from the golden temple, they're like sailors. Sailors, you say? Yes, sir, and do you know why? Because they prefer the windward passage! It's a heading respectable ladies never leave harbour on, no sir, but those temple girls, that's the only way their compass'll point. Due South!"

The general rule for comedians in the halls was to maintain a near-constant flow of banter and puns, but, on this night of subversion, Georgie Parr simply stood centre-stage and laughed along with the men and women beyond the footlights. He laughed and laughed, partly at the bawdy double entendres which were, he now realised, the level on which his humour was at its most instinctive, and partly in jubilation.

This pause, which was as brave and radical a departure from the comedic norm as Sam Collins could remember seeing, might have given George the opportunity to indulge in a little understandable hubris, but it also cemented his relationship with the people. For what they saw, quite apart from a comic unafraid to base his act in the phrasing of their world, was a man who trusted them, who had created an intimacy within the theatre almost clandestine in its power. Everyone who witnessed the genesis of Georgie Parr's scandalous career felt a pioneering pride in belonging to this exclusive brotherhood. What they saw was new-fledged, hesitant and disjointed compared to his later polished performances, but there can only ever be one first night, one birth, with all its attendant magic.

He shook his head, his expression one of contented resignation. "Lovely ladies, to be sure, but we couldn't do without our wives, could we, boys?" There was a somewhat half-hearted response of 'no's'. "No, of course not. God love 'em. Our lawful blankets. And you know why we call them that, don't you? Because they're moth-eaten and thin and never enough to keep us warm in our beds!" The laughter and applause sent a shiver down his spine. "And what about us husbands, eh ladies? How do you describe us?"

"Bleedin' useless!" came a raucous female reply.

It was just this sort of rejoinder that George had bargained for. Not only did it form a convenient link to his next section of narrative, the fact that he had an answer to the woman's comment gave a splendid impression of quick-wittedness. What a revelation it was, this anticipatory gamble, this manipulation of the audience! This was the secret of every top name: their ability to bend an audience to their will, and for the audience to gladly give their consent. And now, out of an act of desperation, he too had discovered this holy grail of the performing arts.

"Useless? Indeed, madam, you have us to a tee! If we aren't out gallivanting with the most accommodating and *flexible* of ladies, we hide ourselves in our study and spend all our time drilling the corporal and his four privates, our own dear army, marching them *up* and down… *up* and down… "

"*Up* and down! *Up* and down!" The audience chanted,

mimicking Georgie Parr's lascivious tone. At first they had been shocked by this staid-looking young comic who used phrases more often heard in gin-houses and brothels, but once over their initial reaction the music hall patrons sensed a curiously liberating cadence to the laughter, as though by embracing their vernacular George was acknowledging the vibrancy and importance of the working class. His dark, conservative clothing, sideburns and neatly manicured nails all spoke of a comfortable position in society. That he was prepared to undermine the cultural mores of this society in so scandalous a manner endeared George to them in a profound way. When, fifteen years later, the appalling news of events at the resort first spread and his name was vilified in the press there were angry gatherings outside the newspaper offices, with both men and women brandishing placards proclaiming his innocence and prepared to face police batons in their defence of Georgie Parr, the people's comic.

"But ladies! Ladies!" He held up a forefinger to make his point. "A soldier needs to be drilled regularly or he will lose the firm resolve required for battle. If he cannot stand to attention on the parade ground then what hope has he of penetrating the enemy ranks? He must be taken in hand and marched, and how must he be marched?" George spread wide his arms, encouraging the audience to reply, which they did with great relish.

"*Up…* and down! *Up…* and down!"

He was almost overcome with emotion at their response. Not only had they picked up the precise cadence of the sentence, reproducing perfectly his own timing, they had also shown George that here was his catchphrase, that seemingly innocuous assemblage of words which a performer could make his own, and which when spoken in another context would nevertheless bring to mind its comedic chord.

The audience's spirited rendition seemed the perfect finale, but in the fierce creation of his act George had lost all sense of time. For all he knew there were several minutes left to his 'turn', and to finish early would cause all sorts of problems backstage, not to mention risk incurring the wrath of Sam Collins. Timing, however, was everything, and the audience was his most accurate instrument. That, and the fact that George felt, for this performance at least, utterly invincible.

"So, ladies and gentlemen," he said, the concluding note in his voice eliciting several groans of disappointment, "I shall bid you goodnight, and remember, if you knock on my dressing room door and I shout out that I am playing with my soldiers, they might not be lead ones!"

With that parting shot, George took his bow and turned to leave the stage, but before he could move Sam, who must have been watching from the wings, bounded on. He stood next to the comic and put one arm around his shoulders, whilst with the other gave a flamboyant gesture of introduction.

"One more time for the Camden Clown, your very own... Georgie Parr!" He roared, before adding in little more than a whisper, "You and me need to 'ave a word later. Now bugger off." And then again in his best compere's voice. "I don't think I've laughed so much since our Molly got 'er bloomers caught in the mangle!"

George headed for the wings, eager for their shadowed anonymity. Having expended so much nervous energy on his improvised performance his body now felt drained, his limbs wooden and obstinate. He was like a puppet, suspended by the threads of applause and cheering, that could collapse in a heap at any moment. And then there was Sam's whispered aside. What had the music hall owner meant? Was he angry and planning to drop him from the bill? Sam knew a lot of hall owners in London; he could make it almost impossible for Georgie Parr to find a booking anywhere in the capital, an embargo which would quickly spread to the provinces, effectively ending his career.

He was so preoccupied with this terrible scenario that he barely noticed the contortionist waiting at the bottom of the staircase that led up to the changing rooms. In the near-darkness, his eyes still adjusting from the bright footlights, and with the girl wrapped in a black cape, George at first thought her pale face was a mask hanging on the wall. But then she noticed him approach and the mask moved.

"Mr Parr, I will speak with you."

All George wanted to do now was change his clothes and go home to tell Katherine about his extraordinary performance. After so many years of unswerving support she would be thrilled to hear that her faith in him had been vindicated at last. They could make plans for the future, rather than living from week to week, chasing bookings and pretending to each other that the shabby accommodation and uncertainty were all part of some quixotic adventure. Circumstance had dictated this romantic blurring of reality, but now they would be able to build something more substantial, more enduring, like Birch and his navvies and engineers conquering the ocean with their magnificent piers.

He could tell, both from the tone of her voice and the fury which lent a peculiar glaze to her dark eyes, that the contortionist had taken the gravest of offences to his introductory lines, but he was not prepared to waste time in what would doubtless be a futile attempt to explain either the circumstances or serendipitous nature of this evening's act.

"I know what you're going to say," he began, "but this is neither the time nor the place to discuss the matter."

His pre-emptive statement delivered, George made to ascend the staircase, but as he brushed past her the contortionist reached out and grabbed him by the arm. This demonstration of such immodest physicality from the opposite sex was shock enough; when coupled with the pain from her vice-like grip it stopped George in his tracks.

"No, Mr Parr," she said, "you must hear to me."

Her accent was peculiar, more Eastern European than Oriental, with a trace of East End in the vowels, as though she had lived in the capital for some time.

"What is it?"

"You cannot say such things, such horrible things. I am not a part of your act. I will not be used as a joke!"

George sighed and looked away from her. A gas lamp, turned down low to acclimatise performers to the gloom of the wings, flickered on the wall behind the contortionist like a will o' the wisp.

"It was not meant as a slight on your character. May I ask your name?"

She hesitated. "It is Zlatka."

"Zlatka," he continued, "I'm a comic. My job is to make people laugh, and if I think of something funny I'll say it. They're only words."

"Words! Yes, I hear your words! Saying I am like a... a common prostitute, that I will do all kinds of things for a man who takes me home! What kind of words are these? Because you are standing on a stage does not make it right to say!"

Her grip had tightened further, and yet George could only marvel at Zlatka's strength. The pain in his bicep, which in normal circumstances would have triggered some form of evasive or retributive action, was instead something to be welcomed, even cherished, a fiercely intimate connection rather than a manifestation of her anger. And enveloping them both, an intangible yet no less powerful bond, was the contortionist's odour, that heady combination of perfume and sweat which had so bewitched him before his act. Cloves and nutmeg mingling with a sappy spice, like the resin released by an axe biting into a pine tree's bark, its bitter notes balanced by a thread of dark molasses. It made his mouth water.

"Will you not say these things again?"

George looked down at her. At close quarters there was an undeniably masculine set to Zlatka's features, from the bushy, straight eyebrows to the angular lines of her jaw. He could make out a thick vein in her neck, throbbing rapidly, which quite repulsed him with its bestial virility. She was more a being shaped and defined by her profession than a woman, so why did she affect him so? How utterly different the contortionist was to the sharp intelligence and delicacy of his Katherine!

"I have to go," he said, placing his hand over hers.

She snatched her arm away as though scalded. "Do not touch me! Because you see me on the stage you think you see *me*, but that is not truth."

*It is not the truth about me either,* is what George thought, but he had wearied of the exchange. If this freakishly bendy girl was so thin-skinned that one mild bit of innuendo gave her the vapours then perhaps she should consider a career outside of the halls. What did she expect? Men never normally saw a woman's body so brazenly defined, especially not in the positions she was able to adopt. Obviously he would not always be following her on the bill, but there was bound to be a similar act on which he could base his opening lines, and if she thought that he was going to tamper with a winning formula for the sake of her or any other performer's vanity then she was very much mistaken.

"We shall have to endeavour not to find ourselves on the same bill," was his final word on the matter, and without waiting for a reply, he began to climb the stairs.

"You should not say such things!" The contortionist called after him, her voice echoing in the stairwell. "God will punish you for your words!"

*Maybe,* George thought, *but the audience will cheer.*

# Victoria

Six weeks after that groundbreaking evening, Georgie Parr was coming to the end of his run at the Collins' Music Hall. Sam Collins recognised a money-making opportunity when he saw one and so had been more than happy to keep the comedian treading his boards, but reaction in both the London press and trade papers to the new act had been unanimous in its condemnation, varying only in its degree of outrage. The closest Georgie came to a sympathetic review was a quote in the *Illustrated Sporting and Theatrical News*, which described his adoption of gin palace slang as 'a regrettable but wholly predictable consequence of limiting the Lord Chamberlain's influence', but the majority regarded his act as 'a disgraceful exhibition of profanity', with an 'utter disregard for the sensibilities of the audience' and even provoked a call for George to be arrested for 'rabble-rousing of the most pernicious kind.' Needless to say, these diatribes from the establishment had exactly the opposite effect to that intended, ensuring full houses every evening and a burgeoning reputation amongst the capital's working classes as something of a folk hero.

Katherine, heavily pregnant now and largely housebound through dizziness and debilitating bouts of cramp, understood that if George stayed in London his continuing presence might provoke the authorities into a more direct form of action, so she suggested a summer tour of the provinces, including several of the most popular resorts. These seaside towns, now accessible to the masses courtesy of the rapidly expanding rail network, shimmered at the end of the line, their crystalline skies and cathedral-like pleasure palaces so far removed from the landlocked black cities that they seemed, to each and every mill and factory worker, every clerk and miner and shopkeeper lucky enough to step off the train and breathe in that unfettered air, like visions of utopia. And it was these holidaymakers who, intoxicated by the resort and yet slightly afraid of it, required the reassurance of music hall for their entertainment. Here, by the sea, was where Georgie Parr's new audience would be found.

First, however, were two more nights working for Sam Collins. George had enjoyed the evening's performance, but as he relaxed in his dressing room he had to admit to a moment of distraction on stage, the faintest hint — born out of the familiarity of his patter and the reaction of the audience — that both he and they were settling into a routine. His reaction to this came as something of a shock to him. How often in the past had he watched other performers on stage and envied their comfort, their *belonging*? And now, having finally reached this point of equilibrium for himself, George was amazed to find that all it left him with was a vague sense of annoyance. For perhaps twenty seconds he had felt like an actor playing the part of Georgie Parr in a biographical play, with fixed lines and scripted movements. The further he left behind that astonishing, heretical first performance, the more he missed its tightrope-like crossing of the abyss. George had never regarded himself as a gambler, but he could not deny a craving for the shock and silence which followed his comments about Zlatka the contortionist. Katherine was right. He needed a new audience, a new town.

Without warning, the dressing room door burst open and Jacob, the hall's carpenter and general factotum, burst in.

"Mr Parr, Mr Parr!"

George started in his chair. "Jacob," he chided, "you must remember to knock on the door before entering."

Jacob, whose senses had been permanently jumbled fol-

42

lowing a terrible rooftop fall as a young man, glanced back out into the corridor, as though debating whether he should leave and properly announce his arrival.

"Never mind," George said reassuringly. "What is it?"

"It's your missus, Mr Parr. Your missus." Jacob's hands twitched and trembled at his sides. He seemed most upset by both the news and his being the bearer of it.

George stood up. A feeling of dread settled on him like an icy web, and the fey light in Jacob's eyes made his scalp prickle. "What has happened?"

"Your missus," Jacob repeated, apparently panicked into repetition by George's reaction.

"Yes, but what has *happened* to Mrs Parr, Jacob? What… has… happened?"

The carpenter took a deep breath. "She… she's taken poorly. Mrs Parr's taken poorly." He nodded to confirm the veracity of his message.

"Who told you?"

"A boy."

"A boy? What boy?" He caught hold of the carpenter's sleeve.

"*What* boy, Jacob?"

"He… I…"

"Try and remember, Jacob. This is very important."

Jacob nodded and frowned. "A boy. A boy." He looked up. "Ralph."

George nodded. His neighbour's eldest. "Thank you, Jacob. You've done very well." He grabbed his coat and hurried out into the corridor, where he almost collided with Sam Collins.

"Has Jacob…?" the music hall owner began.

"Yes, yes, I must go."

Sam gripped George by the shoulders. "Calm down, lad, you'll be no use to anybody turning up frothing at the mouth. There's a cab waiting for you at the stage door. It's already paid for."

George nodded gratefully, moved by Sam's thoughtfulness and generosity. "Thank you."

"Well for God's sake don't tell everyone, they'll all be wanting a free ride home. Now clear off."

The journey home seemed interminable, though it could not have been more than three miles, a jolting passage across the north of London with a driver seemingly oblivious to George's entreaties to hurry. Pedestrians and street vendors at first watched his passing with indifference, their blank faces leached of colour in the gaslights, as though the whole city was complicit in its disregard for Katherine's plight. But gradually, as the carriage headed westward, he began to detect a note of censure in their eyes, a slowly evolving judgement that George, in his heart, could only accept. Because, staring back at this parade of strangers, which drifted by like corpses on the surface of a dark river, he felt only confusion and conflict. Yes, he loved Katherine, and yes, the thought that his unborn child was in danger filled him with dread, but woven into these anxieties was an awareness of his own hypocrisy. Since their confrontation over a month ago scarcely an hour went by that he did not think about Zlatka. Even though it was clear she loathed, perhaps even hated him, he persisted in concocting a series of imaginary assignations, with her strength and suppleness their theme. No matter how he tried to dismiss her from his mind, George knew that within the cab's shadows her brown eyes, their gentle epicanthic fold giving the impression of being half-closed as though in ecstasy, would be shining. Better to endure the reproach of strangers than admit to a craving which made a mockery of all that he claimed to hold so dear.

The unmistakable rhythmic beat of a steam engine nearby told George that they were close to the Great Northern Railway depot. On still summer mornings he and Katherine would often open the window above their breakfast table and listen to the clanking of carriages and engines being coupled together, and conjecture as to the destination of the train being assembled a quarter of a mile away.

George opened the cab window and called up, "For the love of God, man, please hurry!"

"Not far now, sir," the driver said reassuringly. "Just coming into Goldington Crescent."

George slumped back into his seat. Bayham Street South was only a minute away, and yet his mind continued to seethe with conflicting emotions, as though some perverse small fraction of him delighted in this orgy of self-reproach. He pressed his fingertips against his forehead and rubbed them up and down, attempting to concentrate solely on the sensation of his skin moving over the contours of his skull. Now was not the time to indulge in some inner debate! George pressed harder, eager to accept the pain as both flagellation and focus, a cleansing punishment. His resolve was such that the marks would still be visible when he held his daughter for the first time.

The cab slowed and turned right, lurching into a water-filled pothole that was as familiar to George as the stench of its contents, some of which spattered against the side of the cab. He had written to complain that a Gloucester Place sewer was obviously leaking and settling in the hole at the end of their road, but all he received in reply was a long discourse on how Mr Bazalgette's engineering work was set to transform the capital, with only patience and understanding to be asked of its inhabitants.

"It appears our patience has yet to be rewarded," he said out loud, wrinkling his nose at the foetid odour, which nevertheless was of a sufficient pungency to clear his mind of all thought and doubt save a fervent desire to hold Katherine and re-state his love for her.

The first thing he noticed as the cab drew up outside their modest terrace was Edith, their maid and housekeeper, sitting on the front doorstep staring down at her shoes. She looked up, and when George saw the tears glistening in her eyes his stomach lurched. Edith stood, took a deep breath, and made a desultory effort to brush the creases out of her apron. Even in the feeble gaslight of their street George could see the poor girl's red-rimmed eyes, and in the moment before they spoke, a terrible thought leaped unbidden into his mind, as though whispered by some pitiless fiend: *Let it be the child.*

"Oh, sir," she blurted the moment George stepped down from the cab, "why could you not have come sooner?"

Too distracted to notice her familiarity, George took hold of her by the shoulders. "What has happened, Edie? What has happened?"

"It's Mrs Parr, sir. She started with the baby… Oh, she was in such pain, and then I noticed the blood, so I ran to Dr Zimmerman's, and when we got back Mrs Parr was lying on the floor, and Dr Zimmerman told me to boil lots of water…"

George could not bear another second of Edith's rambling. "For pity's sake, Edie! *What has happened?*"

The housekeeper glanced up at her employer. She pressed her fingers to her nose in an attempt to hold back her tears. "She's dead, sir. Poor Mrs Parr's dead, not twenty minutes ago. Why didn't you *come?*"

"I was on stage," George said hollowly. "No one can interrupt a performance. I came as soon as I could."

"I'm so sorry, sir."

The prominent nodes and struts of Edith's skeleton beneath his hands suddenly repulsed him. How thin she was! And hardly more than a child. She could not have done any more to save Katherine. She deserved his praise, his thanks, not this rough interrogation.

"The child!" George cried. "Is it…?"

Edith sniffed loudly. "You have a beautiful daughter, Mr Parr. Dr Zimmerman is attending to her." She looked into George's pale brown eyes, so full of confusion and anguish that she felt her throat tighten with emotion. "If you'll pardon my saying, sir, she has your eyes… and Mrs Parr's hair. I've never seen a more beautiful baby, honest I haven't."

46

George nodded. It was not the child. He thanked God that at least one life had been spared, and detested himself for allowing such a vile thought to even cross his mind. His hands fell from Edith's shoulders. "I should speak to the doctor."

She nodded in agreement. "He told me to send you up the moment you got here."

"Thank you, Edie. Go to bed, now, you must be exhausted."

"That's alright, sir. You'll be needing some errands running." She managed a tight little smile. "Now go on, sir, go and see your daughter."

George nodded. He stepped up to the door but hesitated on the threshold, his hand poised over the doorknob. What tragic tableau awaited him inside? And how would he react to the scene of his beloved Katherine's lonely death? George feared that guilt would overwhelm him; he sensed it already, like a barrier impeding the correct proprieties of grief. Until that whispered vulgarity in the theatre wings he had always thought of himself as a man possessed of quite simple moral philosophies, but now, even though by setting free a more salacious Georgie Parr he had ensured his music hall success, this man's unrestrained sensuality threatened to leach into other aspects of his life and taint them forever.

He opened the front door and stepped into the hall.

What first struck him was how everything could appear normal, unchanged, and yet at the same time be an entirely different world, coloured by the convulsive palette of his wife's death. George's hand patted the umbrella and walking stick handles protruding from their stand, reassured in some strange way by the familiar curves. Only one of the candle sconces had been lit, leaving most of the hall and staircase as little more than an abstraction of shadows. He wanted to call out Katherine's name, as he had done so often in this hallway, and see her appear, either on the stairs or from the kitchen, smiling and eager to put his day's tribulations into perspective. How selfless she had been, and how he had taken that generosity for granted! All those years of struggle, as he searched for his own comedic voice and enduring self-belief, both of these quests bolstered by Katherine's unwavering confidence. And now, so soon after the realisation of this dream, she had been snatched away from him. All their plans for the future lay in ruins. If only he could call her back for a moment, delay her departure just long enough to express his love, and in that expression offer Katherine a vindication of her faith in him. Then George could let her die. That would be fair. That would be just. Not this wrenching away, this incoherent night.

Upstairs a baby cried. For a moment the sound did not register, it did not belong in the house, and again George felt like an intruder. The second cry had him charging up the stairs two steps at a time, across the tiny landing and into the bedroom.

Doctor Zimmerman was seated on the edge of the bed, illuminated by an oil lamp on the bedside table. In the crook of one arm he cradled a small bundle with a casual confidence that unaccountably filled George with resentment, whilst with his free hand the doctor was pouring himself a glass of whisky from a silver hip flask. He looked up calmly, as though impervious to fright or shock.

"Ah," he said, glancing down at the bundle. "Here is your papa."

George stopped dead. The smell of ether hung heavily in the air, its caustic note woven into the darkness, which besieged them and imposed a fierce intimacy on every word. He glanced at the bed, but it appeared to have been newly made up with Edith's customary tautness. Doctor Zimmerman noticed the glance and understood immediately what George was thinking.

"I have placed your wife on the settee in the front parlour," he explained in a deep and heavily accented voice. "I thought it best to separate mother and child in order to prevent confusion in the baby. We do not want her to expect her mother's breast."

This stark medical explanation shocked George, but he saw the sense in it nevertheless. "No, no, I understand."

"Good." Doctor Zimmerman flipped shut and tightened the stopper of his hip flask with a deft and clearly practised twirl of thumb and forefinger, before slipping the flask back into an inner pocket of his jacket. He lifted the glass and spoke while swirling its contents in front of the oil lamp, as though the colour and clarity of the whisky were of equal interest to him as the man before him and the baby in his arms. "I am most sorry for your loss, Mr Parr, but you have the unenviable task of containing your grief, at least for the foreseeable future. In my experience, the living are far more importunate than the dead."

George took a step closer. "Our maid said I have a daughter…"

"Indeed you have." Doctor Zimmerman took a sip of his whisky.

"Is she well?"

"Quite splendid, I should say."

George waited for more information, but the doctor seemed content to supply nothing more than a brief reply to the specifics of his questions, so he attempted to pose a more open-ended inquiry. "How can the child be unharmed when my wife… succumbed to her labour?"

"My dear chap, post-partum haemorrhage has no effect on a child already delivered safely. Once the umbilical cord has been severed its blood supply is entirely self-contained, and your wife insisted that I attend to the baby before her. She would not countenance any other course of action, which I found most admirable."

"Are you saying she sacrificed herself for the baby's sake?"

The doctor looked at George disapprovingly. "You have a tendency to the melodramatic, Mr Parr."

This was more than George could endure. "I have become both a father and a widower in the same day, sir! What would you have me do, pass it all off as of no account?"

She might have been reacting to the note of distress in his voice, or simply its volume, but whatever the reason, George's daughter commenced her own vigorous response: a rhythmic, high-pitched squawk whose vigour was out of all proportion to her size. Doctor Zimmerman jiggled her up and down on his knee, but when this failed to pacify her he dipped his little finger in the whisky and stuck it unceremoniously into her mouth.

Appalled by the doctor's behaviour, which seemed to him both unethical and quite possibly dangerous, George strode to the bedside and snatched the child from Doctor Zimmerman. "What the *hell* do you think you're doing?"

"Simply trying—"

"I will not have my daughter weaned on cheap whisky!" George could feel a rage bubbling inside him, a fury he had never known, tempered only by the surprising weight of the baby pressed against his chest. "Is that what you were doing before you attended my wife? Is that why she died, because you were too drunk to perform your duties properly?"

The doctor's jaw worked, as though he were chewing the accusation like a piece of gristle. "That, young man, is slander! I should have you in court for it!"

"And my wife's corpse will be the first item of evidence!"

There was a moment of silence, a distillation of the darkness that surrounded them, in which both men were presented with an empathetic vision of the other, almost as if the shabby little terraced house could bear no more conflicts that night, no more calamity.

"She was beyond help," Doctor Zimmerman explained, his voice suddenly quiet, professional and detached. He drank the rest of his whisky in one convulsive gulp. "Your wife had lost so much blood by the time I got here that she was barely conscious. The child was showing an abnormal presentation and time was of the essence, which I conveyed to your wife directly."

"I see."

"Yes, and so did she. Mrs Parr showed a quite remarkable clarity of thought, considering the pain she was in. She told me to attend to the baby, and I was left in no doubt as to her insistence that I follow these instructions to whatever conclusion they might bring. Her last words were for me to do whatever I deemed fit."

George felt his daughter shift slightly. He placed one outstretched hand on her back. "She said that?"

"Indeed she did," the doctor confirmed. "I've heard nothing braver, not even on the battlefield." He looked George squarely in the eye. "Believe me, Mr Parr, if I could have saved them both I would have."

George could see the sincerity in the man's bloodshot brown eyes. He nodded, but could not speak.

Doctor Zimmerman took a deep breath. "So, the decision was made." He sighed, perhaps reliving this pivotal moment. "I administered ether, and Mrs Parr summoned the last of her strength for the rigours of childbirth. There was a risk of suffocation to the infant, so there was no time to be lost. The Good Lord must have intervened, however, because events moved quickly and without further complication, but the effort proved too much for your wife. She died soon after hearing her daughter's first cries."

"Did she know she was fit and well?"

"I told her so, Mr Parr. They were my last words to her, and she acknowledged them."

George pressed his daughter tighter to him, hoping against hope that her fierce proximity would be enough to quell the waves of conflicting emotion that threatened to overwhelm him. The fury remained, a simmering undercurrent dictating the tempo of every other thought and feeling. Fury at himself for his absence, for not being able to help, or say goodbye. Fury towards the doctor, who had experienced moments of intimacy with Katherine that should rightfully have been his. Fury towards God, for allowing death to poison his daughter's birth. And fury at the perverse governance of fate, which, having finally consented to bestow success in his professional life, then reduced it to ashes by forever associating it with the guilt and pain of his greatest personal tragedy.

Doctor Zimmerman stood up. "Bring the child to see me in a week, sooner if she shows any bleeding or fever. And you will need to enlist the services of a wet nurse."

George nodded, too overwhelmed by the evening's events to form a coherent response. He followed the doctor out of the bedroom and down the stairs, a descent which he now knew was bringing him closer to Katherine's body. He stared at the door to the front room, hoping against hope that the doctor had been wrong and that a drained, pale but animated Katherine would appear in the doorway and demand to know why she had been abandoned by everyone.

Doctor Zimmerman retrieved his top hat from the coat rack.

"Do you have any milk in the house?"

George replied whilst keeping his gaze firmly on the door. "I don't know. I'll ask Edie."

"Well, it isn't ideal, but the child will need something to sustain her until a wet nurse can start."

"Of course." The door remained resolutely closed, inert and familiar. In one respect nothing but a piece of wood, in another the portal to a colder, less certain world. "Your fee! I must owe you something for your work."

The doctor held up one hand. "Such work as I did should not be associated with commerce, Mr Parr."

"But my daughter—"

"If it will make you feel better, bring a bottle of whisky when you come to see me."

George reached for the doorknob, but Doctor Zimmerman stayed his hand. George looked up, into the doctor's eyes, and was so moved by the expression of concern he saw in them that his own began to fill with tears.

"Allow yourself a night of grief and anger, Mr Parr," he counselled, "but that is all. In the morning, a clarity of purpose will be essential, not only for you but also for your child. You are not the first husband to lose their wife in such circumstances, and you are luckier than many, believe me, to have your daughter in recompense. I have seen stout-hearted men lose all grip on their senses after losing a wife *and* child in childbirth."

George, though shocked by the doctor's astringent medical opinion, nevertheless saw the sense in it. "I bow to your greater experience in these matters."

"Excellent." He picked up his tatty leather bag and allowed the door to be opened for him. "My prescription for you, Mr Parr, is to let your maid feed the child while you pour yourself a large measure of something very strong, then all of you must try to rest. I shall arrange for an undertaker to call first thing in the morning... I know one who has not yet reduced his craft to the level of pantomime."

"Thank you, doctor. For everything."

"You are most welcome." Doctor Zimmerman was halfway out of the door when he stopped and looked back. "Had you and your wife decided on a name for the child, by the way?"

"Victoria," George replied. "She will be christened Victoria Katherine."

# The Pebble

Seagulls chattered and squabbled along the shoreline, picking through the drying seaweed and flotsam with a kind of brutal merriment, as though there was an equal pleasure to be had in the hunt, that plunging of beak into skelpy mass and perhaps uncovering a small crab, as there was in its eating. If there was one thing George hated about living in the resort it was the seagulls. He was not fooled by the purity of their colouring; theirs was a dissembling white, a cloak of purity and innocence thrown over what was in reality a far darker creature, either as recompense by God or the cruel humour of Nature. One had only to look into a seagull's eye to know this. There is nothing more wicked or soulless than a seagull's eye.

"Papa! Papa! Come and see!"

George looked away from the gulls and saw Victoria waving furiously in his direction. Her long blonde hair, curlier than her mother's, but with the same waywardness, the same tendency to break free of whatever attempt at formality was placed upon it, flared outwards in the breeze. Katherine's sister Emily, who had plaited and pinned Victoria's hair that morning, would doubtless have something to say about the appearance of her niece on their return, but George always felt that a certain amount of dishevelment better suited his daughter's whimsical nature. Victoria was certainly something of a free spirit, but whether this was as a result of the circumstances of her birth and upbringing, George's unusual leniency as a father, or simply an inherent trait, he did not know. His preference was to see Victoria's character as a variation of her mother's independent mind, and his greatest sadness was knowing how wonderfully Katherine would have nurtured and challenged her daughter. For all his earnest attempts to provide the love and support of two parents, George often sensed Victoria's need for a more feminine perspective. His sister-in-law Emily, Katherine's elder by nearly six years, a childless widow at the time of Victoria's birth, had offered to become a sort of governess-cum-housekeeper for them, a proposal which had seemed both generous and mutually beneficial at the time, but she lacked her younger sister's empathy, if not her intelligence. As well-read and politically-aware as Emily undoubtedly was, she seemed to be irritated by life, as though nothing quite conformed to the standards she expected of it, an irritation which manifested itself in a thousand ways, from the remorseless way she brushed Victoria's hair after her bath to the constant disputes with shopkeepers, coal merchants, railway porters... in fact, with practically everyone she met. Emily also disapproved of George's music hall work, which she had once described as 'acting the buffoon for a gathering of navvies and harlots'. Even now, with top billing at the newly-opened Pavilion Theatre on the pier, George was left in no doubt as to his sister-in-law's opinion, though she was at least sensitive enough not to bring up the subject in Victoria's presence. It was plain to see how the child worshipped her father, and Emily had no wish to undermine their relationship, which seemed to her to be the most pleasing legacy of her sister's perplexing love for this bawdy showman. She was, then, briskly efficient in her duties, brilliantly able to communicate her disapproval of George's decisions whilst maintaining a polite deference, and completely hopeless as a source of emotional support for Victoria, mainly, it has to be said, because Emily did not recognise the concept. Father and daughter were, therefore, bound closely together not only by their enduring sense of loss, but also because there was no one else available to provide the warmth and indulgence that their somewhat brittle characters required.

George made his way over the loose round pebbles that formed the upper section of the beach to the broad stretch of damp sand where his daughter was waiting.

"What is it?" George enquired as he approached.

"Something strange," she replied, poking the object with the toe of her boot.

George looked down and saw a gelatinous pouch lying tangled in seaweed, its slightly curving sides narrowing to darker ribbons. He seemed to recall it being the egg case of some marine creature, though he could not bring to mind exactly what sort. He did, however, know its more colloquial term. "Oh, Victoria, you are a lucky girl! You've found a mermaid's purse."

She wrinkled her nose in an expression of profound scepticism.

"A mermaid's purse? Are you sure, Papa?"

"Am I sure?" He said, feigning righteous indignation. "Of course I'm sure, young lady! Do you see those ribbons there? They are to tie it to her wrist so that she won't lose it while she's swimming. It must have come undone somehow, unless a crab pickpocket stole it while she wasn't looking."

Victoria was always charmed by her father's flights of fancy, even though there was enough of her mother in her for Victoria to search for the logic in whimsy. "What sort of money do they use?"

"Money?" George replied, warming to his theme. "Oh, they don't use money, at least not like ours. No, no, mermaids use shells, tiny little spiral shells for pennies, round ones for shillings and spiky ones for pounds."

"But what do they *buy*?"

"Lots of things," George stalled. Building his answer, creating a fantasy which was also rooted in a framework of logic, was, he realised, very similar to being on stage and reacting to a shouted comment or recent event. In both instances there was a need to impose discipline on his imagination in order to maintain a thread of believability, without which the audience, or Victoria, would find it difficult to truly relocate themselves to this new world. "They're still girls, after all," he continued, "they like the same things as you do, Victoria. Some nice seaweed ribbons for their hair, pearl necklaces and earrings... special mermaid flutes made out of coral."

"They play music?"

"Oh yes." George knelt down beside his daughter and put one arm round her waist. He knew that to the crowds of people both on the promenade and the pier such a display of affection would be regarded as distasteful, even vulgar, but he didn't care. Years of establishment vitriol and obstruction regarding his act had turned Georgie Parr into something of an iconoclast, always ready to prick the bubbles of pomposity that rose to the surface so frequently in polite society. His audiences, drawn from the vast body of a Victorian proletariat who were more occupied with day-to-day survival than the finer points of social mores, saw George as their spokesman, a mouthpiece for the millions without any real voice. In every performance he could be relied upon to produce at least one caustic comment on some topical subject, and had incorporated several of the more long-lived of scandals into his 'Corporal's Song', which utilised his 'up and down' catchphrase in its chorus. Any degree of censure over his manifestation of paternal love, then, was hardly likely to trouble him.

"Yes," he repeated, "mermaids love to play music. Their flutes make the sweetest sound you'll ever hear... unless you happen to be a sailor, of course."

Victoria wriggled round in her father's one-armed embrace so that she could look squarely at him. "Why don't sailors like the mermaid's music, Papa?"

"Because it lures them to their doom, my little plum duff

and custard. The mermaids are always on the lookout for new men to play with them under the waves, so they sit on rocks, combing their beautiful long hair, until a ship happens by, and then they play their flutes, so sweetly the sailors can't resist. *Crash!* go the ships onto the rocks, and the sailors tumble into the sea, to drown quite happily with the mermaids dancing about them."

A small vertical frown line appeared between Victoria's eyebrows, and for that moment she looked so much like Katherine that George felt his eyes fill with tears. "Well that isn't very nice of them, is it, Papa? The poor sailors only wanted to listen to the music."

He gave her a reassuring squeeze. "They don't mind. They had a spell put on them."

"But they still drowned!"

George grimaced. His seemingly harmless flight of fancy had taken on an altogether more sombre tone because, foolishly, he had not taken Victoria's empathetic nature into account. And yet, performer that he was, George did not want to break the spell, to explain to his daughter the more prosaic reality of the egg case, carried in by an indifferent tide once its usefulness had been exhausted.

"Well, perhaps they would have drowned anyway and the mermaids make it better." He paused, then continued more briskly, "Anyway, I'm not going on a ship, am I? We're safe and sound here."

Victoria pointed to the pier further along the beach. "That's like a ship, Papa, and you *are* on the pier."

"It can't set sail, though, cherry pie. It will always stay right where it is."

"Mmm…" She seemed somewhat mollified by her father's reassurances, but then she reached down and picked up a pebble, which she offered up to him. "Keep this safe, Papa. It's a magic stone that will protect you from the mermaids."

George held out his hand and gave a small bow as Victoria placed the pebble in his palm. "Why, thank you, my lady." He raised his hand to eye level to inspect his gift. Longer than it was broad, the pebble sat comfortably in the hollow between the pad of his thumb and the base of his little finger, a smooth and tactile object that carried its weight with an elegant understatement. Formed from a dark grey stone that he could not name, the pebble's only variance from uniformity was a vein of quartz, which looped part way around the broader end, standing slightly proud of the pebble's surface because of its greater resistance to erosion. George waggled his hand up and down, as though assessing the pebble's heft, its puissance. A minute ago he would have trodden on it like any other element of the beach and not given it another thought, yet now, following its selection by Victoria, this simple stone had indeed become magical. He tossed it in the air, caught it, and dropped the pebble into his coat pocket.

"There, I'm protected! Come on, young lady, time to go home."

That evening, George went on stage with the pebble in his jacket pocket and gave his most controlled, well-timed performance in years, at times coming close to the ferment of his seminal act at the Collins' Music Hall. The perfect weight of the stone, always sensed yet never uncomfortable or a distraction, had an almost hypnotic effect, acting as both a focus and a comfort. It was as though, contained within the pebble's reassuring presence, there was also something of his daughter, a possession strong enough to mean that when he slipped his hand into his pocket and grasped the pebble directly it was like holding hands with her. Fortunately this mediated union seemed free of the embarrassment and constraints that George would have felt if Victoria had actually been in the theatre listening to his act. The pebble's neutrality granted him permission to become *Georgie Parr* more unconditionally than ever before. Indeed, after his final bow and exit, with the prolonged applause and cheers still resonating around the pier's Pavilion Theatre, George headed back to his dressing room with the oddest sensation of having been somehow absent; that the Camden Clown was a third party, a doppelgänger whose lascivious tastes were as disturbing to George as they were to those sections of society who still fought to have his act banned.

Sitting at his dressing table, illuminated by gas lamps on either side of the mirror, George toyed with the pebble and studied his reflection. The hair at his temples was almost wholly grey now, as were his sideburns, but at least his moustache and goatee retained the dark brown of his younger days. He was becoming slightly jowly, with bags under his eyes, a decline exaggerated by the gaslight and stage makeup, but a decline nevertheless. He was now forty-three years old, an age by which a man should have made his mark on the world. Georgie Parr had achieved a certain notoriety, but what of *George* Parr? What would he be remembered for when his feet were not supported by the boards of a stage?

# An Ocean of Forgetting

In his dream George was standing in a small boat, which rocked gently on the mirror-flat surface of a dark ocean. He could just make out the shoreline, a featureless smudge of pale sand broken only by a solitary figure who appeared to be looking in his direction. A tiny ripple running across the water caused the boat to rock more vigorously; George glanced down to regain his balance, and when he looked up again he found he was holding a thin rope which connected him to the figure on the beach. He knew, in that certitude of dreams, that something terrible was behind him, further out to sea, and his only means of evading this monster was to pull on the rope and haul himself and the boat back to land. George also knew that his survival depended on the figure at the rope's far end keeping hold of it to provide an anchor point, but they were too far away to either recognise or communicate with. He began to haul on the rope, sensing that the threat behind him was getting closer. The figure remained impassive, inert, arms outstretched towards the boat. Surely they would tire of such a pose before he reached shallow water? Why did they not find something else to tie the rope to? Could they not see what danger he was in?

An irregular barking noise began to intrude on the scene. At first George thought it was a seal, but as he crossed from dream to waking, drawn away from the enigmatic figure on the shoreline just as their features began to coalesce into tantalising recognition, he realised it was someone coughing… Victoria.

A drab dawn light was filtering through the curtains, and outside several seagulls cackled as though at some coarse and villainous joke. George sat up in bed, listening intently, but Victoria seemed to have recovered, and he was about to settle back onto the pillow when she began coughing again, a dry, abrasive sound which the seagulls mimicked, as though thoroughly entertained by the poor child's distress.

Throwing back the sheets, George stood up, unhooked his dressing gown from the back of the door and wrapped it around him. He stepped out onto the landing just as Emily emerged from her bedroom, a candle in a pewter holder in one hand, her other cupped around the flame to shield it.

"Oh! I'm sorry, I was... I heard Victoria... "

"I'll see to her," Emily replied briskly. "Don't concern yourself, George, she probably just needs a glass of water."

He hesitated. His sister-in-law's conventional opinion regarding paternal involvement had always been a contentious subject between them, but he had no wish to delay whatever form of comfort was required for his daughter. "I think we have some linctus in the pantry, if you'd like me to fetch it."

Emily looked squarely up at him. In the candlelight, with her hair loose, George could plainly see a resemblance to her sister, which normally lay hidden beneath Emily's shield of fastidiousness. He could only imagine how lively the Barnett household must have been when these two sharp-witted yet disparate girls were growing up.

"George," she said, lowering her voice to little more than a whisper, "I am Victoria's governess. She will expect *me* to tend to her wellbeing. Anything else will simply confuse the child and place a burden of expectation on you which, by the nature of your... profession, you will at times be unable to fulfill. Let us avoid future disappointment by establishing a routine now that Victoria can understand and expect." She paused. "You must be tired. I heard you come in just before midnight, let me attend to Victoria now and she can see you after breakfast. I hear there is a puppet show at the winter gardens that could provide you both with some entertainment."

He smiled. "Emily, as always there is an inescapable logic to your reprimand. Go on, see if the poor child has swallowed a feather. Have you mentioned the puppet show to Victoria yet?"

She shook her head. "No, I only saw the poster yesterday. I thought it best to see if you were free to accompany her before I said anything."

"That's very thoughtful of you," George observed.

Victoria's cough began again in earnest. Emily glanced in the direction of the girl's bedroom, then turned back to George. "Any sacrifice I make is insignificant compared to that of my sister's. We must both do our best to make sure that sacrifice was not made in vain. Please excuse me."

George nodded mutely, silenced by the reminder of Katherine's death and the enduring guilt associated with it. Over the years his memories of that night had somehow become conflated with his confrontation with Zlatka, as though the two events had occurred on the same day. And despite correcting himself, despite the entries in his diary that showed, irrefutably, their separation, he could not dissociate the two. His mind, if not the calendar, saw a close correlation. Was he trying to transfer his own culpability into the preternaturally strong hands of the contortionist? In one respect she *had* prevented him from fully attending and engaging with Katherine's death. After Doctor Zimmerman's departure George had plucked up the courage to say farewell to his wife, had entered the front parlour, walked to the settee and gently lifted the sheet. These actions were in themselves quite banal, as though he were rousing Katherine from an afternoon snooze, but of course from this slumber there could be no awakening. He knelt, stroked her hair, wept, murmured tender apologies and fierce promises, and all the while Zlatka nestled at his back, her odour subverting the tang of ether, an unfaithful witness to this final act of penitence.

George watched his sister-in-law cross the landing and enter Victoria's bedroom, leaving him in a palpable darkness formed only partly by the night.

There would be no puppet show.

Victoria's cough appeared to respond well to regular doses of the bitter-tasting linctus, but by lunchtime her temperature had risen markedly, and it was while rearranging her pillows that Emily first noticed the red blemishes on her niece's neck, which stood out so vividly on the child's pale skin. Victoria also began to complain of a sore throat and headaches, a combination of symptoms that Emily recognised from her childhood. Indeed, illness in all its forms was a familiar and reassuring landscape for Emily; plagued with ill-health for long periods as a child, she had come to almost welcome the next bout of infirmity, as its ensuing convalescence at least offered a little time with her mother. Sophia Barnett had married well and given her lawyer husband two children. This, she believed, was a more than adequate fulfillment of her marital obligations; she enlisted the services of a formidable Irish nanny to raise the children, leaving her free to pursue a pre-eminent position within Gloucester's society. The only time any appreciable level of maternal instinct came to the surface was when one of the children became ill, and as Emily appeared more susceptible than her more sturdy sibling, it was she who received the majority of these audiences. A light kiss on the forehead was always the sign that Sophia was being called back to her natural milieu of dining room, salon or parlour. She would bend forward, her long pearl necklace brushing against the bedding with a gently percussive rattle, her perfume enveloping the child like the very essence of a sophisticated and utterly alien world. Even now Emily always associated the hazy days of recuperation with the rustle of pearls and smell of jasmine.

***

When George returned from his constitutional walk along the promenade Emily was able to deliver her diagnosis with a physician's confidence.

"Victoria has scarlet fever," she said without preamble.

George, who was in the process of hanging his hat on a peg, froze. He turned to face Emily, who was standing on the second step of the stairs, looking down at him as though delivering some verdict of the court. "Are you sure? Have you called for a doctor?"

"The doctor has been," Emily reassured him, "and agreed completely with my diagnosis. He was all for taking her into a quarantined confinement, but I persuaded him that to move her would threaten a spread of the disease which could be better contained by strict isolation within the house. The only thing he added to my own diagnosis was a solution of nitrate of silver for Victoria's throat ulcers."

"Ulcers? When I left this morning all she had was a slight fever!"

Emily held up one hand as though to make a point. "George, George," she whispered, "please moderate your tone, you'll disturb her. What Victoria needs now more than anything is rest."

"That's all very…" he began angrily, before lowering his voice but maintaining his vehemence. "That's all very well, Emily, but how can she have declined so quickly? I need to see my daughter."

"And you *will*," she replied, "but not yet. Victoria must be seen by me alone. The doctor was most insistent on this point. The disease is at its most contagious at the moment. Think of where you work, George. The theatre is hot and crowded, hundreds of people jammed in together. If you only passed on the disease to the front row we would have an epidemic on our hands within the week."

George closed his eyes and exhaled loudly through his nose. What Emily had said made perfect sense… *everything*

Emily said always made perfect sense, and yet there was something terribly cold behind her logic. Her unwavering objectivity was at times quite terrifying.

"You're right, of course you're right." He laughed and shook his head. "I wish I had a pound for every time I've said that to either you or your sister. I'd be a rich man."

"Katherine and I were brought up to think logically," Emily explained. "Daddy always said that in a courtroom whoever maintained the most level of heads would win."

No matter the truth of the case, George thought. "I'm sure he must have been very proud of his girls, then."

"I believe he was."

How had this rigorous philosophy been applied equally to two girls with such differing results? It was true that Katherine had shared Emily's analytical capacity, and indeed Emily appeared as capable of subtly winning every argument as her sister. What set them apart, George realised, was empathy. It had been Katherine's ability to see the world through other people's eyes — combined, it must be said, with the sensual way she would slowly brush her fringe to one side with the tips of her fingers — that had caused George to fall in love with her, and it was Emily's detachment which he found so forbidding. Emily would never have been able to look out to sea from the resort's promenade and conjure up a vision of the completed pier as a means of bolstering her husband's self-confidence. The girders and rivets and planking were undoubtedly all there in her imagination, but what Emily lacked was the joy required to build it.

"And how long will this quarantine last?"

Emily stepped down into the hall and helped George off with his coat. "Usually not more than two or three days. I had scarlet fever as a child, so I cannot catch the disease again. What about you, George? Did you have it as a boy?"

He shook his head. "I can't recall… I don't think so, I was quite a robust little specimen."

"There it is, then," she said, shaking the creases out of his coat and releasing a hint of the shoreline's astringency, which had inveigled itself into the material during his walk along the windy promenade. Her every bustling movement was a manifestation of the vindication which she so clearly felt. "I am the perfect nurse for Victoria, and if I stay in the house you can come and go without fear of spreading the disease." Emily looked up at him with an expression of firm resolve. "We must be quite rigorous in all this, George, for everyone's sake."

"Very well, then," he said reluctantly, "I shall keep a safe distance until the worst is over." What he did not say, because there was no way to voice such a thought without it sounding terribly hurtful, was his belief that Emily welcomed an opportunity for rigour in the same way that most people welcomed an opportunity to indulge in their own particular vice, be it alcohol, tobacco, fornication, or even the bawdy ramblings of a music hall comedian. There was something of the martyr in Emily, he realised, a secret longing for the sacrificial altar.

The evening was as still as the day had been windy, with a soft amethyst sky swept clear of cloud. The sea was dark blue with a metallic sheen, its carborundum gloss set off by the single lantern of a shrimping boat. The two elements appeared ill-matched, as though the ocean was reflecting another sky or day entirely, but George had lived in the resort long enough to know how beguiling its light could be, particularly in the evening, when the whole town took on a dreamlike, ethereal air. He could hear the irregular splash of the fishermen's oars carrying across the water, the rhythmic kiss of wave against shore. For a moment the only sounds in the world were those of the sea, a powdery dusk the only light.

For a moment. And then the string of electric lanterns, recently installed the length of the pier, came on, creating pools of red, green and yellow light on the boards, closely followed by the first notes from the rococo steam organ outside the pavilion. The pier had reasserted its brash sovereignty, reducing nature to the role of scene-shifter. George glanced up at the lanterns. He disliked the harshness of electric light; it was cold and austere, like a manifestation of Emily. Gas and limelight left something to the imagination, but the pier's owners had made clear their intention to convert the pavilion to electric within the year, so it would seem he had no choice but to become accustomed to its unforgiving nature at work, in much the same way as he had had to do with his sister-in-law at home.

She would do her best for Victoria, though. He did not doubt that for a moment. George instinctively felt in his jacket pocket, found the pebble, and let his fingers trace the familiar curves and ridge. His touch was as tender as if he had been caressing Victoria's face itself. Indeed, this simple stone somehow bridged the distance between father and daughter as completely and durably as the pier beneath his feet linked the theatre to the resort. Victoria's choosing of it not only lifted the pebble from inanimate fraction of the beach's whole to a symbol of love, dense with memories, it also opened a conduit through which George was able to assuage the guilt he still suffered over the terrible circumstances of Victoria's birth. The stone's weight in his pocket formed a sort of externalised conscience, reminding him that Katherine's death had not been in vain.

Bulbs attached to the pier pavilion, designed to emphasise its exotic outline, came on, as did the lamps inside its four domed towers, highlighting the red stained glass windows which glazed the tops of each one. With the darkening sky behind it the brilliance of the lights lent the theatre a fantastical air, like the fulfillment of Katherine's vision from that day on the promenade.

George smiled to himself. 'You knew, didn't you?' he said silently, astounded, almost frightened, by his wife's prescience. 'You knew what it would look like... that I would be here.' How much of his success was down to that vision?

Or had it been his destiny to walk along these planks, to perform above the waves, and Katherine had merely been granted the briefest of glimpses along an otherwise darkened, inescapable path?

His performance that evening went well. The audience was enthusiastic, roaring 'Up and down' with a collective lewdness that gave George a huge amount of satisfaction, but it nevertheless came as no little relief when he could finally take his bow and return home, to be informed that Victoria was quiet and sleeping. Emily made him a glass of warm milk and brandy and ushered him off to bed, a condescension he allowed to pass without dispute through a combination of weariness and preoccupation with his daughter's wellbeing. When he blew out his bedside candle George fully expected to suffer an unsettled night, but contrary to expectation he sank almost immediately into a deep and dreamless sleep, an ocean of forgetting.

He woke with a start. The bedroom was a confusion of shadows, the window a slate grey rectangle. Morning was clearly still some way off. What, then, had woken him? George propped himself on one elbow and peered into the darkness, straining for any sound. The silence hummed in his ears. The more he listened, the more the silence perturbed him. Surely Victoria would have coughed at least once by now? Or if not Victoria, then Emily, either pottering through the house or tending to his daughter. Wouldn't she have made some sort of noise? He counted to ten, twenty, and still there was nothing. Was it the deceitful quality of the silence that had snatched him from sleep? George's scalp prickled. A thought, too terrible to countenance, burrowed into his mind. The silence was like a huge, remorseless hand, crushing him into his bed.

Almost before his mind caught up with his body, George was out of bed, across the landing and into Victoria's room. A small brass oil lamp, its flame turned down but providing a reassuring glow, stood on a chest of drawers to one side of the bed and illuminated Victoria's tousled hair. George sank to his knees at the bedside and gently brushed the hair away from her face, but even before his fingers touched the cooling skin of her forehead he knew she was dead. Nine years ago he had knelt by the body of his wife and seen for himself the stillness, the way in which what was once a person, with all their complexities and contradictions, becomes in death something utterly simple, and now he saw it again. It was the second time George had been denied even the briefest of farewells, and the realisation of this tore him away from the world as irrevocably as if he had been cast adrift in the middle of an ocean.

A high-pitched moan hummed in his throat with every breath, a sound that can be heard at moments of both ecstasy and devastation: the sigh of exquisite pleasure or absolute grief.

"Oh, my poor cherry pie," George whispered as he stroked her hair. "My poor cherry pie."

The injustice of Victoria's death, fate's snatching away in his absence of the only two people he had ever loved, fuelled a rage within George Parr so fierce that when he called out there was a restraint and calmness in his voice so sinister it frightened him.

"Emily... Emily... " He paused. "Emily?" He called out again, louder this time, but even with this slight increase in volume George sensed the promise of delirium, the uncontrollable babbling roar which churned within him, edging closer. "Emily," he croaked.

The bedroom door opened. Emily was still dressed, though her clothes were crumpled, and she held a dark green shawl closed with one fisted hand at her chest. When she saw the tableau before her it reminded Emily of a painting by Caravaggio, a lament of shadows, but her reading of it was instantaneous. There was something in her brother-in-law's expression, however, that halted her in the doorway.

"Oh, my poor child," she said.

George could not tell whether she was referring to him or his daughter. "Emily," he began, his voice taut and horribly jaunty, "when did you last look in on Victoria?"

"I... it must have been around midnight. I—"

"And how," he interrupted, "did she seem to you then?"

"George, you—"

"How did she seem to you then, Emily?"

"She was tired, George, as was I."

A defensive note had crept into Emily's voice, which caused George to doubt whether she was being entirely honest with him.

"*Tired*?" he repeated incredulously. "Is that all?"

"Well no, not *all*. Her fever had worsened somewhat, but the pains in her stomach seemed to be troubling her less since I administered two or three drops of laudanum on a sugar cube."

George looked up. "Laudanum? You never mentioned giving Victoria laudanum. I never gave you permission to give Victoria *laudanum*! Why did you not consult me first?"

Emily's face flushed. She would not hold his gaze. "You were not available to be consulted—"

"Do not... " George shook his head, outraged by his sister-in-law's superior tone. "Do *not* try to blame *me* for your reprehensible behaviour! I trusted you to care for my daughter. *I trusted you*!"

Emily flinched at the rawness and volume of those last two words, but the young lady who had idolised her father, who had listened enthralled when he related a particularly combative exchange in court, rose in response to what she regarded as a personal slight to her integrity. "Perhaps," she replied haughtily, "if you had pursued a career more befitting of a gentleman rather than prancing on stage as a common clown you might still possess both a wife *and* a daughter."

"Get out," George snapped. "Get out of my house."

"Indeed I shall, and be glad to." The knuckles on the

hand gripping her shawl shone whitely in the dim light. "But know this first, George Parr, for I doubt you will ever have the perspicacity to realise it for yourself. You are a profoundly selfish man, whose vanity has hastened the demise of both my poor sister and now her only child through your…" she closed her eyes to better formulate the perfect phrase, "…pitiful addiction to cheap applause. I only hope it sustains you in the years to come."

Her damning indictment delivered, Emily turned on her heel and marched back to her bedroom. George stared blankly at the empty doorway. He felt numb, as though his consciousness had been transplanted into a wooden body. Movement, purpose, destiny, all these principles of existence seemed devolved to a higher power, a higher power whose sole objective was to destroy everything that was good in his life. Emily's verdict, which had obviously been formed for some time but withheld for the sake of Victoria, silenced him for the simple reason that, in his heart of hearts, he knew it to be true.

He was still by Victoria's bed, a crumpled, diminished figure staring at the wall with an expression of utter incomprehension in his eyes, when Emily reappeared in the doorway fifteen minutes later. She was wearing her hat and coat, and held a large carpet bag in both hands.

"George?"

He turned slowly and looked up at her. "Yes?"

"I'm going to the station now. I shouldn't have to wait long for the first train. Do you want me to alert the relevant authorities regarding Victoria's passing?"

"I'm sure you will do whatever you think is right, Emily. You always have."

"Yes. Very well." She hesitated, moving forward slightly and then stopping, as though a small fraction of her had wanted to comfort the shattered man before her but was then restrained by a more indifferent greater part. "I shall arrange to have the rest of my effects collected as soon as possible. A telegram should suffice to arrange a mutually agreeable time—"

"Just go, Emily," George said. "Please just go."

"I was merely... No, you're right, now is not the time." She took a deep breath and exhaled. "Well, goodbye, George. And I hope, no matter what animosity there exists between us, that you will accept my deepest sympathies for the loss of your daughter. No man should have to suffer such a double tragedy, but many do and still find the strength to carry on, as I hope you will."

He snorted contemptuously. "How very typical of you, Emily, to combine condolence with a sermon. If you understood anything at all about loss I might have been willing to listen, but coming from someone incapable of love your words mean nothing."

Tears glistened in Emily's eyes, and she shook her head sadly.

"You could not be more wrong, George. You could not be more wrong."

Without further explanation Emily turned away from her brother-in-law, who appeared to be fading into the gloom of that sad room, with its blue and grey wallpaper of roses climbing trelliswork which formed, in the dim lamplight, a kind of elegiac bower, shielding Victoria's mortal remains like the impenetrable thickets found so often in the romantic fairytales which Emily adored. From that time on, whenever she saw climbing roses Emily was reminded of her niece, hair shining on the pillow of her deathbed, while her father as good as vanished, erased by regret.

# Hannah

"… but there's a soldier's drill that we boys know
It's practiced every night.
Blow out the candle, Mary,
'Cos I got to get it right.
The corporal and four privates
Are coming to our aid,
To get their marching orders
On a hard and fast parade.
They'll go… come on, everybody, you know the words!
Up… and down,
And up… and down,
We'll give 'em no respite,
Until the fountain's flowing,
Until the morning light.
So if your missus locks the door
Or says that it's too late,
Call up the corporal and his boys
You know they'll put you straight
Just hold on tight and close your eyes
And march them up… and down!"

Georgie Parr opened his arms wide. "All together now! Up…
and down! And up… and down! Just march them up and
down!"

He took his bow flamboyantly, doffing his tatty top hat and
sweeping it in a wide arc before replacing it on his head at a

jaunty angle. And while his right hand was busy with his hat, the left subconsciously slipped into his jacket pocket and closed round Victoria's pebble. How intimately he knew its contours and weight! George was never without the stone — he had even sewn a strengthened lining into every pocket that carried it to ensure its safety — and at night slipped it under his pillow like a lover's note, secure in the knowledge that at least an echo of his daughter was within reach at all times. On stage George had become dependent on the pebble as a form of psychological crutch; one evening he had changed jackets after spilling powder down his front, and in his rush forgot to transfer the precious pebble. When, shortly into his act, his hand had dipped into the pocket and found it empty, George became so terrified that he had lost his talisman he pretended to become dizzy, made an excuse about having eaten a bad oyster, and rushed back to his dressing room, where he promptly burst into tears upon finding the pebble safely stowed in the stained jacket.

Although almost five years had passed since Victoria's death, George was still emotionally numb. With his faith in a just universe shattered, and his requirements reduced to cheap lodgings, the gut-rot gin served in The Three Feathers and the applause and laughter of an audience, the music hall entertainer now regarded any time outside the theatre as an opportunity to hone what was already a finely tuned sense of self-pity. Katherine had recognised this trait in his personality but kept it at bay with a combination of encouragement and gently pointing out to him how comfortable they were in comparison with a large part of the population. Victoria's vivacity had, in its own way, continued this exercise in perspective, but of course without either of these more positive personalities to bolster him George's retreat into melancholia was inevitable. He maintained a minimum of contact with his small circle of friends, who had tried, and failed, to find a lady companion for him. George, however, was no longer interested in relationships. He was not willing to risk making himself vulnerable again, not when that vulnerability seemed destined always to end in unendurable pain.

One night, after drinking solidly for three hours in the Feathers, George ended up in the flea-ridden bed of a prostitute, who coaxed from him both an ejaculation and a cathartic outpouring of grievances against God, fate, disease, and any other malevolent agent he could think of. She sympathised, having lost a younger sister to cholera during the outbreak of 1866, so together they sat at her tiny kitchen table, drinking sweet tea and railing against the world's manifest unfairness. Since that evening he occasionally called upon the services of one of the resort's numerous prostitutes, many of whom recognised him and would whisper his catchphrase in his ear whilst putting on their own performance. Whenever George felt the need to visit one of the 'introduction houses' he always requested a girl with brown eyes. If none were available he would leave and try another house, because George was really looking for a substitute Zlatka, the contortionist from his landmark performance at Collins' Music Hall. The day after their confrontation Zlatka went to Sam, demanding a slot following Georgie Parr in order to circumvent his opening lines. Sam Collins, however, was not a man to take orders from his turns. He refused to alter the running order, suggesting as a postscript that if she was looking for respect she should 'do yer bending with yer quim facing away from the audience'. This was the final straw. Zlatka had left Collins' Music Hall that same afternoon, leaving Georgie Parr with no choice but to modify his introduction. Following her sudden departure he developed the habit of checking every bill and poster he came across, hunting through the aerialistes, escapologists, trapeze artists and contortionists for that unusual name, as well as enquiring amongst other similar performers as to her whereabouts, but all without success. Zlatka had, to all intents and purposes, vanished. George wondered whether she had returned home, wherever that was, driven into retirement by his salacious remarks. He hoped not. Her talents, excruciating though they were to witness, deserved to be seen, and apart from anything else it also meant their paths might yet cross. If that happened then George was determined to obtain her forgiveness, and hopefully even her affections. Until then he found a degree of consolation with his brown-eyed stand-ins, who he instructed to squeeze his arms as tightly as they could whilst he cried out Zlatka's name.

While the applause and whistles, and one or two 'up and downs', were still loud enough to drown out the sound of the waves beneath the theatre, George turned and trotted off-stage. He had learnt, during his time on the pier, that this audible benchmark was the perfect cue to finish his performance; indeed, the sea's slopping and rustling against the piles had become synonymous with out-staying one's welcome, that subtle but significant shift in an audience when, no matter how hard they have applauded, their appreciation of your act is fading, metamorphosing into anticipation of the following performer. Linger too long and you risked irritating the crowd, which would soon make its feelings known with jeers and whistles.

The dressing room was tiny, but at least, as an act at the top of the bill, he did not have to share the space. What George liked best about it, however, was the view from the window. It looked out over the length of the pier, back to the pale gas lamps and shadows of the resort. Even though the pier was only about three hundred yards in length there was a distinct sensation of separation from the town, even from civilisation. The theatre, particularly on nights such as this when fog or heavy rain brought down a further veil, existed on its own terms and laws, an independent state founded on neither land nor sea.

The clock of St Margaret's Church was fading, absorbed by a thickening mist. Outside his window the filmy air took on a reddish glow from the stained glass dome on the roof above. He could hear the skittering feet and petty squabbles of starlings roosting on the roof.

George uncorked the bottle of gin on his dressing table and poured a generous measure into a glass. He lifted it, and seemed on the point of tipping the entire contents down his throat, but then stopped, hand and glass frozen in mid-air, thumbnail almost touching his lower lip. His focus had been on the slick surface of the gin, but as the glass reached its present position his gaze had shifted, if only for a moment, to his reflection in the mirror. What he saw stayed his hand, for it had seemed like an apparition looking back at him, vacant-eyed, pale, with dark hollows beneath each cheekbone, looming out of the dark like something risen from its grave. He stared at the creature in the mirror, which returned his scrutiny with what looked like dismay in its eyes, as though exposed against its wishes. George turned away, unnerved by the wraith. He drank the gin in one gulp and reached for the bottle.

The sound of a door slamming brought George rudely to his senses. He was slumped across the dressing table, his head resting on the crook of one arm, fingers still curled loosely round the empty glass. He blinked, lifted his head slightly and groaned at the shooting pains that immediately danced across his skull. His mouth felt as though someone had packed it with dust, leaching the last drop of moisture from his lips and tongue, and his chest burned with acid indigestion. Forcing himself into a sitting position, George pressed the fingertips of both hands against his forehead and gently rubbed. The skin slid quite freely against the hard curve of his skull; he wondered if, by increasing the pressure, he might push this mitigating layer right off to expose the truth of bone.

How long had he been asleep? George drew out his fob watch and saw that it was almost one o'clock in the morning. Tom would soon be locking the theatre, unless the slamming of the door that had woken him had been the stage door keeper leaving for the night. He considered going back to sleep. George had no wish to return to his lodgings, with its threadbare carpets, a bed whose springs shrieked like the dead in torment at the slightest movement and, overlying everything like the cracked varnish of an old painting, a pernicious air of humiliation which reminded him constantly of his reduced circumstances. George stood and walked to the window. The mist had dissipated somewhat, but still clung to the electric light bulbs along the pier, forming a glowing penumbra round each one. The cold night reached in to him through the glass; he could feel its caress on his cheek. The starlings shuffled on the roof of the theatre. It would always offer a resting place for its dearest confidants. Perhaps it was time to go home after all, George concluded.

Tom Drummond was writing something in a large ledger when Georgie Parr emerged from the gloom. "It's you, Mr Parr!" he exclaimed. "When I 'eard them footsteps I wondered if you was a ghost."

"You don't seem concerned by the prospect of facing someone from the spirit world," George noted.

"Me? Nah. Compared to some of the acts we've 'ad on 'ere there ain't no ghost frightenin' enough to scare me."

"I hope I'm not included in that category."

The stage door keeper laughed briefly. "Don't you worry about that, Mr Parr. I know some folk think you're a terrible man 'cos of what you say on stage, but that ain't you, now is it? It's an act, but they're too damn stupid to see it, if you'll excuse me for saying."

"An act," George confirmed. "Yes, that's all it is. But then we all put on an act in one way or another, don't we, Tom?"

"I don't follow, Mr Parr."

"I mean, we all play a character, to some extent. Sometimes we don't even know we're doing it, but then you catch a glimpse of yourself in a mirror and... it's as though you don't recognise who it is looking back at you. Does that make any sense?" George saw the glazed expression in the stage door keeper's eyes and waved a dismissive hand. "Oh, don't take any notice of me, I talk a lot of nonsense at this time of night. Shall we walk along the pier together?"

"I've still got my records to get finished, but if you want to wait I'll not be long."

"It doesn't matter," George said. His headache had settled and condensed just behind his right eye, a knot of pain that was making his eye water. "I'll head on, if that's alright."

Tom nodded. "You get off home, Mr Parr. You look tired."

"I am, Tom. Dog tired. I'll see you tomorrow."

"G'night, sir." George was opening the stage door, felt the cold night air wrap itself around him, when Tom added, "Just me and the ghosts, now, eh Mr Parr?"

George glanced back over his shoulder. "They're the only ones I really talk to nowadays," he said, before nodding a final goodnight and closing the door.

A small, elongated pavilion stood on either side of the junction of pier and promenade, one containing an aviary of exotic birds, the other a hall of mirrors and tea room. Between these pavilions were three booths, identical in design to the ones positioned halfway down the pier. The central one was the theatre box office, whilst the other two sold sweets, toffee apples and pies. As George neared the booth on his right he noticed a figure, unmistakably a woman, peering in through one of its windows, who turned at the sound of his shoes on the planking and appeared to hesitate, as though debating whether to run away. George slowed his pace to give a less confrontational aspect to his approach, for he well knew that only one kind of woman was abroad at this time of night, and he did not want to scare her. The sight of himself in the dressing room mirror, the residual effect of the gin, and his remark about playing a character, all these had, on first sight of the prostitute, combined to create a huge desire for escape, an absenting of himself which he knew she could effect.

"Good evening," he said quietly, coming to a halt at a respectable distance.

She took a step forward. In the mist-diffused light from the pier's bulbs George suddenly saw how young she was, in all probability not more than fifteen or sixteen, her rounded features still more girl than woman. If Victoria had lived there would have been no great age between her and this street walker, and this realisation truly shocked him. He was not like many of the men who frequented the brothels, forever demanding young and innocent flesh, and prepared to pay handsomely for the privilege of deflowering girls who were often drugged and tied to their bed, trussed up in order to allow their first customer unimpeded access.

And then he noticed her brown eyes.

"Sir," she said.

He took another step forward. "A cold night to be out."

She sniffed. "You get used to it."

Looking at her cracked, chapped lips and reddened finger-tips, George suspected the prostitute was attempting either to fool herself or appear nonchalant, but there was a resonance to her defiance, a reiteration of Zlatka's resolve, that both moved and aroused him. "Maybe... What would you say to a nice cup of tea in front of the fire? My lodgings are nothing if not basic, but at least there is a ready supply of coal."

"I prefer the outdoors for business, sir." She looked up at him with an expression in her eyes that was far older than her years.

"That *is* what you're looking for, isn't it?"

"Well... yes," George confirmed. Even after years of utilising their services he was still somewhat daunted by these girls' unabashed directness. "But where shall we...?"

"Under the pier." The swiftness of her reply spoke of numerous previous assignations in that location. "Unless you've any objections?"

"The pier?" He had never thought of his workplace as extending its facilities in quite so lurid a direction, even though, during the early part of his career in some of the more disreputable London halls he had often been able to watch, from his elevated vantage point on stage, the whores at work round the tables. "Very well."

"Come on." She reached out a hand.

George took her hand in his. He could feel how cold she was through the thin leather of his glove, and her spontaneous gesture spoke to him of the child that remained not so very far beneath the brutalised surface, but he gave himself up gladly to this waif. Some would look at her purposeful stride, her lack of embarrassment, as that of a working girl set upon the completion of her allotted task, but not George. He was, in nearly every sense of the word, lost. This young prostitute's guiding hand offered, albeit temporarily, a sense of direction. To be led, to be touched, was all he craved.

She escorted him down the steps cut into the bluff of the promenade and together they stepped onto the shingle, for all the world like lovers taking a romantic stroll on the beach. A slender moon, gauzy through the remaining mist, dripped silver onto an incoming tide, but beneath the pier an eclipsed realm held sway, full of alien smells and sounds, of water moving and echoing off the boards, and the exhalation of damp iron; to George it felt like he was entering a dark enchanted forest. They made their way through the hundreds of piles on which the pier stood, until the girl was satisfied that they were safe from prying eyes and gently tugged him close.

"So," she said, "what is it I can do for you, sir?"

George looked down. In the gloom her eyes were almost black.

"Touch me, Zlatka."

"What'd you say?"

"I want to call you Zlatka while you touch me."

The prostitute smiled. "She your sweetheart, sir? Won't she do these things for you?"

"That is none of your business."

She patted him rather condescendingly on the chest. "Don't you worry, sir, your secret's safe with me. You can call me anything you like for a shilling."

George unbuttoned his coat and jacket and leaned back against one of the stanchions. Looking up he could see the glow from the electric bulbs through gaps in the planking, but as he felt the girl begin to unbutton his trousers the bulbs went out. *Tom must have finished his bookkeeping*, George thought, then gasped as her ice-cold fingers wrapped themselves round his penis.

"Sorry," she giggled. "I'll have to get meself a pair of mittens. Hang on a minute." She cupped her hands together and blew vigorously into them for twenty seconds or so before reaching down again. "There now, is that better?"

"Marginally." He shifted slightly, pushing forward his hips and using the bulk of the pier as a brace. "Look at me."

Was it the thick shadow of the pier, or a magical trick of the moonlight, or simply the transformational power of his desire that caused the face that gazed up at him to so resemble Zlatka's? Even her eyes, closed slightly as she concentrated on her work, reproduced the contortionist's own with an accuracy that excited him beyond measure.

"My, you were ready for this, weren't you?"

"Don't speak," George snapped, his reverie impaired by the girl's accent. "Grip my arm... higher... as tight as you can... tighter... *tighter*!"

There! At last he could feel again the exquisite pain, a true replica of that administered all those years ago, which, despite attempts with tourniquets and half-hearted squeezes from other girls, he had never previously been able to find. There was a wiry strength to this girl, and an understanding of passion's anarchy that in normal circumstances would have disturbed him.

Footsteps sounded on the pier above them. George tilted back his head and saw the light from Tom's lantern swinging to and fro, a flickering semaphore between the planks. The girl looked up as well but continued her work at a steady pace. As Tom passed by overhead the girl caught George's eye and winked. The silence was such that they could hear the squeak of his lantern's handle between the measured beat of his hobnailed boots. George clamped his own hand over

83

his mouth, as though he did not trust himself to keep silent both the pain and the pleasure which were building within. The stage door keeper's tread receded in the direction of the promenade, leaving George and the starlings as the only living creatures in physical contact with the pier.

"Zlatka... Zlatka... Oh, dear God... " The movement of her hand increased in tempo. George whimpered, engulfed in her brown eyes. He ejaculated into the darkness, the pale arc of semen neatly dodged by the prostitute, who gave his penis a last shake before letting go.

"There," she said with satisfaction. "All done."

It happened so quickly. George, still gasping from the strength of his orgasm, and rubbing his numbed arm with his other hand, was not fast enough to react when the girl's hand, whether for warmth or perhaps a speculative attempt at pickpocketing, slipped into his jacket pocket and brought out Victoria's pebble.

"What's this?" she said playfully, holding the stone away from him at arm's length.

"Give that back!" George cried. The arm she had squeezed so tightly would not obey his will. The panic rising in him weakened the other.

"It's only a stone!" The prostitute laughed, then, with a flick of the wrist, she sent it flying. Moments later a dull clattering could be heard as it bounced and skipped and settled, returned to anonymity with a million others. Lost.

Lost.

This was too much. This was fate, exultant, mocking, voicing its final victory through the girl's laughter. This was the ultimate negation of his life, a vile humiliation. It could not be borne. It could not.

The strength had returned to his arms, an incredible strength, fuelled by the lingering imprint of four fingers and thumb embedded in his bicep. George grabbed the prostitute's shoulders and whirled her round. How light she was! It was like playing with a child. His hands slid swiftly inwards from her shoulders, settling with an appalling comfort around the base of her neck. He did not see the light of fear spark in her eyes: how could he have done? It was so dark under the pier, much darker than the night itself, like a coagulation of night, a condensing of it.

Beneath his fingers and thumbs he could feel tendons, the ridged firmness of a larynx, even a frantic pulse, but George was looking out towards the beach, where two figures stood waiting hand in hand, the moonlight accentuating their blonde hair. He wept, sobbed, pressed harder and harder, because only this unrelenting pressure could open the door that he so desperately wanted to walk through, a door that would close behind him, never to re-open.

The poor girl's flailing arms battered against his. She tried to dig her nails into his face, but they were all bitten to the quick; the best she could do was two small scratches, and to push at his face, turn his streaming eyes away from the figures who waited so patiently. He smelled excrement as the prostitute soiled herself, and then, moments, or perhaps minutes later, she made a soft gurgling sound deep in her throat and sank to her knees, as though George had become an object of reverence. Through the blur of tears he saw Katherine and Victoria beside him. They gently lifted his hands away — Katherine whispered 'Stop now' — but when he reached out they vanished, leaving only the slumped figure of the prostitute heaped in front of him, her crumpled dress pooled about her on the shingle.

George took a deep, jagged breath. The sharp sea air cleared his mind and vision with the speed and impact of smelling salts, rendering the scene before him in the most implacable of focus. This is your doing, was its definitive, incontrovertible verdict. He staggered out from beneath the pier's shadow, fell to his knees and retched. He coughed, wiping the spittle from his lips with the back of his sleeve, aware, with an all-encompassing coalescing of senses, of the rounded pebbles beneath his knees, the susurration of the waves, the cold breeze that had stirred from its rest in the hammock of the moon and was busy ushering away the last of the mist, the pier's presence at his back, the soft chatter of starlings woken from their roost by the change in the air, even the resort's quiet indifference... He smiled sadly, stood, and stepped back into the darkness beneath the pier. Twenty feet away, dangling from beneath a cross-brace, was a length of rope. He patted the cold stanchion, drawing forth a soft resonance from the metal, which he knew was a promise of release.

A young boy, taking his dog for an early morning walk on the beach, found George. The boy was not squeamish; indeed, he possessed an interest in anatomy first fired whilst watching his mother skin and gut a rabbit, and deepened by his own dissection of a frog caught in a nearby pond, so it was with a physician's dispassionate eye that he looked up at the body of the man whose shoes dangled several feet above him. He noted the facial pallor, the purplish hue to the hands caused by pooling and coagulating of the blood, the bruising on his neck where the rope was embedded.

The dog was barking. The boy looked down and saw his pet sniffing at what appeared to be a pile of clothes on the beach at the other side of the pier. He decided to go and see what the dog was fretting at, but not before one last look at the hanged man. The boy shifted position slightly so that he could see the man's face properly, intrigued by how the presumably painful manner of his death had stamped itself on his features. He was surprised to see, beneath the gentle coating of frost on the man's eyebrows and the skin's waxy pallor, an expression of, if not exactly happiness, then some-thing akin to it. It put him in mind of a phrase his mother had used when their old dog, who had been suffering from a tumour, was put out of its misery by a sympathetic veterinary surgeon. The man must have been very sad to have felt the need to kill himself in such a way, but now, at the end, he was at peace.

The boy turned his attention to his dog. "What is it, Billy?" He shouted. "What have you found?"

# 1941

# Observer Corps

Everybody said it was a miracle but I don't know about that. God only shows us when we're good and ready to see it. They said I was a hero. They said I ought to get a medal to pin on my blue overalls but in the end I didn't. It would have been nice to have one of my own like Pa did in the first war. If I had been given a medal Ma and Pa would have been proud. Well, Pa is a ghost now but he would still have been proud because there are such things as ghosts. I saw lots of ghosts because of all the bombs and the houses falling and they aren't scary, just a bit sad. It was all Fucking Adolf's fault.

That's what Norman called him. Fucking Adolf. Fucking Adolf who stood on a stage and shouted and made all the soldiers march and he wanted them to march into our country so me and Norman and Mitch and Taffy sat on the roof of the theatre on the pier in our observation post and waited for Jerry to come. We counted up all their planes and told the people in Ops. I was there because there wasn't anyone better than me at telling what Jerry plane was what, even if it was right up in the sky and dark. I can't explain how I did it, I just did. Dorniers and Junkers and Heinkels and our boys as well.

It was Uncle Walter who got me into the Observer Corps. Well he wasn't really my uncle but I called him that anyway. He was a Warden and one day I went to his house and there was a big white board with lots of black painted planes on it that he was taking somewhere. I pointed at one of them and said that's a Junkers JU 88 and Uncle Walter said how do you know that? And I said because its engines are near enough as long as its nose so he pointed to another and I said that's a Messerschmitt ME109. This was a good game I thought. But it wasn't a game for Uncle Walter. Uncle Walter got all serious and he looked at me and said how many of these do you know? So I looked at the black planes for a bit and then I said all of them. His eyes went a bit funny and starey like he'd sat on something sharp. ALL of them? he said and I said yes because it was true. And that's how I got to be in the Observer Corps and that's how come I was sitting on the roof of the theatre on the pier when the birds came and made me a hero.

I was born in a cottage on the edge of the moors. I remember when I was a baby hearing a strange song. It went pweebbbooeewwbubububeepweepwee all whistles and bubbles like a river talking and I asked Ma what it was and she said it was a curlew. I wanted to see a curlew after that so Ma found Grandpa's old binoculars from when he was a sailor and gave them to me. She said it would make a change for them to see something nice. They were really heavy. My arms ached holding those binoculars but I liked how they put the birds in my head. They were so close you could see their feathers and the shine in their eyes.

I went out on the moors and I waited and waited and then I saw a curlew all brown and black stripes and long curly beak and it sang to me and made me cry. Ma bought me a book of birds showing where they live and what their eggs look like. I copied what it said about curlews and then after that I drew all the birds I saw on the moors and wrote how they sang and what they ate. I decided to write a book that had all the birds in the world in it with drawings by me as well. I'm going to call it *Birds of the World* by Michael Braithwaite. I haven't finished it yet but after what happened I wrote a lot about starlings.

***

Would you like to hear about my family? Well first there was Ma who was called Anne. She was a good Ma. She was skinny but she could beat most men at arm wrestling because Pa got killed at the Battle of Estaires so she had to carry the coal and wood and everything when me and Thomas were young. Ma waited until the men in the pub had drunk a lot of beer and then she used to beat them at arm wrestling and win us some money. Once she won an orange. We ate it with some blackberries we'd picked and my mouth still goes all watery when I think about that teatime. Ma missed Pa. She had a photo of him by her bed and when it was cold she wore his jumper. Once when she didn't know I was there I saw Ma wearing his jumper and she sniffed the sleeve and then pretended to give herself a hug.

I can remember a soldier friend of Pa coming to our cottage to bring his clothes and stuff after he'd been shot. Everything was in a parcel wrapped up in brown paper. I'd been playing outside and I came into the kitchen and heard a strange voice talking so I stayed in the kitchen and listened quiet. The strange man said Harry was a good man but a sniper shot him in the throat and they couldn't stop the blood coming out and the blood made the mud turn red. The mud was red the mud was red. He said it over and over like he couldn't believe what he was saying. Ma started crying so I came in and they looked up. Ma sniffed and wiped her nose with her finger. She had the parcel on her knees. The man tried to smile but it was just his mouth moving. It didn't have any laughing inside it. Is this Harry's son? he said. Yes, Ma said, this is Michael. He's got a look of him, he said. Thomas is his younger brother, Ma said, and the man nodded.

I've got Pa's medals now. When I look at them I always think of the mud turning red.

Thomas was my brother. He was a labourer on Squire Hinchcliffe's farm and then when the war started he joined the navy and went somewhere in the Med. Thomas and me were different because he liked to shoot birds and I liked to look at them. I suppose it was the same difference in the war because he shot planes down and I looked up at them. I hoped Jerry wouldn't drop a bomb on his ship. He joined the navy before I went in the Observer Corps so he never saw my helmet which was made of steel and used to be a copper's because it said POLICE on it in white paint. Uncle Walter scratched off the P and the L and the I and the E so that just left OC on it and that stood for Observer Corps. Uncle Walter was clever to make a new word out of the old one. I got some blue overalls as well which were too short and a bit tight and made my goolies hurt if I bent down too quick. Norman and Mitch and Taffy had berets with a badge on them but I didn't get one of them because I was an honorary observer.

When the next war came, Thomas went off to join the navy, and then Squire Hinchcliffe didn't want us in our cottage any more so Ma and me moved to be with Aunty Irene by the seaside. They had more bombs there but we didn't have anywhere else to go and anyway they said the war wouldn't last much longer. Aunty Irene had a hotel called the Beaverbrook Hotel. It was quite nice with a bright red door and a sign that you could turn one way to say Vacancies and another to say Sorry We're Full! but since the war started it had said Vacancies quite a bit. Aunty Irene always said that Mr Hitler was going to put her out of business. She always called him Mr Hitler like Norman always called him Fucking Adolf.

I liked living in a hotel. It felt like you were on holiday all the time. I used to like walking on the beach and collecting shells but then they put up barbed wire and DANGER! THIS BEACH IS MINED signs on the prom. I was lucky to be in the Observer Corps because I was allowed to go on the pier which was a RESTRICTED AREA. There was an ack-ack gun in the middle and when it fired you could feel the pier shake. The boys on the ack-ack gun shot down a Dornier 215 so they had a bottle of beer each and painted a swastika on the side of their gun. I liked being on the pier especially our look-out on top of the theatre roof. It felt different like you were on a boat. I could see the Beaverbrook Hotel from there. I said to Ma I'd wave to her but she said I'd got to concentrate and keep my eye out for Jerry planes.

Can miracles happen apart from in the Bible? After what happened happened I asked Father Michael and he said that miracles happen every day but people don't realise. Then I said if people didn't realise what was the point in the miracle happening in the first place and Father Michael said asking questions spoils everything and told me not to wear out my brain. I know I didn't see Jesus unless he had changed into the starlings. It's funny because I don't ask questions about anything else important. I ask what we're having for tea and things like that but not miracles. I've never found a proper answer so I still don't know. I don't know why it happened on the pier. I don't know why it happened to me. I don't know how I knew what to do and I don't know how the starlings did it. Later in the war when we didn't have any planes to watch I asked Norman and Mitch and Taffy about it because they were there too. Norman said it was just a coincidence and Taffy said so too but Mitch wasn't so sure. He reckoned there was more going on in the world than just the stuff we can see. Mitch said that a man called Einstein had discovered that time is bendy like rubber. Mitch reckoned that if you could make different bits of time bend and touch then you would end up with two times in the same place. I like thinking of time being bendy. If I'd known how to bend time I would have told Pa not to fight in the Battle of Estaires then the mud wouldn't have turned red. I did save Ma though so that's something.

You don't think about the war happening at the seaside do you? It doesn't seem to fit. Like the ack-ack gun on the pier or the barbed wire on the beach. They don't go together. It makes everything seem like a dream. I didn't dream the miracle though. The story was in the paper with a picture of me that Uncle Walter took ages ago. Ma cut the picture and words out and I stuck it in my diary. The paper is all yellow now but it still shows that I didn't make it up. I hope people read it in a hundred years.

Up until Christmas me and Norman and Mitch and Taffy had been really busy because Fucking Adolf was sending loads of bombers. They didn't come right over us but went past on their way to cities so Taffy was on the radio just about nonstop and my arms nearly felt like falling off after watching the bombers through my binoculars for hour after hour. I remember me and Ma going to the pictures and seeing the Pathé newsreel which showed all the broken houses and shops and factories. Ma leaned close and whispered, you make sure our boys know where these bastards are, Michael. Ma didn't say words like that very often so I was shocked but proud at the same time.

After Christmas Fucking Adolf must have decided to bomb somewhere else instead so we sat on the pier and drank loads of Taffy's tea and listened to Tommy Handley on the radio. One day Norman and me had a nosy round the theatre. We looked in the rooms where the people in the acts got dressed. I sat on a chair and looked in the mirror and pretended to put some lipstick on like Ma does before she goes to the pub. There weren't any light bulbs round the mirror, just the light from the corridor, so you could only see one side of my face. Because I had my blue overalls on you couldn't see my body either so there was just half my face hanging in the darkness with nothing to hold it up. Just then I heard a bump or something out in the corridor. I looked to see if it was Norman but I didn't see anything so I turned back and that was when I saw the ghost. It was another face in the mirror right next to mine. A sad face of a man about the same age as Uncle Walter but he looked more old fashioned like the people in those black-and-white films where everything moved faster. My heart was beating really fast. I thought he was looking at me but then I realised he was just looking in the mirror. Just staring and staring as though he was trying to make up his mind about something. I dared to look sideways but of course there was nothing there and when I looked back the ghost had gone so I went to find Norman. After we'd looked in the rooms we went down the stairs. At the bottom was a door with a sign on it that said Quiet! Stage Access Authorised Personnel and Performers Only in important writing. I wasn't sure me and Norman were authorised and we certainly weren't performers but Norman had the keys to everywhere in the theatre so he unlocked the door and in we went. It was really dark and it smelled of ghosts. I didn't see any but they were there alright. Perhaps they were the ghosts of acts who didn't want to stop. Me and Norman squeezed past big pieces of wood with the insides of houses painted on them and then we came out onto the stage. Someone had left the curtains up so we could see all the chairs looking at us. Hundreds and hundreds of red chairs. I felt like they were waiting for us to do something and that was just the empty chairs so I couldn't imagine what it was like when the theatre was full of people. Really frightening I reckon. Norman must have felt it too because he did a sort of bumping and shuffling dance with his boots banging on the stage making little clouds of dust and then he held out his arms and said thank you folks. His words just sort of vanished like the theatre had swallowed them up. Come on Mickey, let's go for a brew, Norman said and I agreed because stood on that stage I felt like what Taffy calls a sitting duck.

When we were back in the observation post I told the boys about the ghost in the dressing room and Mitch said it might have been the comedian from the olden days who hung himself under the pier. What was his name? I asked but Mitch couldn't remember; he just knew it was right under this pier. Mitch said his nanna was a little girl and she was riding her bike down the prom and saw the police cutting the man down. Mitch said his nanna said the police cut through the rope and then just let him fall down onto the beach without trying to catch him. She said she knew he was dead already but she always remembered thinking the police weren't very kind not trying to catch him.

I remember everything that happened that night like I was sitting at the Regal watching a film though with me in it rather than Errol Flynn. It happened on the third of February 1941.

That day didn't seem any different to begin with. Well no, that isn't quite right because when I got up in the morning and came out onto the landing to go for a wee Uncle Walter was just coming out of Ma's room and he was tucking his shirt in and he looked like he was in a rush. I suppose it was because Aunty Irene had gone to see her sister for the night because she was poorly and Uncle Walter had to cook breakfast for all the guests. There were only three of them though. One man selling vacuum cleaners and a soldier with a girl who I saw putting her wedding ring on outside the hotel. I told Ma about the girl putting her ring on and she said not to tell Aunty Irene or Uncle Walter and to let the kids have some fun because there wasn't much of it about.

After breakfast I helped Uncle Walter wash the car which is his pride and joy though he doesn't drive it very far because of the rationing. Then I helped Ma wind some wool for her knitting. I went for a walk round the park in the afternoon then had a snooze before getting ready for my shift. Ma made me some sandwiches to go with Taffy's terrible tea and then it was off to the pier with my overalls and hat with OC painted on it. Just a normal day. No clues about what was going to happen. I even saw some starlings in the park but they were just hopping about. I wonder if they looked at me and knew what was going to happen?

When I got to the pier I saw John on the barrier talking to two LDV men. John nodded at me and said evening Micky.

Jerry paying us a visit tonight? I looked up at the sky. It's funny isn't it how we look for the answers to questions as though they're written on the sky or the sea or mountains. I don't know John, I said, but if he does I'll know what he's flying in. John and the LDV men laughed but it wasn't really a joke. I walked down the pier. I looked down through the cracks in the planks to see the waves because the tide was in and when you're on the pier you feel like saying ha ha can't get me! to the waves. My ma doesn't like walking on the pier. She says it makes her feel dizzy so it's a good job she isn't in the Observer Corps. I wonder who invented the pier. I think people might have thought they were a bit barmy building something like a bridge that doesn't really go anywhere.

To get to our observation post you had to go up all the stairs inside the theatre then there was a wooden ladder that came down from a square door in the ceiling and then you got into the comms room which was where Taffy sat. When I got there I heard Norman shouting to Taffy De Havilland Dragonfly heading two two five at two thousand feet position effzerothreethreeonetwoeight and Taffy nodded and said got that and it felt like I was at home. I went outside on the roof. Norman was on the Micklethwaite wrinkling his nose to make sure the plot was right and Mitch was looking at the aeroplane through his binoculars so I kept quiet but I couldn't help looking too just to make sure they were right. Yes they were. The lower wing was that shape like Aunty Irene's butter knife so I didn't say anything.

Nothing much happened for a bit after that. They sent me to check the thermometer reading because the box was further along the roof and you had to walk along a ledge and Norman said there's no point having a dog and barking yourself which I thought was obvious really. The thermometer said four degrees and not long after that the first starlings started landing on the roof all chirping away. Norman said they were like a lot of women gossiping. It was good to see the birds so close up without having to use my binoculars. They didn't seem afraid of us. They hopped on to the sandbags and looked into our observation post as though they liked looking at humans the same as we liked looking at birds. Norman wanted to shoo them off but Mitch said no leave them, it's us on their territory and Norman said please yourself which I was amazed at because I'd always thought Norman was the boss of them too. It's a good job Norman didn't shoo them off because the miracle or whatever it was wouldn't have happened otherwise.

The sun went down and it made a thin red line between the dark blue sea and the dark blue sky. Mitch said it was more beautiful than a painting and Norman called him a queer. After the sun went down loads more starlings landed on the theatre roof. They just kept coming and coming. I was surprised how smart starlings are especially in their winter plumage with the white spots. They've got this greeny purply sort of shine on their feathers that you can't see from a distance. It's like they don't want folk to take much notice of them. Anyway down they came and down they came until it almost got a bit frightening like they were planning on doing something. And then like someone had blown a whistle or a hooter to start their shift the whole lot took off at once chitter chattering and got themselves in a big group over us. Me and the boys watched like we were looking at the biggest group of bombers we'd ever seen but you wouldn't ever see bombers flying like those starlings flew. Up down round and round zooming over our heads so close you could hear their wings whispering. It was like looking at a living cloud being blown about in fifty different directions at once. I watched so much I forgot to see anything else. It was like Norman and Mitch disappeared and the pier and the sea and pretty much everything else apart from the starlings. It was like I was flying with them and it made me want to cry.

When they finished and flew away I felt really sad. What was all that about then? Norman said. He made his voice sound as though he wasn't bothered about what the starlings had done but I could tell he'd liked it really. Why does it have to be about anything? Mitch said and he sounded really angry. Why can't it just BE and leave it at that? You're always trying to analyse everything and put it in a box and all that does is take away the magic. I think it was the most words I've ever heard Mitch say in one go. Alright keep your hair on, Norman said. It was just a load of birds. Then he shouted to Taffy to put the kettle on.

It was quarter-past nine. I know because I'd just looked at my watch and it's got luminous dots on the numbers and luminous lines on the hands. I looked at the dots and lines shining and then something strange happened. The dots and lines went whizzing off my watch and up into the sky and they started making the same movements as the starlings had done. When I told the man from the paper he said perhaps you were dizzy and saw some stars but it was cloudy by then so that wasn't it. The dots and the lines followed where the starlings had been and because they were luminous and the sky was black it was like writing. Not English or any other language but it made sense somehow and what it said was go and get your ma and make her safe. Go and make your ma safe. Go and make your ma safe. How could the patterns say that? So many people asked me that question even though every time I said I don't know they just did. They just did and that's all that matters.

I've got to go, I said. Norman said you aren't going anywhere sunshine. Your shift isn't half finished yet. The starlings have sent me a message, I said. Norman said have they now? Well I'm fucking sending you one too. If you go now that's a dereliction of duty and you'll be facing a court-martial. I wasn't sure what a court-martial was but the message was still in my eyes like when you look at a light for too long. I've got to! I said. For God's sake let him go, Mitch said. Michael's a volunteer and we've still got three at the post. He obviously feels something very strongly. Well I don't know, Norman said. Swanning off because the birds have sent him a message? That'd look good on a report. Well DON'T WRITE ONE THEN Mitch shouted and Norman didn't have an answer to that so off I went. Down the ladder down the stairs along the pier with my boots bangbangbanging on the boards sounding so loud with that message in my eyes like it was never going to go away.

What's the rush? said the boys on the ack-ack gun. I've got to make my ma safe, I shouted but I didn't stop. I ran across the prom into town. Everywhere was pitch black because of the blackout but I could find my way home with my eyes shut so it didn't bother me. I ran up Church Street then turned left onto West Street and then through a back alley and onto Copperfield Road which is where the Beaverbrook Hotel is. I came charging into the back room where Aunty Irene and Uncle Walter were listening to the radio. Where's Ma? I said and they looked round. She's helping to sort clothes at the WVS, Aunty Irene said. Why? She's not safe, I said. Where's the WVS? At the Sally Army, Uncle Walter said. On Sunderland Avenue. Do you know how to but I didn't hear any more than that because I'd run back out of the hotel and was aiming for where I guessed the Sally Army was. I hoped the starlings would help and they did because I more or less ran straight into a warden who looked at my tin hat and my blue overalls and decided I must have been authorised. Where's the Sally Army? I said. The warden said you're in the Observer Corps, aren't you? Have you seen something? And I said yes I need to make my ma safe. He thought right quick and said second left straight down half a mile and it's on your right. So I said ta and ran off. Do I need to sound the alarm? the warden shouted and I shouted back no it's just my ma but I didn't stop running. I've never run so fast, it was almost like I was flying. It was like the starlings were carrying me.

Into the darkness past all the dark houses that looked like they were just painted. Like I was running between scenery from the theatre with the message in the back of my eyes going paler because the starlings were further away now. There it was! The Sally Army. I could just see the shape of it against the sky. I ran up the steps and went in shouting Ma Ma Ma. A woman in a brown coat came out of a room and said who are you? So I said I'm Michael Braithwaite, who are you? I'm Mrs Tyler, she said. Are you Anne's lad? Yes I'm Anne's lad, I said. I've come to make her safe. Well, Mrs Tyler said, you need to calm down a bit my lad. Your mum's safe as can be here and if the siren does go the shelter's only on the corner so there's no need to come charging in here shouting the odds now is there? I didn't want to waste any more time with Mrs Tyler so I pushed past her and started shouting Ma Ma Ma again going down the hall and looking in rooms. My heart was beating so much it felt like my whole body was beating. I just knew I had to find Ma fast. I knew it was the most important thing I'd ever do. Ma Ma I shouted and then a door opened and there she was. I was so relieved I felt like crying. Come on Ma, I said, I've got to make you safe.

Mrs Tyler had caught up with me by now and said there you are, Anne, will you please tell your son that it is unacceptable behaviour to barge in here ranting like a madman. I know he has… difficulties but even so.

Then Ma got that look on her face, the one that she puts on when she sees something that needs changing pretty sharpish. For a moment I thought it was me she was going to go mad at but then I noticed she wasn't looking at me, she was looking at Mrs Tyler standing behind me. When I want your advice I'll ask for it Abigail, she said in that calm voice she only has when she's really mad. Anyway you're a fine one to be lecturing me on how to bring up my children. How old was your Veronica when she got in the family way? I turned round to look at Mrs Tyler and she'd gone as red as a beetroot. Then she made a hummph sort of a sound and stomped off. Ma came up and put her hands on either side of my face and looked at me really close like when she was checking whether I'd washed my face properly or not. What's the matter Michael? she asked. I've got to make you safe, I said. The starlings sent me a message. The starlings? she said. How did they do that? By flying around all together, I said. It was like they wrote it on the sky.

Now my ma knows about nature so I wasn't sure whether she'd believe me or not about the starlings. Once a sparrowhawk caught one of Mister Ainsworth's pigeons and ate it really slowly on our back fence. Ma and me were watching from the kitchen and I could tell the pigeon wasn't dead when the sparrowhawk started to eat it so I said it was being cruel. No, Ma said, it's just eating it. Nature isn't cruel it just needs to keep a balance of things. Perhaps that pigeon was a bit slow or wasn't paying attention and then its babies would have been slow as well or not paid attention and so on and so on until all the pigeons were useless and that would make things out of balance. I remember pretending to agree but inside I still felt sorry for the pigeon. Just because it was a bit slow didn't mean it deserved to be eaten alive.

Ma waved her hand to point at all the Sally Army building around us. Isn't this a safe place to be? she said. How do you know the starlings didn't mean to make sure I was safe here? No no they knew you were here already, I said. They come from all over town to the pier. I've seen them from our observation post. They saw you coming to the Sally Army and that's why they wrote the message. Come on Ma you've got to go home. Please! Ma put her hands on my shoulders and looked at me really fierce. She looked at me for ages like Ma's do when they're making sure you're not mucking them about then she nodded. Alright, she said. This is obviously very important to you isn't it? Let me get my coat and I'll say goodnight to the girls. Hurry up then! I said. Ma lifted my helmet with OC painted on it and straightened up my hair at the front which was a bit sweaty from having to run to the Sally Army from the pier. You'd make a good warden, she said and smiled. You're a bossy bugger.

There we were. Me and Ma running home through the blackout like two shadows, me half dragging Ma by the hand because I still wasn't sure she was safe yet and both of us not knowing that we were in the middle of the miracle if that's what it was. I could see a few stars through the gaps in the clouds. Stars look harder in the winter. There's no need to drag me along like a dog on a lead, Ma said. When we get to Aunty Irene and Uncle Walter's we'll be safe I said back and just then I heard the engines in the distance. My ears are just about as good as my eyes at telling what planes are what. I knew right away that they were Jerry engines what with that wumwumwumwum noise but it was too far away yet for me to tell which sort of plane. It sounded quite high up and only one but there were two engines so that meant it was a bomber so that meant bombs. Then Ma heard it too and she looked at me like she was seeing someone different. Can you hear that? she asked and I just nodded. Why hasn't the siren gone off? she asked but the bombers hadn't been for ages so perhaps the boys weren't expecting it. I wished I'd got my binoculars but they were on the pier so I just had to look up at the sky where I thought the sound was coming from. It was getting louder and definitely coming in our direction but everyone in the town seemed to be asleep or at least inside listening to the radio. Only me and Ma knew the bomber was coming.

It's a Heinkel HE 111, I said. Single plane at approx twelve thousand feet. I wanted to shout to the boys but they must have heard it by now and told the ack-ack lads. Wumwumwum and the stars twinkled because they didn't care that Fucking Adolf was coming. Where's the nearest shelter, Ma said. Come on Michael we have to get to the shelter! So we started running down the black street as the wumwumwum caught us up and I imagined the German pilots looking down and seeing us running and laughing. Or perhaps they just wanted to get home like we did and see their families. We'd only got to the corner of Hillingdon Avenue when we heard a big explosion that you could feel through the road. Ma pulled me down onto the ground and she lay on top of me to protect me and that is the bravest thing I've seen but the Heinkel just carried on out to sea. The ack-ack lads had a go at it but I reckon they missed because the wumwumwum got quieter and quieter until it was gone and then it was all quiet for a minute until we heard the bell of a fire engine in the distance.

Ma got up and I got up and we looked at each other and we both just kind of knew where the bomb had landed. We just knew. And then we ran back where we had come from. Towards the flames and the crackle of the fire.

The Sally Army wasn't there any more. It had been turned into a big pile of bricks and wood and stuff by the bomb. There was a big fire in the middle and a lot of the bricks were steaming and it all looked hot. The firemen came and started putting water on the fire which hissed like it was angry. An ARP warden tried to climb over the piles of bricks and stuff to see if there was anybody inside. Ma just stood with one hand over her mouth like she was trying to stop herself from being sick and with her other hand she squeezed my shoulder really hard. The ARP man looked up and saw us standing watching. You! he shouted. You! He pointed at me. Come and give me a hand laddie. I'd forgotten I'd got my Observer Corps uniform on because people treat you differently when you've got a uniform on. In my normal clothes people talk to me like I'm an idiot or something but when I've got my uniform on they reckon I can do just about anything which is fine by me, I know which one I prefer.

So I made Ma take her hand off my shoulder and said I've got work to do Ma. I climbed over the bricks to where the ARP warden was waiting. What's your name? he asked. Michael, I said. Alright then Michael, he said, we've got to work our way through all this slowly to see if there's any survivors. Be careful and don't get in the way of the firemen. Can you do that? Of course I nodded so we got cracking but there wasn't much we could do, it was all in a right tangle and the bits of wood were too heavy for us to lift.

There wasn't much sound just the crackle of the fire and the hiss where the firemen were squirting it with water. More people came, ordinary people and wardens and then Civil Defence and another fire engine. Me and the warden climbed about on the hot bricks and wood which was a bit dangerous but I had to look for survivors. I went a bit to one side of the ARP warden where it was darker and there was a big pile of wood not on fire including a door which looked brand new so I got hold of the door handle and pulled it up. Underneath was an arm buried in the pile of wood and a hand with all its fingers missing but the thumb was still on it. There was a bit of cloth halfway up the arm and I recognised it from only a little while ago which meant that I'd found Mrs Tyler. Well her arm at least. It was difficult to see whether there was any more of her under the wood but one thing I did know and that was Mrs Tyler was dead.

I looked at her arm. Apart from not having any fingers it wasn't much different really from when she'd been going on about unacceptable behaviour and Ma had given her a piece of her mind. It was funny to think that ten minutes ago this thing that I was looking at was all joined together with the rest of Mrs Tyler. She was able to move about and hold a cup of tea and now it looked like something in the window at Mr Gormley the butcher's. It was a shame that Ma and Mrs Tyler had had an argument because now they wouldn't be able to say sorry. I reached down and touched it. The fire made one side of my face really hot and the other really cold. Mrs Tyler's arm was soft and warm. For some reason I thought of my pa and his blood making all the mud turn red. Mrs Tyler died quick and Pa died slow but it all adds up to the same thing in the end.

Did the starlings know Mrs Tyler was going to die? Did they try to tell someone or was it the right time for her to go? I wonder when my time will be.

I looked round to find the ARP warden. Mrs Tyler's here! I shouted and he climbed over the bricks to where I was and looked at her arm. How the hell do you know THAT'S Mrs Tyler? he said. Because I was here ten minutes ago, I said, and he said TEN MINUTES? and that's how I ended up in the paper and everybody heard about the miracle.

It's funny but every time I said about the starlings and how it was them who told me what to do by the way they made the patterns in the sky everybody just smiled and kind of ignored that bit and went on about how I must have heard the Heinkel coming because of how good my ears are or how me and Ma were really close because of Pa dying when I was only a nipper so I had a special intuition about when she was in danger. It's as though nobody dares to believe that the birds knew about what was going to happen. Well I know different. I know the first I heard that Heinkel was after I'd fetched Ma out of the Sally Army. I know the starlings wrote about the future and for some reason or other they let me read a tiny bit of it. Perhaps they felt sorry for me for not having a pa and knew I needed a ma. Perhaps they could tell I loved birds. I don't know.

The war is still going on but Fucking Adolf isn't bothering us so much now. Norman says he's got enough on his hands with the Ruskies but we still sit on the roof of the pier anyway just in case. We drink Taffy's terrible tea and listen to the radio and talk about all sorts of stuff but in the winter come evening time I always watch the starlings and I wonder what it is they are writing about now.

*1965*

# The Inscrutable Glass

Bella Kaminska twitched the curtain of her booth window to one side and looked down at the crowds thronging the beach. Her gaze scanned the seething mass of humanity, united in its determination to make the most of a fitful afternoon sun which, during its brief appearances from behind a succession of large clouds, had managed to muster a sprinkling of bikinis and trunks; tease middle-aged men out of their shirts so that the tapestry of sunbathers was flecked with the convex white of stomach-filled vests; unbutton the waistcoats and cardigans of older couples; and even entice one or two hardy souls into the choppy, brownish-green water of an incoming tide. And if any one of these determined holidaymakers had glanced up at the pier they, like so many others before them, would have been seduced by the expression in Bella's tiny brown eyes, set deeply in a face constructed entirely of soft, smooth, curving surfaces, like sultanas pushed into a ball of dough. Forbearance is what they would have seen, a soothing acceptance of their faults and foibles, but then these were Bella's professional eyes, constructs designed to shield the reality beneath. Reflections of the crowded beach drifted over their brown carapace, under which ran the more truthful currents of both avarice and exasperation.

"Look at them, Tom," she said, nose almost touching the glass. A wistful note entered her voice. "No one's bothered about the future when the sun's shining."

The ginger cat, which was lying on a windowsill to best

enjoy whatever warming rays became available, declined the offer, preferring instead to look rather pityingly at his owner before stretching out even more luxuriously along the narrow ledge.

Bella glanced over her shoulder at the reclining animal. "Don't strain yourself," she said sarcastically, before returning her attention to the crowded beach. "Come on, you lot, *some*body must fancy a walk on the pier!"

Business, despite her exhortations suggesting the opposite, had never been better. Since opening her fortune-telling booth in 1958 Bella had watched the resort blossom as postwar austerity and rationing gave way to a period of vigorous growth, supplying an ever-increasing number of people with sufficient cash left over in their pocket to enjoy a holiday at the seaside, money that Bella was more than happy to relieve them of in return for a few reassuring words on what fate had in store for them. Fate, or rather her own shrewd interpretation based on a fluid formula which combined observation, stereotype, subtle questioning and a modicum of what Bella liked to think of as improvisational resourcefulness. Certainly she was not privy to any genuine foresight; all Bella could see in her crystal ball was an inverted and distorted view of her booth, blotted out occasionally by the looming features of her client as they attempted to witness for themselves the impending events that were apparently parading across the inscrutable glass. Lines on the palm of a hand might as well have been hieroglyphics, and, although she had learnt the basic significances of the Tarot cards, Bella's interpretation of their appearance was always relentlessly optimistic. Even the most doom-laden of spreads was turned into an auspicious vision of the future, dependent only on her client following Bella's guidelines. These postscript homilies were her favourite part of the job. If she liked the person sitting across the table from her she might encourage them to try something new, or persevere, or follow their heart; if, on the other hand, the client had incurred her displeasure in any way (and this was not difficult to achieve), she favoured trying to steer them down a path that would, based on her character assessment of them, cause them the most grief. In this, Bella truly believed she was acting as an instrument of justice, helping to maintain decency and morality in the world based, naturally, on *her* definition of goodness. Her husband Vincent disapproved of his wife's attempts at social engineering, saying that someday it would come back to bite her, but Bella seldom listened to anything Vincent said, so she was certainly not going to pay attention to what she regarded as meddling in her field of expertise.

The sun disappeared behind a large bank of cloud that stretched to the horizon, suggesting that the day's sunbathing opportunities had come to an end. Bella looked up with a conspiratorial smile at the curdled grey slab drifting slowly eastward. "Oh dear," she said to no one in particular, "the sun's gone in. What a shame. Come on, Tom, buck your ideas up a bit, lad, they'll be queueing up for a reading before we know it. Ooh, that's right look, the jumpers and jackets are going on already. Just time for a nice stroll on the pier before going home for tea. And don't bother with that idiot Gypsy Rose Lee, if she's a gypsy I'm a monkey's uncle. I know for a fact she comes from a posh family in Norfolk who chucked her out after some sort of shenanigans with a friend of her father's. Julie from the amusements told me after half a bottle of Crème de Menthe, and those two are thick as thieves. *And* that ridiculous accent is all put on, you know. I've heard her talking on the phone and there was none of that 'oh ja I vos in a caravan living for many years', just a load of oohs and arrs like some sort of country yokel. Why she had to set up here I'll never know, taking away my customers and making out *she* was the original fortune-teller." Bella warmed to her theme. "The bloody cheek of the woman! Plonks herself down not a hundred yards from the pier when there's all the prom to choose from. If that isn't a deliberate… what do they call it? You know, when something starts a war. What is it?"

She looked again at the cat, but he was asleep. "Well you're no help, are you? What is it? What is it? Oh yes, an act of provocation. Yes, that's what she is, an act of provocation. What else could you call it? Well, if it's a fight she's after she'll find she's picked the wrong one to have it with, I'm telling you. I know what her game is. She's after this booth, Tom. She wants all the pier trade. Well, she's got another think coming!"

The velvet curtain that separated Bella's booth from the rest of the pier moved inward slightly, as though caught by a passing breeze, but then she noticed the scuffed tip of a shoe poking under the bottom of the curtain, a shoe she recognised.

"Mickey, what are you up to?" She addressed the curtain.

A voice spoke from the other side of the faded red material. "It isn't too late, is it?"

Bella scowled. "What?"

"It isn't too late, is it?"

"Too late for what?"

"A cup of tea."

"Why would it..." Bella suddenly realised the ridiculousness of holding a conversation through the curtain. "Oh for goodness sake come in!"

The curtain flapped again, before being slowly drawn aside to reveal Mickey Braithwaite, the pier's deckchair attendant. He beamed at Bella, but made no move to enter the booth.

"You don't have to knock, you know," she said.

"Knock?"

"On the door."

He looked up at the door frame, wrinkling his nose to help keep his heavy, dark-framed glasses in place. "You haven't got a door."

"Well, I think you'll find I *have*, sweetheart, but it's open, isn't it, it's fastened back against the... I wasn't being... Oh, never mind, it doesn't matter." Bella leaned forward, settling her broad, stubby-fingered hands on the velvet tablecloth.

The array of gold rings cluttering each finger had a treasure trove's allure. "Why were you lurking outside, anyway?"

Mickey's eyes opened wide. "Slurping?"

"God give me strength," Bella murmured under her breath. She raised her fingers off the table and perused her rings. "No, Mickey, lurking. *Lurking*. To lurk… to hang about in a suspicious manner." The blank expression that greeted her definition prompted a change of tack. "I saw your foot under the curtain."

Understanding sprang into his eyes. "I heard you talking! I thought you might have been talking to me so I got a bit closer to listen. I didn't understand most of it, though, so then I thought you weren't talking to me after all. Then I thought you were talking to someone who wanted to know their fortune, but there isn't anyone here so that's not right either."

Bella sighed. She wondered why the deckchair attendant had become so attached to her. She had never actively encouraged him, unless their passing nods and hellos during her first months on the pier had been misinterpreted as signs of a desire for friendship. Had he been looking for some sort of mother substitute? Bella's aptitude for gossip and the eager dissimulation of any calamitous chapters in people's lives meant that she had soon possessed a sort of potted biography of many of the pier's main characters, which naturally included that of Mickey Braithwaite, who had been a fixture on the pier since the end of the war, dispensing and collecting deckchairs with a meticulousness and seemingly unquenchable enthusiasm that to Bella appeared close to an obsession. She knew that he wasn't quite the full shilling, that he had saved his mother from a stray bomb dropped from a German plane heading home during the war, and that fate had seen fit to balance this woman's serendipitous escape with a brain tumour which killed her only five years later. She knew he still lived with his aunt and uncle. According to several of Bella's most reliable sources his aunt apparently doted on him, whereas his uncle favoured putting him into an institution. She knew his brother had met and married an Italian girl, and she knew that you could show Mickey a picture of any bird and he would be able to tell you which species it was. Of course, Bella being Bella, it was the mother's tale of miraculous deliverance and its subsequent implacable re-balancing that attracted her the most, not only as an example of Death's petulance, but also as a lesson in how ignorance was an essential prerequisite for living a happy life. No doubt Mrs Braithwaite had thought herself incredibly lucky, perhaps even chosen or singled out for some reason. She would have taken an extra pleasure in every day's detail, its careless beauty, a thousand such days before that first savage headache. Bella would never understand why the people who came into her booth were so obsessed with the future and what it had in store for them. As far as she was concerned there was only one, inevitable conclusion, and anything before that was down to either chance or luck. What she had not asked for, however, was some sort of surrogate idiot son.

"Didn't you mention a cup of tea, Mickey?"

He nodded enthusiastically. "I thought you might like a cup of tea. Unless it's too late. It might be too late."

She gave the table a brisk percussive roll, beautifully synchronised, with the fingers of both hands, from little finger to forefinger. "How, in the name of all that's holy, could it possibly be too late for a cup of tea?"

The deckchair attendant wrinkled his nose to push his glasses back up, with limited success. "Uncle Walter says that no one should drink tea after four o'clock."

"Does he now? And what *are* we supposed to drink after four o'clock?"

"Beer."

"That figures." Bella knew all about the philandering Walter Heaton, who at eighty-one was still as incorrigible as ever, always ready with a smutty remark for a barmaid, or to excuse a fumbled grope as simply the result of his infirmity. Val, manager of the pier's Tudor Bar, had told

Bella that she often saw him on the front row during bathing beauty competitions, playing with himself quite shamelessly beneath the cover of his mac.

"You shouldn't believe everything your Uncle Walter says," Bella advised, "he's just a dirty old man who drinks too much."

"He got me in the Observer Corps."

"Did he." The fortune-teller wasn't entirely sure what the Observer Corps was, but presumed it had something to do with the war. "Probably wanted you out of the house for some reason or other."

The character assassination went completely over Mickey's head, however. "He said I was the best spotter in the regiment!"

Bella looked more closely at the middle-aged man in front of her, assessing him as she would a prospective customer. Mickey Braithwaite appeared older than his years, aged by a straggly mop of grey hair, grey stubble and an air of vulnerability that she found both touching and yet also almost impossible to resist taking advantage of. There was very little to be gleaned from his pale, blue-grey eyes, which peered out from behind National Health glasses so thick and grimy that they resembled the blank eyes of the waxworks on display in the resort's Museum of Oddities. There was a superficial likeness to a human eye, in structure at least, but behind the pupil and iris lay a catastrophic void. Bella shied away from too long a contact with this absence. She suspected that if you delved too deeply whilst attempting to determine its extremities there was a danger of never returning. Did the deckchair attendant concern himself with the future at all? She suspected not. His world was defined and contained by the wrought-iron balustrade that edged the pier. Time, like the sea, lapped ineffectually beneath the silvery boards, whilst the rows of striped deckchairs, positioned by Mickey with military precision, provided a perpetual present, a geometry of smaller structures upon a greater whole within which he could safely navigate and know his place. He had no need of a future.

"I tell you what, Mickey," Bella said, "you nip to the cafe and see if they've got any cream buns that need eating up, and I'll put the kettle on. How does that sound?"

"It's not too late?" There was still a note of uncertainty in his voice.

"Mickey, you're just going to have to trust me on this." She stood up and stepped round the table, suppressing an urge to slap him, quite hard, across the face. In an effort to convert this need for physical expression into something more acceptable she gripped his shoulders and shook him gently. "*You* were the best spotter in the regiment, and *I* know when it's a good time for a cup of tea. Alright?"

He seemed to accept quite readily this rather strange conflation of skills as an explanation. "Okey-dokey."

"Okey-dokey," Bella reiterated. She released Mickey from her grip. He remained rooted to the spot. "Off you go, then!"

Some lever or cog in the deckchair attendant's mind clicked into place, turning him round and propelling him away from the booth on a direct heading towards the pier's cafe, the leather satchel flapping at his hip in which he collected the sixpences and two bobs requested for an hour or a day's hire.

On turning round Bella saw a young couple studying the sign in her booth window. She attached her welcoming yet enigmatic smile and stepped across to them. "Hello, my darlings," she purred.

"I've got a feeling this is going to be your lucky day."

# The Corrosive Powers of Birdshit

The rain rattling against the booth's windows was like a massed tapping of fingernails, while below the pier the sea was being whipped into a series of surging waves that crashed into the sea wall and spread across the promenade with an acidic hiss. Seagulls hovered above this brown and white turmoil, excited beyond measure by its unpredictable updrafts. They hung, wings outstretched as though offering themselves up for crucifixion, blanched martyrs screaming their ecstasy in the face of the storm. Spume scuttered over the pavement like the spittle from a madman.

Bella looked up from her *Woman's Weekly* and focused on the rain running down the window. "Not a lot of point us being here for much longer, Tom," she remarked. "Once I've finished this crossword we'll scarper, alright?"

The cat, curled up on her lap, remained silent.

The fortune-teller enjoyed being on the pier in rough weather. She had complete faith in the Victorian engineers and their creation, its roots firmly attached to the bedrock beneath the beach. The pier had remained steadfast in weather far worse than this summer storm, and Bella had no doubt that the resort's century-old attraction would still be here long after she was dead and buried. The storm excited her, it churned up something primeval inside her, and she could think of nowhere better to witness it than from within her booth on the pier, suspended above the chaos with her crossword puzzle and a cup of tea, cocooned in a bubble of comfort and warmth created by an enduring amalgamation of iron, wood and glass. Bella looked towards the promenade and could just discern a face peering out from the window of a hotel bedroom. Were they, she wondered, as spellbound by the rain, the waves and the daunting sky as she was? Were they thinking what it would be like to offer oneself up to the storm?

"I don't know, your mum's going daft in her old age," she said, tugging gently at the cat's ears. "I don't suppose falling into the sea and drowning would be very pleasant really, do you? Although they do say that drowning *is* quite peaceful, once you stop struggling. I suppose that's natural, though, isn't it? To struggle, I mean. We're not going to give in without a fight, are we? It's alright for you, you've got nine lives, although I've never been quite sure whether that means you can have eight really bad accidents and get away with them, or if you can actually *die* eight times and still get another go." She shook her head, persuaded by the vibration of the cat's purring. "No, it has to be accidents, doesn't it, or lucky escapes. Nothing can be brought back to life once it's dead. Unless your nine lives are something like reincarnation, but what would be the point of that? Would you come back as the same cat, or a new one? Would you know that you'd lost one of your lives? And how would you keep a count of them? If you only had one life left you'd need to know so you could be a bit more careful." Bella shrugged, somewhat perplexed by her own philosophising. "It probably just means you're supposed to be lucky," she concluded.

Tom stood up, turned round and settled back in her lap, seemingly unconcerned by the possibility that he harboured the ability to defy death.

Bella looked down at her cat. "Well *you're* lucky, that's for sure. Life of Riley, you've got." She returned her attention to the crossword. "Right, eight down... author of *Lady Chatterley's Lover*, one one eight. Oh, I know that. Val read it not long ago and said she didn't know what all the fuss was about... said it was a lot of talking and not much how's your father. That reminds me, she was going to lend it me... I'll have to... DH Lawrence! That's it. Ooh, that means Keeler's right as well."

Only the D and H had been committed to paper when the door burst open, allowing a gust of wind and rain to sweep into the booth, riffling through the magazine's pages and stirring the red drapes into a frenzy of movement. Bella flinched in her chair, startled and slightly disorientated by the customer's sudden entrance, which seemed for a moment to have recast her booth into a tumult of billowing scarlet. The cat leaped from her lap, its claws piercing her skirt and inflicting pinpricks of pain on her thigh. She caught a glimpse of a young man's face, pale-skinned and with several strands of dark wet hair slicked across his forehead, before he turned and closed the door, returning the room to relative calm. He stayed in that position for a moment, the limp newspaper which he had been using as a makeshift umbrella still held over his head, his gaze seemingly fixed on the theatre at the end of the pier.

"Un-bloody-believable," the young man muttered. He let the arm drop that was holding the newspaper, which he then slapped down on the windowsill, swept back the wet hair from his forehead and made a desultory attempt to brush the worst of the rain from the front of his jacket.

Bella, regaining her composure from her customer's turbulent entrance, coughed in an exaggerated fashion to catch his attention. "This isn't a public shelter, you know," she pointed out.

"I know," he replied, still facing towards the door. "It's you I've come to see."

"Oh?"

"Yeah. Should I have made an appointment?"

Bella thought she detected a hint of sarcasm in the young man's voice, but as his generation had seemingly adopted this combative style as their default form of intonation when speaking to anyone over the age of thirty, for the moment she would give him the benefit of the doubt. "No, that isn't necessary. Looking at the person you're talking to is, though."

"Hmm?" He appeared distracted. "Oh, yeah. Right." He swivelled on the heel of one narrow, pointed boot, rotating with a measured, insolent grace until he was facing her. "Is that better?"

"Much." Bella performed one of her snap appraisals, taking in the young man's pale grey eyes, which looked back at her with a febrile intensity unusual in one so young, his fashionably styled but cheaply made suit, polished boots with worn-down heels, neatly manicured fingernails and an old-fashioned gold signet ring on his little finger. She processed all these observations individually, then combined them and placed the resulting personality on her sliding scale of credulity, all within a matter of seconds. And her interpretation of these details? That she was going to have a tough job convincing this grumpy, hard up, fastidious young man, who was probably close to a dead male relative, maybe his father or grandfather, that she was genuine. He stood quite motionless during this evaluation, unblinking despite the rain still dripping from his fringe. It was as though he knew this process of assessment was taking place, and accepted it without question.

Bella gestured at the chair opposite her. "Take a seat." She watched the young man settle himself, taking care not to crease the back of his jacket. He crossed his legs and hooked his thumbs into the pockets of his trousers. "Well," she continued, "what brings you to see Madame Kaminska?"

He gave her an exaggerated wink. "I'd have thought you'd know that already, you being a fortune-teller and all."

How many times had she heard remarks like that? Everything from which horse was going to win next year's Grand National to knowing whether they were in for a hot summer. "Personal futures are my speciality, sweetheart," she replied. "You don't think I'd be sitting here if I could win the pools every week, do you?"

"So basically you're telling me you're not very good, is that it?"

"No, that's not what I meant at all." His belligerence towards her confused Bella; it went beyond the normal inter-generational exasperation, and she was certain he had not visited her before, meaning he could not be harbouring a grievance over some unfulfilled prognostication. It was almost as though he were there under duress, sent against his will to uncover a destiny he would rather not know.

"Eizel," he muttered.

"I beg your pardon?"

"Never mind," he said dismissively.

Bella took a deep breath, deliberately making it audible as a form of punctuation, a way of moving on the conversation from its present inertia. "First," she said, "you must cross my palm with silver. Half a crown will do nicely."

The young man fished in his pocket, brought out a handful of change and selected two coins. He made a great show of placing them on the table in front of her. "I reckon you're only worth two bob, *Mrs* Kaminska. Take it or leave it."

Bella looked at the two shilling coins. A part of her wanted to pick them up and throw them back at this arrogant young man, to teach him a lesson about manners, and to show him that she was not so easily intimidated, but there was something about him, the sort of truculence that usually masks a bruised, mysterious hinterland many women find incredibly seductive. He reminded Bella of the persuasive, slightly dangerous men who enticed people onto their fair-ground ghost train; you knew there were things lurking in the darkness behind those shabby doors that would make you scream, and yet you boarded the train nevertheless, a willing victim. Despite her misgivings, she picked up the coins.

"Seeing as it's been a quiet day... What's your name, sweetheart?"

He looked down for a moment. "Why do you need to know?"

"Well, so that we can communicate properly. It's common courtesy." She looked at him quizzically. "Have you got a problem with that?"

He scowled. "What's it to you? Does it make any difference what my name is? Won't your," and here he waved one hand in the direction of the cards, "*magic* work properly otherwise?"

"I should imagine so," Bella admitted. She was beginning to feel slightly frightened of this ill-tempered young man, who seemed to take offence at the most innocently posed of questions. For the first time the fortune-teller became aware of the vulnerability of her position; she was, to all intents and purposes, trapped in the booth, which itself was far enough from both shore and theatre for cries of help not to be heard, particularly in the middle of a storm. With its red curtains hiding the interior from view, Bella was at the mercy of any customer strong enough to overpower her, and though she would defend herself as well as she was able, she was under no illusion as to the inevitable outcome of a struggle with her current client. She felt an animosity towards him for causing this change in perception, which would, she knew, burrow into her subconscious and in the future forever colour her time on the pier. To calm herself down Bella reasoned that if he had wanted simply to attack her he would have done so already. Perhaps he was just annoyed by being caught in the storm, and once the reading began he would relax.

"I foresee a hot bath and a change of clothes," she joked in an attempt to lighten the atmosphere, while wondering where Tom had disappeared to.

"Very funny."

He seemed disinclined to add anything to this, so Bella mentally crossed out 'sense of humour' and decided to get down to business. "I presume you'd like me to give you a reading. Is there anything in particular you're interested in? You know, love, work, family, health?"

"Aren't you supposed to be able to guess that?"

"It isn't easy for me to find my way along the path of your destiny," Bella explained, repeating a statement she had formulated years ago as a means of avoiding a huge amount of initial guesswork. "If I'm given an area to look in it saves a lot of time."

The young man leaned back in his chair and studied the ceiling for a moment before returning his dispassionate gaze to her. "Are you a real gypsy?"

Bella smiled. She had expected him to be unpredictable, a test both of her character judgment and initiative, but it seemed he wanted the same questions answered as anyone else. She relaxed slightly, placated by finding herself on familiar ground. "I certainly am, young man. The Kaminskas have been a Romany family since the Middle Ages," she recited. "We've been soothsayers to several courts of Europe, we've been magicians, healers… I'm just the latest in a very long line, and probably not the most powerful, either. My great-grandmother could tell someone's future simply by holding their hand."

"I wasn't after a bleedin' family history. Just a yes or no would have done."

"In that case," Bella said huffily, "yes, I am."

"Well alright then." There was something in his voice, an intonation so subtle it was barely audible, that suggested a requirement ticked, as though he had been primed beforehand by someone else.

Bella, her fraudster's ear finely tuned to such inflections, laid her hands, fingers outstretched, on the table. "So, do I pass?"

The young man thrust forward his head and chest and smiled at Bella's visible flinch. "We'll have to see about that, won't we?"

She could smell the alcohol on his breath, see the skin around his eyes coarsening already from heavy drinking. Bella knew only too well the intense and unpredictable mood swings of an alcoholic; when she was twelve her Uncle Reg began visiting regularly, ostensibly to see Bella's mother, who was his younger sister, but Bella soon discovered she had reached an age that meant his main interest lay with her. 'My, she's sprouting in all the right directions, Janet,' he would say, slapping Bella on her bottom. Further emboldened on each subsequent visit — a squeeze here, a pat there — Reg helped himself to his sister and brother-in-law's whisky and bided his time for the ideal opportunity, which came seven months later when her parents were invited out to dinner. Bella had enquired who was coming to look after her for the evening, and was informed that Uncle Reg had kindly volunteered. On hearing this Bella's blood ran cold, because even at that age she had a fairly good idea as to why he wanted to be alone in the house with her, fears which proved sadly well-founded. Within five minutes of her parents leaving in the cab Reg had poured himself three glasses of whisky, downed each one in a single gulp, refilled for the fourth time and headed upstairs to Bella's bedroom, where she was curled up on her bed, eyes squeezed shut, expecting a knock on the door at any moment. The clink of ice in his glass echoed up the stairwell like the tolling of a cracked bell, and when it stopped outside her door Bella began to weep silently. Uncle Reg opened the door with a slowness that in other circumstances would have been funny, but on that particular evening could only be interpreted as unspeakably cruel. He walked into the bedroom, closing the door behind him, and strode to her bedside. Bella could hear him breathing heavily through his nose. The ice cubes clattered round the glass as he emptied it, clattered again as he banged it down on her bedside table. 'Don't pretend you're asleep,' he said, his voice little more than a whisper. 'I know you're not asleep. Don't pretend, my beautiful little Bella.' And then he roared, a voice so utterly different that she opened her eyes, expecting to see a second man standing there, but it was still her uncle, his mouth slackly open, the skin on his face blotchy and red. 'Don't fucking *pretend*!'

After that Bella could only remember his hands on either

side of her face, pushing her down in front of him, then one hand moving to unbutton the fly of his trousers. The heat of his erect penis on her cheek was like a branding iron. He squeezed open her mouth, held it wide, thumb and fingers pushing down on her jaw, and rammed his penis between her teeth. Bella closed her eyes, closed her mind to what was happening, and instead thought only of her favourite climbing tree, a giant sycamore in the rectory grounds nearby. She began to climb that tree, concentrating on each branch and handhold, as familiar to her as the staircase in their house. Birds sang in the branches above her, a breeze tickled the leaves, and the higher she climbed, the further she retreated from the appalling violation being visited upon her. The tree welcomed her into its sanctuary, a shifting world of dark green and dappled sunlight, where the grunts of Uncle Reg, the pain in her jaw, and, finally, the viscid jet that hit the back of her throat and made her gag, all fluttered away, falling to the ground like the winged seed pods liberated each year from these same branches, leaving Bella to draw up her knees, wrap her arms round her legs, and fall asleep to the sound of rooks squabbling on the graveyard's drunken stones.

"So," she began, "how would you like me to read your future? Cards, crystal ball or palm?"

He stuck out his bottom lip, looked first at the crystal ball on the side of the table, then at the neatly stacked Tarot cards, and finally at the palm of his hand, as though assessing each method's accuracy. Still looking at his hand, the young man spoke, his voice edged with what sounded very much like dismay. "It's all there, then. My life, from start to finish, all done in a few lines." He snorted and shook his head in an expression of mordant amusement.

Bella looked up, surprised by this glimpse of a more contemplative side to his character. "They show the main events, the biggest influences, but what happens in between, and how you use this knowledge, well, that's down to you."

"Oh yeah, right, like a rat in a maze has choices. Hmm, what shall I do today? I know, I'll turn left. Yeah, that should be exciting. Better than turning right."

Bella relaxed in her chair. If she had been given a pound for every time a customer asked her about the possibility of change, of them being able to somehow alter the path of their life, then she would be a rich woman. Her own belief was that almost everyone followed the path of least resistance, a route of ever-diminishing choice dictated by timidity, self-delusion and compromise. Of course there was happiness, and love, and fulfillment, but Bella regarded all such positive outcomes as particularly fortuitous corollaries of certain paths; in other words, luck. The universe did not select winners and losers, and for Bella there was no mitigating God. She knew, however, what to say to her customers.

"The influences are fixed," she asserted, "but there are always different ways of reacting to them. That's where your choice lies. Do you see what I mean?"

"Not really."

Why, she wondered, had this morose man come to see her, and in such foul weather? And why was she taking so much time to explain things that she did not believe in? Perhaps it was because there was something about him that intrigued her, quite apart from his possession of a much older man's fatalistic attitude, and which chimed neatly with her own pragmatism. For all his arrogance and hostility she thought she discerned a dread behind the bluster, and she could not help but wonder what could be haunting someone so young.

"Well, imagine if I turned over the Death card—"

"Oh, brilliant."

"No, no," Bella added hurriedly, "that's my point. The Death card doesn't literally mean death, it means an ending. So you see, if you took it pessimistically you might think it meant you were going to die, or lose someone close to you, but you could also see it as meaning one thing ending and another starting, like a job, or a new girlfriend."

He glanced at the pack of Tarot cards. "All seems a bit vague to me."

"Well, it isn't quite as straightforward as that," Bella explained. "It's all to do with positions, and how one card relates to another, that sort of thing."

"Nah, I don't fancy that," the young man stated. "I don't want to know about any fortune that depends on a card with a bleedin' skeleton on it, whether it's an ending or whatever." He thrust his hands towards her. "'Ere, read my palm, and if there's a skeleton on that as well you can leave it out."

Outside the storm was abating, driven inland by gusts of wind that hummed and keened through the struts and girders of the pier. Rain was still crackling against the south-facing windows, but as Bella reached across to begin her reading an ingot of sunlight crashed across the table, erasing all detail of the palms resting there with its sudden brilliance. And then it was gone again, extinguished, a momentary expiation.

"Are you right-handed or left-handed?" Bella asked.

"Right-handed. What, so my right side's got a different future to my left?"

She laughed. Perhaps she had been wrong about the sense of humour. "No, it's just that your dominant hand gives the best reading. Some say the left is what the gods gave you and the right is what you do with it, or left is past and right is future, but I think that just complicates the reading. Shall we begin?"

His only reply was to take away his left hand and edge the right closer to Bella's side of the table, so taking this as a gesture of approval, she leaned forward to begin her well-rehearsed routine. But then she hesitated. Normally Bella held her customer's hand in both of hers, cradling it for the duration of the reading unless to point out some particular feature, but for some reason she felt a reluctance to instigate physical contact with him. She stared at his hand, with its unremarkable shape, unremarkable colour, and nicotine-stained fingers, and wondered what it was that was pushing her away, a repulsion which reminded her of that invisible yet tangible force felt when attempting to bring together the like poles of two magnets. The nearer her hands got to his the stronger it became. It was really most peculiar.

"What's up? Forgotten what to do?"

"Of course not!" Bella snapped. The tension she had felt earlier had returned, and she found herself wishing that he had chosen Gypsy Rose Lee for his reading rather than her. Bella could see the scene in her mind's eye: the police holding back a crowd of onlookers gathered outside her booth, craning their necks to get a glimpse of the poor fortune-teller lying in a pool of her own blood, and then the image, frozen in black-and-white by the pop and flash of a press photographer's camera, splashed across the front page of the newspaper under the declamatory headline *FORTUNE-TELLER BRUTALLY MURDERED*. With a decisive movement she erased the vision and took hold of his hand, which she was surprised to find both soft and warm. "Let me see... Ah, yes, an interesting life-line." She always began with the life-line. Over the years Bella had learned that her customers' main priorities were longevity, wealth and love, in that order. Clear those concerns and then she could have a little fun with the rest. "Quite long, with no big breaks, so no major health problems, and a nice shape too." What she really saw was a pale crease, almost obscured by a jumble of criss-crossing small lines on its curve near the base of the thumb. Bella couldn't remember what this was supposed to signify, but she assumed it was bad, and therefore not an advisable opening statement.

"Ah, but look here," she continued, adding a sympathetic note to her voice. "Do you see this line, the one that curves away near the top?" This was her first presumption, a necessary but always risky move, when she assimilated one of her initial observations into the reading. This almost always set the tone for the rest of the reading; find an accurate interpretation and they were hers for the taking; miss the target and their suspicions inevitably spoiled the mood and made them less likely to accept any further prediction, no matter how hard she tried.

"What about it?"

"You lost someone close to you, didn't you? When you were quite young."

He laughed once; it was the closest Bella had ever heard someone come to a disparaging 'ha'. "Wow. Unbelievable. A relative dying. How could you have possibly known that?"

Bella was stung by his contempt, and decided to make a guess as to the original owner of the signet ring. She was no expert on men's jewellery, but it looked quite old, with its flat-topped, dark red stone. She would show him. "It was your grandfather. You were always closer to him than your father."

She felt the slightest of movements, an almost imper-ceptible recoiling. If their hands had not been in contact she would never have noticed it, but Bella knew instantly that her speculative arrow had found its target. She glanced up at the young man, preparing to fend off a protestation, even a denial, but he remained silent, his gaze fixed on the palm of his hand as though witness to some form of betrayal.

"You see the way that line joins your heart line," Bella continued quickly, seizing the initiative, "well, that means a very strong bond... One that even death can't break."

"He was trimming the hedge," he said simply. "That's all. Just a bit of gardening because the doctor had told him the fresh air and exercise would do him good. My gran found him when she brought him a cup of tea. He must have been there a while because she noticed a bird had shit on his face."

Bella did not know how to react to this spontaneous, calmly delivered statement. The young man clearly felt a great deal of anger concerning the manner of his grandfather's death, yet at the same time saw nothing wrong in making public the poor man's final humiliation, caused by the simple and unknowing action of a passing bird. And unless he had been there at the time he could only have found out this detail from a third party, either his grandmother or someone to whom she told it, which begged the question as to why they would burden a grieving grandchild with this demeaning particularity.

"A bird… " was all she could come up with.

"Yes, a *bird*. My old man reckoned it was a blackbird getting its revenge for Grandpa pulling out its nest."

"It was your father who told you."

"Oh yes," he confirmed tightly. "My old man doesn't believe in sugaring the pill."

"No," she agreed, "he certainly doesn't." Bella surmised that the young man's father had informed his son about the birdshit as a way of showing him that the grandpa he had idolised was in fact just as fragile and transient as anyone else. Whether that was through petulance, having not been accorded the sort of hero worship he felt was his due, or simply out of a belief in exposing his son to the tenuous nature of life, she did not know, but whatever it was Bella began to feel some sympathy for the man sitting opposite her. His memory of perhaps the only person he had ever regarded as flawless would always be marked by that innocent deposit on his grandfather's face, and who knew what else it might in time corrode.

"Wouldn't it be better to remember him when he was alive?" She offered. "The two of you must have had lots of fun together… I'm sure your grandpa wouldn't want how he died to be the first thing you think of when people mention him."

He looked up. "Tell me what the other lines say."

Bella licked her lips, shaken by the utter lack of emotion in the young man's voice. It was like hearing a corpse speak. "Well… Don't you want to know how long you're going to live?"

"Not really."

The fortune-teller glanced round the tiny room, hoping to find some respite in its familiarity, but all it offered was claustrophobia and menace. Was he seeking one sign or answer in particular? And what would he do if she failed to deliver it? "Well, alright then, we'll go on to the next. You see the line nearest the top of your hand? That's your heart line, which obviously has things to say about love. Yours is telling me that you've liked one or two girls, but you haven't loved any of them... not yet, but there's another you know. She..." Bella smiled and nodded. "She thinks you're *interesting*... a bit of a challenge, but you hardly notice her, because she's quiet, and not quite as pretty as her friends. Not ugly, just a bit on the plain side, but she's a lovely girl, funny and bright. She's your true love."

He frowned. "And I know her already?"

"Yes. You've met several times."

"What colour hair has she got?"

Bella grimaced. "Oh, I can't tell *that*, sweetheart. The lines don't give everything away."

"Thin? Fat? Tall? Short? Black? White? Big tits? Small tits? Blue eyes? Brown eyes? Come on, give us a clue, for Christ's sake! How can you say she's the love of my life when you don't even know what she *looks* like?"

Bella was curiously reassured by her customer's latest outburst. She prided herself on her ability to assess and categorise someone's character, and having spoken to him for several minutes now she had come to the conclusion that his hostility was a defence mechanism, cultivated to disguise an insecurity that presumably stemmed from what had been a difficult relationship with his father. Truly violent people tended not to shout and scream, they just acted; this young man, hardly more than a boy, really, was simply covering his anxiety in the only way he knew how, which made Bella wonder where his mother fitted in to the picture. She began to plot an enquiry into her reading.

"We're expected to put a bit of effort in ourselves," she said.

"*Who* expects it? Who puts these stupid lines on our hand

and then expects us to figure it all out?" He demanded, lifting his hand towards her face. "God?"

Bella stared at the palm laid out before her, hoping against hope that an answer would miraculously form itself from the jumble of creases that taunted her incomprehension. No one had ever entered her booth on the pier and challenged her to a philosophical debate, and she was ill-equipped to respond. Had the powers-that-be decided to check up on fortune-tellers, she wondered, putting into operation a policy designed to root out the fraudulent, and was this young man some kind of inspector trying to catch her out?

"I don't think we need to bring Him into it," she replied, now thoroughly flustered. "It's just a bit of fun."

"So why not invent her?"

"Who?"

"The 'love of my life'. You only had to say a short blonde with big tits, or a tall brunette with blue eyes, and I'd have been happy."

Bella took a deep breath. "I'm just trying to be honest, sweetheart. I tell you what I can see, nothing more." She clung to her performance as affronted authentic like a drowning man to a piece of driftwood. "Or would you prefer me to just make it all up?"

He looked at her with a curious expression in his grey eyes, as though alerted to the possibility of irony, but Bella knew that the brown of her own could easily keep grey at bay, and so it proved. His gaze slid away, and his hand settled back onto the table.

"Alright," he snapped, then, more quietly, "alright, I get it. I'm supposed to fill in the blanks."

"Like a crossword puzzle."

"And the lines are the clues. Very profound. Alright then, *Madame* Kaminska, what else you got?"

"Well," Bella continued, "do you see the line below the heart line? This is your headline... what's going on in your head, basically."

Again he stuck out his bottom lip, mouth downturned in an expression of distaste. "This should be good," he drawled.

"It's not so bad, sweetheart." She stared at the short, wavy line, which sliced straight through his line of fate and racked her brains for a way of explaining this formation whilst simultaneously teasing out some detail about his mother. Had he failed to mention her because she had played a minor role in his life up until now, or did he want to protect her from the grubbier and yet psychologically more influential poles of his father and grandfather?

"Mmm... you're having a hard time making your mind up about what you want to do," she ventured, "but I can see success, once you decide. It'll take a while, but you'll get there in the end... if you keep at it. Oh dear," she said, with a laugh that she hoped would disarm her following words, "I'm sounding like your mother, aren't I?"

He looked at her again. The animosity in his eyes, expressed in a mineral-like flatness that gave Bella the impression she was looking at two pebbles from the beach twenty feet below, encircled her bowels in a cold, relentless grip. "Why do you think that's funny?"

"I just thought—"

"I just thought," he mimicked. "*I just thought*. What? What did you think?"

Bella let go of his hand, not only to break the physical connection, but also so that he would not feel her own trembling. Outside the resort was stirring, drawn out like a snail from its shell by the clearing skies. After a thorough cleansing and reinvigoration by the wind and rain it was now being burnished by the sun, which reflected off the wet surfaces and dazzled the eye in every direction. She heard the rattle of shutters as Eddie opened up his rock and candyfloss stall in the identical booth on the other side of the pier. Soon there would be a steady stream of people passing by, eager to breathe in the purified air, and some would feel the urge to seek out a glimpse of their future, inspired by the reconstituted resort to discover what lay beyond the storms of their own lives. And yet here she was, trapped inside her own booth with a lunatic who was searching for answers she did not possess.

"Why did you come to see me?" Bella asked, and even she could hear the note of pleading in her voice. "What are you looking for?"

"You don't know anything, do you?" he replied contemptuously. "You're pathetic. D'you get a kick out of messing with people's minds? Telling them what they should be doing?"

"I'm not trying to *tell* you anything."

He shook his head. "You probably don't even realise you're doing it. You're like every other woman, you just want to drain all the life out of us and turn us into zombies so we'll do as we're told. You're like a bleedin' *vampire*!"

Bella imagined the young man's father saying something similar, a sentiment perhaps updated by his son through a love of the Hammer horror films that her own husband was so enthusiastic about. "I really don't think I can help you," she said, inching back in her chair to maximise the distance between them.

He stood up, ran both hands through his still-damp hair, then held them, fingers interlocked, at the back of his head. "This was a stupid idea," he said, as though addressing someone else. "I knew I was wasting my time."

"And mine," the fortune-teller added under her breath.

"What was that?"

"Nothing. And if you don't mind I'd like to get ready for my next customer."

His hands dropped to his sides, where they continued to flex and twitch. "So. You've done your worst."

Bella held his gaze with a great effort of will. "Well, what do you expect for two bob?"

"Aw, piss off then," he said, turning away from her. He had opened the door of the booth, letting in a strong breeze that dispersed the tension with a diplomat's touch.

Bella felt released, almost to the point of hysteria, by her booth's inhalation. Never before had the sounds and smells of the resort seemed as sweet and precious, as though she had been buried underground for days and finally found a route back to the surface. "Leave the door open," she requested. "There seems to be a nasty smell in here."

The young man turned in the doorway to face her. "Yeah, it must be all the bullshit you're coming out with."

Bella could not help but laugh. "Very good! You should be on the stage."

He shook his head, either in sadness or disbelief, and then he was gone, reclaimed by the purifying light.

The curtain that separated the main part of the booth from the tiny area where Bella had her kettle and store cupboard moved slightly and Tom peeped out. Noting that his owner's most recent customer had departed, the cat stepped forward and rubbed himself around Bella's legs, purring loudly.

"Yes, I'm glad he's gone too," she said, reaching down to stroke the cat.

# Nightmares

Her nightmare began in the frail hour before dawn.

A crabbed, hunched figure is rushing towards her in a kind of lumpen scramble, boots on darkened pier pounding with metronomic rhythm, terrifying in its unvarying cadence. On and on the man comes, a silhouette, a hole, an animated brutality. His advance is relentless; it shakes the pier to its foundations. Bella can feel it tremble through the soles of her feet. He means her terrible harm, she knows this as unaccountable things are known in dreams, and yet she cannot move, cannot flee. She is rooted to the spot. Boom... boom... boom... boom his footsteps approach. She would not be surprised to see the pier shatter under his boots like a glass ornament. Who is he? *What* is he? It is too dark to make out any detail. A compounding of the terror settles on her as she senses that there may not be detail to be had, that the figure would be black in even the brightest of sunlight, a shadow untethered from its casting form. Closer and closer. The pier vibrates, a low resonance struck from its iron frame multiplying with every footfall into a deep, organ-like chord. He is almost upon her, blotting out all else and still she cannot move, though every fibre screams for release. And beneath the darkness a warped musculature slides, propelling the figure towards her with an inhuman functioning, reaching out, touching...

Bella jerked upright in bed, her heart pounding. The dark bedroom seemed, for a moment, like a continuation of her dream, a place where reason cannot prevail. She fumbled for the switch on her bedside lamp and clicked it on, knocking over one of the cups on the teasmade.

The clatter and light woke her husband Vincent. He grunted and turned over to face his wife. "What time is it?"

"Go back to sleep," Bella said testily. "It's early."

He coughed and rubbed the top of his head, generating a dry, rustling sound that Bella found irritating in the extreme. "*How* early?"

"For goodness sake… " She glanced at the alarm clock. "Ten past four."

"Bloody hell, Bella."

"I didn't wake you up on purpose, I assure you."

Vincent placed one hand over the lower half of his face, slowly massaged his stubbly cheeks and chin, then with thumb and forefinger kneaded at his closed eyes, pushing at them with such force that Bella feared for his sight, before finally dragging down the loose skin below them to reveal a pink meniscus cupping the bloodshot white. "That doesn't make me any less awake, though, does it? Bloody hell, Bella, I've got a busy day tomorrow… today."

"Well, I'm very sorry I spoiled your beauty sleep," she replied, the tone in her voice making quite clear that this was anything but an apology, "but I've just had a horrible dream, probably the worst dream I've ever had. If you were any kind of a husband you'd give me a cuddle and make me feel safe, but that would be too much to ask, wouldn't it? Put your arms around me? Heaven forbid! I can't remember the last time you came near me, and as for sex, well—"

"Here we go," Vincent muttered.

Bella, however, was in full flow. "*As for sex*," she repeated heavily, "I might as well just give up on that idea. You obviously find me so repulsive you can't bear the thought of any sort of intimate contact. I shouldn't be surprised, really, you were never all that bothered about it even when we were young. I'm amazed we ended up with children at all. Not that we would have done if I hadn't—"

"Let's do it now, then," Vincent interrupted, knowing, from long and bitter experience, that cutting across his wife's monologue was the only way to wedge his own opinion into the torrent of words.

"What?"

"Let's do it now. Come on, you obviously want to behave like those youngsters they keep catching under the pier." He plucked at the sleeve of her nightgown. "Come on, get 'em off."

Bella slapped her husband's hand away. "Sod off, Vincent. I said cuddle, but like most men you interpret 'cuddle' as 'sex'. After the dream I've just had the last thing I want is a big lummox on top of me trying to stick his tongue down my throat."

"Thanks a bunch." He had laced these three words with an inflection of deep hurt, but both he and Bella recognised, like most couples who have been together for many years, that this expression of martyrdom had been fashioned entirely for dramatic effect as part of a finely honed verbal jousting, bounded by unspoken rules governing the limits of what could and could not be said without causing real pain. Of course they both possessed the weaponry with which a terrible blow could be dealt to the other; a life properly shared opens up this vulnerability on some flank or other, but love stays the hand unless *in extremis*.

"Well, you pick your moments."

Vincent turned onto his back and stared up at the ceiling. "What were you dreaming about, anyway?"

Bella snuggled in closer to him and rested one arm on his chest. "It was horrible. I was on the pier, and this… *thing* was coming towards me, all bent and black, like a sort of cross between a crab and a human being, and its boots were going crash crash crash, louder and louder, until it touched me and I woke up." She shuddered.

"It was probably one of those daft buggers who you tell they're going to meet a tall dark stranger. Or maybe that *was* the tall dark stranger. You did say he was black."

Bella thumped her husband's chest. "Not black as in Louis Armstrong, you idiot, I meant black as in colour. Just black. Black as the ace of spades. Like something that had been horribly burned. I think I'd remember if one of my customers looked like *that*. I tell you, Vince, he was out to get me, I just knew it, somehow, like I'd done something wrong."

"Guilty conscience, that is."

"I don't hear you complaining about the money I bring home. It's those 'daft buggers' who paid for that Cortina in the garage, so don't come all high and mighty with me."

Vincent looked down at his wife. He knew her remarks regarding their sex life were just Bella being her usual provocative self. Indeed, inciting one of her typically feisty responses had, in their youth, been a favourite method of generating an erotic charge. Their exchanges had often been concluded with a bout of love-making made all the more dynamic for a lingering animosity, the movement, kissing and biting given an added exuberance as a means of exacting some form of retribution for an earlier barbed comment. When he thought back to those times now it seemed as though he was watching a film or documentary about someone else entirely; a frivolous, rather-too-sure-of-himself apprentice butcher who could never quite eliminate the smell of meat on his hands, and a quiet, naive typist with a remarkable hourglass figure. Vincent remembered the first time they met, when he followed Bella up the curving stairs of a Deansgate tram in 1934, admiring the way her calf muscles tensed and relaxed as she ascended the steps ahead of him. There were lots of empty seats on the top deck, but he plonked himself down next to her, bold as you like. When she turned to look at him, Vincent saw suspicion, even fear, flicker in her eyes, so he smiled and introduced himself with a touch of the brim of his snappy felt hat, hoping and praying that she would not dismiss him as some sort of spiv or wide-boy. Luckily his smile had done the trick, with Bella agreeing to meet him later at the Lyons cafe on Piccadilly. The following evening they went dancing, and the moment he had that girl in his arms Vincent knew she was the one for him.

It was sometimes difficult to reconcile that self-effacing young woman, with a waist he could almost span with his hands, with the chubby, combative grandmother now lying beside him, but then again he was sure Bella regarded him in much the same light. His arms and shoulders were still muscular and strong, legacy of a lifetime's butchering, but his stomach had expanded, his legs were wound about with varicose veins — like ivy up a tree trunk — from decades of standing behind a counter, and, worst of all, he found it difficult to maintain an erection for more than a few minutes. On the rare occasions they attempted to make love Vincent found the only way to maintain his ardour was to gently bounce one of Bella's large breasts in the cup of his hand, feeling its soft weight quiver against his fingers. He was under no illusion that Bella derived any great degree of sensual pleasure from this manoeuvre; she had once said it felt like he was weighing out a pound of tripe, but if it kept Vincent in a state of tumescence long enough for her to achieve her own quiet and shivering climax then she was happy to let him do it. They had come a long way, he reflected, since their courtship days in Manchester.

"I'm not complaining," Vincent said, "I'm just saying one of these days you might say something that comes back to bite you."

"I never tell them anything too specific," Bella replied. "Everyone wants to hear the same sort of thing, anyway. You know, a nice husband or wife, a decent job, a bit of money. People don't ask for much, really."

"Why do they bother coming to you, then? Why don't they just enjoy the here and now instead of worrying about what's round the corner?"

Bella toyed with her husband's gold chain. "Because unlike you, sweetheart, most folk have got a bit of imagination, and they want to know more than what they're having for tea that day. It's called being human."

"It's called worrying about something you can't do a damn thing about, more like," he said, still addressing the ceiling. "You think too much you'll just end up a nervous wreck."

"Well that's certainly not something *you* need to worry about."

Vincent laughed and looked down at the crown of his wife's head. "Few more grey hairs there, Bell," he noted. "You must have been thinking again."

"Bugger off."

For several minutes they lay together in a benign silence, broken only by the whine of a milk float passing down the road and the early clamour of seagulls. This quiet communion reminded Bella of simpler times, before the children, when the two of them had lived in a rented one-bedroom flat which was so cold they spent all their time in bed, wound together and still surprised, once in a while, by some detail of the other's naked body. There were no such surprises now, but she didn't mind; there was a profound happiness to be found in feeling her husband's stomach gurgle and shift against her elbow, even when she knew it presaged one of his protein-lover's robust farts.

"Vince," she said quietly.

"Mmm."

"I want to die before you."

He looked down quizzically at her. "Why?"

"Because," Bella explained, "I think you'll cope. I'm not being morbid, and I'm not trying to say you love me less than I love you, I just think you'd be able to manage better."

"You would if you had to."

"No, I wouldn't. I wouldn't at all."

Vincent wrapped his arm round Bella's shoulder. "Well let's die together then. Now shut up and go back to sleep."

# As Old As My Tongue...

The resort could, in some ways, absent itself during the summer months, when its beaches were crowded and its amusement arcades formed a ribald assault on the senses, with their tumult of mechanical clatter and blinking lights; when the pubs reverberated to the sound of jukeboxes, and its promenade was choked with tourists; when the bandstand in Jubilee Gardens was ringed by deckchairs filled with pensioners knitting or dozing or tapping their feet to the phlegmy rhythm of the band; when children tried to lick the dribbled ice cream from their elbow, and were thrilled or terrified by the musky, turbulent progress of their donkey; then the resort stood back, satisfied that its component parts were working as they should, creating a distinctive, heightened reality — brighter, louder, sweeter, scarier — for however long its visitors could tolerate it. And even when the coaches and trains carried them back to their more prosaic worlds the resort lived on in memories and blurry photographs, a special place attached by only the most delicate of threads to the dimmer land of work and tribulation. The resort placed an implicit trust in its visitors' ability to locate it beyond the quotidian, never doubting their competency, for they had to believe that somewhere there was a brighter sun, a clearer sky, a warmer wind.

July began quite promisingly with warm, overcast days followed by a series of spectacular sunsets, but as the school holidays approached a cold wind began to blow, a malicious wind that picked up sand and threw it into the eyes of those on the promenade, a deceiving wind that was welcomed for pulling back the blanket of clouds covering the sun that then, once established, changed direction, bringing an autumnal chill to the days.

It was this duplicitous wind that pushed Mickey Braithwaite's empty deckchairs into bulging convexities, as though mocking the assistant by making it too cold for most customers to rent one of his chairs. Only three hardy souls were currently ensconced, their backs to the wind: two women wrapped in headscarves and identical grey macs, sipping coffee in plastic cups poured from a tartan-patterned thermos, and a middle-aged man whose heavily Brylcreemed hair appeared immune to even the strongest of gusts.

When Mickey saw Bella emerge from her booth to take in her A-board he hurried over to tell her his exciting news. "Bella! Bella! Guess what?"

"What, Mickey?" she said, continuing with her task in the vain hope that the deckchair attendant would take the hint that she had no desire to stand and chat.

"They've asked me to take part! I got a letter."

"That's lovely, sweetheart."

The deckchair attendant, in a display of cunning that Bella did not think him capable of, hurried round her and placed himself in front of the door to her booth, effectively cutting off any hope of escape. "From the council!" he added.

Defeated, Bella leaned her A-board against the booth and straightened. "Come on, then, you've got my undivided attention. What have the council asked you to take part in?"

"The cent… canteen… "

"Centenary?"

Mickey nodded vigorously. "Centenary! That's it. The centenary of the pier."

Bella knew all about the upcoming celebrations to mark the pier's one hundredth year. Indeed, she had recently been involved in an argument with the pier manager Harvey Birdsall concerning his request that she shut her booth for the duration of the weekend, citing 'historical accuracy' as his reason for the temporary closure. She took great pleasure in relating the subsequent exchange to all and sundry, not only as an example of her debating prowess but also to humiliate Harvey, whom she thought a fool. It went:

'The whole pier's going to be Victorian, Bella, and this booth wasn't a fortune-teller's back then.'

'What was it, then?'

'Well, it was… er, well, I'm not sure, but it wasn't a fortune-teller's. I know that much.'

'What about the theatre? That wasn't there back then either. Not as it is now, anyway. Are you going to close that?'

'Of course not. That isn't the same thing at all.'

'What about the arcade? Was that there at the opening? And the electric lights? And the deckchairs? And the sun lounge? Are you going to close all of them for *historical accuracy*?'

'Don't be ridiculous, Bella.'

'If you think I'm going to miss out on the busiest weekend this pier's had for years then you've got another think coming, Harvey Birdsall. I tell you what, I'll wear a Victorian dress. I'll even pay for it myself. You should get yourself an outfit too. I can just see you in a top hat and tails.'

The pier manager had flounced off at this point, leaving Bella to dispense particularly favourable fortunes for the rest of the day and, between customers, doodle dress designs in the margin of her crossword puzzle.

Reminded of this triumphant exchange, and in truth slightly disarmed by the deckchair attendant's childlike excitement, Bella raised her eyebrows and opened her mouth slightly in an exaggerated gesture of surprise that anyone less ingenuous than Mickey would probably have interpreted as sarcastic. "Ooh, how exciting! What are you going to be doing?"

"I'm going to be in charge of the deckchairs!"

"But sweetheart," the fortune-teller pointed out, "that's what you do normally."

"For the show. The deckchairs for the show."

Bella nodded. "Ah. The show. Well that'll be a change for you, won't it?" A temporary stage was being erected in the sun lounge, on which a theatrical history of the pier was to be performed, along with dancers and several 'turns' yet to be announced. The day's entertainment would end with a firework display, thus providing a suitable climax to the weekend's celebrations.

"A hundred years," she said, a note of incredulity in her voice.

"That's a long time to be around, isn't it?"

Mickey tapped one foot on the silver-grey planking. "As old as my tongue and a little older than my teeth."

Bella presumed that he had learned the phrase from a parent or grandparent, who had doubtless thought of it as a simple, humorous response to a question regarding their age, but as quoted by Mickey Braithwaite, with his brittle, sing-song delivery, the phrase took on a more enigmatic quality. Not for the first time she wondered whether there was more going on behind the deckchair attendant's shimmering, empty eyes than he let on.

"I wonder if it'll still be here in another hundred years," she speculated.

Mickey shook his head sadly. "No," he stated unequivocally, before looking up, distracted by a piercing whistle from birds flying overhead. "Oystercatchers! See?"

Bella seized the moment. Grasping Mickey's shoulders with both hands she moved him to one side, opening up an escape route back into her booth. "That's lovely, sweetheart. I'll see you later," she assured him, and with a simultaneous pat on both his arms, she swept past, pulling the door to behind her before he had a chance to reply. Only later did Bella marvel at how insubstantial the deckchair attendant had felt; moving him had taken no more effort than it would have done with a cardboard cut-out, and there had been the same lack of resistance, as though he had anticipated her manoeuvre and complied, or even assisted, with it. She sensed something inescapably fey about Mickey Braithwaite. To the casual observer he would doubtless appear, as he pottered amongst his deckchairs, occasionally making a small adjustment to bring one of them back into perfect alignment, as nothing more than a simple-minded figure, maintaining strict order amongst the deckchairs as compensation for the turbulence and disarray in his head. Bella, however, was not a casual observer. Her livelihood depended on her ability to assess and categorise people, to deduce motivations and desires from a word, a gesture, an object. With Mickey she got the feeling that he had access to something not available to most, though what exactly that was she struggled to define. It was not wisdom, at least not in the normal definition of the word, but he did seem to derive a certain profound understanding from it. There was also no obviously religious perspective, but she believed the deckchair attendant to be content, sometimes to the point of him appearing to be in a state of grace. He possessed a kind of quiet harmony with whatever fraction of the world interested him at that moment, whether that was birds flying overhead, the positioning of a deckchair, or snatching his mother from under a bomb that had yet to be dropped. Paradoxically, behind Mickey's simple acts, Bella caught the occasional glimpse of what closely resembled a quite breathtaking complexity at work. This troubled her, because any evidence of underlying order went against her belief in a random universe, but despite repeated attempts to dismiss these glimpses as either fanciful or simply a mis-interpretation of something essentially haphazard, there was a part of her which responded to the possibility of this intangible structure. Bella likened it to an infinitely long pier, carrying all of life on a framework of fate. Whether it had been fabricated, or had formed quite naturally, was a question that Bella preferred to avoid. It was only because of Mickey's purest transparency that this design could be discerned at all, and Bella was not sure that it was meant to be seen. She felt like a voyeur, peeking through a window at something whose intimacy might be irretrievably compromised by her spying on it, even though she had not intended any harm. It opened itself up to Mickey, allowed him access to its weathered planking, only because he interacted with it on an intuitive rather than an intellectual level. But the pier's deckchair attendant could only walk out so far over the sea of time, and even this admission was not without its consequences. He had saved his mother from the bomb, from a quick death, only to condemn her to a slow one. Which was worse?

# Centenary

The pier had been primped and renovated for its birthday, like some declining dowager who, called upon to attend a ball in her honour, allows herself to be made up into some semblance of youth, even if both she and her guests must then exercise a degree of willful disregard for how the powder has settled in the lines of her face, how the rouge tends to emphasise the pallor of her skin. Similarly, those who walked along the scrubbed decking commented on how lightly the pier wore its century, whereas the maintenance workers who clambered amongst the struts and supports saw at close hand what seventy thousand tides could do to iron.

Union Jacks flew on top of every cupola, and the freshly painted livery of dark green and white shone brightly in the sun, a bold contrast to the unbroken blue of the sky. Bunting, strung along the length of the pier, danced in the breeze, generating a constant whispering sound, as though disclosing the wind's secrets to any who cared to listen. The crowds thronging the pier, however, concerned themselves with nothing more than that the wind was light, and warm, and carried to their noses the smell of hot dogs and fried onions. Nothing the wind knew could compete with the smell of fried onions.

From within the crimson confines of her booth, Madame Kaminska gawped into the capsized lands of her crystal ball, or laid out her Tarot cards, or pointed sagely at creases in a palm, and mentally rubbed her hands with glee at the conversation and laughter which filtered in from outside. She could even feel the thousands of footfalls passing by as the pier's planking transmitted them into her chair, the seismic tremor of potential profit. The bodice of her costume was uncomfortably tight under her bosom and around her stomach, but the expression on Harvey Birdsall's face when she had waved cheerily at him that morning was worth any amount of inconvenience. Never magnanimous in any victory, Bella had pinched the folds of her dress, hoisted them slightly and performed a neat curtsy to the pier manager, who was discussing something with two of his joiners. The men in overalls had laughed and responded with an exaggerated bow, but Harvey merely shook his head and continued with his instructions, studiously ignoring Bella's inflammatory gesture. She had seen the defeat in his eyes, however, and that was enough.

By the middle of the afternoon business was tailing off as visitors headed to either the cafe, bar or sun lounge for the show, so Bella hung up her CLOSED sign and clicked down the latch.

"We don't want another one bursting in like that funny bugger last month, do we?" She enquired of her cat, who had, as all cats are able to do, found the one patch of sunshine available and curled up in it. "I'm sure I don't know what *he* was after, do you, Tom? What an odd-bod."

Bella had been plagued with nightmares for a fortnight after the young man's visit. Always the same threatening advance, always the same coal-black, distorted figure; the only variation was the time it woke her from her fitful sleep, but whatever the hour, the hideous dream never offered any form of explanation or resolution, just another reminder of that inexorable menace. And then, as suddenly as the nightmares had started, they ended, as though their course was run, leaving an imprint in Bella's mind rather like a footprint in the sand, its impression gradually washed away by the tides of her forgetfulness and pragmatism. Already, only four weeks after his melodramatic arrival during the summer storm, she could think of the pale young man and smile at the farcical nature of their encounter.

The fortune-teller hooked one forefinger into the collar of her dress and pulled it away from her neck as far as the stiff material would allow. "It's no wonder everyone looked so miserable on those old black-and-white photos," she said, puffing out her cheeks, "if they had to wear clobber like this all the time. Trussed up like a chicken, I am, Tom. Still, I made sure that Gypsy Rose Lee got a good look on my way here. Gave her a wave and shouted out how I'd got to get here good and early as I was expecting so many customers, and how everybody who was anybody was going to be on the pier." Bella laughed out loud. "Ooh, Tom, if looks could kill! I'd be six feet under by now. Well, it's her own fault. If she wants to play little miss high-and-mighty with me she'll find I can give as good as I get. She must be desperate for business, I saw her lad handing out vouchers on the prom the other day. *And* I know for a fact she's been talking to Harvey about getting a place on the pier. Over my dead body is *that* happening."

Bella, having delivered her ultimatum to a largely unresponsive audience, set about making herself a cup of tea. While she filled the kettle and measured out the tea leaves she thought again, rather more reflectively as this was an internal monologue rather than one of her spoken diatribes, about the possibility of a rival fortune-teller based on the pier. Would Gypsy Rose Lee's presence be so devastating for business? The resort was booming. During the summer months families, young couples and pensioners flocked to the seaside in such numbers that she was turning away would-be customers. There were probably enough people who were either dissatisfied, greedy, frightened, confused or just plain stupid to support half a dozen fortune-tellers in the town. And what was it about being by the sea, Bella wondered, that seemed to cause folk to happily abandon all of their critical faculties? Would they hand over half a crown to a middle-aged woman who set up a stall on the high street of their hometown? Maybe they would. Or perhaps, even though their longing for purpose had nothing in itself to do with the resort, it did provide a suitably fantastical location in which seeking answers from a sphere of glass or a pack of cards would seem less than ridiculous, or even normal.

Once her tea had stewed to the mahogany colour she favoured, Bella poured herself a large mug and settled in her chair to tot up the day's takings. As soon as the cat heard the rattle of his owner's money tin he roused himself sufficiently to amble across the booth, hop up into her lap, circle round several times until he found precisely the right position, and finally curl up in preparation for yet another discourse on the financial vagaries of fortune telling.

"Right then, let's see how we've done," Bella announced. She opened the tin lid and tipped its contents onto the table, creating a clatter to which the cat reacted by digging in its claws. "Ooh… ah," she whimpered, carefully extricating his claws from the material.

"Don't you pull a thread in this bloody dress, my lad, it's got to go back tomorrow. I don't see why we've all had to pay for our own outfits, in any case. I'd have thought for the centenary they might have found a few quid for the workers rather than spending it all on *flags*. Hey, look at all these ten-bob notes, Tom. I reckon the pier ought to have a birthday party every year."

The fortune-teller neatly piled the coins with one hand whilst twiddling the cat's ears with the other, occasionally breaking off to slurp noisily at her tea. Only one further component was needed to make her happiness complete, but she had been unable to locate Mickey Braithwaite in order to send him for a cream bun. "Typical man," was her response to the deckchair attendant's absence.

"Under your feet when you don't want them and nowhere to be found when you do."

It did not take Bella long to separate the coins, stack them in piles of a pound each, and tot up the total. "Eleven pounds seven and six," she declared with satisfaction. "Flipping 'eck, if every day was like that we'd be in clover. Champagne for me and cream for you. I suppose we'd better let Vince have something too, hadn't we? Ten Woodbines should do it, eh Tom?" She laughed at her own joke. "Still, I don't suppose we're going to get another day like today for a while, are we? I think a little celebration is in order." Bella gulped down the rest of her tea and banged the mug back down on the table, as though bringing down the gavel on an auction of possible gratifications.

With the dress' deposit foremost in her mind, Bella carefully lifted the cat from her lap, set him down on the floor, stood up and brushed off any accumulated hairs. "Are you moulting, you mangy mutt?" She ran her hand down Tom's back, to which the cat responded by raising and stiffening its tail. "Your coat's not as shiny as it should be, my lad. I'll get you a tin of salmon on the way home, but we're not going anywhere until I've seen Val for a G and T. You can stay here and stand guard."

The fortune-teller gathered up the takings and placed them back in the tin, keeping one of the ten shilling notes for herself. "I think I deserve a little treat, don't you?" she said, waving the note at Tom. The cat's amber eyes narrowed slightly, perhaps because it had heard its owner's justifications regarding one indulgence or another that many times it had come to doubt whether any significant degree of credit-worthiness was involved in coming to these conclusions.

In the tiny kitchen and store area there was a loose section of skirting board, behind which was a void big enough to take the money tin. Bella knelt with difficulty in the dress, moved the board and manoeuvred the tin into its hiding place, before replacing the board and straightening with a grunt. "I'll be glad to get this flipping straightjacket off," she said, wriggling within the bodice to try and find a more comfortable position. "Now you look after that money, Tom, I won't be long."

Using the bulk of her dress to stop the cat from slipping past, Bella quickly exited the booth, and was about to set off down the pier, a cold and sparkling glass of gin and tonic practically in her hand already, when Eddie hailed her from the other booth.

"Hey, Bella!"

She took a deep breath. Turning, she saw the rock seller, dressed in a straw boater, dark blue striped blazer and cream trousers, re-filling the boxes outside his booth. "Eddie," she replied, pronouncing the word with a plainly false bonhomie.

He brandished the pink sticks as though guiding an aeroplane into its parking position. "I'm running out! What a day!"

Bella smiled politely. She had nothing in particular against the rock seller, apart from his interminable cheerfulness and a tendency to scratch absentmindedly at his crotch, but that gin and tonic was waiting impatiently for her, and she had no intention of letting it down. "Busy," she concurred.

"How have you done?"

The fortune-teller shrugged noncommittally. "Oh, not bad," she replied, already turning in the direction of the bar.

Ignoring this indication that their exchange was at an end, Eddie trotted across the pier, still clutching the sticks of rock, and waved the ones in his right hand at Bella's outfit. "I like the dress. Is it yours?"

"Mine? Of course it is, Eddie, I always wear hundred-year-old dresses. Hadn't you noticed?"

"Er… "

"Of course it isn't mine you narna! I hired it from the fancy dress shop on George Street, though why we should have to fork out for our own clobber I don't know. I've a good mind to send Harvey the bill." Bella made a swift appraisal of Eddie's blazer and trousers. "What about yours?"

"Oh, I had it anyway," he replied. "I sing in a barbershop quartet. I bought it ages ago for concerts."

"Do you? I didn't know that."

"Oh yes. You know…" Eddie struck a pose, one arm raised and bent, the other lowered and straight. "Bye Bye Blackbird… I'll Take You Home Again Kathleen… You Must Have Been A Beautiful Baby."

"Very nice," Bella said.

"You should come and see us sometime. We often provide the star turn at St Luke's church hall do's."

"I'd love to," Bella said, and even she was appalled at the lack of sincerity in her voice.

Eddie dropped one of his sticks of rock, which rolled away towards the edge of the pier, coming to rest against the foot of a chubby young man with sandy-coloured hair who was slumped on the wrought-iron seating. He picked up the rock and offered it back to Eddie, who smiled and shook his head. "No, no, that's alright. You keep it. Finders keepers and all that!"

"Well," the young man murmured shyly, "it wasn't really lost."

"As good as. No, I insist. It's the pier's centenary, you know."

"Mmm, yes, I do. Well, thank you very much."

Eddie beamed. "You're welcome." He turned back to Bella, who had seriously contemplated running away during this brief exchange. "Now where was I?"

"I'm not entirely sure."

"Ah! Yes. I knew I had something to tell you."

"Which was?"

"Someone was asking after you."

Bella felt a slight prickle run down her spine. She could not explain why such an innocuous-sounding statement had produced the reaction it had; there was nothing remotely ominous in those five words, neither had Eddie spoken them with any kind of emphasis, and yet a direct, unequivocal threat could not have triggered a stronger response. It was as though a part of her subconscious had been expecting just such a message.

154

"Oh?" she said. "Who?"

"Young fella," Eddie replied. "Didn't look familiar to me, but he seemed to know you."

Bella glanced up and down the pier. Where was he? What had he come back for? She already had a good idea what the answer to her next question would be, but she felt obliged to ask it anyway.

"What did he look like?"

"Oh, you know." Eddie waved his sticks of rock in a gesture designed to encompass an entire generation. "Slim, dark hair, suit. Quite well turned out, for a young 'un."

"Did he have a signet ring?"

"Blimey, Bella, I'm not Sherlock Holmes!"

"No, of course you're not. Sorry, Eddie. It's just that... well, if it's who I think it is, let's just say I'm not desperate to get reacquainted. What did he say?" the fortune-teller enquired, trying to keep the apprehension out of her voice.

"He asked me if I knew you, so naturally I said yes, and then I asked him if *he* knew *you* and he said very well. He said he knew you inside out, which I thought was a bit strange, because I couldn't remember seeing him before, but he didn't seem to be joking so I took him at his word. I thought he might be family."

Bella could feel her heart beating faster. "He isn't."

"Oh? Oh... Well, anyway, he said to tell you he's been thinking about what you said, and he's going to do something about it."

She waited several seconds, expecting to hear more, but Eddie remained silent. "Is that it?"

"That's it. I explained to him that you'd probably have a minute between customers, what with me thinking he was family, but he said he had other things that needed taking care of. Just tell her that, he said, and then he was gone." Eddie chuckled.

"Disappeared that quick I didn't even have time to sell him any rock!"

"And you're sure that's all he said?"

Eddie, at last alerted to the strained note in Bella's voice, let his grin slowly ebb away, replacing it with an expression of concern. "Yes, that was it, word for word. Why? Who is he?"

Bella glanced up at the sky. She was trying not to let her profound irritation with the rock seller show; after all, he was not to blame for shattering her good mood. Eddie had simply relayed what on the face of it seemed a perfectly harmless message. The trouble was, this well-intentioned act had revived all the more threatening aspects of that fractious reading, aspects she believed had concluded the moment the young man left her booth. "Oh, just someone who didn't like what I had to tell them," Bella explained with a dismissive shrug. "Nothing to worry about."

Eddie's smile reappeared. "Ah, well, sometimes the truth hurts, eh Bella?"

"Yes, sweetheart, it does." She managed to conjure up a smile herself. "Well, thank you for passing on the message, Eddie. I'm definitely ready for that drink now."

The moment she said it, Bella could have kicked herself; the last thing she wanted was the rock seller interpreting her statement as an invitation, but fortunately he appeared to see it as nothing more than a way of rounding off their conversation.

"I'd make it a double if I were you!" He suggested, before noticing a family with two young children peering into the window of his booth. "See you anon. Duty calls!"

As Bella walked down the pier she considered the meaning behind her inscrutable customer's message. Had he deliberately meant it to be ambiguous, or was she reading too much into a perfectly ordinary statement of innocent intent? Remembering the coldness of his eyes, and combining this with the circumstance of his departure, Bella found it impossible to believe the young man's phrase had been conceived as anything other than intimidatory. He did not seem the type of person to take advice, much less make the effort to confirm this change of heart. She sensed a cold intelligence at work, carefully constructing a sentence that would oblige her to replay their entire exchange in the quest to discover a motive, knowing full well that the last thing fortune-tellers wanted was to go back over something meant to be transient, a flimsy construct modelled for and in the moment. Did he know she was a fraud, and took a sadistic kind of pleasure in forcing her to face her own gentle deceit? Bella thought it unlikely. Of course he knew she was a fraud! Everybody with half a brain knew that, and possessing such an understanding meant he also must have realised that pointing this out, however obliquely, was unlikely to cause a great deal of distress. The question Bella returned to, again and again, were his reasons for visiting her on such a horrible day, particularly if he had no real faith in her abilities. And yet there were moments during the reading when she had sensed a willingness to believe, perhaps even a need, but this had then been swept away as though countermanded by a stronger voice. Whatever his motives for battling through the wind and rain to her booth, the young man had left incensed. Whether this anger had been caused by some detail of the reading, or him not finding the answers he had hoped to find, or indeed if he had visited Bella under some sort of duress or obligation, she did not know. The only certainty in all of this was that he obviously believed there remained unfinished business between them. She tried not to let her imagination run away with her as to how he planned to resolve this problem.

The rather grandiosely-named Tudor Bar was packed with customers. The hubbub of a hundred conversations and a smog of cigarette smoke filled the room, pierced irregularly by the cry of a baby or young child, and during the odd moments of relative quiet that settled across the bar, as though orchestrated by some collective subconscious, the Dave Clark Five could be heard, gamely offering to 'show you where it's at' despite a lack of interest from the assembled drinkers.

On entering the bar, Bella glanced around, her vision on high alert for the glimpse of a pale face with those disconcerting, case-hardened eyes, but he was nowhere to be seen. As she stood surveying the room a man with a bushy ginger moustache brushed past carrying two glasses of whisky. Ever since her abuse at the hands of Uncle Reg the smell of whisky always made Bella feel sick; not only did it instantly conjure up the cloying taste of him in her mouth, it also acted as a bitter reminder of her silence. She never told her parents what happened that evening, and even Bella was not sure why. She even managed to stay in the same room with her uncle on his subsequent visits, positioning herself so that one or other of her parents was always between her and her abuser. He would try and catch her eye, but Bella never found out what silent message he wished to communicate because she studiously ignored him, answering any sentence or question directed at her with a sullen nod or monosyllabic reply, her eyes fixed firmly on some piece of furniture or patch of carpet. Less than a year later he was dead, crushed under the wheels of a London Underground train after falling from the platform whilst drunk. Uncle Reg's death was explained as a tragic accident, but Bella, in a rare departure from her usual lucid understanding of human nature, always hoped that her uncle's fall had in some small way been propelled by a pang of conscience. After his death she felt even less inclined to recount the event, not out of any sense that Reg could no longer defend himself, or to spare her mother in particular any further anguish over the loss of her brother, but rather because to dwell on his abuse would hand him a kind of victory. It was neither forgetting nor forgiveness, but a state of mind without a word to describe it that lay somewhere between these two, and that meant she was able to perform a similar act for Vincent and take pleasure in *his* pleasure, like a roar of defiance in the face of her uncle's ghost.

The smell of whisky spurred her towards the busy bar.

As Bella approached, her friend Val caught sight of her and raised her pencilled-in eyebrows in greeting.

Over the heads of men two deep at the bar Val said, "What's it to be, honeybun?"

Several of the men looked back over their shoulder, disgruntled expressions targeted directly at Bella. One of them turned back to Val and held up a pound note as though in evidence. "Hey, hang on a minute. I'm in front of her."

Val looked at him with disdain. "Not very gentlemanly of you, is it?"

"What?"

"Not letting the lady go first."

The man snorted. "I thought you lot wanted treating the same. You can't have it both ways, eh lads?" He looked around, hoping to elicit some form of camaraderie.

One or two of the men made affirmatory noises, but none joined the discussion. Bella did in fact feel slightly embarrassed by her friend's blatant favouritism, so she held up both hands as though in surrender and said, "I don't want you fighting over me, fellas. I'm in no rush."

Val straightened behind the bar. A tall, athletically built woman to begin with, her platinum-blonde beehive hairdo and high heels made her an imposing, if not intimidating, sight. "Alright, boys," she said, slowly scanning the group of men in front of her, "Hands up anybody who's been at work today. Come on, don't be shy." When there was no movement she continued, "Thought as much. Well, I know for a fact that the lady behind you has been slaving away since first thing this morning, helping to make sure you all have a nice relaxing time, so in my book it's the workers who deserve a drink first. Now has anybody got a problem with that?" She paused and looked again at her silent audience. "Wonderful. I knew I could rely on you boys to make the right decision." She turned her attention to Bella. "So, what's it to be, my darlin'? The usual?"

Bella shuffled forward slightly, impressed as always by her friend's ability to take control of a situation by thinking

159

of a logical explanation for her behaviour and then, by apparently offering several opportunities to question its validity, convince everyone concerned that it was in fact the *only* logical explanation, thereby defusing any potential tension whilst at the same time completely vindicating her course of action. It was a skill she envied. "Gin and tonic, please. A double."

"You see?" Val said, opening her arms in a theatrical gesture. "I *knew* she needed serving first."

While waiting for her drink, Bella moved to the end of the bar left clear for glass collection and positioned herself at its junction with the wall. Tucked away, with the reassuring solidity of brick at her back, she again looked round the room. The extra confidence conferred by her strategic location meant she could be more methodical in her second inspection, but the only familiar faces she found belonged to several of the day's customers, all of whom appeared to have been left psychologically unmarked by their reading. In some ways Bella would have preferred to find him amongst the crowds; not only did she feel on safer ground in the bar, but the young man's presence, particularly if some malign intent was obvious, would at least have clarified the situation and made her own response more straightforward. His absence tainted everything, as though the pier and all its visitors were complicit in his scheme, shielding him from view while he plotted his next move. This was paranoia of the highest order, Bella realised, but she could not silence a tiny voice inside that insisted there was a grain of truth to it.

"One G and T."

Bella flinched visibly at the sudden voice to her right, but when she turned and saw Val standing there, still holding the glass she had just placed next to her on the bar, she disguised her reaction by slapping her outstretched hand on her chest and glancing upwards in an exaggerated gesture of surprise. "Bloody hell, Val, don't sneak up on me like that! Give me a heart attack, you will."

The bar manager, however, was too astute to be taken in by such an unwieldy performance. She had seen, albeit briefly, the flicker of fear in her friend's eyes, but Val was also wise enough to realise that someone who so hurriedly and deliberately masked their anxiety would be unwilling to explain its cause through direct questioning. Instead she made a mental note of Bella's reaction and determined to seek an answer later, after several gins had calmed her nerves.

"You can normally detect an approaching G and T from fifty yards away," Val replied. Pleased with her response, which she felt contained both a sort of oblique acknowledgment of her friend's insecurity as well as a touch of humour to help relax her, she jerked her head in the direction of the sun lounge and continued, "D'you fancy watching a bit of the show?"

"Aren't you meant to be working?"

"My shift finished half an hour ago. I was only covering until Jo got here. Come on. You never know your luck, if it's as bad as it was during rehearsals it'll be hilarious." Val tapped the side of the glass with one of her extravagant false nails. "What's up with this, anyway? Taken the pledge?"

"Good God no." Bella took a gulp of her drink, swilling it round like mouthwash and savouring the astringent flavour of juniper, which dissolved her foreboding like acid and left her feeling, for a moment at least, quite ridiculous. She swallowed and exhaled contentedly. "I needed that. You're right, we could do with a laugh. Let's see what they're up to in there."

"That a girl," Val said encouragingly. "Don't let the bastards grind you down, eh?"

"Exactly."

The sun lounge was a comparatively recent addition to the pier, constructed in the early fifties as post-war austerity gave way to a more optimistic period. Essentially a giant conservatory built onto the back of the bar, its main function was to offer visitors a place in which they could sunbathe when it was too cold to sit outside. The lounge also hosted organ recitals and beauty contests, the former attended by an audience of over-forties who, whilst warming their bones, also found a melodic kindling in the medleys of wartime songs, whilst the latter drew young men with cameras clamped to their faces, capturing the girls on films developed later at home and printed in the sour-smelling gloom of a makeshift darkroom.

The hand of Mickey Braithwaite was evident in the rigorous geometry of the deckchairs, which faced the temporary stage in two blocks separated by a central aisle. Every chair was taken, with more standing around the perimeter of the lounge, and a cluster of children sat cross-legged in the space in front of the stage, faces tilted upward in mute expectation. The sun, which seemed fixed in the sky as though reluctant to set for fear of some final, extinguishing immersion in the sea, cast shadows like a tender prison of black bars over the audience, though the stuffy air had induced a torpor so seductive and complete that no restraint was needed. Suffusing this matrix of light and dark was a heady atmosphere of body odour, perfume, tobacco and alcohol: the resort's distillate. And on stage were four men, shirt sleeves rolled, gripping a reddish-grey wooden scaffold that formed a surprisingly emotive reduction of the pier's structure. Through this triumphal arch a man strode, dressed in a dark suit and stovepipe hat, and clutching a large roll of paper. This man was Harvey Birdsall.

The bar manager and the fortune-teller, mismatched in practically every physical way possible and yet identical in their phlegmatic worldview, settled themselves on stools carried through from the bar and prepared for an enjoyably critical dismantling of the centenary performance.

"I might have known he'd give himself a big part," Bella commented as the pier manager stepped on to the stage.

Val leaned closer to her friend. "It's the only big part he's ever likely to see," she whispered, and they both giggled like schoolgirls in assembly.

Harvey made a great show of unfurling his scroll, which had been curled so tightly it snapped shut again twice before he managed to wrestle it under control. A murmur of amusement rose from the audience, who clearly thought they were watching a comedy performance.

"Ladies and gent... ladies... and gentlemen," Harvey boomed, looking round the room with a supercilious air. "This is indeed a *his*toric occasion. You are here to witness the grand opening of our new pier, in the year of our Lord eighteen hundred and sixty-five. I, Eugenius Birch, engineer and designer, have worked long and hard to provide this town with a pier fit for a queen, and this, I believe, we have achieved." He glanced down at the scroll. "Our noble pier, a full year in its making, one thousand feet in length, thirty feet in width, with seven hundred and forty tons of iron beneath our feet, all to offer an unrivalled experience to the visitor, who may perambulate as far out to sea as they would hope to if they were aboard a pleasure cruise, and all, I would greatly hope and desire, without getting their feet wet!"

Val tapped out a cigarette from her packet of Pall Malls and gestured towards the stage. "He's loving this, isn't he? I always thought he'd been born a hundred years too late."

Bella smiled in agreement, but despite her long-standing antipathy towards the pier manager she had to admit to a sneaking regard for his performance so far. Perhaps it was his naturally pompous manner which suited the role, but both the suit and stovepipe hat, as well as the declamatory speech, fitted him so comfortably that she could easily imagine it *was* the Victorian engineer standing there, proudly enumerating his latest creation's vital statistics. Harvey's convincing act, combined with the soporific atmosphere and the effects of a rapidly consumed double gin on an empty stomach, were drawing Bella into a sort of timeless reverie, where past, present and future blurred together. The pier, she mused, was in some ways like a time machine. Yes, certain elements of it had been either added or removed since its opening, but the basic structure was the same, which was more than could be said for almost any other part of the resort. In fact, now she thought about it, earlier that morning, before the day's visitors had begun to arrive and the only people on the pier were employees dressed in period clothes, the sensation of having been transported back a hundred years was utterly convincing. Could time possibly be so flimsy?

"To mark the official opening," Harvey continued, "we have gathered for your entertainment a sparkling cornucopia of stars, a veritable galaxy of song, theatre and laughter, so sit back and enjoy the show!" Hesitant applause rippled through the audience, dying away before the pier manager's outstretched arms had dropped back to his sides. He hurried on. "Yes... ah, please welcome our first act, performing a medley of Broadway classics, the beautiful, the sensational... Alexandra Bright!"

A young, dark-haired woman wearing an acid-yellow mini-skirt and matching short-sleeved blouse stepped up to the microphone, to several appreciative whistles from men in the audience. Harvey edged to one side, his outfit suddenly rendering a jarring incongruity when juxtaposed with the girl's contemporary clothes. After a moment's indecision he turned to leave the stage and narrowly missed colliding with one of two male backing dancers who were taking up their positions on either side and slightly behind Miss Bright. She unclipped the microphone from its stand, causing the PA system to clonk and boom, before beaming at the assembled throng arrayed below her.

"Whoo!" she yelped, "Hi everybody! I can't tell you how excited I am to be here! It's a great honour to be asked to start the show with my two boys Rory," a smile to her left, "and James," a smile to her right. "I'm going to do a couple of numbers, and you're bound to know the words, so sing along!"

The smile still incised into her face, Alexandra nodded

in the direction of the technicians sitting at a small table by the side of the stage. A rhythmic crackle came over the speakers, followed by the opening bars of 'Wouldn't It Be Loverly' from *My Fair Lady*, which brought the dancers to life, spinning them slowly round like some benign galvanic force.

Miss Bright crossed her legs and, holding the microphone in both hands as though in prayer, switched expressions from rictus smile to what presumably she believed was a sort of wistful longing. She began singing in a strikingly deep voice, her cockney accent prolonging the vowels and making her sound as though she was having to dredge up each word from a thick sediment of half-remembered songs.

Val again leaned in close to her friend. "What d'you think? Rory or James?"

Bella tutted in mock disapproval. "Honestly, Val. You're old enough to be their mother."

"So? They need to learn from somebody, it might as well be me."

Bella glanced towards the stage, where the dancers were prancing in opposite directions. "I've got a feeling they wouldn't be interested in any lessons you had to offer, sweetheart!" And they laughed, the more so for the disapproving looks aimed in their direction by some of the audience.

Evening came quickly, as the sun, reconciled at last with a subjugating sea, rushed to its fate below the horizon, leaving behind a stillness that lent the resort a rare eloquence. The pier, its outline now illuminated by strings of bulbs, stood over a reflection of itself so perfect that it became a second, inverted reality. A small group of pigeons circled the amusement arcade roof, but theirs, unlike the starlings, was a utilitarian flight; this was nothing more than a drawn-out landing, with nothing to impart.

The day's warmth was beginning to ebb from the sun lounge, taking with it a number of the audience, who had made their way outside for the firework display. Bella and Val had swapped their bar stools for two of Mickey's vacant deckchairs, and were now only several rows from the stage. Bella felt drowsy, sedated by two further double gins and the reclined position of the deckchair, but she had, against expectation, enjoyed the centenary celebration show and now wanted to see it through to the end. She was not urgently required by either of her men, anyway; Tom had a bowl of water in the booth, and would doubtless find somewhere comfortable to await his mistress' return, while Vince was a better cook than she was, and would probably welcome the opportunity for an evening in the Farmers Arms. Bella realised, with some regret, that nobody depended on her any more.

She and Val applauded as the ventriloquist took his bow, and before Harvey came back on stage she turned to the bar manager. "I'm going for a wee. You coming?"

Val shook her head. "I'm alright. I'll save your seat."

Bella levered herself out of the deckchair, retrieved her handbag from under it and headed in the direction of the Tudor Bar.

There were fewer people in the bar now, but those that remained had grown more voluble as the alcohol took effect, resulting in a level of conversational noise not appreciably lower than when the bar had been at its busiest. The quality of this hubbub *had* altered, however, taking on a palpably more threatening tone. Bella hurried towards the ladies. Without the reassuring presence of Val by her side she suddenly felt very vulnerable, hauled back to her childhood bedroom by the drink-coarsened voices.

Sitting in the cubicle she heard the door to the toilets open, accompanied by a brief increase in volume of the conversation and jukebox out in the bar before the door closed again. The clack of high heels approached, then entered the adjacent cubicle, followed by a resounding bang as the door was slammed shut and locked. A zip was unfastened, its sound metallic in the echoing silence, then the

166

rustle of clothing, and finally a loud and exasperated 'tut'.

"Och, you've got to be kidding me," a young woman's voice said, her Scottish accent thick and slurred.

Bella craned her neck down to look under the gap beneath the partition wall, but all she could see was the pointed tip of a dark red shoe and the frilly edge of lowered knickers. "What's up, sweetheart?"

"There's no any paper in here. Would ya credit it, hey? And here's me just got maself nice and comfy."

"Don't you worry," the fortune-teller replied, "I've got plenty in here." She unrolled a handful of sheets and passed them under the partition, letting them go when she felt her neighbour take hold.

"There you go. Is that enough?"

A brief, gravelly laugh emanated from the cubicle. "Aye, that'll be fine. I'm no havin' a shite."

Bella smiled. "Glad to be of service." She flushed her toilet, opened the cubicle door and walked over to the sinks to wash her hands. Moments later the other toilet flushed, the door was unlocked, and she was joined by a red-haired girl in her early twenties.

The two washed their hands in an amicable silence. Bella was aware, out of the corner of her eye, that the girl was swaying slightly, so she assumed that their brief exchange in the cubicles had perhaps exhausted the girl's inclination, or indeed ability, to communicate.

As she turned off the taps and yanked a towel from the dispenser, however, the girl turned to Bella. "Are yous on holiday?"

Bella looked into the girl's green eyes, which if they had not been so bloodshot would have been incredibly beautiful. "No, not me, sweetheart. I live here."

"*Live* here?" The concept appeared to baffle her.

"That's right."

"Live here," she repeated. "Aye, well, some folk have all the luck."

Bella took a paper towel for herself. "Where are you from?"

"Paisley." She crumpled her towel and threw it at the bin, missing by several feet.

"Oh. Is it nice?"

Again the bark of a laugh. "No, it is not. It's a shite-hole. And then we come here every year and when we go home again it seems even *more* of a shite-hole. I cannae think why we do it to ourselves. We'd be better off no' coming at all."

Bella dropped her paper towel into the bin, retrieving the girl's from the floor at the same time. She straightened and gave the girl's arm a reassuring rub. "No you wouldn't. Everybody feels like that when they go home after a holiday. It just means you've had a good time."

The girl ran one hand through her hair. "Aye, but you *never* have to go home, do you?"

With her inscrutable message delivered, the girl from Paisley nodded farewell and tottered away, back to the Tudor Bar and all its temporary delights, to be paid for later with a more abiding disappointment. Bella stood by herself in the stark, echoing light of the women's toilet, and as the cisterns filled and a pipe hammered and gulped behind the wall like some insatiable beast clamouring for release, she realised that she *was* lucky; lucky to have the sea so near, lucky to be able to breathe in its iodine purity whenever she wanted, lucky to work in a town that most people regarded as an exemplar of all that was fun and exciting in life. She took all this for granted, and it had needed an empty toilet roll to make her realise her presumption.

She came out of the toilets and was walking past the bar when a familiar voice stopped her in her tracks.

"Well, well, well. If it isn't the Wicked Witch of the West."

Bella turned to face the young man, who was standing at the bar, one foot resting on the polished brass rail at its base. "What do you want?"

He waved one hand in the air, dismissing her concern

with a loose-wristed gesture. "Ah, don't panic. I'm not after a refund."

"Well what is it then?"

He shrugged. "Who knows? Do you? Get your crystal ball out and let's see. Tell you what, I'll buy you a drink while you're having a look. Can't say fairer than that, can I? Come on, what's your poison?"

Bella found it hard to look him in the eye, particularly as she recognised the over-precise and combative manner of someone both drunk and angry. "I'm really sorry, but my friend's waiting—"

"No no no no no," he said, closing his eyes and shaking his head with a smile, like a teacher hearing the wrong answer from a particularly troublesome pupil. "You're not listening. Just one little drink. I'd take it very personally if you said no." He licked his lips.

"Don't let me down, now."

"I can't."

The fortune-teller made to walk away, primed and ready to shout, or even scream, if he tried to stop her, but it was as he reached out, misjudging the distance between them so that only his fingertips brushed against the back of her hand, that it happened.

In an instant, Bella felt engulfed in a heat so fierce, so all-consuming, that the young man, the bar, the pier, everything vanished, and all that was left was an overwhelming need to escape, to flee from this terrifying inferno. Indeed, even as she stumbled into a table, heading blindly towards the exit, Bella could not look down for fear of seeing herself on fire. Her clothes must already have been stripped away, seared off in moments. The appalling heat was now peeling away her skin, layer after layer crisping and curling, her hair gone in a brief, incandescent flare, the very meat of her bubbling, tightening, separating from her bones.

Vaguely, as though seen through a trembling sheet of flame, Bella could make out the bulb-lit perspective of the pier. The heat behind her was just as intense, but ahead, in the direction of the resort, she sensed a cooler world. Gasping, crying, she ran towards land.

The heat. It was following her. Like the blackened figure from her nightmares, Bella knew she was being pursued. The fire desired nothing more than to consume her, as it had consumed everyone in the Tudor Bar, the sun lounge, the theatre, gobbled them up with its insatiable appetite, and now the fire had seen her trying to escape, and it was beyond rage.

The pier groaned beneath her. The fortune-teller's legs were weakening and the heat grew closer, wrapping itself around her like some hellish blanket. She heard her voice being called by a gentle, sing-song voice, and moments later Mickey Braithwaite loomed out of the dark, but this was not the Mickey Braithwaite she knew, this was a terrifying, incandescent version of the deckchair attendant, ablaze and yet seemingly impervious to the pain, revelling in his immolation.

"Bella! No!"

She hesitated, slowed by the cooling tone of his voice, which seemed to pacify the fire behind her somewhat, but then she looked into the great void of his eyes and Bella saw the flames there, dancing victoriously. She pushed him aside and never heard his last words to her as they turned to ash in the night air.

"Wait! You don't need to go." And then, quieter, almost to himself, "It isn't happening yet."

Was it instinct that brought her to a halt outside her booth, or the faint yowling of a cat that recognises the footfall of its mistress? Whatever it was, the fortune-teller could not leave Tom to suffer a captive, agonising death. With trembling hands she unlocked the booth door, opened it slightly and slipped through the gap, stopping the cat from escaping with the shin of one leg.

Inside the booth, shadows cast by the flames outside flickered and skipped over the familiar items, the tools and props of her trade animated by their impending destruction. Bella could not look directly at her crystal ball on the table; it burned a dazzling scarlet, like a miniature sun. Grabbing the cat's basket, she opened its barred door, crammed Tom unceremoniously inside, fastened the buckles and opened the booth door, not really knowing what she would find outside.

The heat hammered Bella to her knees, but somehow she found the strength to stand, and to attempt to close and lock the booth's door. The key was red hot, however, and burnt her hand, so she dropped it, abandoning the booth to its fate. A crackling noise above her made Bella look up, and she saw winged embers wheeling in a black sky; they were starlings, burning, red-hot starlings, weaving a net of glittering trails across the night.

Managing to keep one step ahead of the flames Bella lurched towards safety, expecting at any moment to be swallowed up by the fire and praying that, if and when she succumbed, it would be quick. She thought of Vince, and Paul and Sarah, her children. She thought of Val and was overwhelmed with guilt at her selfishness. Bella had abandoned them all without thinking: Val, Harvey, Mickey, the young woman from Paisley, she had condemned them all by her despicable actions. No one else had escaped the flames, and if, by some miracle, Bella did survive, she would have to somehow reconcile herself with the consequences of her cowardice.

There seemed to be the slightest diminishing of the heat's intensity as she rushed away from her booth, but the fortune-teller did not stop. She would not stop until her feet touched the promenade, leaving the pier behind her for good, and so Bella never saw the solitary starling hop down from the roof of her booth and watch her figure diminish into the night, until all that could be seen of her was the glint of gold on fingers wrapped tightly around the cat basket's handle. And then that last spark was extinguished, leaving the pier cold and empty, its planks a pale smear across the darkness. At the end of the pier came a small, explosive bang, followed moments later by a burst of colour as the first fireworks spread across the sky. The starling ruffled the feathers on its back; from a distance, the gesture could almost have been interpreted as a shrug.

*1989*

# Hats

Early morning light seeped through grubby net curtains and highlighted the group of Capo di Monte figures neatly displayed in their glass-fronted cabinet. A large oval mirror above the fireplace reflected the china pieces, but its dusty glass made them look more like a collection of disfigured bones, exhibits in a museum of degenerative diseases. Nubs and knuckles of cold, unthreatening bones. Below the mirror an ancient gas fire hissed and popped, its centre burner glowing bright orange from being on for most of the night. A plastic vine straggled across the fire's brick surround; its leaves had been singed and distorted from being in close proximity to the heat, paradoxically making the fake plant appear more realistic. Next to the display cabinet was a large dining table, and at this table sat archivist and local historian Colin Draper.

Colin was forty-six, but most people thought he was at least ten years older, partly because of his unkempt greying hair and crumpled, nondescript clothes, but also because he behaved like an old man, and had done since the age of twelve, when his father died and Colin became, in his mother's words, the 'man of the house'. He occasionally pondered how fate had lifted him clean out of puberty's clutches and dropped him down into a world of responsibility and obligations, but Colin was not a man to dwell on life's 'what ifs'. Studying the past had shown him how lucky he was to be alive in the twentieth century, when similar circumstances only a hundred years ago would have put the Draper family in the workhouse. It was also fair to say that, had Colin been given the opportunity to rebel, sleep around, marry and become a father, he would undoubtedly have run a mile in the opposite direction.

"Look at all those hats!" he exclaimed out loud, then pulled a face when he remembered how early it was. His mother's bedroom was across the hall, a room that had become, as her multiple sclerosis gradually, inexorably, tightened its bindings around her limbs, the limits of her world. Following her diagnosis almost fifteen years ago Colin had found himself, practically by default, as the person charged with her care. Other family members made their apologies, professing a variety of commitments or reasons why they would be unable to help, but in all honesty, both Colin and his mother would not have wanted it any other way. For the best part of a decade her mobility remained relatively unimpaired, giving Colin the time to build himself a reputation in the resort as its definitive chronicler. As the council's archivist, Colin Draper spent his working life in basements and dimly lit offices, absorbing the slightly bitter odour of old documents until the two coalesced. With his clothing's palette of beiges and browns he became a form of document himself, a covenant telling the story of how a meek history graduate found his voice through a fascination with the resort which grew to become an all-consuming passion. In many people's eyes the archivist was as much a part of the town as its theatre, winter gardens, promenade and pier, not only because of his encyclopedic knowledge of its history, but also because Colin exhibited an utter lack of ego. It was as though the resort spoke through him, channelling its thoughts and memories with a clarity made possible only by his own happy absence. Having read the words and studied the photographs of those long dead the archivist regarded his own existence within this same historical perspective. His fleeting consciousness was both a privilege and a wonderful gift, but any claim to its importance lay solely in what could be bequeathed to the future. Colin's rigorously intellectual way of life appeared dry and joyless to some, but this was not a vision he would have recognised. Researching, indexing, recording. He was not being selfless by dedicating himself to these activities. These were the things that brought him joy.

His greatest dream was to see the creation of a museum for the resort, where its role as a catalyst for social change, as well as for entertainment, could be properly celebrated. From its first great expansion and period of popularity in Victorian times, through the town's heyday in the 50s and 60s, to its present decline, his faith in the resort was unshakeable. Colin was its staunchest advocate and defender, despite those voices, including some of the town's own public figures, which predicted a lingering and inevitable death. He would not see this wonderful place dismantled like some sort of redundant liner hauled into dry dock. If history had taught him anything it was that the resort's time would come again.

He looked at the photograph. The hats in question belonged to a sea of Victorian faces crowded onto the pier, the people so tightly packed that the planking could not be seen; faces that looked out at Colin across the years in faded monochrome, and yet somehow had lost none of their humanity, none of the quirks and characteristics that had made them who they were. The archivist angled the photograph towards the window. The hats! Every single person in the picture was wearing some sort of hat, creating a perfect graphical representation of the social classes gathered on the pier in that pale afternoon sunshine. One or two highly polished toppers rose above the masses, there was a scattering of bowlers, and the rest wore flat caps, with the ladies' creations standing out like fanciful meringues. It could have been staged, so neatly did this ubiquitous wearing of headgear demonstrate the era's sharply delineated social strata, yet Colin knew it was simply folk, probably in their Sunday best, enjoying a brief respite from their labours as they took the sea air with a stroll along the pier.

A toff, wearer of one of the top hats, was poised, about to take a drag from his cigarette; two women giggled in the foreground, clearly amused and slightly embarrassed by the photographer's presence; one of the bowler-hatted middle-class gents, wearing a pair of small round glasses and sporting a severely clipped moustache, looked alarmingly like Doctor Crippen. They all had purpose, *life*, but then they had walked past the camera and were gone, back into the mystery of their resumed, unphotographed existence. What had happened to them after that second, that moment's immortality? Who had they loved? What had they hoped for? It was this immense unknowability to history that Colin loved above all else, the dozens of questions posed by even the simplest photograph or artefact; this, and the uncovering of an answer to just one of these questions, when his spotlight picked out another detail on the dark hull of the past.

Colin gently slid the photograph into a plastic folder, attached a circular self-adhesive label to the folder and printed *VA341* on the label, then added the code to his Victorian Archive file and wrote *Crowded Pier — late nineteenth century (HATS!)* alongside the code. He smiled at this touch of whimsy, which was all the more conspicuous for its positioning amongst the dispassionate numbers and phrases elsewhere on the page, like a Hawaiian shirt at an undertakers' convention. The professional in him baulked slightly at this lapse into subjectivity. In five hundred years scholars looking through this archive could be influenced by the word, with its bold lettering and exclamation mark, and come to a skewed conclusion as to its importance. He thought about Tippexing the entry out and writing another, but then what would those same hypothetical scholars think? They might be sufficiently intrigued by the correction fluid to use some sort of X-Ray scanner to reveal the original entry, discover *HATS!*, and make assumptions about why the word had been erased. This would, Colin, concluded, be a more disruptive intervention than simply leaving the word as it was, so he moved the archive file to one side and reached into the shoebox for another photograph.

This one depicted a street scene, with a horse and cart carrying what appeared to be bales of cotton or cloth as its main focal point. The cart's driver stood next to his horse, one hand holding the reins while the other was tucked, somewhat awkwardly, into his jacket pocket. Colin could imagine the man's indecision leading up to the photograph being taken, as he tried to decide what to do with his free hand. Being photographed in Victorian times would have been an unusual, if not daunting, experience, so for the drayman to find himself the subject of this street photographer, with his intimidating contraption of wood and brass, it was not surprising he affected a somewhat stilted pose. His parents may have been able to afford a photograph of him as a baby or young child, and if he had served in the armed forces or some other official organisation he could well have posed as part of a group, but apart from such possibilities this image may have constituted the only visual record of the man. Had he understood its significance, and placed his hand in several positions before, undecided and unnerved by the photographer disappearing beneath his cloth, thrusting it into his pocket? At least, if this was the drayman's only image, he had managed to bequeath a dignified expression to history, unsmiling but with a compassionate light in his eyes. The young man sitting on top of the bales, presumably an assistant or apprentice, had turned his head as the picture was taken, reducing his identity to a grey blur.

The archivist turned his attention to the background. He enjoyed trying to match the grimy, soot-stained facades and buildings in historical photographs to the present-day resort; any small detail which could flesh out the town of a century or more ago was precious, because to Colin it was these fragments that brought the past to life, far more so than the extensively documented national figures and events of an era. It was then he noticed a bill poster attached to a fence and half-obscured by one of the cart's wheels. By its layout Colin could tell it was advertising some form of theatrical entertainment, but the graininess of the image, combined with his need for a new, stronger pair of reading glasses, meant some assistance was needed to reveal more detail. He reached for his magnifying stand, placed the photograph underneath it and manoeuvred the desk lamp into position next to the stand. When he looked down again Colin felt his heart thump as the white 'Pavilion Theatre' masthead came into focus, below which could be made out, in bold type, '*Georgie P—*', the rest of the name being covered by the cartwheel. To the local historian, however, the name's visible portion was more than enough to know that this poster was advertising Georgie Parr, the Camden Clown, a name synonymous with one of the resort's darkest episodes. Naturally Colin knew about the music hall star's suicide beneath the pier following the brutal murder of a young prostitute, but there were precious few facts to be found regarding the terrible incident. It was almost as though there had been some form of cover-up, perhaps instigated by certain of the town's authorities in order to protect the reputation of the resort. A scandal involving one of that era's most well-known and controversial entertainers, who had been celebrated and condemned in equal measure by his contemporaries, may well have tainted the resort's hard-won pre-eminence. There had been, of course, one or two lurid headlines in the papers, but the story appeared to vanish from the collective consciousness with amazing alacrity. Now, seeing the poster guilelessly advertising that infamous name triggered a burning desire within the archivist to find out more, regardless of the difficulty. There was something terribly unresolved about the whole affair, not only for Georgie Parr and the prostitute but also for the resort. These two deaths had been overlooked for too long, their voices ignored, and this treatment had to have left a sense of shame within the resort's psyche. Colin was sure that an explanation could be found, that he could bind together sufficient fragments to offer at least some degree of closure. He did not believe in an afterlife, nor could he discern any kind of benevolent guiding hand behind the blood and struggle of history; facts were his only gospel, and if they were hidden, or remote, then surely this made them all the more important.

*VA342* he wrote on a label, before sticking it to a new plastic folder and sliding the photograph into its new home. *Draymen with pier Pavilion Theatre poster — Georgie Parr top of bill* he wrote in the file, and this time his entry seemed to him a model of understatement, like the unruffled surface of a deep, and very dark, lake.

"Colin?" came a thin, high-pitched voice from across the hall.

He leaned slightly towards the lounge doorway, as though this marginal reduction in distance would help his mother hear him more clearly. "I'm in here, Mum."

"What time is it?"

He glanced at the mantelpiece clock. "Half-past six."

"Is that all?"

"Yes."

"Oh." There was a pause. "Colin?"

"Yes?" he said, a note of long-suffering forbearance elongating the word, stretching it from the lounge to the bedroom like a pennant of servitude.

"Is it too early for a cup of tea?"

# The Rusting Truth

Colin's large, hairless hands operated the microfilm viewer's controls with a practised and casual dexterity, spinning the spools backwards and forwards as he hunted for a certain front page from November 1880. Outside the viewer's metal hood the reference library's quiet industry continued — the soft rhythm of books, an occasional rustle of newspaper, a cough, a sniff — but within the nineteenth century held sway, re-animated in the archivist's head by so many wonderful trivialities: a paragraph detailing the transfer of a licence for the Unicorn Inn from one Gareth Humpage to a Miss Martha Lomas; an advertisement for 'Beautiful French Millinery'; a flowery article on the joys of railway travel; the matter-of-fact reporting on the devastating bombardment of Alexandria by the British fleet; all these and more he could place within an imaginary three-dimensional template that, as the number of details grew and coalesced, formed a separate, entirely habitable world.

The headline slid past and was gone again, but the archivist's eyes were attuned to these briefest of glimpses; it was not reading as such, more a kind of subliminal absorption, so when *TERRIBLE TRAGEDY ON PIER* swept across the screen his hands were stopping the spools and rewinding almost before Colin had thought consciously about his actions.

The page re-appeared. Colin adjusted his reading glasses and leaned in towards the viewer.

# TERRIBLE TRAGEDY ON PIER

## Music Hall Performer Hangs Himself After Brutal Murder

*A scene of the utmost depravity was to be found this morning when early mists lifted from the beach and pier to reveal the body of popular music hall entertainer Mr George Parr, hanging by the neck from a length of rope, having evidently taken his own life beneath the very pier upon which his work and reputation rested.*

*Indeed, this would by all accounts be a tragic enough circumstance, but further horrors awaited the observer if he were to conduct no more than a cursory examination of the scene, as on the beach but a short distance from the sad remains of Mr Parr there lay the body of a Miss Hannah Goodwin, a young woman of fallen virtue, whose bruised and torn throat indicated that she had been most brutally strangled.*

*Upon discovery of these two corpses the police were summoned, and an expeditious removal of the sad remains was swiftly ordered, with officers cognisant both of the sensibilities of visitors to the beach and pier, as well as the uncontrollable and pressing attentions of an incoming tide.*

*As we describe this tragedy there have been no witnesses either called upon or who have volunteered to cast light on what may have transpired, so it seems the inescapable conclusion to be drawn is of a most villainous deed perpetrated by Mr Parr, who then, seized by some great remorse, fixed upon his own destruction as the only action remaining open to him. The reasons behind this savage act remain a mystery, notwithstanding the best efforts of the constabulary, but we can at least be somewhat eased in our sorrows with the knowledge that the family of the unfortunate Miss Goodwin has seen swift justice served on their daughter's behalf.*

*The results of a post-mortem examination on both players in this calamitous drama are due presently, their details to be found here together with any further developments.*

Colin levered his reading glasses up on top of his head and rubbed the bridge of his nose between thumb and forefinger. The report, with its typically Victorian style of journalism, combining moral outrage with a salacious eye for gory detail, appeared to be wholly confident in its assessment of the situation, presumably encouraged by the lack of anyone to contradict its conclusion. Without witnesses, and with both protagonists taking their own account to the grave, it was perhaps tempting to put forward a likely scenario, particularly if it helped to sell newspapers, but the archivist was far more wary of such conjecture. All he saw was a hanged man and a strangled girl; what the circumstances of each death were, and whether or not there was a connection between the two, would be a matter for research. And even following a determined and exhaustive effort to uncover the truth, Colin was well aware he might never find it. Over one hundred years lay between him and that misty November night. The remote possibility of anyone still being alive who could have witnessed it first hand was hampered still further by their being little more than a baby at the time, and even if, allowing for a truly precocious feat of infant memory which was then recalled a century later with total accuracy, the likelihood was that their parents or nanny, on seeing the police activity or the corpses themselves, would have rapidly turned the pram around to spare their child from having to see such a distressing sight. No. If answers there were, they would be found by nothing more than methodical inquiry. Letters, diaries, newspapers, official records, death certificates; if anyone could coax the past from paper and ink it was Colin Draper.

His first, simplest piece of groundwork was to see what the paper had subsequently to say, so the archivist scrolled through the rest of that day's paper, moving the roll of microfilm along to the following day's front page. Here, however, he could find no mention of the double death, neither as the main headline nor a smaller article, which surprised him. Undeterred, Colin worked his way through the entire paper. Nothing. This silence continued for another two days, until suddenly there it was again, second lead on page one.

# Music Hall Star's Secret Vice

*No one in this thriving yet close-knit community can have studied the recent events relating to the music hall star Mr George Parr, known to many thousands as 'Georgie Parr the Camden Clown', and failed to be appalled by his treatment of the young prostitute Hannah Goodwin, who, little more than a child herself, was through sorry circumstance obliged to find work in this basest of professions.*

*As regular readers will know, it is the steadfast stance of this newspaper to fight against immorality in the resort, as such behaviour can only tarnish its hard-fought reputation as the ideal recreational destination for decent, hard-working folk and their children, but we have a heart, and so feel only sorrowful pity for Hannah, who did not deserve to meet her fate in so ghastly a circumstance. There has been a good deal of detailed and scientific investigation into the case since last we reported on it, and we shall presently allow the man in charge, Inspector Henry Price, to explain in his own words his findings and conclusions, but first we must pass on the shocking revelation that George Parr had been an habitual guest of this town's seamier inhabitants, regularly calling on their services for purposes that modesty precludes us from expounding upon.*

*It seems, then, that Mr Parr's behaviour took its lead from the coarse and licentious tone of his music hall act, which has for some years sailed perilously close to the wind in its choice of material, often causing outrage amongst the greater public whilst, we have to admit, garnering a devoted following in the halls themselves.*

*Recent tragic events, therefore, seem to supply a compelling argument in favour of curbing the wilder excesses of these 'comic' turns, as they clearly have a disastrous effect on the morals of those exposed to them for any length of time. Granted, Mr Parr has had* to endure tragedies in his personal life, losing first his wife and then his only child, but so have many folk, if not worse, and they have faced such adversity with fortitude and without recourse to immorality and murder.

To close this tragic chapter we hand over editorship to Insp. Price, who provided us with a statement which, in its professional and objective analysis, offers the definitive version of events that transpired beneath the pier on the 14th November 1880, in the fervent hope that we never again have to relate such a harrowing tale.

'I was assigned to this case,' Insp. Price begins, 'less than an hour after the discovery of the two bodies, so on arrival at the scene they were in situ and I could make an initial assessment. Mr Parr's corpse was quite advanced in its state of rigor mortis. My calculation was that death had occurred approximately eight to ten hours previously, by asphyxiation due to a makeshift noose. I also noted two scratches running along his jawline, and his jacket sleeve was slightly torn away. Moving to Miss Goodwin, I ascertained that her own death must have been concurrent with Mr Parr's due to a similar degree of rigor to the limbs, and that death had been due once again to asphyxia, as evidenced by the severe bruising and tissue damage to her throat. I examined the area around both bodies and could find no other weapon, or indeed anything other than that which one would expect to find on a beach. There was no blood, and no visible wounds to either body.

'I instructed my men to remove the bodies, which were then transported to St Barnabas' Hospital morgue and prepared for autopsy. These were carried out by Dr Jonckheer, a gentleman of huge experience and skill in these matters, and on whose findings I have always placed the highest of regard.

'As expected, both autopsies confirmed my initial thoughts. Mr Parr's windpipe and oesophagus were greatly compacted, which would have cut off all supply of air, though his spinal column was only slightly distorted. Dr Jonckheer remarked that 'This man went calmly to his death, without struggle or second thought', a phrase I interpret as further evidence for George Parr's guilt. He knew what *he had done was unconscionable, and saved the courts the time and bother of coming to the same conclusion. I cannot in all honesty picture any other scenario. If a third party had strung him up there would surely have been a great disturbance in the surroundings, and signs of struggle upon the body, but there were none. Similarly, Miss Goodwin's oesophagus and larynx were crushed by a force exerted on either side, i.e. by the savage application of pressure from two strong hands. She was a slender thing, without the strength to resist such an assault, and despite her occupation I can only commend her poor soul to the Good Lord's mercy, for no one should meet their end in so brutal a fashion.*

*As to motive, I put forward two alternatives. The first is of a business transaction gone terribly wrong, perhaps when Miss Goodwin demanded more for her services than Mr Parr deemed right or proper; the second is the need to silence Miss Goodwin, who perhaps threatened to tell her story regarding the predilections of a well-known entertainer to some unscrupulous representative of the press. Having questioned those who knew both parties I could uncover no previous relationship of any kind, which eliminates an historical grievance or need for vengeance. I cannot countenance any kind of third party involvement, for reasons already outlined above, which leads me to the inescapable conclusion that George Parr murdered Hannah Goodwin, then took his own life. Some may seek to find complexity and subterfuge behind this act, but it is my experience that often the simplest of explanations is the truth of the matter, and I am sure that, in this sorry affair, this is the case.*

*Inspector H Price 17th November 1880*

Colin slumped back in his chair and breathed out noisily. Reading the articles had brought the case's grim details back into the forefront of his mind, details which, even in an era that was soon to witness the Jack the Ripper murders, had the power to shock. In the nineteenth century life could be brutal and short, and often traded as another form of commodity. There was hypocrisy and hubris, both wonderfully illustrated by the editorial tone, yet Colin saw through all this, freeing

George and Hannah from the distorting lens of historical context to leave them standing on the shingle, a man and a woman destined to end their life in the shadow of the pier, the same shadow that fell now, less than half a mile from where he was sitting. Colin felt a sudden urge to go down to the beach. He wanted to stand where they had stood, even though the articles never explained the exact positioning of the bodies. He even thought, with a sniff of derision and a shake of the head only moments later, that he might find some vital clue overlooked by Inspector Price. Yes, the archivist had heard of Georgie Parr's terrible crime, and he vaguely remembered reading the first of the newspaper articles before, but that must have been twenty years ago, when he was sufficiently young and ignorant to regard deeper research into his hometown as an admission of failure. The Colin Draper of 1966, fresh from Durham University and somehow left untouched by the sexual and social revolution sweeping through his generation, wanted nothing more than to continue his studies at postgraduate level, hopefully complete his doctorate and then immerse himself in a research post, like a tick burrowing under the skin of academia. He had written twenty thousand words of his thesis detailing the slave trade's influence on the formation of the British Empire when the call came regarding his mother's diagnosis, and Colin had abandoned his doctorate without a moment's thought, returning to the resort and becoming the council archivist, a post he would come to make his own.

Only now, for some reason, had the Georgie Parr story fired his imagination. Colin wondered why that was, when it was clearly one of the most intriguing events in the resort's history. Did he, in some way, identify more with the music hall performer now than he had back then? The newspaper articles had not mentioned George's age, but reading between the lines Colin estimated it to be fairly close to his own, so perhaps he had needed to age, to develop a middle-aged perspective, for the story to come alive. Whatever it was, the archivist could sense that tingle of anticipation he always felt when an interesting and challenging project presented itself. He also, despite the best efforts of the Victorian journalists, believed there was more to the case than had been reported. Why, for example, had the paper not said anything about the investigation for three days after its initial headline? Why was Inspector Price so dismissive of the possibility of a third party? And what were the circumstances behind George Parr's family tragedies? Were they in some way connected to the terrible events beneath the pier? There was a lot of work to do, but for the present Colin, like Inspector Price, wanted to see for himself the crime scene. Research and analysis could provide the facts, but for that flash of insight, that momentary inhabiting of another age, there needed to be a tangible connection, and what better example of this could there be than the pier?

Warm sunshine, an almost cloudless sky and a gentle onshore breeze combined to create the perfect spring day, and yet the beach and promenade were almost empty, metamorphosed into a bleak wilderness by the scattered family groups and individuals, who appeared vulnerable and lost within such a featureless tract. Colin looked at the sweep of sand and concrete, saddened by the stark contrast to how he remembered it only twenty years ago, when there was hardly a patch of sand to be seen for holidaymakers. Cheaper air travel and a taste for more exotic climes had exacted a terrible penalty on the resort; in the space of one generation it had gone from being a byword for fun and frivolity, drawing people from all over the country to its beach and theatres and arcades, to a neglected, down-at-heel place having to rely more and more on the raucous stag and hen parties who rampaged through its pubs and clubs at the weekend, leaving it stained with urine and vomit and then abandoned for the rest of the week, until Friday brought the next wave of revellers. The resort echoed to their marauding cries. It had become possessed of that febrile atmosphere prevalent whenever an empire collapses, and Colin hated to see it accept these reduced circumstances so meekly.

He reached the wrought-iron railing at the edge of the promenade and leaned against it for a moment to catch his breath. The archivist had decided to walk from the library to the pier, a decision he regretted now, even though the two were only half a mile apart. Colin had grown to loathe all forms of organised exercise at an early age. Chubby and uncoordinated, he had been taunted and bullied by his teachers as well as by his fellow pupils, but this had merely made him seek comfort in food, creating a vicious circle which saw him dumped in goal for football, where he would then spend most of the game surreptitiously munching on sweets smuggled onto the playing field in his shorts. His higher education was entirely sedentary, as was his career, so Colin slowly put on more and more weight without really noticing. His mother, in a mother's wilfully blind vernacular, described him as 'strapping', but he was under no illusions as to his size; he expected to have to pay for his unhealthy lifestyle, presumably with either a heart attack or something similar. Colin was quite sanguine about this. He had even formulated a sort of rough guide to his own expected mortality, basing it on his father's coronary, then adding a decade to Malcolm Draper's lifespan for never having smoked (unlike his Senior Service-loving dad), another decade for the lack of physical exertion required in his work, and a further five or six years from his very moderate drinking, again unlike his father's fondness for beer. This total, which Colin regarded as having been calculated with scrupulous honesty, took him to his late seventies, which he felt constituted a decent enough innings. It was more than the vast majority of mankind had enjoyed, after all, and would have been beyond the wildest imaginings of a fellow proletarian from any century before his own. And, having watched his mother's decline, to the point where she could now do little more than push buttons on the television remote control, he had no desire to reach an age that brought with it a similar level of incapacity. Better to take one's leave of the planet with a lingering sense of what more could have been achieved than feel as though purpose and relevance had long since been left behind.

Restored to the minor aches and hindrances that passed for equilibrium, the archivist made his way along the promenade and began his descent. The steps cut into the promenade were deep and stained with rust from the flimsy chain fence that formed a makeshift handrail, and led him down onto the band of shingle which formed the upper section of the beach, fist-sized stones that the sea would, with its infinite patience, reduce to the tiniest of particles. Colin stumbled several times negotiating their shifting, convex surfaces. The pebbles ground against each other as his scuffed brogues settled on them, the one beneath his shoe binding to those surrounding it until, his full weight pressing down, the limits of friction were exceeded and the stones gave way, like a series of booby traps. The high tide mark was delineated by a straggling line of seaweed mixed with pieces of driftwood, plastic bottles and clumps of tangled netting; sandflies busied themselves amongst the detritus, whilst further along the beach several brown-and-white birds Colin did not recognise bustled in and out of the seaweed as they feasted on the insects.

Finally, with a grunt of relief, he reached the firmer footing of sand, and for the first time could look up at the pier. From down on the beach it appeared less poetic, more a collection of corroded iron pillars than a fine spun statement of mankind's mastery of the elements, and Colin realised that he was not meant to scrutinise the pier from this angle, to lift its skirts, as it were, and squint upwards. Here was the rusting truth, the view of the pier as appreciated only by an engineer, a prosaic land of support upon which life could be sustained… and death found, of course.

Moving into shadows which seemed as solid and unbending as the iron piles they wrapped around, the archivist thought again about Georgie Parr, who had walked beneath these very same props and struts knowing he would never re-emerge. A sudden idea came to him: what if George had indeed committed suicide, and some devious villain had discovered the entertainer's body and seen it as the perfect scapegoat upon which to foist the blame for their own violent crime? They could strangle the girl, dump her body near George's suspended corpse, and walk away with impunity, secure in the knowledge that the police would associate the two deaths. This was long before any kind of forensic examination, apart perhaps from fingerprints or imprints of shoes; as long as detectives could concoct a convincing scenario they were unlikely to delve too deeply. They would even avoid the tedium and cost of a trial, as the prime suspect was, handily, already dead. He was only a music hall entertainer, after all, and the victim a prostitute. The whole sorry affair could be quickly concluded as a dispute between two representatives of the lower classes that had got out of hand, leaving the resort to forget the whole episode as an unnecessary distraction from its primary function as opiate to that very same stratum of society.

The more he thought about Inspector Price's dismissive and condescending attitude, the more Colin felt convinced he was on the verge of uncovering a terrible miscarriage of justice. The authorities had assumed George's guilt from the outset, without looking properly at his background, circumstances, motivation or character. They were both lazy and prejudiced, a privileged coterie of Freemasons and civic figureheads who saw the cash flowing into the town and were determined not to let a scandal cause alarm. That would explain the newspaper's silence. He could see them now, gathered in some wood-panelled room with their brandy and cigars: the inspector, the town clerk, the magistrate and the newspaper editor, formulating a tale of sordid urges and violence with all the loose ends neatly tied together in a bundle of speculation and supposition.

The archivist patted one of the iron pillars. "If only you could talk," he whispered.

Stepping out from beneath the pier, Colin felt as though he had returned, not only to the sunshine, but also to the present. He made his way towards the steps, but something made him turn and look again at the pier. A figure was leaning on the gently undulating back of the wrought-iron seating that ran along the pier's edge, a figure who was clearly staring down at him. Colin shaded his eyes with one hand and squinted. He recognised the frizzy tufts of hair and bald pate which belonged to Mickey Braithwaite, the pier's longest-serving employee, who had been arranging deckchairs along its length for over forty years. Colin wondered whether Mickey would know anything about the George Parr story, and made a mental note to seek out the attendant as soon as possible. He waved, and Mickey waved back.

# Angel Delight

Edna Draper's bedroom had become her world, and therefore contained strange vistas that could be seen by her and her alone. The light, too, possessed a translucent quality found nowhere else in the bungalow: gauzy, tinted blue from the thin curtains which were always drawn, as Edna's eyes were sensitive and could no longer bear direct sunlight; it appeared at first glance as though she was lying at the bottom of a still, pellucid pool. At bedtime, Colin would switch on a child's night-light to keep the darkness at bay. There was an indefinable quality to the light that gave the impression of it being very old, light that had perhaps witnessed too much and was tired now, reluctant to move from the large, bay-windowed room that contained it, the kind of light which stands guard over sleeping princesses who wait, insensible, in their rooms at the top of ivy-clad towers, dreaming, as all the persecuted do, not of their rescuer but their tormentor. Edna was, appropriately enough given her tenure cradled in this light, a romantic. She regarded her own plight in romantic terms, as a curse to be endured. She even referred to the multiple sclerosis as her 'poisoned apple', as though the disease had been visited upon her due to some innocently made but fatally flawed decision on her part. Her son did not attempt to alter this peculiar mindset, guessing quite correctly that it was simply a form of coping strategy, and that pointing out its obvious shortcomings could prove disastrous. The elegiac atmosphere in Edna's bedroom, however, exerted little influence on the prosaic and ordered mind of Colin Draper. Stepping into that room was, to him, like nothing more than entering a familiar hospital ward.

Her single bed jutted out from the wall like a soft white promontory, surrounded on three sides by the things that made her life bearable. On one side stood a table which could be swung round so that it projected over Edna's midriff, its top crammed with juice cartons, bags of sweets, bottles and boxes of tablets, magazines, books, a small radio, and a box of tissues. On the other side was a large electric fan, permanently switched on, its low hum as much a part of the room as the aquatic light. To one side at the foot of the bed was a trolley carrying a television and VCR, with videotapes neatly stacked and labelled on the lower shelf. The only other items of furniture in the room were a chair next to the fan and a huge wardrobe, constructed out of a dark wood with unusual jagged streaks of graining, which made it look as though someone had vented a terrible fury on the wardrobe, slashing and slashing at it before attempting to cover up their senseless act with a thick, treacly varnish. As a child, Colin had been terrified of it, and would refuse to go into his parents' bedroom at night if there was no one there. He could never understand why they had chosen such a brooding piece of furniture, but his mother would not hear of it being removed, and so it remained, glowering at Colin like some malevolent guardian whenever he entered the room, ready to intervene if it suspected any form of threat against its immobile and vulnerable charge.

Mrs Draper herself, habitually clothed in a white nightie, and possessing skin as pale and smooth as cream, merged with her bedding so perfectly that, in the dim light, the bedroom appeared empty, as though either by some miracle she had recovered and left to re-acquaint herself with the wide world, or else had perished and been taken away in her coffin, a place of confinement which would hold no fear for her. And then her hand would move, perhaps to dip into her bag of sweets, or press a button on the remote control, and her whole form would coalesce, a collection of mounds and curves so amorphous as to resemble a bank of clouds rather than a person. Her hazel eyes, however, always her best feature, shone out from these pale foothills with undiminished life. Visitors invariably remembered Edna's eyes, much more so than her failing body, or the room.

Her illness dictated that she lay for the most part on her right side, so arranged on the wall opposite was a collection of her favourite paintings, mingling with family photographs which to her were as precious as any Monet or Van Gogh. If there was nothing on television, and Colin was not available to feed a tape into the video machine, Edna could quite happily while away the hours studying her wall of images. She particularly enjoyed a game she had devised, whereby she transposed one or more family members from a photograph into one of the paintings, imagining how they would react, and what the people in the painting would say to them. As a lover of Impressionism, Mrs Draper realised that the painted characters were more than likely to speak French, but she ignored this small inconsistency and granted everyone subjected to her experimentation perfect communication in some form of *lingua franca*.

This, then, was Edna's world; a cool land of permanent twilight, peopled by ghosts, never completely silent, never completely rooted in any one particular time, perfumed by the sherbet sweets she adored, and wonderfully tranquil, so much more tranquil than would be expected in a place of such cruel illness.

Into this world, for the first time, came Georgie Parr, and by this simple introduction was granted some small measure of peace.

Colin, having cleared the movable table beforehand as he always did at mealtimes, carried his mother's tea into the room and placed the tray on the table, swinging it round so that the bowl of finely chopped Spaghetti Bolognese was within reach of Edna's functioning hand and arm, before returning to the kitchen and bringing his own. He settled in the chair, and the two of them ate for several minutes in companionable silence before, with a clatter, Edna dropped her spoon.

"Oops! Butterfingers," she said.

Colin put down his food and leaned forward to retrieve the utensil, which was resting on the base of the fan. He picked it up and studied it, checking for any signs of dirt.

"It's lost nothing," his mother noted. "A bit of dust won't do me any harm."

"You don't know that," Colin replied. He gave the spoon a perfunctory polish on his shirt and handed it back. "Who knows what germs are lurking in dust?"

"Oh, for goodness sake, Colin, stop fussing me. I'm not a baby."

Her son placed both fisted hands on his hips and gave her an 'oh really?' look. "It might have escaped your notice, Mother, but—"

"Yes, yes," Edna interrupted, "I'm well aware of my situation, Colin, and the more you wrap me up in cotton wool the worse it is. All anyone in my position wants is a little bit of normality... to be treated like anybody else. We don't need constantly reminding of our... " She searched for the word.

"Plight?" he suggested.

"Oh, Colin!" Edna laughed. "You really are a miserable so-and-so at times."

"What's wrong with plight? If I was in your position I'd think it was the perfect word to describe it."

Mrs Draper closed her eyes for a moment and exhaled, a long, deliberately toned expulsion of breath, as though she hoped it would carry off some bothersome notion with it. "And at times I do too, love, I do too, but there's no point shaking your fist at God and asking 'why me?' all the time. It doesn't get you anywhere but to a very angry place."

"Particularly when God doesn't exist," Colin said pointedly.

"Says you."

Colin retrieved his bowl and sat back down. "No, Mother. Empirically, he doesn't exist."

Edna scooped up a spoonful of pasta and sauce and guided it into her mouth. She sometimes wondered how she had managed to raise such a dogmatic individual, who seemed somewhat frightened of life. Her husband Malcolm had occasionally slipped into a sombre mood, but after being propelled, physically if need be, out to his garden shed for a few hours he always returned with dirt under his fingernails and a renewed sense of humour. She missed his dry wit. Colin, bless him, had his father's nose and broad, thick-fingered hands, but there was none of Malcolm's sense of the absurd. If Edna challenged God about anything, it was his taking away of her husband at the age of fifty-three. This was the only injustice that truly tested her faith.

"I don't want us to fall out, Colin," she said, a note of chastisement in her voice, "so can we please change the subject? Thank you." Edna continued in a cheery voice. "Well, what have you been up to today?"

The archivist recognised the tone and knew it was pointless trying to argue, so he paused, indicating to his mother that his reply was a concession rather than a capitulation, then continued, "I've been researching a Victorian music hall comic who hung himself under the pier."

"Oh dear. What on earth did he do that for?"

"The papers seemed to think he'd strangled a prostitute, but I think there's more to it than meets the eye."

Mrs Draper tried to lever herself into a slightly more comfortable position, pivoting her body on her elbow. She managed to move no more than an inch, but to her it felt as though she had rolled from one side of the bed to the other, such was the easing of pain at the points where her body's weight rested. "Ooh, Colin, you sound just like Columbo."

He gazed witheringly at her. "This is not one of your lurid American programmes, Mother, this is a man scapegoated by a cabal of worthies in order to safeguard the town's tourist trade. I think they were hiding the killer in their own ranks. I'm not even sure he committed suicide. He was a successful comic, top of the bill in the pier's theatre... Why would he kill himself?"

"A lot of comedians are miserable as sin," Edna remarked.

"Really? How many comedians do you know?"

"It's a well-known fact," she countered. "'The tears of a clown', that's what they say. Most of them can hardly crack a smile once they're off-stage. Perhaps he was fed up with all that laughter."

Colin edged forward in his chair. He already felt a sort of proprietorial protectiveness towards George Parr — his defender against a century of misinformation — that he knew had the potential to turn his research into a subjective, unscientific endeavour, but he somehow sensed the righteousness of his cause. Was the truth, supressed for all those years, finally pushing its way to the surface, assisted by his investigative work?

"*Fed up*? Mother, your mastery of the understatement never ceases to amaze me. People do not hang themselves because they're 'fed up'. Apparently his wife and daughter had both died, though not at the same time, if the wording of the newspaper article is to be believed, and he didn't commit suicide then, so I hardly think an excess of laughter would push him over the edge."

"Well I didn't know that, did I?" Edna put down her spoon and frowned. "The poor man. Losing your other half is bad enough, but then to lose your child as well."

"Rather vindictive of your kind and righteous God, don't you think?"

"God doesn't have anything to do with these things."

"Ah!" Colin said triumphantly, "So he isn't all-powerful after all. He's just as helpless in the face of fate as anybody else."

Edna felt tears starting to cloud her vision. "I don't know why you feel the need to constantly mock my faith, Colin. It isn't hurting you, is it? It doesn't make any difference to your life, does it? Why can't you just let me believe what I want to believe?"

He noticed the tears glistening in his mother's eyes and realised he had gone too far. Like she said, what harm did it do? And yet the archivist felt duty-bound to try and prepare his mother for that devastating moment, as the blackness of death descended, when even the strongest faith was snuffed out like a candle, and each individual was obliged to understand that not only their life, but all life, all creation, was nothing more than an effect, following on inevitably from the Big Bang's cause, and that effect did not require meaning, any more than the ripples spreading out across the surface of a lake after a stone was thrown into it required meaning. Water was being displaced, in a concentric and agreeable form, but it *meant* precisely nothing. Colin had come to terms with this; indeed, he found a degree of comfort in it, but he feared for his mother. He did not want her final moment of consciousness to be one of pure terror, as everything she had expected to happen failed to materialise.

"I just don't want you to expect answers, that's all," he explained, "when there isn't really a question."

"I've been answered already, but you wouldn't understand what I'm on about. Oh well, I suppose that's as close as I'm going to get to an apology. Here's a question for you: how did his wife die? And his daughter?"

Colin wagged an appreciative forefinger at his mother. "Good question. I don't know. I don't know how they died, or when they died, in relation to George." He tried to recall the newspaper article's exact wording. "From what it said I think they died a while before he did, and not at the same time. We need to get hold of the death certificates. They'll give us the timing and the circumstances. I'll drop Neil a line at the PRO, he'll dig 'em out. Thanks, Mum. That was an obvious follow-up and I hadn't thought of it. Too busy thinking about Georgie Parr."

"Mum!" Edna exclaimed. "Blimey, I don't often get one of them. I am honoured."

Colin stood up. "Indeed you are. I tell you what, as a reward, how do you fancy a bit of Angel Delight for afters?"

"Strawberry flavour?"

"Of course. What other flavour is there?" Colin replied, and mother and son laughed, relieved to have navigated their way back into the safer waters of shared whimsy and domestic detail. There was a darkness around George Parr that seemed able to reach across the years, infiltrating and staining both the mind and wider world of anyone who came too close to him; Colin and Edna had sensed it too, even in the limpid tranquillity of her bedroom, even one hundred and nine years after George's death, and despite being able to pull free of this darkness because of their deep-rooted love and symbiotic relationship (and a well-rehearsed exchange concerning the choice of pudding), there remained an echo of his former presence, creeping across previously inviolable boundaries as easily as an incoming tide washes over a child's sandcastle.

# The Euphoria of Uncertainty

A single fluorescent tube illuminated the town hall base-
ment, its austere light softened by the dust and cobwebs
that had collected around it. From this shrouded source the
light percolated downward, filtering through a thick, musty
gloom, until it reached tea chests and cardboard boxes,
then wooden plaques and pennants exchanged with much
pomp and handshaking before being consigned to obscurity,
their bestower forgotten. It continued, to pick out framed
photographs of former mayors now stacked together so they
could discuss the ignominy or justness of their abandonment;
old furniture, and broken lamps meant at some juncture to
be repaired. Finally what remained of the light settled on the
balding pate of Colin Draper, who sat, very much at home,
in a threadbare armchair next to the shelves containing the
oldest council meeting records, an archive which began in
1870 when the council was formed.

The tube gave off an incessant, high-pitched buzzing noise
that to some would have proved infuriatingly distracting, but
not Colin. Anyone who worked with him could attest to the
archivist's prodigious powers of concentration, which were
sometimes mistaken for ignorance or rudeness by those
unfamiliar with his singlemindedness. He had the ability
to shut out everything except the document or task in hand,
effectively isolating himself within a bubble that contained
nothing but Colin and the voices of those long dead. As a
young boy he would think nothing of sitting for hours at

the tiny desk his uncle had made for him, either drawing or reading. Later, to block out the taunts and bullying which seemed to follow him wherever he went, Colin developed this incredibly narrow field of focus, so much so that during his latter years at grammar school his tormentors largely abandoned their campaign, so impervious to its blows had he become.

Behind a dividing wall, built much later from breeze blocks, the wumph and clatter of a boiler could be heard, followed by a metallic resonance from the pipes which ran over Colin's head. Subconsciously the archivist must have glanced at his watch and concluded that Dougal, the small, fearsome mayor's attendant, had turned up the council chamber's thermostat in advance of a meeting that evening, but consciously he was wholly immersed in the leather-backed ledger resting on his knees, and the copperplate handwriting it contained.

"The twenty-second of November," Colin read out loud, as was his habit. "That's eight days after George and Hannah's deaths." He flipped back a page to check the dates. "No special meetings convened? No committee formed? Just the normal council, on its normal day? Come on, you lot, aren't you *bothered*?"

But then he remembered the social standing of those present on the resort's council, which back then consisted solely of (though Colin hated the term) middle-class professionals: lawyers, doctors, civil servants, businessmen and clergy, none of whom would have wanted to be associated with the sordid events under the pier. By even raising the subject before full council on its allotted day they would have attracted attention, if not suspicion, for involving themselves with such a typically proletarian demonstration of immorality.

"Let's see if anyone's brave enough to say anything in the chamber," Colin said, turning back to the minutes from that November evening so long ago.

There was an introductory statement from Councillor

Allardyce, at first congratulating the mayor on the recent birth of his first grandchild, before continuing with the minutes of the previous council meeting. These were followed by the town clerk, who reported on a variety of applications to the council, consisting mostly of requests to build or alter a property, as well as what seemed to be an ongoing dispute over boundaries to a proposed park on the northern edge of the resort. Normally Colin would study these apparently trivial items with the same thoroughness and interest as he would a royal proclamation — he regarded both as of equal importance, because whereas the proclamation undoubtedly wielded greater influence over the entire country, and therefore dominated the macro-historical picture, the minutes and applications from a council meeting illustrated what was happening on a day-to-day basis, at the level of ordinary people... where history began, in other words — but today his mind had narrowed its field of view further; today all it was concerned with were the words *Parr*, or *Goodwin*, or *pier*. Anything else may as well have been written in hieroglyphics.

His eyes skimmed over the immaculate copperplate handwriting, attuned to its slender loops, long, vigorous crossing of 't's, and the slight thickening of certain letters as the clerk dipped his nib in the inkwell and continued his notes. Had this faithful recorder ever questioned the relevance of his work, all those thousands and thousands of words? Had he ever been tempted to simply write down what he fancied, or even put down his pen altogether and allow the spoken words to be heard by those present and then vanish forever, unrecorded, and perhaps the better for it?

The word *pier* brought his scanning to a halt, but it was only a request from the company that owned and ran the pier to be allowed, from next May, to run pleasure boat rides from a mooring at its seaward end, the request being made now so as to allow them time to construct steps, a ticket booth, and to procure a quantity of advertising posters for the new venture.

Lured in by mention of the pier, Colin continued reading

at a more sedate pace. The polite debate, and the subtle political manoeuvring that could be discerned running below its surface, delighted the archivist, but for all the coded insults and the proposals made with one eye on getting their name chiselled into a foundation stone or engraved on a plaque, Colin had to admit that there was an obviously genuine desire to promote and develop the resort. These men seemed well aware of their responsibilities as founding fathers, whose decisions would shape the town for generations to come, and he had to respect them for that. He wondered what they would think if they could see it now, with its penis-shaped sticks of rock, marauding packs of stag parties, and the older parts of its infrastructure — the pier, winter gardens, theatres and hotels that these men watched rise from their foundations — crumbling and corroding for a lack of investment?

And then he found it. Following a jocular interlude concerning a group of passengers who alighted from their train only to find themselves face to face with an angry chimpanzee that had managed to escape from its cage as it was being transported to the resort's new zoo, Councillor Hind then proposed a motion calling for an additional rental to be levied on traders whose businesses were either on, or adjacent to, the promenade, as this was clearly the most profitable area of the resort. This was seconded by Councillor Routledge, but then the Reverend Thomas Fearnley spoke, and Colin could almost hear the booming, denunciatory tones echoing round the council chamber.

'There is one trade,' the Reverend Fearnley had stated, 'that makes a good part of its despicable profits on the promenade and pays not one penny piece in rent! These harlots seem to think that they can behave with impunity wherever they please, and decent folk will rightly shun anywhere such a business is being plied. And where these women work, so too does every other disreputable trade, along with its basest of associates, as was amply demonstrated by the events of Tuesday last. If the full weight of the law is not brought to bear on these women, and the men who control their purse-strings, then we shall see a great deal more such tragedies, and our promenade will become nothing more than a latterday Sodom and Gomorrah.'

Colin puffed out his cheeks and widened his eyes. "Don't beat about the bush, reverend," he said. The similarity in tone between the vicar's outburst and that used in the newspaper articles amused him, but also lent added credence to his idea of a group of influential people working together to steer public opinion. They obviously wanted to create a distraction, but from what? The archivist continued to read.

Councillor Ibbotson, the mayor, called for order. 'We are all painfully aware of what happened last Tuesday, reverend. The death of Mr Parr and the girl will undoubtedly go down as one of our town's darkest chapters, but it is all in the hands of the relevant authorities. We must let them do their work without interference.'

"What's that supposed to mean?" Colin enquired of the shadows.

He read on. Reverend Fearnley. 'My parishioners will not venture into certain areas after dark for fear of being propositioned or robbed. If the promenade develops a similar reputation then the very resort is in jeopardy.'

Councillor Ibbotson. 'Indeed, which is why I have asked for a thorough investigation into the matter. Any further comment would be nothing more than speculation, and as I hardly need remind all those present in this chamber, to act on nothing more than hearsay would be imprudent, to say the least. On receipt of this investigation's findings we will debate the issue fully, and take the appropriate steps.'

Councillor Appleby. 'I gather there are certain street vendors selling lengths of rope which they claim are from the one on which Mr Parr chose to suspend himself, but I suspect that if we joined together all these pieces we would have a rope long enough to comfortably hold the Great Eastern at bay!'

And that was that. The council went on to debate the proposed draining of marshland, a dispute between cab drivers and a blacksmith who, they alleged, was over-charging for shoeing their horses, and the cost of extending gas lighting to all parts of the resort, but there was no further mention of George Parr. With some reluctance Colin closed the ledger, returning it to its place on the shelf, and with this short sequence of actions brought himself back into the twentieth century and all its banal coherence. The archivist always felt this disappointment on withdrawing from history; he felt so much more at home within its blinkered borders, where photographs or artefacts or musty pages shone a pale light into the gloom, but where all else waited, silent and fragmented, indifferent to the possibility of its discovery. Colin understood how the words *terra incognita* on a map had exerted such a pull on certain individuals. Fame, fortune and glory awaited the favoured few, but failure or even death were equally likely outcomes, that death sometimes occurring in a manner too grisly to contemplate. No. *Terra incognita*'s literal translation might be 'unknown land', but it could equally be interpreted as the euphoria of uncertainty.

Evening rainclouds had brought a premature twilight to the resort, leaching the colour out of everything but the neon signs of the amusement arcades, which now broadcast their red and yellow promises with an acidic fervour in this drab and diminished world. Wet roads and pavements mirrored these pledges, but a footfall was sufficient to break them and prove how flimsy they were. One or two family groups shuffled along in the cold drizzle, shrouded in cagoules or huddled under umbrellas, their faces creased as though in pain, penitents on some dour pilgrimage.

The windows of the bus had been rendered almost opaque by a combination of rain and condensation, turning what was normally an everyday route into an enigmatic, featureless journey, its only landmarks traffic lights and the blurred neon signs of the arcades. Those passengers familiar with the route sat calmly, either counting the number of stops, or waiting for some illuminated landmark to appear like an amorphous beacon, while others, visitors perhaps, rubbed portholes in the condensation and peered out anxiously, hoping to recognise something in the murk.

Colin sat next to the window, pressed up against the cold glass by the presence of a huge woman next to him. He had known she was going to take the vacant space to his right from the moment he first noticed her lumbering down the aisle of the bus with two large shopping bags, and sure enough she did, collapsing onto the seat with a grunt and a sigh, the bags clasped in both arms on her knees. He had shuffled as far as he could towards the window in order to accommodate her bulk, but Colin was no lightweight himself, and the two were forced to continue their journey pressed together in reluctant intimacy. What most alarmed the archivist, however, was the fact that the heat from her body, combined with the bouncing of the bus, had given him an erection no amount of mental effort seemed able to dispel. His stop was only a few minutes away, and the prospect of manoeuvring past her whilst still in a state of arousal appalled him, so Colin decided to analyse the brief interchange he had found in the council meeting records, in the hope that a little dry Victorian debate would have the desired effect.

There had clearly been some degree of tension between the mayor and vicar, but without further research into their respective characters or the council's hierarchical structure Colin was reluctant to conclude that the discord reflected either a wider power struggle or significant personal animosity. Of course Councillor Ibbotson and the Reverend Fearnley may well have loathed and detested each other, but Colin Draper, council archivist and local historian — a man whose scrupulous adherence to the facts managed to co-exist with a sort of crusading subjectivity, a man who could display a passionate empathy for the dead and yet feel nothing but clumsy indifference to the living — refused to acknowledge any such rivalry without documentary proof, while at the same time remaining utterly convinced that they were complicit in some self-serving smear campaign against George Parr. Who were the 'relevant authorities' that the mayor had referred to? If he had meant the police why had he not simply called them that? And to defer any detailed debate on the wider implications of George and Hannah's deaths until some nebulous investigation had been concluded was one of the oldest political tricks in the book. Awkward questions can be deflected whilst maintaining a sense of propriety, of being sufficiently humble to defer your own wish to reply to the greater good of due process, which then allows time to come up with either a convincing answer, or for the original question to be forgotten. Councillor Ibbotson must have been privy to details he felt unwilling or unable to relate in the chamber, and so employed a delaying tactic that he knew the vicar could not argue against. Colin made a mental note to seek out a painting of the man; he wanted to look him in the eye and see whether there was any sign of duplicity there, or if the mayor had merely been doing what he thought was right for the resort. An honourable man unnerved and, perhaps, overwhelmed by the savagery visited upon his town.

Had any of that group of wing-collared, mutton chop-whiskered and rigid gentlemen looked towards the council chamber's stained glass windows with fear and incomprehension at what they perceived to be the forces of chaos clamouring outside, or had they unleashed these same forces as agents charged with a particular task, the consequences of which had been engineered from the outset? But how could the death of a young prostitute and a well-known music hall entertainer possibly be of benefit to the resort's ruling elite? If benefit there was, it would have to be substantial, given the risk of political and social suicide if any evidence emerged linking the council member to such a violent crime. Colin stared out at the phantasmagorical night, willing it to conjure up a logical explanation, but all it could offer was wet pavements and the diffracted lances of streetlamps, which cast orange splinters against the greater darkness without appreciable mitigating effect, like flecks of paint spattered on a black canvas. The bus drew up at a stop. Colin rubbed away a small patch of condensation and looked out. Quite close by, on the other side of a narrow front garden, was the bay window of a guest house, its curtains drawn back to reveal a brightly lit dining room. Seated at a table in the window was a man eating alone, hunched forward over the table as though the contents of his bowl were drawing him in with inescapable force. He lifted a spoon to his mouth, and Colin could see a portion of the watery soup dribble down the man's front. He appeared not to notice, however, and again dipped the spoon into his bowl, a slow, deliberate movement, before raising it once more, only to lose a little more soup before the spoon reached his mouth. A small queue of people was joining the bus and paying their fare, so Colin had time to count fifteen identical scoop/spill/mouthfuls before the vehicle's two sets of doors came together with a hiss of compressed air and it set off from the bus stop, drawing the archivist away from the robotic ingestion of the man in the window. Colin imagined the soup stains down the front of the man's shirt and wondered whether or not he would be concerned by them, or even if he would notice them at all. Had the man started his meal without waiting for his wife to settle at the table, or was he alone? Had the presence of the bus, of Colin, impinged on him at all? He did not appear to be particularly old, but everything about the man, from how he had huddled over the table to the mechanical, undeviating method of his eating, exuded an enormous weariness, a weariness that he had learned to exist within by committing himself entirely to its natural frequency. He was sitting at the table. The bowl was on the table. The soup was in the bowl. The spoon was in his hand. The spoon was in the bowl. The soup was in the spoon. The spoon was in his mouth. The soup was in his mouth. The spoon was in the bowl... and so it continued. The bus, and its passengers, and the cold, rainy night, simply did not exist.

Colin knew something was wrong the moment he opened the front door and stepped into the hall. Every day, on his return from work, his mother would call out from her bedroom 'Is that you, Colin?', and he would inevitably reply with something along the lines of 'No, Mother, it's a mad axe murderer', but tonight there was silence.

"Mum?" The word seemed to hang in the air, unanswered and unadorned, almost mocking in the way its cracked, high-pitched sound filled Colin's ears, forcing him to acknowledge how much he depended on the stanchion of his mother's response.

He threw his keys onto the hall table. A part of his mind registered that at the bottom of the pile of post — neatly arranged on the table by Pam their next door neighbour, who came in to give Mrs Draper her lunch — was a large buff envelope with IMPORTANT DOCUMENTS PLEASE DO NOT BEND stencilled across it, and, if he had had the ability to detach himself from the situation, to analyse it with scrupulous honesty, Colin would have been forced to admit to a moment of quite ferocious resentment towards his mother, whose stricken existence was delaying him from the joy of opening that envelope. This was the dark undercurrent of their interdependence: the quiet rage he sometimes felt at being hampered in his work, in his *life*, by the needs of his mother, and the inevitable feeling of self-loathing which always followed. This was not a moment for objective analysis, however, so Colin left the envelope and hurried into his mother's bedroom.

A pale amber glow from the streetlamp at the end of the garden seeped in through the curtains, accentuating the pulpy mound in the bed. The fan, its enduring hum imperturbable during those few seconds of tumult, blew a sweet and cloying odour towards him that Colin thought for a moment was the smell of death, until he realised that a bag of fudge lay open in the path of the fan's current of air. He hurried round the bed, both dreading what he would find and yet desperate to determine the reason behind his mother's silence.

Edna was slumped against the chrome guardrail, her forehead pressed against its burnished bar. Her eyes were closed, but as Colin knelt beside her he could discern a gentle fluttering that played across her eyelids like a breeze ruffling the surface of a lake. Her breathing was rapid and shallow, not laboured, exactly, but rather as though she would be happy to relinquish the tedium of drawing air into her lungs.

"Mum? Mum?" Colin laid his hand on her shoulder, which had slipped free of her nightie, and shook gently. The softness of her skin beguiled him, soothed him. How very pale she was, lustrous in the filtered light, emollient and utterly formless. Her skin was cool, but not cold.

"Mum?"

Her lips parted slightly. Some sort of white material had gathered in the corners of her mouth; it stretched like gum as she tried to speak. "Malcolm?"

"No, Mother," Colin corrected her, irritated beyond reason by her mistake, "it's me... Colin. *Colin*. Your son."

Edna's breathing lost its rhythm for a moment, and when she spoke again the words were so quiet they seemed little more than appendices to each exhalation. "Tired, Colin. Let me sleep. Let me go."

This last sentence filled him with dread. The archivist knew, of course, that the nature of his mother's illness meant she would deteriorate over time, until the creeping paralysis reached her vital organs and slowly squeezed them to a standstill, but he was not ready for her to die. Not yet. Just the dislocation of entering the house, the absence of her unvarying welcome, had been enough to show him that.

Colin stood up. "I'm going to phone the hospital," he said

decisively. "I won't be long. Don't go to sleep, Mother. I'll be back in a minute."

The only reply she gave was a brief noise, somewhere between a grunt and a sigh, deep in her throat, and again her eyelids fluttered. As Colin made his way back into the hall he could not help wondering about this sporadic movement. Did it reflect some inner distress, perhaps, or was she searching for something or someone in the darkness, a familiar image or figure that could offer solace and guidance in the face of a solitary death?

Hours later, as he sat, neat and upright on the couch, cloaked in the silence of the house and with the unopened envelope across his knees, Colin thought back over all that had happened since arriving home after work, the emotions and sounds and smells, the movement and voices, and found that everything had been whisked together into a thick paste of sensory overload, an indigestible mixture of sirens and clattering trolleys, the tired eyes of a doctor, a hospital's austere light, the trembling needle of a ventilator dial, reassurances spoken in terms which could never bring reassurance, tea which tasted of plastic and, having been drunk whilst staring blankly at the wall in a seating area, had become conflated with a poster about HIV, and, finally, a ride home through the same chimerical landscape as his bus journey, only this time accompanied by the haunting choral wash of Enya playing on the taxi driver's cassette. Colin, bizarrely, could recall his brief exchange with the driver as they set off far more accurately than his conversation with the doctor.

'Mind a bit of music?' the driver had enquired.

'No. No, that's fine.'

'Let's have a bit of Enya, then. Calms folk down. Bit of Enya, everyone's off. Sort of meditation, know what I mean? They won't have been listening to her in the clubs. More likely some of that dance rubbish. Thump thump thump. All that gets you is wound up, but that's no good in your cab, is it? I'm not going to put something like that on, there'd be a bloody riot. Bit of Enya, you're going to have it nice and quiet. You look like an Enya fan.'

'Do I?'

'Yeah. Sensible. Brainy.'

'Oh. Well... '

'Ha! I knew it.'

Why had his mind seen fit to store such prattling nonsense, when all he could recall from the hospital was a collection of phrases, clumped together in a barely comprehensible aggregate of medical diagnoses and platitudes? Pulmonary complications... comfortable...fluid build-up... get some rest... best place for her... cardiac arrhythmia... doing all we can. He had no real idea how ill his mother was, whether she was likely to recover or if she had entered the final stages of her illness, and yet he could explain an anonymous taxi driver's psychological manipulation of his passengers through his choice of music. Did this discrepancy mean that, on a fundamental level, he did not really care if his mother lived or died? Colin was appalled with himself. His mother deserved a far more attentive and caring son, and, if she pulled through, he vowed to become that son, even if it meant spending less time on research. George Parr was dead, as was Hannah Goodwin. They had waited patiently for over a century for him to uncover the truth; surely they would not mind waiting a little longer; surely they, more than most, would want Edna Draper's transition from life into death to be as gentle as possible.

Thinking of George and Hannah reminded the archivist of the large envelope on his knees. Opening it now, he admitted, would be an instantaneous renunciation of his pledge to put the living before the dead, but Colin did not feel tired, and how, by leaving the envelope unopened, would that benefit his mother?

He carefully peeled open the sealed flap and drew out the papers. Clipped to a thin sheaf of photocopies was a note from his old university friend Neil Hanlon, who was now a senior archivist at the Public Records Office in London.

Colin read out loud the typed note. "I've enclosed the death certificates you wanted. Sounds like another Victorian tale of woe. What are you up to these days? Found a girl blind or crazy enough to get you into bed yet? Masturbation at your age is so undignified. Give me a ring when you're next in London. Neil."

The archivist shook his head despairingly, unclipped the note and brought that incredible focus to bear on the neat copperplate writing that lay between the regular dividing lines of the death certificate.

"Where and when died," Colin read. "The twenty-sixth of March, eighteen sixty-six, Bayham Street Camden. Name and surname: Katherine Jane Parr. Sex: female. Age: twenty-five. Occupation: teacher of piano. Cause of death: postpartum haemorrhage. Signature, description and address of informant: Doctor Ezra Zimmerman, in attendance, Cranleigh Street. When registered: twenty-eighth March, eighteen sixty-six." With barely a pause, Colin removed the top photocopy and began reading the second, which had been written in a less flamboyant hand and with a thicker nib, making the words appear bleaker, as though they had become infused with the sorry facts they imparted. "Where and when died: eleventh of August, eighteen seventy-five, Henry Street, Hinton Moss. Name and surname: Victoria Katherine Parr. Sex: female. Age: nine. Occupation: blank. Cause of death: scarlet fever. Signature, description and residence of informant: Emily Tindall, governess, Henry Street."

Colin looked up. He knew Henry Street. Located perhaps half a mile or so from the centre of the resort, Hinton Moss had, as its name suggested, originally been a boggy area of land dotted with small farmsteads, but was drained and built on as part of the town's huge expansion in the mid-nineteenth century, mostly to house those working in the burgeoning leisure industry. The archivist was surprised a music hall star such as Georgie Parr had chosen Hinton Moss as his home, when the wider avenues radiating out from the park were becoming popular with the town's more affluent citizens. It was an intriguing choice, one that only added to Colin's admiration and interest in the man. Georgie Parr, the Camden Clown, who had built his act using the robust argot employed by the working class, who had been castigated for his choice of material by those agencies within Victorian society that saw him as a destabilising influence and yet stubbornly refused to dilute even one aspect of his act, who had walked on the same silvered boards above the waves as Colin, had now shown himself to have remained true to his empathetic connection with the underprivileged by living with them, even when his earnings would have dwarfed those of his neighbours. How could such a virtuous man, whose sympathies so clearly lay with his audience, end up murdering a girl who, in both profession and circumstance, represented that stratum of society so perfectly? It just did not make sense. Hannah Goodwin, hardly more than a child herself, would surely have brought out George's paternal and moral instincts. He would have been more likely to make sure she returned home safely than kill her with his bare hands. Colin could not conceive how a man who had lost his own daughter would then deprive another father of his.

With his hands resting on Victoria's death certificate, and his grey eyes staring out into the shadowed recesses of the living room, the archivist saw an alternative scenario, a sequence of events that, the more he thought about it, the more likely it seemed. He knew that there had been a strong masonic lodge in the resort, with a membership that tied together the legal, administrative and religious ruling elite. Even though some of these worthies had doubtless enjoyed the company of the likes of Hannah Goodwin, they nevertheless exercised a righteous indignation at their existence. Might they not have created and financed a course of action which would rid the resort of these immoral women? Perhaps they had gathered together a small group of thugs, operating with impunity because those whose duty it was to uphold the law had been told to look the other way, who targeted vulnerable working girls whose disappearance would hardly be noticed, and whose violent end could be neatly annotated by the editor before his paper went to press. Perhaps George Parr had stumbled on this gang, had gone to Hannah's rescue, and ended up as the perfect, silent, scapegoat.

"Oh, George," Colin murmured, utterly convinced by his own narrative, "they stitched you up good and proper."

Carefully placing the papers to one side, Colin levered himself off the couch and walked over to the roll-top desk. He opened the top drawer, brought out a notepad, chose a silver-capped biro from a cigar tin bristling with pens, flipped open the notepad and wrote, in bold capital letters, *THE FRAMING OF GEORGE PARR*. Beneath this he began a list of items that required further research.

1) *Masonic membership of council members*
2) *Extent of prostitution in resort*
3) *Pier theatre records*
4) *1871 Census for Henry Street*
5) *Police records for deaths of prostitutes*
6) *Georgie Parr — music hall society archives*

Satisfied with this initial agenda, Colin returned to the couch. There would, of course, be no documentary evidence relating to such an illicit enterprise — no one involved in such a thing would be stupid enough to implicate themselves — but, he hoped, by approaching the subject laterally, and finding out where apparently separate facts overlapped, there might be a chance of revealing what really happened beneath the pier on that November night in 1880.

Colin looked again at Victoria's death certificate and shook his head at how those few columns of starkly related facts summed up the brutal realities of that age, when a quarter of children died before their fifth birthday, many from illnesses that could now be cured with nothing more than an injection or a few tablets. He wondered if future historians would study death certificates from the late twentieth century, shake their heads at entries such as 'cancer' or 'heart disease', and try to imagine what it must have been like to live in such a barbaric world. Such a projection, Colin realised, proved just how condescending such an attitude like this was. These same historians, poring over their documents with late twenty-first-century eyes, could not help but regard all those deaths from diseases now conquered as tragedies, visited upon individuals who had the misfortune to have been born in a more primitive age. And yet within that age, despite the prayers and heartfelt wishes for just such a cure, there was an understanding that things *were as they were*, and that in many ways life was better than in the past. The child mortality figures, for example, appeared shocking now only because they could be compared to statistics from the twentieth century. When little Victoria had succumbed to scarlet fever she had, despite the anguish of all who had loved her, simply re-stated that era's close acquaintance with death.

Only then did Colin notice a third sheet of paper. He drew it out from under the death certificates to find a photocopy of another official document, though this was not a birth or death certificate, and also contained a small photograph. Beneath the photocopied section was a note in Neil's handwriting: *Found this with our newfangled computer... you should get yourself one. I put in the names you sent and this came up.*

"Particulars of a person convicted of a crime specified in the 20th section of the Prevention of Crimes Act 1871," Colin read. Then: "Name: Hannah Goodwin 2175. Age when liberated: 13. Height: 4ft 2. Hair: brown. Eyes: brown. Complexion: dark. Offence for which convicted: simple larceny of meat pies. Date to be liberated: 11th March 1878.

Colin placed one hand over the photograph, a reaction that he found difficult to explain. Here she was, the girl found strangled beneath the pier, who until now had been nothing more than a name, the victim regardless of whatever scenario represented the truth. He had almost certainly stood within a few feet of where her body was found, and again the archivist felt the century between them dissolve. She may have spoken to George Parr, or watched him perform — one of music halls' most controversial characters — on stage in the old pier theatre, the one modelled on an Indian palace and demolished in 1948 to make way for a newer, more practical design that possessed none of the flamboyance and charm of its predecessor. How he envied her that experience! All Colin could ever have were black-and-white photographs or pieces of paper, and despite his love for these remnants he was under no illusion that they were anything more than that: faint echoes from a distant voice. Historians of the future would have access to a far more complete picture of life, with video, news coverage, documentaries, and the proliferation of cameras filling in many of the blanks left in computerised records. Before 1900, however, the world was essentially static, represented solely by words, still images and objects. Hannah had witnessed the Victorian resort as very much a dynamic entity, filled with details now lost forever. Until Neil had unearthed an obscure police record, which but for the cross-referencing powers of a computer might forever have remained in dusty obscurity, how Hannah Goodwin had looked was just such a detail, one that Colin, after drawing a blank in every archive he could think of that might have contained it, had reluctantly concluded did not exist. And yet here she was, beneath his hand. Her presence unnerved him; what if her appearance was a disappointment? Colin Draper's passions were limited to the inanimate, which of course made him all the more susceptible to becoming infatuated by the intensity with which George Parr had seemingly lived his life. If Hannah, in one way or another, had been George's nemesis, how she looked mattered enormously. Colin wanted her, *needed* her, to possess an allure, some quality that George Parr, who was already a hero in the archivist's eyes, could not have resisted.

"Come on, Colin, pull yourself together," he chided. What was happening to his professional detachment? Covering up a photograph for fear of disappointment was the behaviour of an infatuated teenager, not an objective historian. But then again, he reasoned, was it surprising for him to be feeling particularly sensitive and emotional after coming home to find his mother in such a perilous state, and then having to sit for hours at the hospital waiting to find out if she was going to make it through the night?

He moved his hand and looked down.

The background appeared to be a grimy wall, and Hannah was sitting on a round-backed wooden chair, which was paler at the top where the varnish had been worn away. She was wearing an ashen, crumpled dress, and around her shoulders was wrapped a thin tartan shawl, partly obscured by the slate hanging round her neck with the number 2175 chalked crudely onto it. Her long dark hair was loose and matted, her skin pale, but it was Hannah's eyes that wholly dominated the picture, shining out of the humiliation and squalor with quiet determination, as though she was intent on showing the police, the judiciary, in fact anyone who looked at her criminal release record, that she was unrepentant, unbroken.

And did he also detect an air of abandonment to the frankness in her gaze, as though Hannah had set her mind to something the moment she was released, something that she had fought against but which she now realised was inevitable? Colin wondered whether knowing her profession when she died was colouring his interpretation of the photograph, so he looked away, tried to partition off the story of George and Hannah in his mind, then returned to the release form of prisoner 2175 as though it were simply another document to be examined. Still those eyes burned effortlessly across the decades, her dark irises conveying a frankness which Colin found quite beautiful. He had to remind himself that Hannah was little more than a child who, judging by her criminal record and subsequent occupation, had been forced to grow up far too early, adapting to whatever life threw at her in the only way she knew how. If he could track her down in the 1871 census there might be an answer to her 'reduced circumstances', but in an age where the only social safety net was the workhouse Hannah had clearly faced up to her predicament with a self-possession and fortitude that went way beyond her years. For her to die less than two years after sitting down on that rickety old chair and fixing the police photographer with her unequivocal stare was, the archivist realised, not only a tragedy but a waste. He imagined what a girl with such resourcefulness could achieve now, born into the relative comfort and luxury of the late twentieth century. Dyed-in-the-wool socialist though he was, Colin had nevertheless also seen more than enough documentary evidence to convince him that, irregular and selective though it often seemed, there *was* progress in the world. He disapproved of the large-scale social engineering project that he perceived the Thatcher government's policies to be, but even in this era of inequality there was no reason why a teenage girl would have to steal a pie in order to feed herself or become a prostitute to pay for a roof over her head.

He looked into her eyes. "Who did this to you?" Colin enquired of the photograph. "Who was the last person you saw?"

# Home Sweet Home

Nine days after being rushed into hospital Mrs Draper returned home. Her lungs, the hospital had informed Colin on the phone, were now clear, and her heart had settled down, with only the occasional palpitation. They had again enquired about finding her a nursing home, but her son was adamant; no one was capable of looking after her more effectively than he was, he had taken time off work, knew exactly what his mother liked and how to make her as comfortable as was possible, and that was the end of the matter.

The archivist had been sitting in his customary place at the dining table, poring over and editing his day's notes, when the ambulance drew up outside. He was shuffling down the drive in his shirt and slippers, oblivious to the unwavering drizzle, before the ambulance men had had time to open the back doors, then he dithered at the margins of activity as they manoeuvred his mother out of the ambulance and up the drive. Once she was safely transferred into her own bed and made comfortable, the medics handed Colin a paper bag of tablets, politely turned down his offer of a cup of tea, and left, leaving mother and son ambushed by an awkward silence.

Edna found the suitably mundane words to steer them past the joy and relief they both felt but could never express. "Well," she noted, "here I am again."

Colin looked round the bedroom as though seeing it for the first time. "Home sweet home."

"It's true," she concurred. "I never thought I'd say it,

but I missed this room… my pictures, my fan, how quiet it is." Edna looked at her son. "Why is it always so noisy in hospitals? There's always somebody crashing about with a trolley, or someone coming to take a sample, or take your temperature. Don't they know poorly people need a bit of peace and quiet?"

"It's probably some tactic by the NHS to free up more beds," Colin remarked. "They don't want to make you feel too much at home otherwise they'd never get rid of you."

Mrs Draper settled into her pillow. "Well now I *am* home, and it's lovely to be back."

"Yes, well, it's nice to *have* you back, but let's not have any more shenanigans like last week, eh Mother? I don't think my heart could stand another evening like that."

"Oh, Colin," she said, laughing, "you really are the most self-centred person I know. It's a good job you never got married, it wouldn't have lasted five minutes."

The archivist adopted an offended pose, but in reality he knew his mother's assessment was true, and moreover saw no reason to be apologetic about it. "You have to be single-minded to achieve anything in this world, Mother. Wasting time being dragged round shoe shops or sitting silently in a cafe after forty years together because you've got nothing left to say to each other is not my idea of achievement, I'm sorry to say. Well actually I'm *not* sorry, that's just how I feel."

"I agree."

The reply surprised him. "Really?"

"Of course. I can't think of anything worse than being stuck in a bad marriage. Just imagine having to live with someone who drives you crazy all the time!"

Colin looked suspiciously at his mother. "What's that supposed to mean?"

"Oh, nothing." Mrs Draper affected a hurt tone. "You didn't think I was referring to you, did you? How could you think that?"

"Mmm... "

"Seriously, though, Colin, that's not the only sort of marriage, you know. There are good ones too... like mine and your dad's. That's when your other half *wants* you to achieve whatever it is you're aiming for. You've always got someone to get things off your chest with, laugh at things with, discuss things with."

"I can do that with you."

"It isn't quite the same, though, is it?" Edna looked at her son, whose unremarkable features had been rendered even more forgettable by the putty-like fleshiness that had grown over the years, whose red, flaky scalp could be seen through his straggling hair, and felt a pang of fear for him. "And I won't be around forever, will I? Who will you talk to then?"

Colin shrugged. "I see people at work. I'm quite happy on my own when I'm here."

"Charming."

"You know what I mean."

"I'm only teasing." Mrs Draper nodded in the direction of the chair. "So what have you been up to while I've been away? Got time to chat for five minutes?"

"Of course I have. Tell you what, I'll put the kettle on and make us a brew, and I'll tell you the tragic tale of Georgie Parr and Hannah Goodwin, star-crossed lovers who died under the pier a hundred years ago."

Edna, whose bedside table was always piled high with Mills & Boon romantic novels, raised her eyebrows in anticipation. "Ooh, that sounds good."

Colin had reached the bedroom door when he stopped and looked back. "I made up the bit about star-crossed lovers."

Beyond the bedroom and the bungalow, past streets where puddles reflected the stony evening clouds like melted pewter, across the suburban hinterland's varnished rooftops where seagulls squabbled on television aerials, the resort persisted, intent only on the moment: hen and stag parties shrieking, shouting, fuelled by the bravado of the pack, or teenagers discovering, within graffiti-frescoed bus shelters, the ability of kisses to erase the wider world, or pensioners anchored to a promenade bench, staring out to sea and hoping for one more beautiful sunset, they were all, all of them, an affirmation of the resort's ability to carve a niche in time, excising past and future and offering instead a continuous present, a sensual *now*. This was why, on warm sunny days, there were many visitors moved to employ the adjective 'heavenly' to describe their situation; here they could glimpse the rapture of being liberated from time.

Within the confines of the bungalow, however, there was no present. What held sway was a form of hybridised past, because for both Colin and Edna the past was where they preferred to be. For Edna it was a specific period: 1937 to 1954, the years she spent with Malcolm. Colin's affinity with the past was rather more imprecise; it was as much a doctrine as a calendar of events, and lacked a personal reciprocity, but despite not being able to place the events of his own life within the larger frame of the nineteenth century, the archivist felt no less affection for it.

As the two of them settled, then, Colin the storyteller and Edna the audience, both fortified with a cup of tea and a Mr Kipling bakewell tart, they knew, and were comforted by, the fact that the past was at hand. Mother and son regarded the contemporary as a most unforgiving of mirrors, reflecting truths about their lives that neither of them wished to dwell on; much better to look instead through history's darker glass, and the consolations that such vision brought.

Colin opened the notebook and laid it on his knees. "George Parr," he began, "was born on the twenty-fourth of February 1832 in Kentish Town, London. His father Charles was a railway shunter, and his mother Charlotte was a whitener." He glanced up from the page. "That was someone who bleached cloth," he explained, before returning to the notebook. "He had two brothers, David and Roderick, but

Roderick died at the age of fifteen and David emigrated to Australia, so he had no sibling support as an adult. He married Katherine Barnett in 1862, a lawyer's daughter, which is very unusual."

"Why?"

"Well from what I can gather George wasn't doing particularly well when they got married. I rang the British Music Hall Society, and their records on him only start in 1866, so presumably before then he was so low down on the bill that nobody noticed him. Even if he had been doing well he certainly wasn't the type a lawyer would have wanted for his daughter. She must have been very single-minded, because her father would have done his best to end the relationship and find someone more suitable for her, like an army officer, or a doctor, or even another lawyer. Music hall performers were regarded as rather subversive by the middle classes, so a lawyer certainly wouldn't have wanted one as a son-in-law, even though in the end George became very well-paid... he was probably earning more than Mr Barnett by the time he got to the top of the bill."

"I bet there were ructions when *that* marriage was announced," Edna remarked.

"Undoubtedly. But married they were, in Camden Parish Church. George registered his address as Bayham Street, which is where Charles Dickens once lived, but they weren't there at the same time, which is a pity."

"Why?"

"Because Dickens had a habit of incorporating characters he met into his books, and George must have been a very strong character." Colin looked up from his notebook, the tone of admiration in his voice clear. He presented his left hand, fingers held wide, and emphasised each point by tapping the end of a finger with the index finger of his right hand. "One: he was a music hall comic, which wasn't a job for the faint-hearted. Two: he was a *successful* music hall comic. Three: he married a lawyer's daughter. Four: he didn't go to pieces when his wife died in childbirth. And five: he didn't go to pieces when his only daughter died. In fact he was top of the bill for another five years before he... before that night. Don't you think that's the sort of character Dickens would have been impressed by?"

Edna smiled gently, but her expression was a way of disguising from Colin her grimace and gritted teeth as a shooting pain coursed up her right leg. It was a paradox of her illness that these numbed and useless limbs, which she had, for the most part, disassociated herself from, regularly mocked her lack of governance by generating a brief but intense discomfort that travelled along nerves supposedly silenced. Worse than the pain, though, was its tingling after-effect, which always stirred in her the slenderest of hopes that some miracle had occurred, that the feeling in her treacherous body was returning. Even though Edna knew that, following on from every previous spasm, the tingling soon dwindled, consumed by the heavy silence of her flesh, she could not help but cherish the possibility that this time, against all odds, her paralysis was somehow in retreat.

"Certainly," she replied, though her mind was elsewhere, traversing the prickling cables which delineated the leg resting on the mattress. Was the sensation lasting a little longer this time? Had the pain jolted some linkage back to life? *Oh, grow up Edna,* she chided silently. A thought came to her. "Don't forget the other side of the coin, Colin."

The archivist pulled a perplexed expression. "What?"

"You're saying all this about your... you know, your comedian man."

"Georgie Parr, Mother. Try and keep one or two facts in your head for longer than ten seconds."

"Yes, him. Well, what I'm saying is, don't forget about the other side... Georgie's wife."

Colin leaned forward. "Katherine?"

Edna nodded. "She must have been a strong character too, you know. Imagine her going to tell her father that she wanted to marry a comedian. I bet she loved her dad, but her love for Georgie was stronger."

Colin groaned. "For goodness sake, Mother, this isn't a Barbara Cartland novel."

"How do you know?" Mrs Draper was surprised by the vehemence in her voice. She realised that it was not the condescension in her son's reply which had provoked her outburst — she was accustomed to that — but an instinctual protectiveness towards a woman who she sensed had been anything but a submissive or secondary character in her son's narrative. "Just because you think love stories are rubbish doesn't mean they never happen. I bet she had to give up a lot to marry him."

"Alright," Colin conceded, "alright, so Katherine was strong as well. Perhaps her family cut her off without a penny, but George succeeded on his own *after* she died, *and* he had a baby daughter to bring up at the same time. I'd say that was positively heroic."

Edna let her head sink deeper into the pillows. The tingling had gone, leaving her feeling like the queen termite she had once seen on a nature programme: a tiny creature attached to something bloated and numb. "You just have to get on with it, Colin. When your father died I found a job in a florists that meant I could be home by the time you got back from school. I was dog-tired by tea time, but I didn't let it show because you'd been through enough already. I made sure you did your homework, I made sure you always had a clean shirt for school the next day, and then I fell asleep by eight o'clock, but I wasn't being heroic, I was just doing what had to be done, that's all."

The archivist gesticulated his frustration. "You see? You're being heroic about being heroic! It's not normal behaviour, Mother, it's above and beyond the call of duty, it's superhuman."

"You'd be surprised what you can do when you have to."

"Well, let's hope I never have to find out, eh?"

"God willing. And you say she died?"

He returned to the notebook. "On the twenty-sixth of March, giving birth to their daughter Victoria. It was a risky business in those days."

"That almost happened to you."

Colin looked up again. What other revelations did his mother have in store, and what was it about the story of George Parr that was proving so cathartic for her? "I'm sorry? I thought you just said I almost died when I was born."

"That's what I *did* say."

"I see. And you didn't think to mention this before any time in the last forty-odd years."

Edna pulled her mouth into a downwards curve. "Haven't I? I must have. You've probably just forgotten."

"I *think* I might have remembered that small fact, Mother," Colin said heavily. "Was it supposed to be some terrible family secret?"

"Not particularly," Edna replied blithely. "You were just in a funny position, and getting all agitated, and the cord was starting to get tangled up, but the midwife managed to get her hands in and hoiked you out. You were a funny colour, but she got you breathing and you were fine after that."

"You make it sound so matter-of-fact."

"Well, I'm sure it was a bit more hectic at the time, but there wasn't a good deal I could do, not with my legs all akimbo and—"

He held up his hands in horror. "Whoa, too much information, Mother!"

"She saved your life, that's for sure," Edna continued, ignoring her son's histrionics. "Joan Sexton. I'll never forget that name. Afterwards she told me she'd only been a midwife for eight months, but saving your life had evened things up for her, because during the war she'd been helping out at the old Salvation Army building when a lad came in shouting for his mother, saying he needed to take her and make her safe. They tried to shut him up, because there'd not been

229

any sirens, but he wouldn't have it, and eventually his mum agreed to go with him. Well, Joan had heard him talking, and he was going on and on about the starlings, about a message, and she thought he was crazy, but there was something in his voice, how certain he sounded, and before she knew what she was doing, she'd left as well. And you know what? About a minute after she'd left the Salvation Army a bomber on its way back to Germany—"

"A bomber on its way back to Germany found it had one bomb left jammed in its cradle, so they managed to loosen it and decided to drop it on the town they were over, and that bomb just happened to land right on the Salvation Army building and killed seven people," Colin finished. "It was this town's worst tragedy of the Second World War. And that lad was Mickey Braithwaite, who'd run all the way from the pier where he was a spotter for the Observer Corps." He hesitated. "Hang on a minute. Are you telling me that if Mickey Braithwaite hadn't rescued his mother from the Salvation Army building then I would have died at birth? Is that what you're implying? That I owe my existence to Mickey Braithwaite's *premonition*?"

Edna glanced at the prints on the far wall. Her eye was drawn to her wedding photograph, her most treasured possession. It was the only picture she had from that day, and she had no idea where the negative was, if indeed they had ever possessed it. Malcolm looked so pleased with himself, having finally won his girl from what he always imagined was a long line of potential suitors, a notion Edna had done little to discourage, even though in reality she had loved him from the moment he vaulted over her parents' garden gate with one hand on the gate-post and the other clutching a sprig of wild flowers he had picked along the lane.

The photograph was in black-and-white, but she remembered every colour perfectly, from the bright red carnation in the lapel of Malcolm's grey double-breasted suit to the aquamarine necklace she had worn, an heirloom given to her as her something blue, and which still nestled in her cleavage, just below her delicate gold crucifix.

She returned her attention to her son. "These things are meant to happen, Colin. It's all for a purpose."

"Oh, *please*, Mother, are you suggesting some sort of divine intervention?"

"Why not?"

"How many times do I have to tell you? Because *there is no God*. It's just… chance. Luck. Being in the right place at the right time. Or the wrong place at the wrong time."

"But how did Mickey *know*?"

Colin tilted back his head and spoke to the ceiling. "He didn't *know*. He either heard the bomber approaching or else they got a message on the radio, and he thought he'd better warn his mother just in case. There's no mystery to it."

"He said the birds told him."

Colin snorted. "Oh! Right. And you think that's a reasonable explanation, do you? Knowing what Mickey's like."

Edna looked back to the wedding photograph, stung by the condescension in her son's voice and unwilling to hold his gaze. She remembered feeling the warmth on her back, which was radiating from the sun-soaked dark red brick of St Michael's, and the slightly unsteady cadence of the church bells. She remembered the soft material of Malcolm's jacket sleeve brushing against her bare arm like a gently expressed promise of protection. "You can't find the answers to everything in a history book!"

The archivist slammed shut his notebook. "Well in that case," he said, standing up, "you won't be interested in what happens to George and Hannah, will you?"

Edna closed her eyes and sighed. "For goodness' sake, Colin, there's no need to be so touchy."

"Isn't there?" he said venomously. "You've just demolished my profession… Everything I hold dearest, and all because it doesn't include warnings about German bombers given by a flock of birds to someone whose only purpose in life is to make sure his deckchairs are all neatly lined up! Bloody hell, Mother, and you wonder why I'm being touchy!"

For once, however, Edna did not back down, did not appease her son. She spoke to Colin, but her eyes were fixed on Malcolm in his wedding day suit. "Don't you twist things, Colin Draper, that isn't what I said. I said you can't find *everything* in history books. Some things can't be written down… like faith, or love, but it doesn't mean they don't exist, and it doesn't mean that they can't make strange things happen."

"That's a lot of double negatives, Mother."

"Well I'm not as clever as you, am I? A fact that you remind me of at every opportunity. But do you know what?" Edna frowned up at her son, willing him to look back at her and take note of the conviction in her eyes. "I'd much rather have my faith than your… well, I don't know what it is. Is it anything? Do you believe in anything, Colin?"

"The truth," he replied quietly, genuinely hurt by his mother's unsparing analysis.

"And who's to say what the truth is? You? Have you got all the answers?"

The archivist sat back down. He studied the front cover of the notebook in his hands, tracing with one finger the subtle pattern printed into the cardboard. For a moment he glanced up, but the expression in his mother's eyes, a combination of pity and disappointment, which darkened their normal hazel to the colour of molasses, pushed his gaze back down to the notebook almost instantly. When he spoke again Colin resumed his aimless mapping out of the cover pattern. "No one has them all, do they, but I just need to base my beliefs on the ones I *can* find. The answers that history provides."

"There are answers in other places too, love," Edna said, her voice softening. "Places you don't expect them to be, sometimes. Maybe watching the starlings drew Mickey's attention up to the sky and he saw something there, perhaps another bomber much higher up, and being in the Observer Corps he knew it was German and there were likely to be others nearby. Isn't that an answer?"

Colin looked up again, surprised and touched by his mother's reasoning, which he realised was entirely for his benefit. She didn't believe in so prosaic an explanation because it did not fit her model of the world as an interdependent and meaningful work of creation, and yet she had formulated it nevertheless. It was an offering of such generosity he felt tears well up in the corners of his eyes. He smiled. "It certainly is. Plausible, logical, rational... everything you're not!"

Edna chuckled, pleased that her peace offering had been accepted. "I surprise myself sometimes." She paused. "So, what happened to Georgie after his wife died?"

Colin flicked through several pages of notes. "In the 1871 census George and his daughter Victoria had been joined by George's sister-in-law Emily Tindall, who was described as a governess, so I assume she'd stepped into the breach while George was busy in the music halls."

"That was good of her."

"Indeed. And she must still have been with them when Victoria died in 1875, because she was the official informant named on the death certificate, so George must have thought very highly of her. I should imagine he relied on her for support quite a lot, especially when Victoria died.

"Georgie Parr appeared in halls and theatres all over the country for the next few years," Colin continued, "building his reputation. His 'Corporal and Four Privates' song was as well-known and popular at the time as 'Any Old Iron' and 'My Old Man' were later on; they used to queue round the block whenever Georgie Parr the Camden Clown was in town."

At the mere mention of their titles Edna could not help but sing the opening lines of both songs to herself, but she could not recall anything of George Parr's. "I've never heard of that other one," she admitted.

Colin smiled ruefully. "You probably won't have. It might have been a hit with the audiences, but the 'Corporal and Four Privates' was a very controversial song for its time. It didn't go down well with the authorities, or the church. They tried to get it banned as a moral outrage, and George was even arrested once outside the Britannia in Glasgow when he encouraged the crowd waiting to go in to sing his song. The headline in the *Herald* read *Appalling Scenes of Decadence as Music Hall Star Soils Glasgow's Pavements with Loathsome Act.*"

"Goodness," Edna exclaimed, "what on earth was all the fuss about?"

"Well, it wasn't really a song about soldiers, Mother. It was metaphorical, and fairly heavy-handed at that, though that was how the music hall audiences liked their songs."

"Well what *was* it about, then? Come on, Colin, don't keep me in suspenders."

He squirmed in his chair. "This is very embarrassing —"

"Colin!"

"Masturbation!" The word breached the defences of his tightly closed lips, which in addition gave added impetus to its first syllable and propelled the word out into the bedroom with a vigour and comedic brio that Georgie Parr himself would have appreciated.

"He was singing about masturbation. There, satisfied now?"

Mrs Draper mouthed a silent 'oh'. "And did everyone know that that was what he was singing about?"

"Of course they did! That was why it was funny."

"It all seems like a lot of fuss over nothing, if you ask me," she remarked. "I mean, everyone's done it, haven't they? At some time or another."

Colin's eyes widened. "Mother, you never cease to amaze me. This is not a subject that we should be discussing. It isn't relevant, anyway."

"Of course it is," Edna contradicted. "If that song was what he was most famous for."

"It was until he met Hannah Goodwin. After that the song was more or less forgotten; no one had the heart to sing it again."

"And he was here, on the pier?"

The archivist nodded. "Georgie Parr was a big name, and one of the first to get a long-term contract in one venue. Before that top of the bill usually meant dashing about all over the place, particularly if they were performing in London, but George must have liked the seaside because he came back here several times, and then like I say he managed to negotiate a contract that kept him at the pier theatre. Not the one that's here now, the old one... the one that looked like an Indian palace."

Edna looked again at her wedding photo. "Your dad took me to see Jessie Mathews there not long before they knocked it down. It must have been just before the war. I remember the seats were terribly uncomfortable."

"But that was the same stage that Georgie Parr stood on," Colin said, a note of censure in his voice. How often had he spoken to generations before his own and witnessed the envy he felt towards their direct contact with what he could only ever experience through documents or photographs turn, often within seconds, to annoyance, as they recalled some ridiculous or trivial aspect of that irretrievable world?

"Well I didn't know that then, did I?" His mother protested. "I'd never heard of him. All I knew was that the place looked old and tired and the seats gave you a numb bum."

"Philistine."

"Well they did!"

"Georgie Parr brought the crowds flocking in," the archivist continued, "but he was nearly fifty by now, which was pretty old by their standards, and all those years of touring must have taken their toll. I wonder if he was thinking how much longer he could carry on."

Edna sighed. "Perhaps it took his mind off the empty house that was waiting for him."

Colin looked at his mother. "Is that how you felt... after Dad died?" he enquired cautiously.

"Oh, love, it's how I feel *now*." She saw the hurt expression and quickly continued, "And that isn't meant to be horrible about you, before you start. You've been a wonderful son to me. I don't know what I'd have done if you hadn't been around, but when someone you love so much is taken from you before... before you're ready for them to go, that pain never goes away. Never. Poor George lost his wife and then his daughter as well, which must have been unbearable. Perhaps that's why he was still working."

"To numb the pain." In some ways Colin was grateful to his mother for these insights, for offering him a glimpse into the mechanics of a long-term relationship, which was something he had neither experienced nor felt any particular need for, and yet this gratitude was tinged with resentment, born out of a suspicion that his mother would always be closer to George Parr, in emotional terms at least, than he ever could. A thought occurred to him. "Do you think he might have harboured suicidal thoughts?"

"Oh, without a doubt," Edna replied without hesitation. "I'm sure there were plenty of times when he wished he could join his wife and daughter. And then there'd be times when he would be so angry he could scream, and times when he'd wonder if he was being punished for something he'd done... and then sometimes he'd feel all those things at once, and they'd be the worst days. The days when you know that Hell can't be any worse than what you're living through."

The archivist pinched his bottom lip and nodded. Clearly his mother was describing her own condition as much as Georgie Parr's, but what troubled him the most was that, having heard her candid and heartfelt description of long-term grief, he had to concede the possibility that events beneath the pier *had* played out in precisely the manner described in contemporary reports, and that, far from being the wronged victim, George was in fact a murderer. Had all his weeks of research, cross-referencing and analysis been rendered futile by one moment of empathy? And if so, what did that say about him?

"Colin? Are you alright?"

He managed to assemble a smile. "Me? Yes, yes. I'm fine. Just a bit tired."

Edna glanced at the clock on her bedside table. "You ought to have an early night. It's nearly time for *Dallas*, anyway. We can finish your story tomorrow."

"Alright." Colin felt chastened and ridiculous, his crusade to find justice for George Parr sabotaged because he had been unable to comprehend, much less assign as a pivotal influence, the fierce emotional tides which must have ebbed and flowed within the music hall entertainer. "I'll pop back later to make sure you've got everything you need for the night."

"There's no need, love, I'm right as rain. You get off to bed, you look shattered."

He exhaled through his nose, the slightest hiss of wry amusement. "That's precisely the word I would have chosen." Colin stood up, leaned over and gave his mother a kiss on the cheek.

"Night night."

"Night night," she replied. "See you in the morning."

The archivist had almost reached the bedroom door when he stopped and turned round. "Mum?"

Edna, who had been manoeuvring the television remote control into position with her good arm, looked up. "Yes, love?"

"Do you really believe Mickey Braithwaite can see into the future?"

"Yes, I do," she said simply. "Why?"

"Oh, no reason." Colin smiled. "I just wondered, that's all. Night night."

# Counting The Seconds

Days passed, and the unfinished story of Georgie Parr and Hannah Goodwin slipped from the forefront of their minds, displaced, in Colin's case, by the demands of an upcoming exhibition charting the resort's history of political conferences, whereas Edna, inspired by Sue Ellen's decision to make a feature film about her marriage to JR, spent many a happy hour thinking up scenes for a film of her own. She imagined it in black-and-white, shot in the sort of gauzy light that seemed to soften all her favourite films, and, unlike Sue Ellen's Texan melodrama, Edna's movie would be a much quieter affair, illustrating how many years of the commonplace, the routine, can become quite exceptional when viewed as a whole.

Perhaps unconsciously both mother and son had sought a brief respite from the story's intensity and darkness. Certainly neither of them mentioned George or Hannah; their conversations instead centred on either Colin's work (and Edna's rather jaundiced opinion of nearly every politician he mentioned) or the weather, which was becoming extremely hot and close. Edna asked Colin to turn up her fan, and even allowed him to crack open the smallest of her bedroom windows, despite her staunch belief that hordes of intruders lurked outside, waiting patiently for an opportunity to ransack the bungalow.

And then, late one afternoon, she heard the distant rumble of a thunderstorm. As it approached Edna began, just like her grandfather had taught her, to count the seconds between a flash of lightning and its corresponding echo of thunder, plotting the storm's advance with that atavistic combination of excitement and fear felt by humanity whenever it is faced with a force immeasurably greater than itself.

The window, whose closed curtains had filtered brilliant sunshine since early morning, filling the room with a tender glow, grew darker. As the light leached away, Edna reached instinctively for the lamp's extension cord with its white rocker switch, but as her hand groped in an unseen emptiness she remembered Colin moving it to one side while he rearranged her pillows. He must have forgotten to replace it, either that or he had reasoned that on such a bright and beautiful day she would not require the lamp.

A dazzling flash of lightning lit the window. "One, two, three, four, five," she counted out loud, her sequence silenced abruptly by a prolonged rumble of thunder that reverberated across the sky

The curtains began to twitch, galvanised by a strengthening wind. Mrs Draper shivered. The temperature in her bedroom was dropping rapidly, yet all she had on was a thin cotton nightie and a sheet draped loosely over the bed. She glanced at the fan, whirring away on its stand, the blades and mesh surround sweeping slowly backwards and forwards and propelling chilled air the length of her body. Edna knew that switching off the fan would reduce her discomfort, but there was a supportive, soothing quality to its movement, its benign touch, that stayed her hand. She regarded the fan almost as a companion. Switching it off now would mean facing the storm alone, a far worse prospect in Edna's eyes than having to endure an hour or so of feeling cold.

The wind strengthened still further, blowing the first drops of rain against the window and carrying a thick, musky scent of honeysuckle into the room. Normally she loved to breathe in the plant's fragrance; on warm spring evenings Edna would listen to the industrious hum of bees as they delved into the rambling mass of foliage which sprawled over half the bungalow's south-facing wall and, from within her own immobility, be transported by their ceaseless movement. Now, however, the scent appeared to have been subtly appropriated by the approaching storm, turning it from a heady statement of vitality into something darker, like the pungent odour of an animal. A final burst of sunlight illuminated the bedroom, only to be extinguished moments later, plunging Edna into a forbidding twilight.

Lightning bleached the room. "One, two, three—"

The thunder made Edna jump. She instinctively tried to curl up beneath the sheet, but of course there was no response from her mutinous body, which simply lay there, offering itself up to the storm. A memory came to her of Fay Wray, trussed and defenceless as something huge and terrifying came crashing through the jungle towards her. That was how Edna felt now, and, for the first time in years, she wept quietly at her utter vulnerability.

A sudden squall of rain clattered against the window, followed moments later by another flash of lightning. "One, two—"

This time the thunder was more physical, like a huge hammer being brought down on the roof of the house. Edna felt for her crucifix. Gripping it tightly, she peered through the gloom, her gaze locking onto her wedding photograph as though it had become the only stable reference point in a world of tumult. In the darkness the image was reduced to little more than a collection of further shadows, but Edna knew every detail so well she could see it perfectly.

"Dear Lord," she whispered, "what are you keeping me here for? What am I supposed to do? All I want is to see Malcolm again." Her voice took on a slight tremor. "I don't want to be on my own any more."

Outside she could hear the wind shaking their neighbour's beech trees, generating a sort of static that filled the silence between thunderclaps. Lightning flared. Edna flinched, and as she did so her gaze slipped away from the photograph, flicking instead to the incandescent instant of her bedroom, and in that starkness, that brief eternity, she saw within it a figure, whose sloping shoulders she knew so well, as though it had been carried into the room and deposited there by the lightning. And then, in a blink, it was gone, snatched away. Rational thinkers, like Colin, would have found a ready explanation for the vision; after staring at the picture, and then having it so dazzlingly illuminated by the lightning, Malcolm's image would have been preserved on Edna's retina for some seconds. As her eyes re-focused that image would therefore have been superimposed on the room, thus creating the illusion that there was a figure standing near her bed. It was a perfectly natural combination of the brain's retention of vision and the deep psychological longing as evidenced by her prayer. If Mrs Draper had ever had the chance to tell her son about the event then this would doubtless have been his response, along with, perhaps, some gently mocking comparison to Mickey Braithwaite. But Edna was not rational, especially when it came to her husband; her belief could take the preposterous and re-cast it as not only probable but necessary, in the same way that by touching two thin bars of gold joined perpendicularly to each other and declaring one's loneliness to an empty room you could bring back a man dead and buried for over forty years, bring him back and find such comfort in his momentary presence, and not for one second even consider that this was the alchemy of delusion, or be terrified by the implications of such an appearance. *Then* you would know the meaning of the word faith.

Malcolm was nowhere to be seen in the next flash of lightning, but he had no need to be. Edna had already snuggled further into her pillows, reducing the thunder to a muffled percussion, and though she tensed slightly at the lightning, half-expecting some calamity, like the ceiling caving in, the bang and grumble carried with it an air of resentment, as though the storm was well aware that this tiny life far below, damaged and pathetically flimsy though it was, had defeated it. The storm rattled the glass in Edna's window, but her eyes were already closing. She had overcome.

Colin turned the key in the front door and stepped into the hall. He had lost all track of time during a protracted and at times heated debate with the town's head librarian over the relative merits of displaying the conference exhibition in chronological or party political order, a dispute that not only ended in what to him was a muddled and unsatisfactory compromise, but also caused him to miss his bus. The next one had sped past the bus stop, already crammed with workers on their way home, so by the time he finally turned into Rosemere Crescent his stomach was rumbling and he was steeling himself for a dressing down from his mother.

For the second time in less than a month the archivist was greeted with silence.

"Mum?" Once again he spoke into the impartial quiet, and once again he heard the child in his voice, the boy who, on being told of his father's death, ran to his bedroom, connected the transformer to his model railway and spent the rest of the evening lying on his stomach, watching the engine and its solitary carriage go round and round whilst imagining, from his proximate viewpoint, how wonderful it would be to climb aboard the train and be carried away.

He placed his keys in the brass bowl on the hall table, as was his habit, but even that clattering, tuneless ringing, which had for so long signalled the demarcation between adulthood, work, being Colin Draper, archivist, and becoming son and carer, sounded different, because a part of him already knew what he would find, and how that discovery would alter everything. Pam had, as always, placed the day's post on the table with admirable neatness, even taking the trouble to position the envelopes in size order, largest at the bottom. Colin rested his fingers on the letters for a moment, their symmetry a comfort to him. He looked down and began to study the handwriting on the topmost envelope; Colin recognised the style, with its 'E's formed from a 'C' split by a horizontal line, but he could not remember who wrote like that. He examined the postmark, hoping for a clue from the letter's source, but it was smudged and illegible. Obviously the post had been delivered during the thunderstorm, the archivist reasoned.

He glanced at the door to his mother's bedroom. A soft, lustrous glow radiated out of the room and into the hall, tinged with a delicate cornflower blue. It reminded him of the light to be found in Renaissance religious paintings, bathing the saintly and protecting them from the medieval gloom which pervaded the rest of the canvas. This thought led in turn to the memory of his childhood night-light, modelled on the Virgin Mary, who held back the darkness which hung in dusty swags beyond her beatific radiance, a flimsy boundary that, if he watched it long enough, would creep slightly closer, extinguishing a little more of the Virgin Mary's glory.

"No," Colin said, though he would not have been able to say what he was denying. His declaration voiced, the archivist pushed himself away from the hall table as though it were the jetty of a last outpost on some uncharted river, took the three long strides along the hall and stepped into the light.

At first the glorious early evening sunshine almost blinded him, bleaching every detail in the bedroom in a silent explosion, but as his eyes adjusted the familiar items of furniture drew themselves back into a solid existence, coalescing from the light like a stage set at the beginning of a play. This was no act one, however, but rather a coda, made more poignant by a daring directorial decision to keep the set unchanged, except in one hugely important regard.

Colin walked round to the far side of the bed, his heart thumping.

Edna appeared asleep. Her good arm was folded across her chest, the single sheet slightly corrugated and creased beneath it, as though she had tried to pull it further up over herself, an impression reinforced by the sight of her feet and ankles, which were protruding from the bottom. The skin of these exposed limbs appeared pale blue, but how much was inherent and how much was due to the quality of the light was impossible to tell. Colin reached out to touch her foot, and even as he registered how cold the skin felt, and what that coldness inevitably signified, he could not help but be beguiled by the wonderful softness of the soles of her feet. He remembered passing the bedroom's open door once and seeing the district nurse massaging his mother's feet with moisturiser. After the nurse had left he queried the efficacy of massaging feet which were, to all intents and purposes, 'dead', but Edna retorted that it was 'good for her circulation', before adding, in what was for her a rather caustic tone of voice, that he had no need to worry, because it 'wouldn't be long before the rest of her caught up with her feet' and she would no longer be a 'burden' to him.

And now it had happened.

Now she was gone.

Colin gently lifted his hand away. How many times had he mentally rehearsed this moment and speculated what his emotional response would be? For all that their relationship was characterised by its incessant bickering, mother and son had, since Malcolm Draper's death, forged a powerful bond, providing them with the emotional strength to face bullying, bereavement, insecurity and illness. And this mutual support had continued, a stable structure of more or less balanced forces, until Edna's deteriorating condition threatened its equilibrium as she became increasingly physically dependent on her son. Her reliance on him, though Colin attended to his mother with unfailing commitment, would by turns dismay, frighten and infuriate him. What he never realised, or at least never admitted to himself, was that his mother's dependence created an essential bolster for his fragile self-esteem, so even if Colin saw himself as the one shouldering the greatest burden, theirs was in fact the perfect symbiotic relationship, an alliance against what seemed to them to be a harsh and unforgiving world. If only the archivist could have acknowledged this parity he would have found his reaction to Edna's demise far less surprising.

In every imagined deathbed scenario Colin had seen himself as a blubbering mess, either collapsed in a heap by her side, or wandering aimlessly about the house, or even railing against his mother through the tears for having had the audacity to abandon him, but now, as he actually touched the leniency of her death, all he felt was happiness. Colin could see no possible reason, be it biological, intellectual or even spiritual, for a life after death, but he had also been forced to acknowledge the tenacity and comfort of his mother's faith. The archivist had always regarded such convictions as nothing more than an inability to see the universe for the beautiful hiatus that it was, though Edna had occasionally alluded to some sort of corroborating evidence for this belief, without ever giving him a full explanation. Maybe she had been waiting for some sort of indication from her son that his attitude towards her religious convictions had softened, or perhaps she found it difficult to put this evidence into words; maybe there never had been anything more than simple faith, and she had been trying to couch it in terms that her son's empirical mind might understand. Whatever the reason, the simple truth of the matter, a truth written on her quiescent features, was that his mother had died without fear, and for that Colin was truly grateful.

As he had done for so many years on his return from work, the archivist manoeuvred round the television on its trolley and sat down in his chair next to the fan. Outside a group of starlings chattered amongst themselves, and in the distance a dog barked; all life's threads, woven together to form the most beautiful and fragile of materials, remained intact, save one.

"You wouldn't believe the trouble I've had at work today," Colin began. "Janet… the head librarian, you know, the one with the moustache and bad breath... the one who thought terrorists were going to blow up the library last year because the council leader insisted they have a copy of *The Satanic Verses*... well, anyway, her, she wanted the conference exhibition to be arranged by party, but I said that was ridiculous because it wouldn't flow properly, and it wouldn't reflect how the parties swap around, and it'd be tedious, because who wants to read a huge chunk on Labour, then Conservatives? Better to spread it out, vary it a bit, year by year, but oh no, Janet wasn't going to have that, she said that my 'fragmented approach' was confusing. Confusing! What's confusing about taking it year by year? I said anyone who could grasp the basics of a calendar would be able to follow an exhibition laid out how I wanted it, and that only an idiot would be confused. She took that personally and started going on about my 'sexist' attitude and how the council was full of misogynistic dinosaurs who belonged in a museum. I might not have helped matters when I said that if the museum was set out by her no one would want to look round it, but then James intervened and said that the town was very lucky to have two... how did he put it? Oh yes, two 'passionate and unique visionaries', but we had to find common ground and that we all needed a break. Of course Janet's idea didn't seem any less ridiculous after a cup of coffee, but we ended up arranging the displays in chronological order by political party, which I thought wasn't a true reflection of the conference pattern but James babbled on about an 'amalgamation of genius', even though you only have to spill a can of paint on a canvas these days to be called a genius... " Colin exhaled, one of his sneeze-like laughs, and shook his head. "Oh dear, I have officially lost my mind. I am performing a monologue for my deceased mother." He felt tears begin to prickle his eyes, and realised that he would have to do something or else give in to the collapse and lamentation that he could feel bubbling in his chest.

"Well," he stated, "we can't let the undertakers see you

in this condition, Mother. Let's find you something more appropriate to wear, shall we?"

Colin pushed himself out of the chair and crossed to the wardrobe. It loomed over him, in some ways still the ogre from childhood, so much so that when he reached for the handles Colin half-expected some sort of angry reaction to his intrusion. Its doors were stiff, having clearly not been opened for years, so when he finally managed to yank them apart the vigour of his action was heralded by the clatter of empty wire coat hangers, several of which banged against the back of the wardrobe as though to alert their master to an intruder. Hanging to one side was a pathetic gathering of dresses, together with a camel hair coat, its fur collar conjuring up a memory of being on a railway platform, surrounded, or so it seemed at the time, by huge packing cases, and being terrified by the hissing and clanking of a steam engine as it drew up alongside. Colin reached into the wardrobe and stroked the fur collar, but physical contact revealed no further details; the coat clung on to the meat of the memory — what station it was, the contents of the packing cases, their destination — with a tenacity he could only admire.

"Which do you think?" Colin enquired, still facing into the wardrobe, which contained, he was surprised to note, the same ammoniacal freshness of the steam, which had engulfed him on that anonymous railway platform so long ago. "There's a black one... no, that isn't really appropriate, is it? We don't want you to be mistaken for one of the undertakers. Well, it's either the spotty one or the blue one. I like the spotty one best. We'll go with that."

He lifted the dress out of the wardrobe, hung it on the outside of the door, gave it a perfunctory brush with the back of his hand and stepped back, the better to assess its ability to contain his mother's substantial bulk which had, he felt sure, grown somewhat since she last wore the dress.

"What do you think? This isn't really my area of expertise, you know. It *looks* about right." He shrugged. "We'll just have to see. I might have to leave it unfastened, but whatever we do I am *not* letting you be seen by complete strangers in nothing but a nightie. There's absolutely no reason why they need to mess about with you… no reason at all. I'll get you ready and then they can do the rest."

Colin took a deep breath. He thought for a moment of George Parr, who, despite living in an age more accustomed to the proximity of death, had been obliged, within the space of nine years, to bury the two people he held most dear, and yet somehow managed to step out onto that stage every night and make his audience laugh. How had he done it? Was every performance in some way a tribute to his wife and daughter, demonstrating to the world how they had helped him become the star that he was? Or was it a means of forgetting, for a few minutes at least, how alone in the world he was?

"Come on, Colin," he admonished, "if George could do it so can you."

He walked back to the bed. Gently lifting Edna's arm, he slid the sheet off, letting it pool on the floor at his feet, unveiling, in that simple subtraction, the brutal mechanics of her illness, from the wasted, dimpled flesh of her legs, the catheter draining into a bag attached to the side of the bed, to her useless arm, which was angled, palm away from her body, so clearly a forsaken appendage. Gripping her shoulders, as he had seen her carers do, Colin rolled his mother onto her back, straightened out her legs and positioned her arms at her sides.

"Like a regimental soldier," he commented. "Now, how am I going to get this dress on?" He laughed. "How *do* you put a dress on? Does it go over your head, or is it legs first? Bloody hell, Mother, why couldn't you have preferred trouser suits? I don't even know if I'll be able to get it over your nightie. I won't, will I? Even if I did it'd look a bit weird. I'm really sorry, but the nightie's going to have to come off. I know, I know, but you'd rather it was me doing this than some stranger. I'll be as quick as I can."

The archivist began his work. First he drew up the night-dress, carefully lifting his mother's body to one side, then the other, until the material was bunched under her armpits and across the top of her breasts. The mound of pillows which had kept Edna propped in a comfortable position for reading and watching television now assisted her son as he manoeuvred one arm at a time out of the nightie, a task made easier by the garment's voluminous size, finally lifting it clear whilst taking care not to disturb her hair, which she had insisted on being neatly trimmed and styled once a month by a mobile hairdresser.

Encouraged by the success of this first stage, Colin returned to the wardrobe, opened the drawer at its base and drew out a bra. It looked brand new, crisp and white, though it appeared comically large in comparison to the only other bras Colin had any experience of, the ones belonging to Siobhan O'Connell, a skinny post-graduate researcher from Cork who had managed, after spiking his lemonade with vodka and impressing him by being the first person he had met to not only finish James Joyce's *Ulysses* but also enjoy it, to finally deprive him of his virginity at the age of thirty. They had remained together for six months, until Siobhan returned to Ireland. She had asked him to come with her, but Colin declined, citing work commitments and a reluctance to leave his mother on her own. The real reason, however, was fear. The idea of moving to another country, and the commitment to their relationship that such a move would surely endorse, terrified him, and so they said their rather awkward farewells in a cold ferry terminal, where Colin promised that he would write, and Siobhan shook her head and replied 'no you won't', and then he stood and watched her leave, watched the bright red of her rucksack until it was swallowed up in the black maw of the ferry, before turning away, bewildered by how such powerful feelings of both relief and regret could co-exist.

He held up the bra. "You could make four of Siobhan's out of this."

Before the onset of her illness Edna Draper had fought a long, arduous and ultimately unsuccessful battle with her weight. She was not greedy, but she belonged to a generation that abhorred waste, a habit which when combined with a family preponderance for the women to thicken around the waist in middle age meant that as the multiple sclerosis tightened its grip, limiting her physical activity, she inevitably became increasingly rotund. And after a particularly traumatic episode, when within the space of a month she lost nearly all feeling in her left leg, Edna sought comfort in buns and cakes, consuming them with an almost fatalistic abandon. Until her recent collapse it had been her habit to enjoy a vanilla slice or bag of doughnuts with her afternoon tea, a routine frowned on by her doctor yet actively encouraged by the district nurse, who regularly stated her philosophy that 'a girl's got to have some pleasure in her life', and so, as Colin returned to the bedside carrying the bra, he saw, with new clarity, what a peculiar shape his mother had become. Edna's soft white torso had settled into the equally white mattress, and with the evening sun blurring the boundary between flesh and material still further, it appeared she had morphed into a sort of bed/human hybrid, with her belly button and broad, pale brown nipples the only reference points marking out her former unconjoined self. Attached, as if quite arbitrarily, to this embryonic form were her limbs: the attenuated legs, made all the more meagre by their proximity to the broad spread of her stomach and hips, and the arms, more robust, but with the flesh sagging from the bones like sallow wattles.

Colin placed the bra on his mother's chest, but the cups sat in a space occupied by nothing but her crucifix and the necklace with the pale blue stone, while her breasts drooped, like slabs of dough, towards her armpits. Colin's hands dithered above the bra as he tried to work out the mechanics of large breasts, before reluctantly concluding that he would have to first fasten the clasps behind her back and then manoeuvre each breast into its respective cup.

"Brace yourself, Mother," the archivist warned, "this is going to be far worse for me than it is you."

Tilting Edna forward, as he had done so many times in the past when rearranging her pillows, Colin positioned himself so that her weight was supported by his shoulder. He then looped the shoulder straps into place, pulling the elasticated band around her back as he did so, and to his surprise and delight managed to line up the hooks and eyes and fasten them securely at his first attempt.

"Well, that wasn't too bad, was it? Now for the awkward bit."

And then Colin hesitated. For the first time since making the decision to dress his mother the archivist considered his actions as if seen from the outside. Would people understand that his number one priority was to ensure her dignity? That his mother would not be mauled about by a complete stranger who, God forbid, might even take some sort of perverse pleasure in their work? What he was doing was surely right, and if certain individuals thought otherwise then that was their problem. He had tended to her for well over a decade; surely he had earned the right to perform this last task, and to discharge it with love.

Convinced of the righteousness of his actions, Colin lifted the bra's right cup, which in itself was quite difficult as the elastic was surprisingly strong, and tried to shepherd the slack flesh of his mother's breast underneath the material, but he soon realised that using the flat palm of one hand in an attempt to maintain a minimum of contact was hopeless.

"Bloody hell, Mother," he muttered, "you're not making this any easier, you know." Colin tried to remember how Siobhan had put on her bra. She had fastened the hooks and eyes at the front and then rotated the whole assembly, he recalled that much, but her breasts had been little more than neat conical protuberances that fitted into the cups without the need for anything but minimal adjustment, nothing like his mother's recalcitrant bosom.

"Right," Colin said firmly, "I'm afraid this calls for rather more direct action." His explanation voiced, the archivist spread his hand wide, took a firm grip of the breast, and tucked it under the bra's cup, letting the elastic snap back before the contents had a chance to slide free. A sausage-shaped section of flesh bulged around the lower curve of the bra, which he poked under the elastic with two fingers, before standing back from the bed to admire his handiwork.

"There you go. Nothing to it."

He repeated the technique for Edna's other breast, then took her dress, guided her legs through the hole at its top and, by gently rocking her body from side to side and inching the dress upwards at the same time, eventually had the garment in position. Leaning her against him one last time, Colin reached behind and pulled up the zip, which came to a stop several inches from the top of its travel. "Oh dear, too many cakes, Mother." He let her sink back onto the pillows and straightened the material. "Not to worry, you can't tell from the front."

What, Colin wondered, was the accepted protocol for the deceased's arms? Should they be at their sides, or crossed over their chest pointing slightly upwards, or crossed horizontally, hands overlapped? He tried all three poses, concluding that whether or not it was the norm the horizontal cross-over looked best; the 'by the sides' seemed overly formal, whereas the 'angled cross' made Edna look like an Ancient Egyptian mummy. He arranged her hands so that her fingers interlocked, and it was during this careful placement that Colin realised she was not wearing her wedding ring. He vaguely remembered there being some medical reason for its absence, but equally he knew Edna would want to be buried with her ring on.

"Where did you put it?" He wondered out loud, looking round the bedroom, but its spartan furnishings offered no clear answer. He returned to the wardrobe, searched through every pocket, lifted out every blanket and pillowcase in the bottom drawer, but all he found was a dry cleaning receipt and an empty perfume bottle. Had she entrusted the ring to his safekeeping? Colin racked his brains. If he had tucked it away somewhere with his most treasured possessions and then forgotten its location he would never forgive himself. "Think, Colin, think," he nagged. What *were* his most treasured possessions? Might he have put the ring with them? This train of thought quickly led him to the surprising and, for someone who regarded himself as a political radical, gratifying realisation that he had no such things, at least not anything of significant monetary worth. In fact the body of cross-referenced documentation, postcards, photographs, letters, articles, newspaper cuttings and ephemera which he valued most highly Colin did not see as a possession at all; it was, rather, an archive in the literal sense of the word: a store or repository, assembled by him, certainly, but not, ultimately, *for* him. One day he would offer the archive to the town, and on that day it would become public property. Colin also hoped, because he was not quite as devoid of ego as he liked to think, that the archive would contribute in some small way to the resort's cultural heritage; he saw his carefully constructed assembly of disparate parts as his own pier: a gestalt creation brought together by the vision of one man for the enjoyment of many.

And just as Colin was enjoying his moment of gentle hubris the location of the wedding ring popped into his head. "Of course! It's in the pot in front of Dad's photo on the mantel."

He plodded across the hall and into the living room, reaching under the shade of the standard lamp as he passed by to switch it on, as he did every day on returning from work, because the living room faced north and remained fixed in a gloomy half-light no matter what the time of day, and after saying hello to his mother the archivist would, without fail, make himself a cup of tea and spend half an hour with the paper before starting tea. He would also follow this routine today, having dressed his mother's corpse. He would slump in the armchair next to the standard lamp, sip at his tea, and read every headline, study every photograph, without any of it seemingly registering, and yet in twenty years time he would be able to recall every detail of the front page, as though the newspaper had been reporting the death of Edna Draper rather than the start of an official enquiry into the Hillsborough disaster.

Malcolm Draper was grinning his lopsided grin, pale blue eyes framed by black plastic spectacles. His checked shirt was partially unbuttoned, revealing the inverted triangle of suntanned chest and the pale skin that surrounded it which marked the limits of his casualness. He was leaning on the wooden handle of a garden tool, its precise function lost beyond the photo frame's border, but Colin always imagined it to be a spade, judging by the soil under his father's fingernails.

"She's all yours now, Dad," he said, addressing the picture.

Colin lifted the lid of the Wedgwood dish, retrieved Edna's wedding ring and replaced the lid, its ceramic clink so very loud in the room's hush. He returned to her bedroom, brandishing the ring. "Look what I found," the archivist said. "Can't have you setting off without this on."

Gently lifting her left hand, Colin slid the ring onto her third finger, but it came to a halt at the second joint. He thought for a moment, then remembered a tip his grandmother, or an aunty, someone, had mentioned, so it was out of the bedroom again, this time turning left and into the kitchen, the fridge, to return with a tub of margarine. He rubbed a little of the margarine on the knuckle and thickest segment of Edna's ring finger, then manoeuvred the slim gold band into position, before finally wiping off the greasy film with his handkerchief. The archivist unfolded a duvet cover, draped it over his mother so that just her head and shoulders remained uncovered, and stepped back to admire his handiwork.

"All done," he announced. "You're fit to be seen out now."

The brilliant evening sunshine that had filled Edna's bedroom with light the entire time Colin was dressing her faded abruptly as clouds began to build, and the sensation of an ending, like the lowering of stage lights at the conclusion of a play, was so powerful that it made his presence seem intrusive, as though he was impeding some vital moment of transition. The skin of Edna's face, which had been kindled into a semblance of life by the sun, now revealed its truth. Colin could hardly bear to look at the waxy mask thus exposed, and he realised that without the lambent effect of the sunshine, which had warmed her skin as well as lending it colour, he would never have been able to perform this final service. Now, in the sudden twilight, Colin looked on his actions in amazement; where had he found the objectivity, the composure, to dress his mother's lifeless body? Had she too become, in effect, an archive? Had he subconsciously deemed the bra, dress and wedding ring as necessary codicils to the far greater anthology that was Edna Draper's life?

The archivist, for that was what he was, in all things, reached out for the fan's switch and turned it off. The whirr of the blades subsided, returned after so long as a translucent disc to their component parts, and it was this simplest of endings which finally broke through his composure, offering up a pristine silence in which his sobs could take the place of their hum.

# The Plausible Tide

The sea had turned from its lowest ebb and was beginning to wrap itself around the pier's outermost stanchions like the coils of a glittering grey snake. How patient the water was, touching the iron posts that impeded it with a beguiling tenderness, stroking each one briefly before creeping further up the beach. No one could have seen the malice lurking behind each caress; no one except Mickey Braithwaite, who lay sprawled, belly down on the floor of the sun lounge, peering through a wide gap in the planks to the sands below, and the plausible tide.

Prostrate, a most penitent of disciples, Mickey loved the intimacy with the pier that lying spread-eagled on its planks afforded. It was almost like becoming part of its structure, some malleable strut or span. Every part of his body was in contact with the pier, from head to toe, allowing for a much more satisfying communion than simply walking along it or sitting in one of his stripy deckchairs. It was only by performing this act of obeisance that he could detect the faint tremor running through the structure beneath him as the pier, appalled by the tide's silky touch, which whispered of destruction and a victory only briefly deferred, anticipated its inevitable defeat. Twice every day it had to endure this gloating embrace, knowing full well that the ocean was correct, that it would one day wash over rusted stumps protruding from the sand like the blackened bones of some half-buried corpse, and then, in a million years, remember the pier as nothing more than an ephemeral hindrance, its grandeur commemorated by a scattering of iron atoms dissolved in the cold belly of the sea.

Mickey thought of the sea's everlasting consciousness, and the cruelty that inevitably accompanied it. What a dreadful cage immortality was, a limitless cage, and yet it offered such temptation to the mortal soul; only after succumbing to such temptation, and having stepped willingly through its portal, did immortality reveal the true horror of its towering, impregnable barricades. Then there was nothing to be done except seek some form of unknowing through madness, or else become a god and dispense cruelty to all those happy creatures who could count the days of their existence.

Further along the pier Colin Draper was slumped in a deckchair, unaware of the tide's intentions, or indeed of anything except the lengthening shadows which were creeping gradually nearer to the scuffed toes of his shoes, and the gossiping of starlings flying in small groups to and from the theatre roof, carried on the rhythms of their own headlong tides.

The funeral had been and gone, interminable at the time and yet now little more than a crowded moment. He remembered the uneasy smiles of mourners, the sharp edge of his mother's coffin cutting into his shoulder, the sunshine on his neck as Edna Draper was committed to the soil next to her husband, and the overpowering sensation of needing to be away from the house within minutes of the last guest leaving. Colin hadn't even tidied away the cups and plates. He had simply grabbed his coat and caught the first bus that came along, a bus that had deposited him on the promenade only yards from the pier. The resort had known where he needed to be, and had guided him there.

Since then Colin had wandered up and down the silvery-grey boards, barely noticed by the tourists. The archivist was already one of those people whose unremarkable physical presence rendered them, if not transparent, then extremely easily forgotten. Wrap this persona in a raincoat whose grey was a close match to the weathered boards and what resulted was an almost chameleon-like level of camouflage. And so he wandered, trailing what appeared at first glance to be an untethered shadow, until his feet ached and he sought refuge in the blue-and-white striped haven of a deckchair. He had looked up and down the pier for Mickey, not wanting to deprive the attendant of his fee, but Mickey was nowhere to be seen, so Colin settled himself at an angle that gave him a panoramic view of the returning sea, the beach, and the resort.

As an intellectual exercise and distraction the archivist began to mentally strip away every modern encumbrance and alteration within his field of vision, peeling back the layers one by one, reconstructing buildings or features that had been lost, until what lay before him was the resort as George Parr would have seen it: raw, vigorous, confident, a New Jerusalem for that most evangelical of eras. And it was during this process of imaginary restoration that the sadness already within him diverged, so that Colin found himself in mourning not only for his mother, but also the resort's lost innocence. Having painstakingly renovated the entire sea front in his mind, Colin could now switch from the 1989 version in front of him to his mid-nineteenth century simulacrum and back again, like clicking between two slides in a projector, a process that only emphasised how much had been lost. Where once restraint and optimism had proclaimed the town's vigour, now there was only garishness and despondency. The resort, like every other in the country, had been left behind, abandoned by all those thousands that once thronged its beach in favour of sun and sangria. It still catered for those who wished to escape their normal lives, certainly — all resorts function, to a greater or lesser degree, as fairground halls of mirrors — but there was an abandonment to its revellers that in Colin's eyes came perilously close to despair.

How had it come to this? What had transformed ladies

in crinolines and lace gloves into the lewd, mini-skirted young women who, quite frankly, terrified him? Why had the gents, all wearing their splendid hierarchy of hats, seen fit to metamorphose into packs of raucous, predatory young men?

"Mr Draper?"

Colin started. A figure, silhouetted by the sun, loomed over him, but even had he not recognised the tangle of hair that glowed like a threadbare halo, the soft, enchanting quality of the voice could belong to only one person. "Mickey... I was looking for you earlier."

"Were you?"

"Yes. I thought I needed to... " the archivist patted the arms of his deckchair. "I haven't paid for my chair. Someone else must have left it."

Mickey Braithwaite turned to look along the pier. His halo caught the breeze and fluttered slightly as if in response to a less than wholesome thought. "That's alright," he decided finally. There was a silence that lasted several seconds. "I was watching the tide. Do you like the tide best when it's in or out, Mr Draper?"

Colin looked past the deckchair attendant to the glittering sea, as though the mere sight of it might supply an answer to Mickey's gnomic question. "Out," he said, more to satisfy the sudden fervour in Mickey's eyes than anything else, and then he realised that he really *did* prefer to be on the pier or promenade with the sea at a safe distance, knew it with a certitude that bordered on the revelatory.

"It's coming in now. It wants to swallow everything up."

The archivist was one of those people whose desire to educate only ever manifested itself as condescension; not, in his case at least, through any feelings of superiority, but rather because of a lack of communication skills. "I wouldn't worry about that. The tides are controlled by the moon's gravity, Mickey, they'll only come up so far."

Mickey squinted upwards. He had still not moved from his position between Colin and the sun. "I like looking at the moon through my binoculars. Have you ever looked at the moon through binoculars, Mr Draper?"

"I once saw it through a telescope," Colin answered, and he was not the first person to be surprised at how quickly and easily the deckchair attendant could turn a conversation to his own agenda.

Mickey nodded. "What did you see?"

"Oh, the usual. You know, craters, the 'seas'."

"But they aren't really seas, are they? It's all dust."

"That's right," Colin said, surprised by Mickey's astronomical knowledge. "Darker areas of dust."

The deckchair attendant sighed, as though the lunar topic was cause for some regret. "With dust fishes."

Colin smiled. "No, I don't think so. Mickey—"

"And dust whales... and dust dolphins. Does it have tides? Does the dust move about because of earth's gravy?"

"Gravity. Well, not as far as I'm aware."

The deckchair attendant, presumably encouraged by their conversational momentum, settled himself in the deckchair next to Colin, shifting his bus conductor's ancient lever-operated ticket machine so that it rested on his thigh. "My binoculars used to belong to my grandpa. I used them when I was in the Observer Corps."

"I bet you did. You kept this town safe from the bombs, Mickey. You should be very proud of what you did."

"Fucking Adolf wanted to put Aunty Irene out of business."

Colin was shocked by the abrupt expletive, but he reasoned that Mickey, like many others who lived through the war, had every reason to feel so strongly about Hitler. "He wanted to put a lot of people out of business, Mickey, but it was thanks to people like you that he didn't. I've seen photos of the pier during the war. It looked a bit like a battleship with its gun, and there you were up on the bridge like the captain."

Mickey turned towards the theatre. He wrinkled his nose to push his spectacles back up his nose. "We were on the roof, Mr Draper, not a bridge."

"No, no, the bridge of a ship. It's where the captain and the officers are."

"My brother was on a ship."

"During the war?"

Mickey nodded. "He didn't die in the war like Pa, but he died afterwards."

"I'm sorry to hear that," Colin said. "It was my mother's funeral today. I thought... I thought I'd cry from start to finish, but I didn't feel anything. It was like we were burying an empty box. Is that wrong?"

The deckchair attendant sniffed. His hands, which were almost freakishly large, flexed and shifted as though following some compulsion quite detached from his motionless body. "Your mum went away in the storm. A bomb came and took Mrs Tyler away. There's always something that takes you away, Mr Draper. Bella thought the burnt man was coming to take her away but he wasn't, he was just angry with her, but it won't be her fault. Even when things we do take people away it's not our fault, not really. It would've happened anyway."

Why, thought Colin, am I attempting to have a meaningful conversation with Mickey Braithwaite? All I'm ever going to get in return is a meaningless stream of consciousness. Even if there *is* some sort of meaning to it it's nothing anybody but Mickey would be able to understand. But then he remembered hearing the thunder whilst in the middle of his argument with the librarian, and the waterlogged streets on his way home that evening, the evening he found her. "What do you mean, my mother went away in the storm?"

The deckchair attendant's hands performed a brief, explanatory dance in the air on either side of his head.

"Onetwothreefourfive... boom!" He chanted. "Onetwothree... boom! Two... boom! That's how the storm takes you away, Mr Draper. You shouldn't count the numbers. Don't count the numbers."

"What do you mean, Mickey? What numbers?" The

archivist was becoming increasingly disorientated by the surreal turn to the conversation, a sensation not helped by the strobe-like reflections and distorting layers of Mickey Braithwaite's thick lenses, which at certain angles appeared to reveal a depth of glass that went far beyond the frame's boundaries.

But Mickey had seen a middle-aged couple settling themselves in two of his deckchairs, and without a word set off purposefully in their direction. By the time he returned Colin knew it would have been hopeless to repeat the question, so he tried another tack.

"Would you like an ice cream? I fancy an ice cream. We can have a nice ice cream and a chat. How does that sound? If you're not too busy working, that is," he added, sensing that he was talking as if to a five-year-old.

"A ninety-nine, please," Mickey replied decisively. "With monkey's blood and hundreds and thousands."

Colin grimaced. "What?"

The deckchair attendant elbowed him playfully in the ribs.

"Raspberry sauce! It isn't really monkey's blood. I wouldn't want monkey's blood on my ice cream."

"I'm glad to hear it. Two ninety-nines it is, then."

To the casual observer the two men might have been father and son, enjoying an ice cream in the sun. There was even a passing resemblance between them, not only because of their windswept straggly hair, but also from a certain similarity of demeanour. Colin would probably not have been conscious of it, as he lacked the ego required for prolonged self-analysis, but as a socially inept obsessive-compulsive he had much in common with Mickey Braithwaite. However, as he watched the deckchair attendant carefully lick any dribble of melting ice cream before it could reach the wafer cone, rotating it round and round continuously on a constant look-out for new drips, Colin perceived only a huge gulf between them. Mickey appeared to inhabit a different world, a place of wonder and infinite possibility, hidden from most people's view behind the theatre scenery of the tangible. What rules there were seemed concerned solely with repetition, as though these behavioural mantras served to anchor the deckchair attendant and prevent him from being carried off on some prodigious tide.

Colin extracted his chocolate flake and bit off the end clumped with ice cream. A sharp jab of pain in his jaw reminded him of the cavity in one molar that he had been meaning to have filled, but which he always forgot about as soon as the pain receded. He pressed the palm of his hand to his cheek and groaned. "This flipping tooth."

"Taffy's tooth... went all brown," Mickey noted, his anecdote punctuated by pauses as he continued his hunt for stray trickles of ice cream. "Mitch and Norman wanted to pull it out... with a pair of pliers, but Taffy... told them to f – off." He laughed, a short, bark-like sound. "Taffy was always telling them to... f– off."

Colin sensed an aperture, a gateway into Mickey's world that might remain open for only a few seconds, so he decided to hazard an educated guess. "Were they your Observer Corps colleagues... friends?"

"They gave me a helmet with OC painted on it. Well, it did have police painted on it, but Uncle Walter scratched off the other letters so that just the O and C were left. That meant they were quite far apart. They looked a bit like two eyes when it was dark."

Colin gestured with his ice cream cone at the building next to them. "And there you were, up on the roof of the theatre. Lords of all you surveyed."

Mickey turned and looked up. He was silent for perhaps ten seconds, then returned his attention to his own ice cream. "Do you know what hundreds and thousands are made out of, Mr Draper?"

What, the archivist wondered, was the best method of dealing with Mickey Braithwaite's tangential changes of conversational direction? Go along with them and hope to steer him back to the subject, or treat them as diversionary tactics — maybe even a form of test — and continue the theme? He chose the latter. "Yes, I know all about the Observer Corps post up there. You had a radio room above the dressing rooms, and a platform on the roof. I remember seeing photos of it all. You were a very important part of this area's defences during the war, Mickey. You and your colleagues must have saved a lot of people's lives."

The deckchair attendant dabbed one fingertip onto his ice cream, collecting several of the hundreds and thousands, which he then examined closely, his eyes crossing with the effort.

"Then there was that terrible night when the Salvation Army was bombed," Colin persisted.

"They look like tiny little tablets."

"Do you remember? When the bomb fell on the Salvation Army?"

Mickey stuck his finger in his mouth and sucked. "They're all different colours, but they all taste the same."

"That night when you rescued your mum."

"You'd think different colours would taste different."

"The bomb fell on the Salvation Army, but you rescued your mum just in time. Mickey, do you remember?"

The deckchair attendant withdrew the now clean fingertip and turned to look at Colin, who smiled encouragingly, even though the eerie light in Mickey's eyes sent a shiver down his spine.

"Everybody says it was a miracle," Mickey said, "but I don't know about that. I don't even know what a miracle is. Do you believe in miracles, Mr Draper?"

Colin, thrilled and terrified in equal measure by his success in bringing Mickey's mind into some form of focus, sensed also that honest responses were essential if the deckchair attendant was not to revert back to his normal arbitrariness. "No. No, I don't."

"No," Mickey repeated, his tone of voice suggesting that the reply was a regrettable but inescapable truth. "It's just people being frightened of something that's supposed to happen. That's what I think."

"Have you thought about what happened a lot?"

Mickey licked his ice cream and nodded vigorously. "Every day. It's like it got stuck in my head. I can still see everything. It's like watching a film."

The archivist leaned forward. "What else can you see? Can you see Georgie Parr? Or Hannah Goodwin?"

Mickey frowned. He twitched his nose, but a slight film of perspiration meant that his heavy glasses slipped back to their previous position almost immediately.

"They lived a long, long time ago," Colin expounded. "Georgie Parr was a comedian who worked in the theatre before this one, and Hannah, she died, right here." He pointed downwards. "Under the pier. Can you see them, Mickey?"

The old attendant took a deep breath, sank back in his deckchair and then, to Colin's horror, began to weep quietly, his body shaking in time with his sobs.

"Oh, Mickey, I'm sorry. I didn't mean to upset you."

Mickey Braithwaite looked at the archivist, and the torment laid bare in his eyes not only shocked Colin but also made him fearful for his own safety. He had always regarded the deckchair attendant as a harmless eccentric with mental incapacities which were, in certain areas, compensated by a rare, even unique, insight; what he had just seen was rage, pure, unadulterated rage, and though he sensed it was not directed primarily at him, Colin suspected that he could well be swept up in some all-consuming outburst if these emotions ever breached whatever defences Mickey had put in place to contain them.

"I don't want to see anything else!" Mickey cried. "I don't want to see *anything*! I saw what the birds were telling me and so I rescued Ma, but they didn't say anything about Mrs Tyler. Why didn't they say anything about her? What had

Mrs Tyler done wrong that she had to be blown to bits? My ma was all in one piece and all I found of Mrs Tyler was her arm and they were in the Sally Army doing the same thing ten minutes before." The deckchair attendant wiped his nose with the back of his fingers. "If I'd told *every*body to get out *that* would have been a miracle but I didn't, did I? I just told my ma because that's all I saw, so really it was my fault all those ladies died, not Fucking Adolf. Mrs Tyler was right there in front of me all in one piece and I never said anything and then the bomb came down and afterwards all that was left was her arm. I never thought about anything but rescuing my ma... all those other ladies died and they said it was a miracle, but how could it be? How could it be, Mr Draper?"

"You saved another girl too," Colin said quietly.

Mickey sat forward in his deckchair. For a moment his mouth moved, as though speaking silently. Only after this brief phantom sentence did anything audible begin. "Another? There was just my ma—"

"No," Colin corrected, "a younger girl heard you talking to your mother... to your ma, and she decided to get out of the Sally Army building as well before the bomb dropped, so you saved her too, Mickey, without even knowing you'd saved her. And a few years later that same girl became a midwife... a sort of nurse who helps ladies have their babies, you know? Well anyway, when I was being born it wasn't happening right, and this girl saved my life, so really you saved *me* as well." A thought came to him, an extrapolation of his last sentence. "And I bet she saved lots more babies as well as me, so you saved all of them too. You see, Mickey? You didn't just save your ma that night, you saved lots of people, including me."

A light aircraft droned overhead, drawing the deckchair attendant's eyes upwards in a reflex action so ingrained it was as much a character trait as his spectacle-adjusting nose twitch.

"Cessna 172," he declared, before popping the last piece

of ice cream cone in his mouth and standing up. "Time to start packing up now, Mr Draper. Thank you very much for my ice cream."

The archivist managed a weak smile. He hoped a little of what he had said had registered, because what he had seen during Mickey's moment of disclosure, when Colin's persistence had broken through a crust of ingenuousness to reveal the magma of self-recrimination and anguish bubbling beneath, was a life forever compromised, pulled this way and that by the dilemmas posed by his unearthly powers. Would a keener intellect have been better able to cope with Mickey's premonitions, and the decisions that they demanded? Colin thought not. Such deliberations and intellectualising would only end up going round in circles, whereas a gut response was the only appropriate action. Colin could not think of anyone better qualified to have these gifts bestowed on them, but he did not envy the deckchair attendant, not for a moment.

"You're welcome," he replied. "Thank you for talking to me. It's helped put things in perspective." The archivist manoeuvred his bulk out of the deckchair and stretched his weary bones. "I suppose it *is* time to go home."

Mickey half-turned, apparently on the point of leaving, then suddenly turned back to face Colin, drew up neatly to attention and gave him an impeccable, crisply executed salute. "They're all waiting for us, Mr Draper," he said simply, the tone of his voice implying some deep and abiding consolation. Then he turned again, away from the reassuring mass of the theatre, and headed off down the pier, a mystical figure in the evening light; hair aglow, ticket machine glinting, a figure that paused as a small group of starlings flew past, and tracked their business-like direction, before setting off once more as soon as the birds were safely settled on the roof of a booth.

Colin thought of the dirty plates and cups waiting for him in the bungalow. Before their discussion the post-funeral detritus had seemed like a callous reminder of his loneliness and loss, but now it was simply a chore to be completed. Mickey had somehow waved his magic wand over them, drawing their sting, and for the life of him the archivist could not explain how he had done it.

As for George Parr and Hannah Goodwin, Colin had no idea whether the deckchair attendant knew anything about the events of a hundred years ago. There was a part of him, the chronicler, the assiduous gatherer of detail, the *archivist*, that felt disappointed by his failure to unlock the mystery of George and Hannah's deaths. Mickey Braithwaite had, however, demonstrated how extraordinarily high the cost of such knowledge could sometimes be, perhaps even at the risk of losing one's grip on reality, so there was another part of him that recognised and accepted this cautionary footnote bound up in certain secrets. Yes, perhaps the answers were out there somewhere, but could he be sure they offered enlightenment or merely confusion?

Colin began to walk back towards the promenade, his scuffed shoes finding consolation in the weathered boards as they carried him safely back over the unfathomable sea. It was then that the archivist realised the pier was the perfect metaphor for civilisation and everything it represented, lifting humanity above the chaos which boiled and churned not so far beneath. And the pier was also a bridge, linking solid ground, the prosaic and understandable, to an entirely different realm, one of delicacy and magic. George and Hannah had crossed this bridge, as had his mother. As must we all.

# Today

# The West Wind

The west wind has returned, and the gulls cry welcome to its enduring songs. It knows the resort, as it once knew the dunes and marshland that existed before the resort, and the warm shallow sea that covered the coast long, long before the dunes and marshland. In time it will know whatever is to come after the resort. But the wind is immortal, so there will be no record of its understanding, for what are stories if not an attempt to outwit death? Yet if the wind is content to play, there are others whose greatest purpose is to document and preserve. They write their own rhythms on the wind's transparent pages in a shifting, swaying, shimmering form of calligraphy, a beguiling language within whose ebb and flow lies the resort's history. And who can they be, these peerless narrators? Why, the starlings, of course.

# TV's Very Own

"Why did my wife cross the road?"

A robust, masculine cheer went up in the theatre as the audience recognised one of the comedian's old, oft-repeated jokes. He paced the stage, question posed, his erratic movements leaving the spotlight behind. Thrown into shadow, one arm illuminated, Sammy Samuels was as though fallen from a dream. He paused, and the beam caught up and glistened once more off his evangelist sweat. He draped one arm over the microphone stand and thrust his head out towards the audience.

"Hey, never mind why she crossed the road... what was she doing out of the fucking kitchen?"

Laughter, from men who knew the line and shared the sentiment, but this was a thin, early season audience and their timing was out. They weren't giving Sammy the space to hone his act, pissing him off even more than their coughs and farts and frequent trips to the toilet. The offbeat crashing of the waves against the stanchions below broke up what remained of the theatre's rhythm, leaving everyone unsure of their role.

"Yeah, well, there isn't a lot of point my wife being in the kitchen anyway, she's a shit cook," Sammy continued. "She says she doesn't need any of those poncey cookbooks, she just uses her own rule: if it's brown it's cooked, if it's black it's fucked. She's started experimenting with those foreign foods now. The other night she said to me, 'I'm going to make one of those *coq au vin*s,' but I said the only *coq au vin* I'm interested in is if I'm shagging some bird in me Transit!"

Smoke from the cigarette in a tin ashtray curled and looped around the four working light bulbs and two blown ones. A tatty-edged poster advertising last year's end-of-pier summer show depicted Sammy in his trademark Hawaiian shirt, pointing thumb up index finger out, the way children turn their hand into a gun. The pockmarks on his cheeks had been airbrushed out and a cartoon glint on his teeth added. The show's other acts were positioned around him, smaller photos, smaller captions, as Sammy had demanded.

He peered into the mirror and was gratified to see a profound absence in the pale grey, bloodshot eyes staring back at him. As a boy Samuel Rosenberg had made friends easily due to a knack for remembering jokes, coupled with an innate sense of timing in their telling, but even then he cared little for these schoolmates aside from the gratification of their laughter. Their games were dull, and their own attempts at humour seemed to consist largely of how loudly they could fart. His brother David, eight years older and groomed by their parents from an early age as heir apparent to the family's law firm, treated his younger sibling with a condescending arrogance that infuriated Samuel. It was like having two fathers in the house, constantly pointing out his shortcomings and offering advice on every aspect of his life. His switch to Sammy Samuels when setting out on the club circuit was ostensibly to provide him with a more poster-friendly name, but the real joy he derived from it was the effect it had on his father and brother, who were both appalled at what they regarded as a betrayal, not only of the family but also of his Jewishness. Contact became increasingly sporadic, particularly after his television breakthrough, which resulted in a hectic diary of appearances and shows designed by his then agent to make him a 'household name'. When Sammy appeared on the Royal Variety Performance he sent a telegram to David that read *If only I'd listened to you and Dad*.

He picked up the cigarette and took a long drag. Still holding it between his fingers, Samuels pulled down the skin below one eye: he saw pale pink, capillaries, some yellow round things.

"Are you alright?"

Sammy jumped. "Shit!" He turned from the mirror to see David Clark, the pier manager, leaning round the door. "Ever thought of knocking?"

"It *was* open."

The comedian studied the cigarette between his fingers. "So that's an invitation to just barge in, is it? Hoping to catch old Sammy doing something he shouldn't be, hmm? A quick Jodrell after the show? I get somebody else to do that for me, pal."

"I didn't wish to know that," David replied. His checked shirt was too tight, making him look fatter than he really was. A hankie protruded from one pocket of his jeans. "Is there something wrong with your eye?"

Sammy glared at the younger man. "Would it make any difference if I said there was? If I said I couldn't go on, do the show without me, it's terminal, I've got two weeks to live. You'd still expect me up on that fucking stage, wouldn't you? How many seasons have I done here? Who do the punters keep coming back to see? Sammy Samuels!" He threw his arms wide, like some flamboyant compere announcing the top of the bill. "TV's very own, star of stage and screen, like it says on the poster." He laughed disparagingly. "When I did the Royal Variety Performance I never thought I'd end up in a shit-hole like this."

The pier manager looked away from his star act's compassionless eyes. David remembered the 70s footage of Sammy on stage at Drury Lane, bowing to the Queen, frilly shirt and lapels flamboyant even for that decade. There was regular television work after the appearance, even talk of his own series, but tastes changed, and vodka provided Samuels with a comfortable refuge from rejection. Alcohol helped his fall from grace, but his own behaviour sealed it, leaving Sammy to coarsen his act and scratch a living from incoherent club turns, drunken rants which the audiences enjoyed because they could witness fame unravelling before them, until too many years had passed and the draw of a collapsing talent turned to apathy. The comedian woke to find himself a cliché, the boozy has-been, and this epiphany was enough to turn him teetotal. Sober, he climbed back onto the lower rungs of showbusiness, but there was something moribund about him now. Former colleagues spoke of lost potential, but David saw only self-delusion and malignant fury.

"Morecambe and Wise played this 'shit-hole'," the pier manager pointed out, "as did Tommy Cooper, *and* Norman Wisdom, *and—*"

Samuels held up his hands in surrender. "Alright, alright, enough already. I get the picture. I should be honoured, right? I should be paying you to work here. That better?"

David decided not to pursue the matter. "All I wanted to say was there's a meeting to discuss the season with the MD tomorrow in his office at eleven. He said he wanted you to be there."

"Did he now? Did he ask whether I'd got anything on? Whether I was free to come to his *meeting*?"

"No. Why, have you?"

"I might have. Just depends whether I get lucky or not." Sammy sucked hard on his cigarette and blew smoke in the pier manager's direction. "I want extra for working on a Sunday."

"It's hardly going to be work. I think Julian's got a few ideas for acts that he wants to discuss, then he said he'd take us out for lunch."

"Fuck me, that's worrying. What's he after?"

David flapped at the cigarette smoke in an effort to dispel it. "I have no idea."

"No change there, then."

"Ha ha. I did hear a rumour that a couple of the acts from Margate might be moving here, but I haven't seen any paperwork yet. Whoever it is, I'd appreciate it if you could keep on speaking terms with them for at least a couple of weeks."

"Depends whether they're like the dickheads we had last year, sunshine. I can work with anybody if they know what they're doing and don't give me any hassle." The comic pointed the glowing end of his cigarette at the pier manager. On the other side of the window the iridescence of starlings flashed past like the portal to a more vivid world. "Didn't you use to run amateur night at the Tavern? Perhaps that's why we keep ending up with such a bunch of no-hopers."

David felt the anger begin to well up, making him flush, stinging his skin. He was annoyed at himself for reacting, knowing that Samuels used his bullying as a force for destabilisation. "I think we ought to be concentrating on making next season a good one, Sammy. Julian's already told me there's more money in fairground rides than a theatre."

"Smart kid. He'll go far."

"That I don't doubt, but if everybody spends the entire summer bitching and stabbing each other in the back it'll be all the excuse he needs to knock this place down and put some bloody rollercoaster up instead. And *I* happen to think this theatre is something worth saving."

"Oh, just listen to yourself, will you?" The comedian ground out his cigarette. "This is nothing but a poxy little theatre on the end of a poxy little pier in the middle of a poxy little has-been…" He cast around for another suitable adjective. "… shit-hole of a seaside town. *You* might think we're on Broadway, but don't bother trying to convince me, okay?"

There was a moment's silence between them. Beneath their feet the sea surged round the Victorian ironwork, sending a tremor through the floorboards. "Just meet me at the EuroEnts office tomorrow at eleven o'clock," David finally managed, then with the hand which had never left the door frame he pulled himself backwards out of the dressing room like someone saving themselves from an abyss. Sammy noted this act of salvation, derived satisfaction from it and from the trepidation it denoted. He picked up the paper, lit another cigarette, and re-read the small ad he had circled, whilst forty feet below him the tide turned, happy to deposit its plastic bottles, condoms, jellyfish, seaweed, and one dead seagull on the drying shingle. Amongst the detritus, however, lay the beautiful curling labyrinth of a broken shell, its destiny to be either crushed under the wheels of a beach patrol Land Rover or picked up by a five-year-old girl, her eye drawn to its laid-bare helix. She would keep it in her jewellery box for the rest of her life and never realise that she loved it so much because the shell, in showing the world its equilibrium and elegance without vanity, was like her.

# Glitterball

There were no windows in the lap dancing club, only mirrors to give the illusion of size, but the men who came here would not look out even if they could. A platform took pride of place in the centre of the room, illuminated by red spotlights and a rotating glitterball. In the centre of the platform was a gleaming metal pole that acted as the room's hub, remaining stationary whilst the bar, padded alcoves and reflecting walls all turned in faithless orbit. Cigarette smoke stacked up in spotlit layers, gliding over the expressions of appraisal and assessment.

Dry ice spurted out from the bottom of a spiral metal staircase, eliciting a cheer from those men who knew its role as overture. Lights dimmed, Madonna began to sing, bottles of beer hung halfway between table and mouth, held in a forgotten trajectory. She descended. High heels, a dancer's legs, satin mini-skirt, bright white vest which glowed in the ultraviolet striplights, nipples perked up with a quick tweak in the changing room, long straight brown hair that swayed round her pretty face and genuine smile. There was nothing calculating in those brown eyes, which made the least drunk feel a momentary unease, so they concentrated instead on her tits and thighs and arse and found them comforting. She strode round the platform, her arm reaching out, fingers caressing the pole, just in passing; fixing herself, a bearing on which to navigate this dark, thudding, disorientating world.

Sammy Samuels knew her, knew them all: their bodies,

at any rate, moles and dimples and tattoos. He could put a name to them as well, but only so that when he rang the club he would know who was performing on any particular night. Here she was, then, Amanda, his favourite, the only one whose eyes did not betray her as she thrust and pivoted above an erection reined in by trousers and a libido growing colder each year. He could see the other girls' production-line glaze or contempt, but Amanda was different, Amanda saw herself as a kind of sanctuary, where men adrift in the world could seek brief refuge, and if their only gratitude was shown by ten-pound notes tucked as far down her knickers as their fingers could reach, or the pained expression as they came in their pants, then she felt vindicated by a job well done. All those wives and girlfriends, in fact all of womankind, were freed from the pent-up frustrations of their menfolk who, if Amanda did not perform her act of discharge, might subsume their tension into violence. Hers was a preventative dose, and Sammy needed to taste its sweetness.

"Tits are too small," remarked the man sitting on the other side of the table. Each of the fingers wrapped around his beer bottle carried a large gold ring. His nose was large and bulbous, with broken capillaries running down either side like the tributaries of a forgotten delta. "What d'yer reckon, mate? Bit flat-chested or what?"

Samuels, still cocooned in the temperate waters of Amanda's body, glared at his distractor. "*I* like her."

"Yer no a tits man, then."

Sammy looked more closely at his unwanted companion. He had the generic look of his theatre audience, enlivening a life in the doldrums with alcohol, fantasy and a brittle camaraderie with others of their creed. He was wearing a pinstriped jacket over the virulent green of a Celtic shirt, and even in the semi-darkness Sammy could see the dark brown nicotine stains on his fingers.

"You'd prefer Kara," he replied, puzzled by his own forbearance. "A tit man's dream."

"Aye? She on tonight?"

"No."

Amanda wrapped herself around the pole and the music slowed, took up a languid rhythm which Amanda replicated with a thrusting of her hips, an arching of her back, a tilting of her head. With little apparent effort she lifted herself up the pole, then, thighs locked around its burnished shaft, she let herself sink backwards until her hair brushed the stage. Only the tremors in her leg muscles betrayed the effort required to make this move prolonged and elegant. A silver crucifix slid onto her chin and Jesus sparkled.

Her inverted beauty smiled at Sammy, but the crescent of her mouth appeared to turn down in sadness. He stared at the glistening collagen-plump lips, imagining what it would be like to kiss them, or watch them open as they neared the end of his cock. For a moment he was back at his flat, the yellow glow from his bedside lamp reflected in her lip gloss. It was so wonderfully shiny, like varnish, glistening as her mouth opened wider and wider until, like the maw of a whale, she engulfed him and swallowed him whole: the ultimate blow-job. Because this was all Sammy had ever allowed the ladies to perform on him; now he had a perfect excuse in HIV and AIDS, but even back in the 70s, when the comedian first made use of call-girls and the occasional groupie, he had balked at penetrative sex. He regarded it as demeaning, awkward, undignified. There was something about being inside another human which made him feel uneasy. He could not help thinking of all those organs and processes, pumping and squirting and *functioning* only inches away from his penis. To Sammy sex was as unacceptable as dropping his trousers in an operating theatre, climbing onto the patient and thrusting himself into their open wound. Even the look of a woman's sexual organ reminded him of an injury. Their mouths were so much more appealing: warm and soft and inviting, just like Amanda's.

The flecks of light drifting round the lap dancing club left streaks on his retinae. He closed his eyes, waiting for the after-images to fade, but instead they intensified, began to burn, and the music lost all treble, folded itself into the beat of the darkness. Amanda crouched, hands caressing her thighs, a purple spotlight making her look like a putrefying toad. Sammy's mouth was dry, his top lip cold and sweaty, and the white streaks in his eyes still weren't fading. Amanda flicked a huge tongue, caught a fly, munched it down and her eyes were filigree gold. The glitterball accelerated, its reflections elongating into bands of white light pulsing in time with the bassline, which was all Sammy could hear. What's happening to me? he wondered, near to panic. He had snorted two small heaps of cocaine from the back of his hand in a graffiti-daubed cubicle less than an hour ago, but had never experienced anything like this reaction to the drug. Was it a contaminated batch? Or was this what a heart attack felt like? He tried to stand up, but the floor was whipped from under his feet, like jumping off a speeding roundabout and not running when you land. His head caught the edge of the platform. Amanda's clear plastic stilettos clomped and twirled only inches from his face, and bizarrely he noticed that the left heel was worn down further than the right. High in the darkness the glitterball hummed, about to fly loose from its mountings such was its speed. Samuels gawped. It looks like Telstar, he thought. Then it was eclipsed by the Scotsman bending over him. Sammy read 'Carling' across the man's shirt.

"Y'alright, man? Come on, let's have ye up before the bouncers see yer."

"Fuck off… I'm not drunk."

Amanda had sashayed off into the club to bring succour to those on its fringes. Sammy, still sprawled on the floor, watched her transparent shoes recede into an uncertain distance, refracting the dollops of light which were returning to a more sustainable speed around the room. He felt a tingling in his fingertips and toes, but his heart was still beating strongly, unequivocal and cold.

Before he had a chance to clamber back into the protective darkness of the booth, however, Sammy felt someone take a firm hold of his jacket collar and haul him unceremoniously to his feet. An awareness of the strength required to do this instantly stifled the comic's anger at such treatment, but not without it being followed by a silent caveat of deferral.

"No touching, pal, you know the rules."

Sammy tried to shrug off the bouncer. "I wasn't *trying* to touch her. I fell over."

"Yeah, right. Had a bit too much to drink, have we *sir*?"

"I don't drink, dickhead! Look, there's my glass... " The comedian gestured at the booth table. "Taste it if you don't believe me."

"You're leaving, pal. Right now."

The grip tightened on Samuels' collar and the same inexorable force that had raised him from the floor now began to propel him through the club, away from the music and the glitterball and the resonance of his dizzy spell. A group of men cheered his ejection — 'dirty bastard!' — but they never saw the irony of their jeers. Sammy caught a last glimpse of Amanda's arse, neatly bifurcated by her sparkly G-string, as she bent over a customer whose strained features were smoothing out, brought back onto the path of righteousness by virtue of her confessional skills, before the swing doors opened and he was expelled, banished from the womb of the lap dancing club, up the stairs and out into the night where a leaking downpipe spattered like vomit on the pavement.

Deprived of the club's warmth, Sammy turned up the collar of his jacket against the spring chill. Why is it always so fucking windy here? Wet and windy and dying on its arse. Normal people didn't go to the seaside in England for their holidays any more, not when a fortnight in Spain cost less than a week wiping the kebab stains off the nylon sheets in a damp B&B where the fairy lights round the bar tried to dispel the ennui of the guests but in fact only emphasised the watered-down whisky in its wobbly optic and there was a smell of dog, and burnt toast, and cheap air freshener; where the landlady jacked up her apron to polish the strobe-lit fountain in the bay window of the dining room, the window which looked out onto the terrace of guest houses opposite who all had VACANCIES, still, it was early in the season, it might pick up, Easter was only round the corner, pity the show on the pier won't be anything to write home about this year, but it'll never be the same as it was...

No. Sammy interrupted his own reverie. That's not true: it's *always* been the same. It always was shite, and it always will be. Different kinds of shite, maybe, but shite nevertheless. Because people will always want shite, they've got an insatiable appetite for it. Appetite for shite. The comedian smiled to himself inside the tweedy confines of his lapels. It could be the title of his autobiography.

He walked the mile or so to his flat in an agreeable daze, still able to glimpse the white blurs from the glitterball dancing in his peripheral vision and welcome their portent. Certain details of the town were all Sammy recalled from his journey: two doormen, like overstuffed undertakers in their long black coats, joking with a group of girls shivering in skimpy summer dresses; the red LED on a CCTV camera glimmering in a shadowed doorway like the only witness to the bad in the world; litter whirling in a patch of neon-lit pavement. The resort felt enervated, in need of a transformation as drastic as it would be invigorating. Maybe, Sammy wondered, he could be the catalyst, like a comic book hero letting loose a shockwave of cleansing destruction while he emerged, awesome, triumphant, a top billing the likes of which had never been seen before.

Carlton Apartments was once an address to be proud of, a social yardstick that could be quoted with confidence in any context. Four storeys high, with wide steps up to a porticoed entrance and stucco detailing, it was all there, no expense spared. These were no ordinary flats, catering as they did for professionals who were looking for either a weekend retreat or retirement home, and perfectly positioned to supply a constant flow of rejuvenating seaside ozone to fill ageing lungs, a little bit of Riviera class to take the edge off post-war austerity Britain. Fifty years down the line, however, the optimism that had built the place was long gone, along with the social strata counted on to fill it, who had been lured away by the glittering come-on of the Mediterranean. In order to survive Carlton Apartments had had to lower its sights somewhat. Its residents were still decent enough folk; no DSS, no students, but they weren't chic, or exotic, they didn't trot up to that grand entrance with an aspirational spring in their step and a warm feeling of pride at the success in life which had enabled them to buy into the Dream. No, these people were tenants in the literal sense of the word, fully aware of the temporary nature of their possession, knowing their livelihood depended on a declining tourist trade. When Carlton Apartments were built the crowds were thick enough to obscure the sand; now the small groups of donkeys and sunbathers scattered over the beach looked more like lonely outposts on a desert frontier, preparing for a last stand from behind the flimsy protection of their windbreaks.

Sammy trudged up the steps, turned the key and pressed his foot against the bottom of the door frame as he pushed it open because the door had warped, years ago, yet despite repeated requests to the landlord nothing had been done and now Samuels was so used to this extra manoeuvre that when other doors opened normally it unsettled him. He reached for the large white button that would give him twenty seconds of light in which to unlock the door to flat two, winced at the bare bulb's harsh light, then frowned at the dried blood on the knuckles of his left hand that it revealed. When had that happened? It must have been his fall in the lap dancing club, but the comedian could not recall any pain at the time. Amanda's body must have anaesthetised him, like the drug that she was.

He turned the key, and as the door to his flat opened a

new wave of fatigue and dizziness washed over him. Sammy staggered into the hallway, scattering unopened junk mail with his scuffing feet, and let the spring-loading slam shut the door behind him.

"Fuck me," the comedian muttered. He leaned on the bathroom door jamb one-handed and with the other gripped his face as though to let go would see it fall from the front of his skull to the floor. Bright spots of light flitted over the darkness of the hallway, swirling together before separating and vanishing with a blink. Sammy heard the entrance timer switch off the light, and like the click of a hypnotist's fingers its sound restored a delicate equilibrium to his mind, but his trust in this stability had been greatly diminished.

Samuels groped for the lounge light switch and flicked it down. For a split second the room looked utterly foreign to him, but then its jumbled elements resolved themselves into the spartan setting that he openly acknowledged said more about his life than any amount of psycho-analysis. Three of his Hawaiian shirts were drying on hangers hooked over the dado rail; an overflowing ashtray, two mugs and an empty takeaway foil tub lay on the coffee table; a rack of porn and science fiction DVDs stood next to the television; three weeks' worth of newspapers were jammed into a wicker basket, and on the walls were photos, mostly black-and-white, of Sammy with various stars of TV and theatre, together with a framed front cover of the *TV Times* depicting Samuels dressed as a cowboy tilting back his stetson using the barrel of a revolver, a promotional picture for some long-forgotten game show which he had always loathed but which his agent had insisted would 'widen his appeal'. So you're saying hardly anybody likes me at the moment? Sammy remembered replying. Isn't that *your* fucking job? They had parted company not long after that.

He threw his jacket onto the back of the couch and slumped into its worn cushions. For perhaps ten minutes he sat motionless, wrapped in the gentle patter of rain on the window, staring vacantly at the blank television screen. He had always been able to do this, to clear his mind of all conscious thought and simply *be*. Sammy found this waking coma, what he termed his 'lobotomy mode', invaluable before a performance. It seemed to clear away the detritus of everyday life and leave his jokes and observations in sharp relief, categorised, cross-referenced, together with a selection of put-downs for hecklers and some specific comments on the town he was playing. He had no idea where this meditative skill had come from, nor did he want to. In his experience it was the performers who analysed their work too closely that ended up as politically correct castrati, bleating out tedious observations and petrified of losing market share by causing some offence.

Sammy held up his right hand and studied it carefully, from the nicotine-yellow fingernails to the clumps of black hair on the first joint of each finger. He traced the course of the blue-green veins — like creepers slowly throttling the life out of a tree — to the white crescent scar on the side of his thumb left by a dog bite on his twelfth birthday, and the skin, translucent and shiny like paper wrapped round greasy food. What was happening beneath all this banality? He flexed his fingers, balled them into a fist. Sammy thought back to the signet ring he had once worn on his little finger, and the damage it had caused.

"Fuck it," he said out loud, baulking at his train of thought. Sammy switched on the television and flicked through the channels, anything to detract from the emotions clammering for admission. There was the usual crap, the endless exhortations to decorate improve buy buy buy which the comedian understood were all variations on his own profession. He plucked a DVD at random from the rack, placed it in the player's tray and returned to the couch. First came titles outlined in fluorescent purple, then teasing five-second clips, and finally the film itself began, set in a hotel where all the guests appeared to be nymphomaniac teenage girls. Samuels unzipped his trousers and settled back. He needed to wank himself into the right frame of mind for tomorrow's meeting, and if his cock was sore by the time he had achieved some degree of tolerance towards the half-wits who ran the pier's parent company then that was a risk Sammy was prepared to take.

# The Karmic Imperative

The doodle was a series of concentric isosceles triangles, immaculately drawn, with precise straight lines and equal spacing. Julian J Walker took great care with each triangle. Indeed, if anyone had asked him at that precise moment whether he was concentrating more on the telephone call or the doodle he would probably have been unable to say with any degree of certainty. He found the symmetry of the triangles soothing, which was as well, because the longer the phone call went on, the shorter his patience grew.

"I can't make a decision based on something you might have heard at a party," he protested. "I'm not writing a bloody gossip column."

"C'mon, Mr Walker, you know me better than that." The woman on the other end of the line possessed a strident Mid-Western American accent which, during its fibre-optic journey beneath the Atlantic, had acquired a sibilant quality that was setting the managing director's teeth on edge.

"Do I?" Julian countered. "You told me not long ago that Matt Damon was going to be filming here. I made sure all the local media got the story, then when nothing happened I had to sack one of my PR team so that *I* didn't look like a complete idiot."

"His publicist," she persisted heavily, "told me that Matt had seen a documentary about the town and he said to them that it looked like a cool place. Don't shoot the messenger."

Julian finished another triangle. "Why not? Why shouldn't

the messenger be shot if they keep bringing the wrong message? If I had a gun and you were standing in front of me now, Carmen, *I'd* shoot *you*. Bang. Right through the forehead. You wouldn't feel a thing."

"That isn't funny, Mr Walker."

"Who says I'm joking?"

Five thousand miles away Carmen took a deep breath of pine-scented San Fernando air. "Okay. It's late, I should be in bed, but I rang you first because I figured you ought to know what I'd heard. If you don't want to listen…hey, that's up to you. You're the boss."

Julian glanced at his watch. "What time is it there?"

"Nearly three in the morning. Why?"

"Just checking to see how dedicated you are."

"And have I passed your little test?"

"Oh, without a doubt."

There was a pause. The phone line was so clear Julian could hear the unmistakable sound of an American police siren in the distance.

"Mr Walker?"

"Carmen?"

"Nathan, you know, the guy I was talking to, he *is* an associate producer, and he *does* get to hear about casting decisions. We're not talking about the catering assistant here."

Julian started to shade the innermost triangle. "They're often the ones who know the most. As far as the sort of people you mix with are concerned catering assistants and such-like are invisible… plates just magically appear in front of them, then *poof!* they're gone again, but these invisible people have ears. They can *hear* what's being discussed."

"Every now and then you remind me how you got to be MD, Julian." Carmen unclipped one earring and gently massaged the lobe of her ear. "Okay, here's the deal. This guy Mike Kavana, the one from the Aussie soap *Sunset Beach* who's trying his hand at singing… the guy that's supposed to be coming to *you* for the summer season, is being lined up for a big part in the next Michael Mann movie. He's as good as signed, if he hasn't already. I don't want you to lose a chunk of your star billing halfway through the season, or maybe even sooner than that, because you'd blame me for not doing my job. He'll sign for you, because he's not stupid and he knows a studio contract might never materialise, so it's as well to have a back-up plan, but if Hollywood says yes he'll be out of your theatre so quick you won't have time to bring the curtain down."

The EuroEnts Managing Director smiled ruefully to himself.

"You've lived in LA for too long, Carmen. You can't tell the difference between a script and real life any more. I've got Mike Kavana's signature on a contract, and he'll be here next month to honour that deal. I only hope he doesn't find out how little faith you have in him." He glanced at his watch. "Anyway, you're missing out on your beauty sleep, so I won't keep you any longer. Thanks for the call."

"Okay, Julian, but don't say I didn't warn you. Call me the next time you're in town. I'll take you to Spago's for dinner."

"I will. Goodnight, Carmen. Sweet dreams."

He replaced the receiver and sat back for a moment, then swivelled round to his laptop and keyed in the password. Opening an anonymous folder tucked safely away in a remote corner of the computer's hard drive, Julian clicked on a sub-folder labelled *Pier Theatre* and moved the cursor down a list of headings until he came to *Summer Season Spoilers*. Clicking again, he read the bullet points and added the line *Mike Kavana leaves to star in film*. Re-reading all the entries, including his latest addition, Julian tapped out a staccato rhythm of pleasure on the laptop's hard plastic deck. When the decisions of others, taken in offices and boulevard cafes and cocaine-fuelled parties thousands of miles away, so dovetailed and enhanced his own plans, it could only mean that *his* was the righteous cause, the karmic imperative.

There was an inevitability to the sequence of events that gave Julian a feeling of destiny, as though some higher power were guiding him towards greater and greater success. Business rivals had always regarded his uncle's acumen and foresight with envy, even wonder; thirty years later the company his uncle founded had become a household name, a byword for leisure and entertainment, and now that he was in charge they would have to accord him a similar degree of respect.

He closed the secret folder. The computer's desktop displayed a tranquil palm-fringed island, sandwiched between a turquoise sea and cobalt sky. Julian wondered what it felt like to be wealthy enough to buy an island like that, to possess the kind of mindset which meant that whatever you thought of, no matter how extravagant, you could have, without having to consider either the cost, the process or the consequences.

He wrote *WorldEnts* next to the triangles. *GlobalEnts.* What other words were there for the planet? *Walker Worldwide. WorldWalker. Walker—*

The intercom buzzer startled him out of his reverie. Julian pushed the flashing button. "Yes?"

"David Clark's arrived? The pier manager? Your eleven o'clock meeting?"

Samantha, his PA, was an efficient young woman, with a truculent air he approved of, but she suffered from a habit which seemed to afflict many of her generation, that of ending each sentence with a rising intonation that turned every statement into a question.

"Oh, right." Julian exhaled loudly. He had arranged the meeting as a means of reinforcing the impression that he was committed to the pier theatre's long-term survival, even though plans for its re-development were safely stored on his laptop. To defuse the anger of both staff and conservationists Julian had realised quite some time ago that he had to seem to be trying to keep the theatre going, and part of this charade involved going through the normal business processes: booking acts, setting up seasonal shows, fixing maintenance schedules, in short, appearing to be fully involved with the day-to-day running of the pier. Hence that morning's summer season planning meeting, even though he regarded David Clark as just the kind of old-fashioned, *laissez-faire* manager who had no part to play in the future of EuroEnts. Sammy Samuels was even worse, a foul-mouthed comic whose heyday lay thirty years in the past and who had only taken up residence at the end of the pier because there was nowhere else for him to go. Having these anachronisms cluttering up his schedule irked Julian greatly, but he was sufficiently astute to recognise their importance in bolstering the impression of business-as-usual. If he could convince David and Sammy that the company was not operating a secret agenda then their confidence in the theatre's future would percolate through to the rest of the staff, leaving Julian free to orchestrate its demise without interference, whilst at the same time appearing blameless as to the outcome.

He pressed the intercom button. "Send them in in five minutes, Samantha. I've got a personal call to make."

David Clark squinted at his reflection in the stainless steel plaque as he attempted to adjust his tie, bending his knees to avoid the etched lettering *EuroEnts Ltd & Walker Holdings*.

Sammy Samuels watched the pier manager with undisguised contempt. "What the fuck are you pratting about at? Anybody'd think you were here for a job interview."

"That's what it feels like," David replied. "With Julian *every* meeting's like a job interview. He said to me only last week that the company was facing a challenging year, and that the days of a guaranteed job were over."

The comedian shook his head. "He's just playing management mind games with you, but you're too bloody naive to see it. They always come out with crap like that before the start of the season… it's supposed to make us all work like niggers and not complain."

"I find that word offensive, if you don't mind."

"What? Complain?"

David patted down his fringe. "You know what I mean."

"You worry too much," Samuels concluded. "A fella your size shouldn't be getting so stressed. You'll keel over with a heart attack and then it won't matter to you *what* happens to the theatre."

"Thanks for your concern." The pier manager pressed the intercom button, and moments later a metallic voice enquired, "Can I help you?"

"Oh, yes," he stuttered. "Hello...it's David Clark and Sammy Samuels... We've got a meeting with Mr Walker."

There was a pause. "Ah, yes." The lock buzzed, and as David pushed open the door he stopped and turned to Sammy, who bumped into him. "You do realise that whatever you say in this meeting will affect a lot of people, not just you? Headliner or not, you're part of a team, and it doesn't matter whether you think Julian is playing 'mind games' or not, people's livelihoods are on the line. Just try to remember that you're in the managing director's office, not on stage. The same rules don't apply."

Samuels backed away slightly. Pursed lips and a nod of the head seemed to suggest that he was seriously weighing up the pier manager's words, an impression strengthened when he placed one hand on David's shoulder in what appeared to be a gesture of solidarity. But when David saw the cold malevolence in Sammy's eyes he knew there was to be no concurrence.

"I'm Sammy Samuels," he whispered. "People recognise me all over the country. D'you know how I know? I see them looking. I see them pointing. They *pay* to come and see me. They'll pay to come and see me wherever I am. Any theatre, any town. Doesn't matter where. Speak like that to me again, sunshine, and you'll be looking for a new star of the fucking show. You got that?"

For a moment the pier manager wondered whether it would be worth calling the comedian's bluff. If Samuels did walk out he would be free of his jibes and bullying, with the added bonus of seeing him fined for breach of contract, and yet if he stayed Sammy's position would inevitably be weakened. Either outcome was tempting, but then a mental image flashed into David's head, an image of him walking on stage to explain to the audience that the main act would not be appearing, that of course their money would be refunded, and that as he spoke there would be Julian J Walker in the front row, stony-faced as he made a note in his electronic organiser.

David Clark turned away from the rain-flecked abstractions of the resort and headed into the bright, anodyne, rational offices of EuroEnts, all too aware that he had gifted the comedian yet another victory in their ongoing battle of wills.

"Does anybody actually know what these things *mean*?" Sammy enquired, peering at one of the framed motivational posters outside Julian's office. "Success depends on brave decisions," he read out loud, then tapped the photograph of a solo climber dangling one-handed from a precipice. "Presumably this fella made the right decision, because they wouldn't use a picture of someone who fell off and spread 'emselves all over the rocks at the bottom, would they? Mind you, you could use a photo of that instead. A body all bashed up, brains and guts all over the place. Underneath it could say *Don't applaud when you're climbing*."

A buzzer sounded on the desk of Julian's PA. She picked up her telephone. "Yes? Yes, they're both here? Certainly." She glanced up at them. "You can go in now?"

David Clark leaped in front of the comedian. For some reason he felt it was essential to enter the managing director's office first.

"Once more unto the breach," he murmured, opening the door.

The EuroEnts empire encompassed two theatres in the

resort as well as the pier, along with a casino, amusement arcades, hotels and a go-kart track. There was also an amusement park in Herefordshire, a theatre in London, numerous villa and apartment complexes dotted around the Mediterranean and, the chairman's latest baby, a non-league football club who, he insisted, would be playing Manchester United within ten years. All this had grown from William Walker's first business venture, an apartment block in Torremolinos purchased just as the British began to flock to Spain. Further shrewd investments along the Costa del Sol made William a millionaire by the time he was thirty, and since then he had developed his company into one of the major players of the leisure industry, timing each acquisition to perfection as he anticipated a succession of trends. Thirty years of success saw William become one of the top five hundred richest people in the country, but his wealth never seemed to sit easily with the boy from Salford. He drove a ten-year-old Mercedes, frequently turned up to board meetings wearing golf shoes and the jacket and trousers from two different suits, and once famously pronounced that anyone who says they like caviar is a liar. Happily married for forty years, he and Esther had two daughters, neither of whom showed any desire to have a role in the family business, which left the way open for his brother's son, who signalled his intent whilst in charge of the amusement park by tripling its profits within two years. Julian achieved this by re-writing employment contracts, bringing in more cheap foreign labour, increasing the rent for all franchises in the park, and lowering the age limit for an adult ticket from sixteen to twelve. None of these measures, naturally, were accepted without protest from both staff and visitors, but a board dominated by accountants saw only the bottom line and recommended him for promotion. William, whose deteriorating health overcame any misgivings about his nephew's suitability for the role, agreed to the move, in effect signing over the day-to-day running of EuroEnts to Julian whilst retaining the notional title of chairman.

Less than eighteen months after this transfer of power, William had become marginalised to such an extent that his appearance at the company's AGM consisted of nothing more than a slightly rambling introductory statement, followed by lunch with the only two members of the board he still knew by name. Julian naturally showered praise on his uncle during his speech, asserting that his own business plan was only a natural progression from William's pioneering and shrewd empire-building, and that under his guidance EuroEnts would benefit from greater financial stability and efficiency. William, and his few remaining allies, predicted a turbulent and diminished future for the company.

Julian stepped from behind his crescent-shaped desk and strode towards David, right arm outstretched. The ceiling spotlamps reflected off his narrow, angular-framed glasses like the warning sweep of a lighthouse.

"Hi… David!" he enthused, shaking the pier manager's hand whilst gripping his forearm with his left hand. "How are you? Good? Great! Great. Excellent." His gaze drifted past David to Sammy.

"Ah, the star of the show!"

"Too fucking right," Sammy muttered under his breath.

"I'm sorry?"

"Nothing." The comedian beamed unconvincingly at Julian. "Just chewing on a brick. I'm under strict instructions not to say a word."

"Really? Why's that?"

"He's just joking, Julian," David said hurriedly. "You know what comedians are like."

"Ah… yes," Julian replied, his tone of voice implying not only that he did *not* know what comedians were like, but also that he regarded such knowledge as supremely unimportant. "I must find the time to catch your show one weekend, Sammy. I hear the numbers aren't bad for this time of year."

"Could be worse."

"Don't be modest," David interjected. "We're up on last year—"

Samuels snorted. "That wouldn't be difficult."

"We're up on last year," the pier manager persisted, "and Ian's karaoke nights seem to be bringing in a fair few on Fridays."

"Excellent," Julian said, removing all connotations of jubilation from the word and reducing it to a collection of workman-like syllables. "Hopefully we can take advantage of Club Tropicana's little licensing problem, which I'm keeping a *very* careful eye on. I can't understand why underage girls would want to go to an Eighties club anyway, it's hardly their musical era, is it?"

"Eighties music's enjoying something of a revival with teenagers, apparently," David explained.

"Really?"

"Well, it is according to my daughter," he continued, anxious not to make the managing director seem ignorant or out-of-touch.

"She's been borrowing all my Ultravox records... She says they're 'retro', which makes me feel *extremely* old."

Julian smiled briefly. "I wouldn't worry about that too much, David. Retro seems to mean anything more than five years old these days. Still, it might be worth our while setting up an Eighties night somewhere if you think there's enough of a market for it. Club Tropicana doesn't have exclusive rights to that kind of music, does it?"

"And it'll give all those underage drinkers somewhere to go," Sammy added.

"I don't think Julian—"

"I'm *kidding*," the comedian replied heavily. "It's a *joke*. You remember them, don't you? Like, what's the similarity between a woman and a tornado?"

The pier manager glared at Sammy. "This is neither the time nor the place... "

Julian, who had studied this brief exchange with a

psychiatrist's analytical interest, touched his top lip with one index finger as though gesturing for silence. "No, no, let him finish." The finger pointed briefly at Samuels like a floor manager's cue. "What *is* the similarity between a woman and a tornado?"

Sammy paused, just for a moment. There were only two men in front of him, but they still constituted an audience, and his innate sense of timing took over. "They both moan like hell when they're coming and then they take the house when they leave."

For one terrifying moment, as Julian's expression did not alter, David thought the managing director might throw them out of his office. Following on from this ejection, like some devastating chain reaction, he saw the summer season cancelled, the theatre falling into disrepair, its closure and demolition, all within the time it took for Julian to smile faintly and nod some sort of benediction in the direction of Sammy's joke.

"Ah, yes. Very good. I should imagine that sort of material goes down well with the stag parties."

Samuels tried to detect an expression of sarcasm or ridicule in Julian's eyes, but the window's reflection in his glasses turned both lenses into concealing mirrors. "I've had no complaints."

"I'm sure you haven't. Anyway, we'd better get on to the business of sorting out next summer's season. Once that's out of the way we can have lunch. I thought we might try Franco's... my treat."

David's eyes widened. "Franco's?"

"Would you prefer to go somewhere else?"

Sammy stepped in front of the pier manager. "Pay no attention to this pillock. Franco's'll be fine. It's all tax deductible anyway, isn't it?"

"I think you'll find that the taxman keeps a far closer eye on things than he did in your day, Sammy," Julian replied. The tone of his voice was so neutral that it was impossible to tell whether he meant the statement to be derogatory or informative.

The comedian, disarmed by this inert style of speech, sat down in the seat offered to him without further comment, followed by David, who sank into the adjacent chair. The pier manager felt that some kind of crisis point had been negotiated, but as little more than the introductions had been completed he could not afford to relax just yet. He felt drained by the verbal jousting and powerplay, and by the sense that, unfairly or not, he would be held responsible for anything controversial Samuels said. And yet, no matter how torrid the meeting turned out, it would have been worthwhile if only to witness how Julian handled Samuels. The managing director's deadpan technique, coupled with a sort of amused tolerance, certainly seemed to strike a responsive chord within the comedian. Was this, David wondered, the kind of template he should be employing?

Julian's finger hovered over the intercom button as though about to initiate a nuclear holocaust. "Tea? Coffee? Fruit juice? Mineral water? Something a bit stronger? I think we've got most things. Name your poison."

"Coffee's fine, thanks," David said. He chuckled and added, "I don't think the sun's quite over the yardarm yet, anyway."

Sammy shifted round in his chair so that he could glower directly at the pier manager. "Who d'you think you are, Prince fucking Charles?"

"Right, gentlemen," Julian continued, blithely ignoring this display of animosity and settling himself in his black leather swivel chair, "How are we going to make this year our best summer ever?"

Two hours later, with ideas mooted, figures discussed, musicians and dancers shortlisted, and a theme for the show decided on of classic Hollywood films combined with 80s music, the EuroEnts Managing Director clicked shut the lid of his laptop with a satisfied flourish before looking back up at the two men on the other side of his desk. *Jesus, what a pair of losers,* he thought.

"Nice work, boys," he said out loud. "I think we've created something truly dynamic between us that will appeal to a broad demographic."

"Come again? Could you say that in English?" Sammy remarked.

Julian looked amused. "I'm sorry, Sammy, I sometimes forget not everyone is quite up to speed with the current terminology. I spend too much time in meetings... we tend to develop a language all of our own." He patted the laptop. "What I meant was it's a good show with something for everyone. Mmm," he savoured the sentence, swirling it round in his mouth like a fine wine. "There's something to be said for plain speaking, isn't there. Making a connection to the man in the street. My uncle would have approved."

The comedian scrutinised the younger man's face, hoping to glimpse the slightest sign of condescension, because if he had he would punch him and accept the consequences later, but there was nothing but a bland, even scrupulous neutrality.

David and Sammy were being ushered towards the office door when the managing director suddenly stopped. "Oh, I almost forgot. Sammy, can I have a word in private? You don't mind, do you David? It'll only take a minute."

The pier manager smiled and gestured magnanimously. "No, no, of course not."

"Good man. Appreciate that."

As soon as the office door clicked shut Julian walked over to the window and looked out. For perhaps ten seconds there was silence. Sammy stayed where he was, indifferent to whatever was to come.

"Come and look at this," Julian said at last. He glanced back over his shoulder. "Come on, it sums up what I've got to say to you."

Sammy sighed extravagantly, walked slowly over to the window and looked out. The EuroEnts offices were on the corner of the promenade and a street that led into the town centre, and from the managing director's office there was a clear view of both the promenade and the pier. Several small groups of tourists could be seen battling their way along the prom, a firm grip on the hoods of their cagoules. There was also a young man in a T-shirt and combat shorts, posing near the promenade railings for his girlfriend as coffee-coloured waves crashed over the sea wall.

"The British public at play," Julian observed drily. He looked to his left at Sammy Samuels. "I get the impression you're a man who favours plain speaking. Am I right?"

"You are."

"Yes. Well, in that case, allow me to speak plainly. You do not fit in with my long-term plans for this resort. Your time has been and gone, and you're now relying on former glories to draw in an audience." Julian saw that Sammy was about to say something, so he raised one hand in a conciliatory gesture. "Which is fine, it really is. Honestly, it's what most performers do, the ones who've been lucky enough to have had a career high point, anyway. It just doesn't suit my plans. However, EuroEnts has a number of hotels and leisure complexes along the Spanish Costas whose clientele would, I'm sure, thoroughly enjoy watching a comedy legend at work. An hour a night, with the rest of your time free to soak up the sun and enjoy the rather more... relaxed tax arrangements out there. How does that sound? Be honest."

Sammy puffed out his cheeks and raised his eyebrows. "It sounds too fucking good to be true."

Julian's expression altered subtly, conveying both an acknowledgement of the suspicious assessment and a rebuttal of it. "What if it wasn't?"

"Then it'd be fucking marvellous."

"That's what I hoped you'd say." Julian had turned back to continue his perusal of those hardy souls on the promenade, as though emphasising the clandestine nature of their conversation.

"There's only one problem standing between us and an outcome which will suit both parties."

"Which is?"

"I've gone through your contract, and our solicitors have done a very thorough job — as I would expect them to, of course — but it seems the only way you're going to be jetting off to the Costa Brava is if it's impossible for the summer season to go ahead."

"What d'you mean?"

"I mean something physically prevents you from being on that stage. It's the only get-out clause I can find."

Sammy's line of sight raised slightly to the pier, which appeared both flimsy and vulnerable from this distance, a child's model of papier-mâché and matchsticks that must surely succumb to the boiling seas around it. "Why not just sack me, and then sign me up again for the Spanish gig?"

Julian grimaced, as though Sammy had thrust something unpleasant under his nose. "That brings my decision-making into question, don't you think? It's too obvious, anyway." He ran the fingers of both hands through his hair. "I'm sure you'll think of something, you're a resourceful chap. Come on, we've kept David waiting long enough. He'll be thinking we're talking about him."

Sammy turned away from the rainswept promenade. "Oh, on a different subject altogether, there *is* one thing I've always wondered, and if I don't ask now I never will."

"What's that?"

He reached the desk and lifted the heavy, prism-shaped black marble name plate engraved with Julian J Walker. "What does the 'J' stand for?"

The EuroEnts managing director laughed. "You really want to know? If I tell you, can I trust you to keep it a secret?"

"Cross my heart and hope to die."

"If you tell anyone you will. It doesn't stand for anything. I haven't got a middle name, but I once read an article that said using a middle initial confers added gravitas and memorability, so I thought I'd give myself one." Julian took the lump of marble and rotated it, as though entranced by either the reflections or joyous concatenation of his engraved name. "I tried quite a few letters, but I liked how the 'J' sounded best. It does scan rather well, don't you think? Julian J Walker. Much more interesting than plain old Julian Walker. I might even become JJ Walker when I'm a bit older, or even just JJ. You know you've made it when just two initials are enough. So, now you know my secret. We should pledge an oath of allegiance."

Sammy again looked closely at the younger man, and again failed to discern any particular emotion. "The only allegiances I trust are signed contracts."

"Very wise." He replaced his name on the desk, positioning it carefully so that it faced the office door. "Come on, let's get over to Franco's before they give my table away."

# A Heart Less Rosy

*MASSAGE*, proclaimed the flashing pink neon sign in the window, its strident voice softened somewhat by the net curtains, which were a grubby grey save for the sign's aurora, grubby grey curtains with a beating coral heart. MASSAGE was its collection of letters, but it might just as well have spelled out FRESH FISH, or NUCLEAR MISSILE SILO, for all that it related to the business within. But when the inaccuracy of its declaration was so widely ignored could it be seen as deception? Or was the sign's fiction necessary in order that it might disarm the truth?

Whatever the answer, Sammy Samuels was unconcerned with its procurement. He had been distracted with what the bogus-initialled Julian J Walker had said to him, in their slightly surreal moment of candour two days ago, regarding his future employment within EuroEnts. The shock of his brutal relegation, followed almost immediately by the managing director's startling proposition, dangled before him like a mocking vision that could never be realised. At first the comedian had felt simply bemused, but now, now he was angry, not only because it had so clearly been formulated without any kind of acknowledgement of his standing in the business, his *pedigree*, but also because such blatant manipulation reflected Julian's low opinion of Sammy. Was that all he thought of him, that he judged a crude good-cop-bad-cop stratagem sufficient? And what was he expecting him to do in order that it would be 'physically impossible' for

Sammy to perform? Hire an assassin to bump off the rest of the cast? Feign temporary madness? Burn down the theatre? And then there was the business about his middle initial; was all that bullshit as well? Did that cretinous J really exist, or was it nothing more than the bastard offspring of Julian's ego and some nonsensical bit of cod-psychology? And whatever the truth, was the managing director sharing his 'secret' as a roundabout way of eliciting some form of allegiance?

The comedian decided, after going over these questions again and again without coming to any kind of satisfactory answer, that there was only one way to clear his head, which was what had brought him to his present location outside the massage parlour, silhouetted in the glow of the neon sign, a head full of cocaine and a heart less rosy than the one possessed by the grubby grey curtains. One of the girls would take his mind off the conundrums of Julian J Walker and give him a good night's sleep into the bargain; it seemed the only times he slept well these days was after visiting one of these anaesthetising establishments.

Sammy opened the door with the calm indifference of someone entering a newsagents, and the two girls, one behind a desk, the other perched on a stool next to the desk, turned to examine the customer and immediately noted this composure, because their senses were necessarily attuned to the demeanour of men. This was not a first-timer, they deduced, the ones propelled across the threshold with the slightest of hesitations, all stag night bravado lost in that one step, or virgins brave enough to seek professional assistance in the removal of their innocence. Here was a man well-versed in their trade, and in many ways as detached from it as they were themselves.

"Hi there, love," the girl behind the desk greeted him in a broad Scouse accent. "Y'alright?"

Sammy looked at her huge hoop earrings and fake tan, then at the girl on the stool, and back to the earrings. He shut the door behind him with a bang. "Does it matter if I'm alright? Are you really interested? Yes, I'm alright. Is that what you wanted to know?" He made a dramatic show of taking his pulse at his wrist. "Yep, still beating."

There was a prolonged silence. The tan and earrings seemed unsure how to respond to this irascible customer. The tan paled, the earrings swayed backwards and forwards, dragging their suspending lobes with them, a fleshy undulation. Then the girl remembered her smile, which she brandished like some gaudy trinket, revealing large, slab-like teeth smudged with lipstick.

"That's good." She shuffled slightly on her chair. "Are you looking for a bit of business, darlin'?"

Sammy looked round the room, as though seeking some clue as to the nature of the business. "Well I'm not here looking for a lost cat."

"Alright," she replied, finding her courage from the solidity of the desk between them, "there's no need to be sarky. We only want to give you a good time."

"A good time," he repeated, as though she was referring to some event from ancient history.

"So, who would you like for your massage?" she said, maintaining the parody of the sign.

The comedian looked from one girl to the other. The one behind the desk had dark hair scraped back into a ponytail, gentle hazel eyes and a curvaceous body that would, he thought, soon run to fat, her flesh constrained by a tight-fitting black-and-white striped dress. There was a tide-mark along the side of her neck where she had forgotten to rub in her fake tan. The other girl, who had remained silent throughout, had shoulder-length blonde hair, blue eyes, and pale skin stretched over a skinny frame. Her collar bones jutted out and there was a haunted quality behind her eyes, a shadow that spoke of some deep melancholy.

"Is it just the two of you?"

"There's another girl normally, but her little girl's ill so she's had to stop at home to look after her."

"I'm not interested in your staffing problems," Sammy snapped. He looked at them both for a moment longer. "You'll do," he said to the blonde, who immediately hopped off the stool and walked over to a cupboard, took out a towel and tucked it under her arm. She appeared to be completely insensible to the comedian's disparaging acceptance.

"Come on," she said, making her way towards a doorway shielded by a curtain of sparkling silver ribbons.

Sammy followed her through the curtain, which parted to reveal a dimly lit staircase. As he followed her up the steep stairs Sammy could see below the hem of her short skirt to the crease where buttock met thigh, alternating as she took each step, and a white lace pair of knickers, but for Sammy there was nothing remotely erotic about this view. A warm mouth and a lively tongue were all that interested him.

She lead him into a sparsely furnished room, illuminated by nothing but a string of Christmas tree lights draped over the headboard of its rumpled bed. The only thing on the walls was a Johnny Depp calendar. Placing the towel on the bedside table, the girl sat down on the edge of the bed, crossed her legs and looked up at him.

"So... what would you like?"

Sammy looked down at her. In the oblique white light from the tree lights he could see small, scabbed puncture wounds on the girl's forearms. Like so many of the resort's addicts, this one funded her habit through prostitution. "A blow-job," he pronounced.

She nodded. "That'll be twenty quid. Do you want to come in my mouth?"

Sammy, who was already unzipping his trousers, looked up.

"Yeah. Why, is that a problem?"

"No, but it's another fiver."

"A fiver?"

"Yeah. Toothpaste... mouthwash... they all cost money."

The comedian had taken a shine to the girl's candid,

prosaic attitude. "Fair enough. I don't want to leave you with a nasty taste in your mouth."

"Ha ha," she said heavily.

He unbuttoned his trousers, let them fall to the floor and stepped out of their crumpled concertina. When Sammy saw his legs — white and hairless, with almost no muscle tone to give definition to their bony cylinders — they reminded him of the ones which had dangled from beneath his father's shorts during that last summer before he died.

The girl began to unfold the towel and spread it over the bed, for all the world like a young mother smoothing the duvet cover of her child, because sometimes the only difference between the most virtuous and wanton of acts is context.

"No, no," Sammy said, "I prefer to be stood up. You can kneel on the floor in front of me."

The girl looked back over her shoulder. "Aren't you the bossy one?"

"That's just how I like it." The comedian had been accustomed to taking his pleasure in the prone position until, one evening in Newcastle, a bad back forced him to remain standing. The feeling of dominance and control had proved so satisfying that he had adopted it as his default option.

The girl pulled an expression that said 'fair enough, it's all the same to me', then without another word re-folded the towel, lay it at Sammy's feet, knelt on it and reached up for his underpants. In an attempt to bring at least a notional eroticism to the act that was both touching and yet, in the circumstances, quite pathetic, she ran her fingers round the elastic waist of his pants for a few seconds before slowly pulling them down, then opened her mouth and began to suck vigorously on his flaccid penis. Sammy lifted the flaps of his shirt out of the way to better observe the prostitute, whose centre-parted hair formed a dark-rooted pathway to his belly button. She was no expert, but the girl took to her task with a vigour that might have been relish, or more likely a desire to have the deed done as quickly as possible, and was encouraged in her work as she felt his cock grow firmer. Sammy sighed and closed his eyes. The swish of traffic on the wet street faded, carrying away on its flowing static the questions and internal debate that had plagued him, until all his mind could hold, all it *wished* to hold, was the wet roaming warmth around his penis and the occasional snag of teeth that, far from distracting or lessening the rising pleasure, served only to heighten the vulnerability demanded of him by the act, the vulnerability which a deeply buried remnant of Sammy Samuels craved.

Her tongue ran around the rim of his circumcised glans, a deft manoeuvre that proved decisive, extracting a sudden tightening of his scrotum and a brief but intense orgasm. He ejaculated with a grunt, and to her credit the girl hardly flinched, accepting this stranger's semen as professionally as she knew how. He managed another small dollop before withdrawing, the girl reached over to a box of tissues, plucked one out and spat her mouthful into it, folded it neatly and dropped it in a small metal bin which had Disney cartoon characters transfer-printed around it.

She rose from her position of prayer, knee joints cracking, and sat down on the edge of the bed. "There," she said, and there was job satisfaction in that word, but also a concluding note, a reminder that their transaction was only half-finished. "Was that alright?"

Sammy replied whilst hoisting his underpants. "Not bad. I haven't seen you here before, have I? What's your name?"

"Debs. What's yours?"

"Sammy."

The girl clicked her fingers and pointed at him. "I *knew* I knew you! You're the bloke on the pier, aren't you? The comedian. I've seen you on posters and stuff."

"That's me," he confirmed. Sammy reached down for his trousers and pulled them up. Their brief intimacy was at an end. He had no desire for it to be prolonged any further. "I suppose you'll be after some free tickets now."

Debs eyebrows lifted. "Can I?"

"I'll sort something out." He opened his wallet, counted out several notes and held them towards the prostitute, but when she reached for them Sammy withdrew his hand so that the money remained just out of her grasp. "How much did you say? Fifteen quid, wasn't it?"

"Twenty-five! You said that was alright."

His expression shifted to incomprehension. "Sorry, darling, I don't remember that. I'm sure it was fifteen."

Debs again made a grab for the cash in his hand, but again Sammy jerked it away. "Come on," she pleaded. "Don't fuck me about. You know we agreed twenty-five."

The comedian laughed and shook his head, but this movement dislodged the white beads of light from the Christmas tree decorations, which began to float around the room like the smeared gobs of light from the lap dancing club's glitterball, creating a similarly disorientating effect. Sammy opened his eyes wide, squeezed them shut, opened them again, but the phantom glitterball was still rotating, spinning faster and faster. "We agreed fuck all, darling. Now, are you going to take this fifteen quid or what?"

"You bastard," Debs said vehemently. "I'll put the word out about you... You won't get away with this crap again." He shrugged. "There are girls under the arches on west promenade that'll do it for a fiver, love, so you can do what you fucking well like." The comedian threw the three five-pound notes in her general direction, then watched in confusion as instead of fluttering to the ground the notes were swept up by the lights as though they had fallen into an illuminated tornado, and then a voice from many years ago, spoken less than a mile from where he was standing now, slipped through his head like a piece of debris spat out from the storm. 'You always loved him more than your father.'

Sammy shook his head, glanced up at the ceiling and was astonished to see a Winnie the Pooh lampshade, laughed out loud at the incongruity of it, and when he looked back down the money was lying on the thin carpet amongst the cigarette burns and other stains, about to be picked up by Debs. When she scowled at him the shadows in her eyes had assumed the tempo of the spinning lights and were drifting across her pale blue irises like clouds in a November sky. "I bet the newspapers'd be interested in the sort of things you get up to... *and* what a cheating bastard you are," she surmised. "I might just give 'em a call tomorrow and tell them all about it."

The lights were spinning ever faster, dragging the bedroom into their orbit. Sammy squeezed hard on the sides of his nose, fighting back a sudden wave of nausea; it felt exactly the same as that night in the lap dancing club, and for a moment he wondered whether this was some sort of divine punishment for a life of such blatant immorality. The prostitute's narrow features metamorphosed into a skull-like mask which hung before him, malevolent and triumphant, a composite of all the people who had tried to take advantage of him over the years, their smug, contemptuous faces which regarded Sammy Samuels as though he were something they had found on the sole of their shoe, and now this *whore*, with her crude threats, thought that she too could treat him like a fool.

His hands flexed, contorted into fists, and before he really knew what he was doing Sammy flailed out, his left hand catching the girl on her temple, his right just below her eye. "Don't fucking try to blackmail me!" She dropped to the floor and curled into a foetal position, her arms tucked around her head in an instinctive protective embrace. He continued to pummel at the exposed side of her body and hip, the blows timed to accentuate his words. "I know... everybody... in this... town! Everybody! You haven't... got... a fucking... chance... of proving... anything! Don't even... think about it."

And then it was finished. His hands dropped to his sides, all the fury in them suddenly extinguished, but the swirling lights continued to cocoon him in his own personal galaxy, following as he turned and stumbled out of the room, clattered down the stairs, crossed the reception area without acknowledging the other girl, where the neon sign in the window, now brazen without its mitigating curtains, burnt its cryptic brand ƎƆAƧƧAM into his eyes. Out, out he went, his heart hammering, fear gripping his stomach as a tingle arced along the nerves in his left arm, into the night whose gloom only heightened the disorienting lightshow that Sammy could not shake off, could not even decide whether it was inside or outside his head. "What's happening to me?" he asked silently once more, but the moon beamed down and remained silent, for it spoke only through the tide, which was diligently binding a dead seagull in discarded netting and would not be distracted from its task.

The comedian was expecting the police, and they duly came, a knock on the door waking him from a dreamless sleep. Their black bulk and crackling radio messages filled the doorway of Sammy's flat with an unequivocal authority, but they were polite and non-judgmental, young men whose self-righteousness had been blunted by their work. Humanity is weak, the resort had taught them. It has constructed many gods in order that, once led into temptation, men and women can rail at these deities, crying out that they demand too much, and then blame them for their flaws. Terrible things are visited upon the good, while the bad prosper, and what most call morality is in fact a simple fear of anarchy. These were the resort's lessons. Of course the resort attracted a disproportionate number of hedonists and drifters, whose weaknesses were more pronounced, but perhaps they were simply being honest; perhaps the resort was more magnifier than distorting mirror, a realm of indulgence bordered by the more unforgiving sea. And so the policemen disapproved of Sammy's alleged unprovoked assault against a slender and vulnerable young woman, but it did not shock them. A far more profound level of violence was required to do that. What they had retained, however, was their faith in procedure. The resort might have broadened their minds, but they truly believed its excesses would always require the formality and structure of procedure to contain them.

"Are you Samuel Rosenberg?" enquired the older of the officers, whose eyebrows joined in the middle to form a black barrier dividing his face neatly in two and lending him a strangely pious air.

Sammy rubbed his forehead with the palm of one hand.

"Nobody calls me that. I haven't used that name for years."

The policeman glanced at his colleague. "We *are* aware of your stage name, sir."

"Oh right. In that case, yes. That's me."

"Do you mind if we come in?" The policeman gestured, encompassing the whole of Carlton Apartments. "This isn't very private."

"What's this all about?"

The policemen, taking this question as an offer of admittance, shifted their authoritative blackness into the flat's entrance hall. As they did so the second of them, who to Sammy looked hardly old enough to be out at this time of night, said, "An allegation of assault has been made against you, Mr Rosenberg. We need you to come with us to the police station to answer some questions. It shouldn't take too long."

Sammy edged past the jacket and protective vest of the other officer and led them into the lounge. Both policemen cast a professional eye over the framed photographs depicting a fresher-faced Sammy Samuels mingling with royalty and celebrities in a monochrome world that seemed to them utterly removed from the present; the couch and dining chairs draped with clothes, the plate with its smears of dried ketchup, the wooden fruit bowl containing two over-ripe bananas, and a copy of the evening paper lying next to the plate which together formed a sorry tableau on the dining table. They saw all this and understood how meagre the reality behind showbusiness' dazzling facade could be.

"Assault? Who the fuck am I supposed to have assaulted?" Sammy enquired. "Jesus, it's five o'clock in the morning."

The younger officer brought out a small notebook from his breast pocket. "We know what the time is, Mr Rosenberg," he said pointedly, opening the notebook. "Were you in the Jewels massage parlour on Edward Street at around 8pm last night?"

"What?" Sammy looked from one to the other.

"It's a simple question, Mr Rosenberg."

"Oh, I get it," the comedian said, nodding slowly. "I don't know what that stupid bitch has told you, son, but you should know what those girls are like when they don't get their own way. She tried to get more money out of me than we'd agreed and when I refused she started screaming and shouting about going to the papers because she knew who I was, so I chucked some money at her and left."

"So you deny hitting her?"

Sammy raised both arms in a gesture of incomprehension. "Is that what she's saying?"

"She's got a black eye and bruising."

"So what?" A possible defence sprang into his mind, for which he gave silent thanks. "Anybody could have done that." The comedian cast about for examples. "Another 'customer', her fucking *pimp*—"

The officer with the solid eyebrow reached for his radio. "Please don't use language like that, Mr Rosenberg, we're only doing our job. It might be acceptable on stage but I don't want to hear it here." He turned his head slightly and lifted the lapel of his jacket so mouth and radio were close. He pressed a button. "Sarah? We're bringing Mr Rosenberg in for questioning. Can you tell DC McKenzie we'll be there in about fifteen minutes? Thanks." He turned back to Sammy. "Samuel Rosenberg, I am arresting you on suspicion of assault. You do not have to say anything, but it may harm your defence if you do not mention when questioned something which you later rely on in court. Anything you do say may

314

be given in evidence. Do you understand everything I've just said?"

Sammy laughed in disbelief. "You've got to be fucking kidding me. You're going to believe somebody like her rather than me?"

"I haven't said anything of the sort, Mr Rosenberg, and may I remind you that you have been cautioned. Any more abusive language and you'll be leaving here in handcuffs. Is that what you want?"

He shook his head, suddenly subdued. "No, of course not."

"Well calm down then and get dressed. Have you got a lawyer you can call to be with you during questioning?"

Sammy gripped the top of his nose with thumb and middle finger and closed his eyes. "I don't believe this is happening to me. A *lawyer*?"

The younger officer flipped shut his notebook and managed to convey, in that small operation, a feeling of both disdain and condescension that his older colleague disapproved of but which was missed by Sammy, whose eyes were still shut. "Assault is a serious charge, Mr Rosenberg," he advised. "You need to know what the implications are."

Sammy opened his eyes. "Now you're *really* shitting me. What d'you mean, the 'implications'?"

"What he means," the eyebrow interjected, the tone of his voice making clear that he had had enough of the conversation, "is that you need to get your clothes on, get yourself in the back of the car and tell someone where you're going and what you're being arrested for. I presume if you're under contract with EuroEnts they'll have a legal department who can sort out a lawyer for you. Tell them you'll be at the central police station." He fished in a pocket, brought out a bunch of car keys and tossed them to the younger policeman. "Go and open her up, will you?"

The comedian watched the policeman leave, waited until the front door closed and then turned back to the other officer.

"He's a bit up himself, isn't he? Fancy himself as a bit of a tough guy?"

The eyebrow shifted upwards, a miniscule movement and yet more than enough for the comedian's questions to be answered.

"Come on, Sammy," the policeman sighed, "let's get you down the nick. I've had enough of this fucking shift."

"You and me both, mate. You and me both."

# The Spanish Carrot

The Bangles' 'Walk Like An Egyptian' boomed out from speakers on either side of the stage, distorting slightly on the bass notes, whilst on stage five dancers were attempting, with varying degrees of success, to skip across the boards at the same time as holding their hands and arms in the favoured Egyptian dance cliché of straight lines and right angles. They succeeded in reaching the other side of the stage, but while spinning round to head back in the opposite direction two of them caught each other's arms and lost the song's rhythm.

Paddy McNeil, the summer show's director, sprang out of his chair in the auditorium, waving his arms wildly. "Oh my *God*, what are you *doing*?" he cried, his high-pitched, soft Scottish accent overly dramatic and emphatically camp. "Can ye not just even turn *around* without crashing into each other?" He gesticulated to the sound engineer at the back of the theatre. "Stop the music! Stop the music!"

The song's insistent rhythm came to an abrupt halt, leaving the girls stranded mid-stage.

McNeil edged along the row of seats and out into the centre aisle, then strode down to the front of the stage. "It isn't difficult! Just keep the same spacing as you had when you're coming across! Why do you keep bunching up? I know it's a quick rhythm, but honest to God, girls, I've seen more grace and elegance in a post office queue."

Sammy Samuels watched the director's fit of pique with amusement. He had positioned himself some distance from

317

the stage and its bright lights, comfortably concealed in the shadows from where he could observe the dancers and assess both their bodies and whether any of them appeared likely to be interested in a sexual encounter with the star of the show. The added allure of celebrity, even on his relatively minor scale, had never failed to surprise and delight Sammy who, particularly during his early years as a recognisable star, had taken full advantage of it. There had been a more than adequate supply of girls looking to claim either a vicarious trace of fame or a showbusiness opening from their liaison with the comedian, and if their illusions were shattered by the banality of the encounter or Sammy's avoidance of them afterwards then in his eyes at least he had taught them a valuable life lesson, demonstrating to these innocent creatures that the magic of the stage began and ended in the spotlights. There seemed far fewer young women these days who possessed such a naive nature, which could of course have had something to do with his grey hair, yellow teeth and pot belly, but there were still one or two ambitious enough to ignore his physical shortcomings. Sammy had learned over the years to identify certain characteristics which implied such a charitable disposition. A liveliness, perhaps, or sense of humour, or even (and these were the ones that Sammy liked best, as they were the least complicated and understood his own requirements) a scalp-hunter with the unquenchable appetite of any avid collector. These attributes were what he had been looking for in the dancers, but all he had seen so far was a giggling infatuation with their own ineptitude.

The comedian was about to resume his appraisal on a rather more basic level — in other words, which of the dancers had the best legs — when David Clark appeared at the end of the row of seats.

"Sammy? Can I have a word?"

Samuels continued to watch the girls on stage as they prepared yet again to perform their Egyptian dance. "What is it? I'm busy here."

"This is important."

"So is this."

"So is *this*," and on the last word the pier manager took the newspaper he was holding and threw it at Sammy. It hit him on the leg and fell to the floor.

Sammy turned and glared. "What the fuck?"

David pointed angrily at the newspaper. "*Look* at it."

The comedian sighed, leaned down and picked up the paper, which he recognised as the resort's local evening edition. "Injury woes for keeper?"

"The front page!"

The moment he turned the newspaper round to reveal its lead story Sammy understood the pier manager's anger. *ASSAULT ALLEGATION AGAINST STAR* proclaimed the headline, under which was a stark photograph of the girl from the massage parlour, her bruised and swollen features accentuated not only by the harsh flash of a police camera but also by her neutral, even forgiving expression.

"Shit," was all Samuels could think to say.

The pier manager sat down in the seat next to him. "Exactly. And when were you going to tell me about this?"

Sammy frowned. "I didn't think she'd go to the papers. She got a thousand quid out of me. I thought that was the end of it."

"Obviously not."

"No. That fucking bitch. If I'd known she was going to do this I wouldn't have coughed up so quick. Jesus."

David exhaled. 'Walk Like An Egyptian' started up again. "This is all we need. God alone knows what Julian's going to do when he sees this… if he hasn't already."

"I hardly touched her!" Sammy protested, staring down at the photograph.

"You hardly touched her?" The pier manager sounded incredulous. "For God's sake, Sammy, *look* at her!"

The comedian lifted the newspaper out of the shadows, angled it towards the stage lights and peered closely at the picture. "They must have doctored it... you know, on a computer. To make it look worse."

"You really are unbelievable," David said. "You beat up a woman, a *prostitute*, and then accuse the newspaper of fiddling with the picture. Unbelievable."

"They do it all the time!" the comedian protested. "It's just so they can sell more papers. They don't give a shit about her, they just want to embarrass me."

The pier manager leaned away from Sammy, as though suddenly appalled by his proximity to him. "You don't think you've done anything wrong, do you?" he said, the revulsion clear in his voice. "You think this is all some plot to make you look bad. Bloody hell, talk about paranoid. You're going to have to start taking responsibility for your own actions, Sammy. This sort of thing is a clear breach of contract. If Julian wanted to get rid of you you've given him the perfect excuse."

Samuels looked closely at David. Did the pier manager know more about the comedian's private discussion with Julian than he was letting on? Could he even be in league with the EuroEnts boss? Were the two of them playing some sort of game with him for their own amusement? "What makes you think Julian would want to get rid of me? Why would you say that?"

"Because I know what Julian is like. I know he doesn't give a shit about this place, and I suspect he has a similarly cavalier attitude to the people who work in it, which includes you, amazing though that may seem, you being the 'star of the show' and all. We're all just chess pieces on a board to him."

"Yeah," the comedian countered, "but there's normally two people playing chess, isn't there?"

"What?"

"You heard. Strange how you've never said a word about Julian wanting to get rid of me before, and then you both come out with the same thing within a few weeks of each other."

"Julian's *said* that to you?"

"Julian's said that to you?" Sammy repeated, exaggerating the tone of surprise in the pier manager's voice. "Don't treat me like a fucking idiot. I know what the two of you are up to." He tapped the side of his nose. "Well, Sammy's got one or two things up his sleeve as well, sunshine. You just wait and see. Julian *J* Walker's in for a big surprise. My old man didn't teach me much, but he showed me how to recognise a cunt, because there wasn't a bigger cunt on the planet than him. Him and that stupid fortune-teller tried to lay some sort of psychological bullshit on me but I saw straight through them, just like I can with you and Julian. First he dangles the old Spanish carrot in front of me and then you come in with your breach of contract bollocks, and I'm supposed to go down on my knees and beg for forgiveness. Well it won't fucking wash! You won't get me like that!"

"What the hell are you on about? You're not making any sense! Spanish carrot?"

"You know! You fucking know!"

The dancers on stage, distracted by the outburst from the stalls, again lost their rhythm and stumbled to a halt. McNeil sprang out of his seat in the front row and turned to see what the disturbance was.

"Could you two gentlemen *please* find somewhere else to have your argument?" The director pleaded. "These girls are finding it hard enough without you two ranting at each other."

"Sorry, Paddy," David said loudly, then turned back to Sammy and continued speaking more quietly. "We need to have a proper discussion about this, because a) I don't know what the hell you're on about and b) we need to think of a reason why Julian shouldn't just cancel the whole bloody season and stick one of his sodding rollercoasters on the end of the pier."

Sammy, however, was already levering himself upright. "You," he snapped, screwing up the newspaper and throwing it on the floor, "can go fuck yourself."

The comedian edged along the row of seats, holding on to the backs of the row in front to help mitigate the dizzying swirl of lights which had flowed down from above the stage to encircle him and form an amalgamated reality, part pole-dancing club, part prostitute's bedroom, part pier theatre, where Amanda and the prostitute and the dancers blended into some sort of combined uber-eroticised girl. She pirouetted in front of him, this creature of pure carnality, tantalisingly out of reach, her smile gleaming like a beacon in the darkness beyond the red and green blurs. She guided him into the soft harbour of her ever-willing mouth, while also leading him away from the puzzled eyes, up the central aisle and out of the double doors, through the foyer and out, out onto the pier.

While its unquestionable solidity brought some measure of calm to Sammy Samuels' turmoil, there was a part of him now that welcomed the tumult, found both solace and impetus within it, a freedom that the linear, the cast iron, could never offer. Perhaps, he concluded, if the world was spinning out of control the only way to cope was to follow a similar trajectory.

He weaved and tottered as quickly as he could towards the resort, hoping to be free of the pier's influence quickly enough so that he could reach his flat, masturbate while the dizziness lasted, and watch enchanted as his ejaculation added a stream of glowing semen to the churning maternal lights.

# The Friable Fabric of History

A balding, shambolic figure stepped warily onto the pier, scuffed shoes barely clearing the boards with each step. It appeared their owner distrusted the silver-grey planking, believing it might vanish from beneath him if contact was lost between sole and wood and leave him, like some cartoon character, suspended in mid-air for several seconds — complete with a comedic double-take — before the inevitable plunge to the beach below. Where had this phobia come from? Why did stepping onto the pier now feel like stepping onto a tightrope, when for years its boards had offered nothing but comfort and clemency? Colin suspected the extraordinary vision of Mickey Braithwaite was to blame, which had, as the decades passed, gnawed away at the cosy fabric of his observable world like some sort of slow-release acid, dissolving his-tory's friable fabric to reveal the chasm beneath. Colin often wondered what the deckchair attendant had done to him on that glassy afternoon more than a quarter of a century ago when, after his mother's funeral, they had eaten ice cream together on the pier and talked about the sea, and the moon, and the girl whose life Mickey had saved without even knowing it. He honestly believed Mickey had somehow set a psychological corrosive in motion, perhaps by means of a subliminal message, perhaps simply through a coded flash of his spectacles, which had slowly, inexorably, dismantled the pillars upon which the historian had constructed his faith in the observable universe's ability to supply an answer.

Bedevilled by these new uncertainties, Colin took early re-tirement soon after his sixtieth birthday because, although the archivist in him remained, his indexing and cataloguing had taken on a sandbagging aspect, a somewhat frantic building of barricades against the ever-rising tide released by Mickey Braithwaite. Now he spent his days pottering around the bungalow on Rosemere Crescent, helping out in the local Oxfam shop, and writing what even he admitted was a rather po-faced and overly technical novel set in a Victorian workhouse. And, though what had once been his mother's bedroom was now a book-lined study, steeped in the musty tranquility which Colin seemed the very manifestation of, there remained several of the touchstones which had punctuated his and Edna's life together; the clatter of keys in the brass bowl on his return home; the early morning cup of tea during which he would often converse with his absent mother; a tendency to cook enough tea for two; these things endured, like the smallest of echoes, a sort of living archive into which Colin had filed himself.

As for George Parr and Hannah Goodwin, Colin had collated all his notes, together with the Public Records Office documents, the newspaper articles, and a selection of photographs of the resort contemporaneous to the tragic events of 1880, to create a pamphlet which had successfully laid their ghosts to rest. Until yesterday, when he had picked up the evening paper from the hall carpet and seen the headline, with the prostitute's battered and bruised face looking up at him. In that moment Colin felt not only a surging return of the crusading zeal which had characterised his investigations into the baffling events beneath the pier, but also dismay that history appeared to be repeating itself. The archivist already carried with him a kind of assumed guilt for failing to either exonerate George or provide Hannah with an explanation that would give her at least a modicum of peace. It was intolerable to contemplate failing again, in circumstances so strangely consonant that Colin felt himself being drawn physically back into the nineteenth century, which was why he now found himself stepping once more onto the pier, determined to make amends for previous shortcomings and prevent Sammy Samuels from following Georgie Parr down the same, catastrophic path.

He found it easier to navigate his way along the pier by keeping his eyes fixed firmly on the theatre at its end. This way the planking remained in his peripheral vision and Colin could more or less convince himself that he was on a solid pavement, and not a one-hundred-and-fifty-year-old collection of wood and cast iron which tiptoed out into the sea with all the grace and infirmity of a dowager taking her first dip.

Evening sunshine raked long shadows across the pier, which to the former archivist looked like cracks or crevasses to be negotiated, as though the entire structure were coming apart, but he found a modicum of comfort in the unhurried demeanour of the other visitors. If the pier was indeed undergoing some form of silent disintegration then surely they would not be soaking up the last of the sun with quite such equanimity.

He passed the first of the booths with their onion-shaped roofs, both of which were empty and boarded up. Their redundancy saddened him; Colin remembered visiting the pier as a young man and thinking himself so superior to all the tourists who handed over good money to the fortune-teller dispensing her bogus prognostications from this very booth. Madame... What had she been called? He could picture the booth with its red curtains, and the fortune-teller's disgruntled-looking cat, which seemed to spend most of its time draped along the windowsill, but all he could remember of her were her tiny eyes and huge bosom. Madame? Madame? No. Perhaps it would come, unbidden, at a later date. How he had scoffed at her claim to be able to see into the future! And yet he had never dared take that test himself.

A rather forlorn single row of deckchairs bore the exacting

geometrical hand of Mickey Braithwaite, but Colin dismissed the idea that he could possibly still be working on the pier. Mickey would have to have been approaching ninety by now, and even if he was still alive surely the unsentimental accountants at EuroEnts would have pensioned him off long ago. Even so, Colin stopped, braced himself against a lamp post and glanced up and down the pier, on the lookout for that wild mop of white hair and the dazzling reflections from improbably thick spectacles.

Strangely, the moment his shoes touched the slightly darker boards which were set perpendicularly to the ones running the length of the pier, and which delineated the wider section carrying both the theatre, bar and sun lounge, Colin's vertigo disappeared. Was it the theatre's reassuring solidity that calmed him, or did the increase in width of the pier take it beyond some dimensional limit of his phobia? Whatever it was, he felt hugely relieved to have reached the darker boards. The first part of his mission had been successfully negotiated.

Colin glanced at his watch. Ivan, the pier theatre's stage door manager for over thirty years, had suggested when Colin rang him that the best time to catch Sammy Samuels was half an hour before the start of the show, as the comedian was notoriously uncommunicative and preferred to turn up as late as possible in order to avoid having to talk to either fellow performers or theatre staff. Ivan had also warned Colin that Samuels was unlikely to prove particularly welcoming, but the archivist had emphasised the importance of his visit, alluding to recent events without being too specific.

On entering the theatre foyer a young girl behind the ticket desk looked up from her bags of change and addressed Colin. "We're not open yet."

"I know," he replied, "I'm here to see Sammy Samuels. Ivan has sorted it all out."

"Oh. Right. Do you know where to go?"

Colin smiled. "I used to be the council archivist. I know this pier like the back of my hand."

Her face registered a moment's interest. "Oh? Well, best of luck then."

"Luck?"

"With that arsehole." The girl suddenly blanched. "I didn't... You're not a friend of his, are you? You won't—"

Colin shook his head and held up both hands in a gesture of reassurance. "No, no, don't worry. Your secret's safe with me."

She smiled again, the sincerity evident this time. "Thanks. My big gob! I've only been here a couple of months, I don't want to get sacked for dissing the stars of the show." She gestured to her right. "It's through that door marked private... but you knew that already, didn't you? Sorry."

He glanced in the direction of the door, feeling, for one moment, like Theseus about to enter the Labyrinth, with the kiosk girl his Ariadne. "Perhaps I should have brought a ball of thread with me," he remarked.

She smiled a third time, and now there was uncertainty tightening the curve of her lips, but her relief at escaping censure for her indelicate comment made some sort of response an obligation. "Oh? Well, yes, maybe you should've."

The door opened onto a corridor lined with framed billboards announcing both the stars and support acts from over a hundred years of entertainment on the pier, printed in a cluttered hierarchy of font size and colour. Colin had to suppress an urge to read every one, and perhaps even find Georgie Parr's name, but he knew full well that he would almost certainly lose his nerve at the first sign of procrastination. What he had to say was controversial, if not defamatory, but it needed to be voiced, no matter what reaction it provoked.

He did not stop.

The corridor stretched out before him, elongating and narrowing to a bright point of light in the distance. His footsteps were silenced by the grimy red carpet, making Colin feel as though he were watching a film with the sound turned down. And even though he tried to focus on the far end of the corridor, certain names shouted from the billboards, ebullient, potent, refusing to be denied — George Robey, Gracie Fields, Arthur Askey, George Formby, Tommy Cooper — they were all there, lining the corridor, applauding as he passed, encouraging Colin to do the right thing.

He eventually reached the fire doors at the far end, pushed one open and stepped down into a gloomy hallway. The bare plastered walls were painted bright yellow, but a grubby fluorescent tube leached all joy from the colour, leaving it merely jaundiced. Through a small window in the wall opposite Colin could see Ivan eating a sandwich in his tiny office, surrounded by signed photographs from performers and acts.

"Hello, Ivan," Colin said.

The stage door manager looked up. "Mr Draper! Long time no see!"

Colin stepped across to the window. "Indeed it is. Must be ten years."

"Where does the time go, eh?" Ivan shook his head. He stood up, placed the sandwich back in its plastic box, brushed both hands down the front of his jumper and thrust his right hand through the window to shake hands. "How are you, Mr Draper? You look well."

"Really?"

"Yeah! You haven't changed a bit. Few more grey hairs, maybe, but then haven't we all!"

For a moment Colin, as Ivan was actually speaking, felt both disarmed and flattered by the stage door manager's opinion, but the cheery assessment had hardly concluded before Colin remembered what a relentlessly optimistic outlook on life Ivan possessed, a trait he had always envied. What he envied even more, however, was Ivan's treasury of anecdotes concerning practically every star, celebrity, has-been and never-would-be that he had signed in since the 1970s. He had met everyone from Frank Sinatra to Bonnie

Langford and could recall some little-known fact or tale about them all, but the stories he told were never malicious or derogatory. As far as Ivan was concerned his role was not only to filter out anyone without the proper credentials from accessing the theatre's inner workings, but also to do exactly the same thing with any information he received concerning a performer, be they a top of the bill star or a dancer. Colin coveted this vast wealth of confidences but he had tried and failed on many occasions to persuade Ivan to let him document his tales, even when he offered to sign a legally binding agreement that none of them would ever be published. 'It would be a crime to let all those wonderful stories die with you,' he once said, only for Ivan to reply, 'Well, I'm not planning on dying just yet, Mr Draper.'

"You're too kind," Colin responded, before adding, "I'm alright, I suppose. What about you? Not tempted to call it a day yet?"

"Naw." He looked round the tiny room, his personal fiefdom. "I wouldn't know what to do with meself stuck at home."

Colin nodded. "I know what you mean. When Mum died I wandered round the house like a lost soul for months."

"I'm sorry to hear that."

Colin shrugged. "She'd been ill for a long time. It was probably a relief for her, but she left a big hole." He looked away from the solicitude in the stage door manager's rheumy eyes and focused instead on a photograph that had caught his eye. It showed a ventriloquist and his dummy which, with its bright green mohican and studded PVC jacket, was clearly supposed to be a punk. The ventriloquist was looking at the dummy, mouth agape in an exaggerated gesture of shock at its two-fingered salute towards the camera. *To Ivan, all the best, Kenny Lomax* read the dedication, whilst beneath this was an untidy *Piss Off! from Karl*, presumably added by the dummy.

"I know what you mean," Ivan said. "I couldn't bring

myself to get rid of Dad's stuff for two years after he died. As long as it was there he wasn't totally gone, d'you know what I mean? In the end I just had to bag it all up and give it to the binmen when they came round. If I'd left it on the doorstep I'd have brought it all back in again. I sort of had to give meself no choice, if that doesn't sound weird."

"No," Colin confirmed, "not at all."

There was a moment's awkward silence, as the two men contemplated how the lingering presence of their dead parent had affected them, and how, like an unseen cobweb brushing against your face, that death still had the power to be both gentle and startling.

Colin suddenly thought of something to say. "As I was walking down the pier I noticed how neatly the deckchairs were lined up, and if I didn't know better I'd have thought Mickey Braithwaite had set them out, but he can't still be working, can he? He'll be knocking on ninety by now."

Ivan smiled. "Oh, he's still here, Mr Draper, believe it or not. He's only supposed to do weekends now, but he's here most days, for a few hours at least. There's a new lad who's supposed to be in charge, but I'm afraid Mickey doesn't seem to think too highly of his efforts. He's always rearranging the deckchairs, which drives the poor lad to distraction," he chuckled. "You know what Mickey's like."

"That's incredible."

"I know. He doesn't look a day older than he did twenty years ago, either, the sod. I don't know what his secret is but I wouldn't mind a bit of it meself. Must be all the fresh air."

"Good old Mickey. He's been on this pier since the war, you know."

"Amazing, isn't it? Makes us two look like part-timers."

"Amazing," Colin concurred. The archivist was aware that his heart had begun to beat faster, and a prickling sensation was creeping across his scalp. He desperately wanted Ivan to begin another topic of conversation to delay his inevitable confrontation with Sammy Samuels, but the stage door manager appeared to have reached a natural end-point to his observations on life and simply sat back down, his wistful expression a jarring incongruity amongst the background of beaming showbiz smiles.

"Well," Colin said, "I suppose I'd better get a move on."

Ivan straightened the signing-in book. "Aye... Mr Samuels is expecting you."

"Is he? Oh."

"I thought I'd better tell him after you rang. I didn't want you turning up and Mr Samuels not to be here. Did you not want me to tell him?"

The prickling across his scalp was intensifying. "What did he say? Was he alright?"

Ivan shrugged. "He wanted to know what you wanted to see him about, so I said it must be something about the show. That's right, isn't it?"

"Sort of."

"I haven't spoken out of turn, have I? You didn't say much on the phone, so I just assumed... Would you like me to ring his dressing room?"

"No!" Colin coughed, embarrassed by the note of panic in his voice. "No, no, that's fine. I'll just go up, thanks."

The stage door manager leaned forward, resting his forearms on the wooden shelf that separated him from the corridor, the theatre, and the rest of the world. "Are you sure you're alright, Mr Draper? You look a bit pasty."

"Oh, I'm just weary, Ivan. Old age catching up with me, you know?" Colin tapped the window frame, as though some percussive note were required to signal an end to their discussion.

"I'd better get cracking."

"You know where you're going, don't you?"

Colin laughed. "I should hope so!"

Ivan shook his head. "Of course you do. Daft question. You know this place as well as I do."

"Almost," Colin corrected.

"They'll never be able to knock it down in our memories, will they, Mr Draper?"

"No, Ivan, they won't."

The archivist began to climb the stairs, eyes fixed on the stained linoleum and the worn patches on every step. The sounds of the theatre and pier resonated in the stairwell: the gulls' callous shouts, old metal beneath his feet shifting slightly as it mustered the strength to withstand another incoming tide, the sudden howl of an electric guitar on stage, voices from somewhere in the building that were so indeterminate they might have been whispers from another century, all funnelled into the air around Colin and transmuted, by his ears at least, into a perfect melody. At that moment he knew he would always remember these sounds, bundled together with the worn lino, his tingling fear, and his astonishment at the continuing presence on the pier of Mickey Braithwaite. An indivisible, complex and yet beautifully clear memory. The future would never be totally unknowable as long as these enduring moments of clarity were capable of being woven into the present.

He reached the first floor. The dressing rooms were here, a row of identical green doors with laminated name-cards slotted into brass brackets, the doors arranged on one side of a corridor almost brutal in its strict functionality, with bare walls and concrete floor, pipework and fire extinguisher. Colin's hands were shaking, but he was still able to see how these doors and signs would make an eloquent installation piece on the theme of fame's transient nature. The doors, offering access to celebrity, money and privilege were permanent, always ready to be opened by those who possessed the correct key, and yet the rooms' stars would not occupy them long enough to warrant any specific identity more enduring than a thin piece of card printed on the pier manager's computer. Whose names would be fixed there next season? And how many of those attached there now would be remembered in a hundred years' time?

He walked past the first door: *Kerry Hunter*. The second: *Mike Kavana*. He stopped outside the third: *Sammy Samuels*. The archivist stared at the two words, their neat and memorable alliteration, the sturdy capitalised font David Clark had chosen, and tried to imagine standing outside a similar door, spatially in much the same position as the one now in front of him, with *Georgie Parr* written on it. What, Colin, asked himself, was he doing there? What did he hope to achieve? What possible relevance could a nineteenth-century music hall comic have to this foul-mouthed twenty-first century comedian? He was about to turn away when he heard laughter coming up the stairwell, so, not wanting to be discovered loitering in the corridor, Colin watched with a kind of detached horror as he raised his hand, balled it into a loose fist, and knocked.

"Yes?" came a voice from inside the dressing room.

"It's Colin Draper... Ivan said—"

"*Who?*" Already the comedian sounded irritated.

Colin cleared his throat. "Colin Draper. I used to work for the council. Ivan on the stage door told you I was coming."

"Is this going to take long?"

"No, no."

"Come in, then. You've got five minutes."

With a speed of response that echoed Ivan's throwing away of his father's effects, Colin pushed open the dressing room door and stepped inside.

The first thing he noticed was the heavy pall of cigarette smoke which filled the room and instantly brought to mind a question regarding fire regulations, but Colin thought it best not to voice his concerns, at least not until he had delivered his message. Samuels was sitting at his dressing table, dabbing gently at his forehead with a piece of sponge, his other hand holding a cigarette over a metal ashtray half-filled with ash and butts.

"Five minutes," Sammy reiterated, without turning away from the mirror. "I've got a show to do."

Colin closed the door. He looked round the room for somewhere to sit, but the only piece of furniture, a tub-shaped armchair, was tucked away in a far corner beyond the comedian, a position the archivist sensed would leave him vulnerable if Samuels became violent. He decided to edge closer to the table, but in so doing accidentally kicked a metal wastepaper basket, which tipped over with a loud clang and deposited its contents onto the dressing room floor.

"What the fuck?"

"Sorry, sorry, I didn't see it," Colin explained. He made to bend down and begin tidying up the mess, but Samuels wafted the arm holding the sponge in a dismissive gesture towards the upturned basket.

"Leave it," the comedian instructed, "somebody'll sort it later." He turned slightly in his chair and studied the portly, dishevelled-looking old man for the first time. "So, you wanted to see me. What's your name again?"

"Colin. Colin Draper."

"Okay, Colin Draper, you've had a minute already, so I suggest you get on with whatever it is you're here for."

The archivist tried to hold the comedian's gaze, but there was such a profoundly cold *absence* in the pale grey eyes looking up at him that he found himself addressing instead the reflection in the mirror, as though hopeful that this doppelgänger possessed a more tolerant and benign nature.

"Yes... um, I realise you're very busy... I appreciate you giving me a little of your time." How on earth was he to begin? Ever since his decision to confront Samuels Colin had struggled with an internal debate as to how to introduce Georgie Parr, but for every imagined scenario he could always see a disadvantage. There was, he had reluctantly concluded, no method without risk. He took a deep breath. "There was once a comedian who worked on the pier called Georgie Parr, and he died here in 1880... they found his body hanging under the pier, but no one knows whether he committed suicide or if he was murdered. And nearby, on

334

the beach, they found the body of a prostitute called Hannah Goodwin. She'd been strangled. The police assumed Georgie had murdered her and then hung himself in some sort of act of remorse, but whatever the circumstances, he was dead. It came out afterwards that Georgie had been a frequent visitor to the town's brothels, but he *had* lost both his wife and daughter in tragic circumstances, so that wasn't so surprising. He must have been very lonely."

Sammy, whose dabbings had slowed during the archivist's short speech, now placed the sponge back in its pot of concealer and swivelled his chair round to face Colin. "This wouldn't happen to have anything to do with what was on the front page of the paper last night, would it?"

Colin, who could feel his bowels loosening at the quiet menace in Samuels' voice, tried to smile reassuringly. "Yes, but please, *please* don't think I've come here to judge you, or… or, well, anything. I just don't want you to make the same mistake as Georgie Parr, that's all. I don't want history to repeat itself, is what I'm trying to say."

"I see."

"You do?"

Sammy ground out his cigarette. "Oh, yes, I think so. You think that because some stupid tart talked herself into a black eye this time I'm going to murder the next one that comes along. That's it, isn't it? You think I'm going to kill a prostitute. And then I'm going to string myself up under the pier."

"No, no, not… well, not quite as literally as that, but—"

Sammy stood up. Colin took a step backwards, but he was still within reach of Sammy's forefinger, which jabbed him in the chest on each emphasised word, inching him further and further backwards with every painful contact. "No, that's *exactly* what you're saying. *He* was a comedian, *I'm* a comedian. *I* hit a prostitute, he *strangled* a prostitute. *He* worked on the pier, *I* work on the pier. Isn't that just fucking *peculiar*? Oh, hang on. Do you think I'm this murderer reincarnated? Is that it? Have I been possessed, d'you think? Is he telling me to do things?" Sammy spread his fingers and gripped the sides of his head. "Is that what the voices are all about?"

Colin felt the dressing room wall against his back. His breast-bone was hurting from Sammy's prodding, but what alarmed him most was the psychotic glassiness of the comedian's eyes. He imagined the battered and bruised girl in the newspaper photograph cowering before this same impervious surface, wondering, as he did, where the assault would end. Had Hannah Goodwin also been witness to some similar expression? The thought of it being the last thing she saw appalled him.

"I want to help! That's all. Please, just read this." The archivist felt in his coat pocket and brought out an A5-sized booklet, bound in pale blue card, which he held out like some armistice agreement.

Sammy knocked the booklet out of Colin's hand and leaned closer to him so that their faces were only inches apart. "That, you fat fuck, is what they all say. Agents, women, fortune-tellers... 'I want to help, I want to help', but you know what's really funny? All they really want to do is help themselves. So what is it you're *really* after? Eh? What?"

Colin wondered if he was right. Was there something he wasn't admitting, not even to himself? Were his amateurish attempts at psychoanalysis with Mickey Braithwaite and his new desperate hope in synchronicity both just pitiful diversionary tactics to delay the inevitable; that was, his failure to solve the mystery of Georgie Parr and Hannah Goodwin?

"Nothing," Colin replied, his voice flat and blunted. "I'm sorry I've wasted your time."

"You will be, sunshine, if you say a word about this to anyone." Sammy took a step back. "Who else have you talked to about this bullshit?"

"No one. Honestly, I wanted to speak to you first."

"Well now you have, so you can fucking well forget you ever thought about it, can't you. And if you don't keep your trap shut I'll know where to find you. D'you get my drift?"

The archivist nodded. "I won't say anything, I promise."

"You'd better not." Samuels pointed at a spot between Colin's eyes. "You're in my sights, you crazy bastard. Now piss off, I've got a show to do."

Colin reached for the door handle, opened the door and left the room without looking again at the comedian.

With the archivist gone, Sammy slumped onto his chair, lit a cigarette and scrutinised the back of his hands, dismayed by the brown blotches and grey-green veins, the loosening skin and sparse clumps of hair; they were an old man's hands, which had somehow been grafted onto his arms at some time during the last ten years. He turned them over, squinting in an attempt to bring the voiceless fissures across his palms into focus, but they writhed and blurred, reluctant to supply any kind of answer. What was it she had said? Something about his grandfather's death, a girl he was meant to love, and being successful. It had all been so obviously vague, subjects that could equally have been applied to anyone stepping in to her stupid little booth, so why had the fortune-teller left such an enduring impression? What was it that bound them together? He remembered — with a clarity made all the more remarkable because when he looked back to his drinking years there were precious few memories with any kind of reliable definition to them — the look of terror in her eyes when he had touched her that night in the bar. There was no way she could have faked such a primal fear, and what made her reaction even more ominous was that it had been conjured from nothing but the slightest of contacts. What had she sensed through his fingertips that sent her blundering out of the bar as though being pursued by all the hounds of hell? And now here was this crazy old fool babbling on about a comedian who murdered a prostitute over a hundred years ago and saying the same was going to happen to him! Why were these lunatics allowed to roam the streets, and why did they all gravitate towards the pier or, more to the point, towards him?

Samuels snorted and shook his head, and in so doing caught sight of the pale blue booklet lying on the floor. He bent down, picked it up and read out loud the title. "Laughter and Tragedy — The Life and Death of Georgie Parr."

Colin needed a brandy to calm his nerves. He could still feel the comedian's finger jabbing at his chest, still see that shark-like blankness in his eyes; perhaps Sammy would glance through the booklet out of curiosity, and hopefully realise that Colin had meant him no harm.

Just inside the doorway a group of young men were clustered around an electronic quiz machine, raucously debating the answer to one of its multiple choice questions.

"Is it bollocks."

"It *is*. Daz's mate's been there."

"So what? Daz knows fuck all about anything."

"It's Toronto, I'm telling yer. Hurry up and press the fucking button."

"Oi, mate."

Colin realised that the last phrase had been aimed at him. He stopped and smiled at their bland, alcohol-flushed faces which glistened like lacquered masks in the bar's gloom. "Yes?"

"What's the capital of Canada?"

"Ottawa," the archivist replied without hesitation.

His questioner frowned. "You sure?"

"Yes. It's in the French-speaking area—"

"Okay, we don't need a fucking lecture!" The young man turned back to the machine, punched a button, and was rewarded by a brief electronic fanfare. The group cheered.

"Get in!" one of them said.

Colin lingered for a moment, expecting some small in-dication of gratitude for his contribution, but their attention had returned to the quiz machine, a dismissal which irritated but did not particularly surprise him. These young men were typical of the type of visitor that seemed endemic in the resort these days: groups of girls and boys who tottered from bar to bar, shrieking and bellowing because, deep down, they knew they had nothing to say. The girls draped in sashes, their bare legs mottled in the chill wind, boys cavorting in ill-fitting comic book hero costumes, outfits deeply ironic given their mundane existence, and all of them propelled by a belief in the redemptive power of a hedonistic lifestyle as espoused by their celebrity gods.

As he walked away Colin heard their blundering debate move on to the next question.

"Who wrote *Moby Dick*?"

"Sounds like a porno."

"Nah, it's that thing about a whale."

"Moby Dick! That's me!"

"In yer dreams."

"Fuck off."

'Herman Melville, you idiots,' Colin said silently, thankful to the general hubbub of the bar for absorbing the conversation at that point. He needed a large brandy, then home on the bus and the sequestered hush of his study. How he longed to be safely concealed behind the barricades of books, to put himself beyond reach of the world, with all its volatility and unanswerable questions. To interact with this world was to open oneself up to its disorder, a vulnerability Colin now knew he could not withstand. If Sammy Samuels and Georgie Parr were indeed following identical paths then it was incontestable and inviolate, a destiny he could now be nothing more than a bystander at. He was an archivist, a bringer of order; there was nothing more to be done.

When the five minute call came crackling through the dressing room speaker Sammy Samuels closed the booklet and dropped it into the now upturned wastepaper basket, knowing that it would be gone by the time he came off-stage later that night, carried away in a black bin liner, its riddles silenced.

But as he bawled and hollered his jokes and observations, Hawaiian shirt flapping around him like some flag of acrimony, Sammy knew that Georgie and Hannah were beside him, and when he returned to his dressing room he checked, the moment the door was closed, that the booklet had been taken from the wastepaper basket. Yet still he heard them, whispering entreaties of redemption and release. The answer to their pleas, however, was to come from a most unlikely of sources.

# ... And A Little Older Than My Teeth

Sammy had been leaning on the railing at the pier's end for almost half an hour, gazing out to sea as his mind danced between fractured glimpses of Amanda's perfect symmetry, the photo depicting what his hands had wrought on the prostitute's face, and the letter that had been waiting for him at the stage door. The plain white envelope bearing his name, printed in an austere lower case and containing a letter on EuroEnts-headed paper from Julian J Walker ordering... ordering!... him to attend a meeting the day after tomorrow. One short paragraph, strangely lacking in the kind of management-speak that Julian usually employed; it was this clarity that alarmed Samuels the most, and which spoke far more eloquently than any of the carefully phrased sentences. The managing director was sending him a message through the letter's restraint, a message that, so the comedian concluded, was unequivocal and signalled the end of his career.

And so he stared, smoking one cigarette after another, hypnotised by a flickering orange flame on the horizon, a will o' the wisp that danced so prettily on the boundary between the steel-blue sea and mauve sky, until a wooden clatter behind him made him jump and turn to see what had caused it. A white-haired old man was bent over a jumbled pile of deckchairs, clearly having just dropped his load, which flapped at his feet as though in its death throes.

The comedian flicked his cigarette into the sea and walked

over to the old man, who had begun to mutter to himself as, stiff-limbed, he attempted to untangle the chairs. "They fighting back, Pop?"

The old man looked up in surprise. "I dropped them," he said by way of explanation.

Sammy took in the white hair, thick-lensed glasses and arthritic demeanour and shook his head. He vaguely remembered seeing this hermit-like character on and around the pier ever since his first visit in the early sixties, but he had always felt uncomfortable dealing with either physical or mental disability and had therefore never even spoken to him before. What struck the comedian most forcefully now was a surprising feeling of sympathy for the old man, whose loyalty was obviously being callously exploited by EuroEnts. Continuing to employ this relic, presumably on some piddling retainer that the poor guy needed to supplement his pension, for a job which was clearly too physically demanding for him, summed up for Samuels everything that was wrong with the company. "Jesus, Julian, I thought *I* was a bastard," he muttered, before continuing in a louder voice, "you shouldn't be doing this, not at your age. Come on, I'll give you a hand. I'm Sammy Samuels, by the way."

The old man stuck out his hand in greeting, his broad smile revealing a lustrous set of false teeth which appeared slightly too large for the mouth in which they resided. "You're on the posters!"

"I am." Samuels struck his child's-gun pose, pointing straight at the old man's forehead, and even as he moved his hand into position the comedian felt astonished, and slightly puzzled, by how much he wanted to impress this antiquated deckchair attendant.

"What's your name?"

"I'm Mickey Braithwaite."

"Well, Mickey," Sammy said, "let me give you a hand." He knelt, separated two of the deckchairs and picked them up. "Where were you going with them?"

"Over here." Mickey led him to a large wooden door set into the back of the theatre. He fumbled in his pocket, brought out a bunch of keys and worked his way methodically through them until, selecting one, he unlocked the padlock. The deckchair attendant then lifted the padlock out of its hasp and swung open the door to reveal a large storage room piled high with deckchairs, cardboard boxes and tins of paint.

"In we go!"

Samuels followed Mickey into the room. "I've always wondered what was in here. Where do you want these putting?"

Mickey patted a low stack of deckchairs, so the comedian placed his two on top and stood up, only to watch, more in amusement than irritation, as the old man carefully manoeuvred each deckchair until it was perfectly aligned with those below. "Perfectionist, eh? A regular Rain Man, aren't you? Away with the fairies. No wonder you're still working."

"Pardon?"

"Never mind. I'll get the other deckchairs, you wait here."

"Pardon?"

"You... wait... here."

Sammy stepped back out into the gathering twilight. He noticed a second gas platform flare now flickering out at sea, but as he looked, more and more sparked into life, until the entire horizon was a solid shimmering line of yellow. He imagined the sea brushing against the pier stanchions, leaving them gilded in its wake. Sammy no longer cared whether these hallucinations were a result of his prolonged drug abuse, not when they could produce something as disarmingly beautiful as this. In fact he welcomed them, welcomed them as a means of escape from the moribund reality he found himself in.

He gathered up the rest of the deckchairs and carried them into the storeroom, where again Mickey ensured their exact arrangement. Satisfied at last with the neatness of his work, the deckchair attendant straightened with a slight grunt and smiled his disconcerting smile. "Finished! All shipshape and Bristol fashion."

"Why are you still working?" Sammy enquired. "Don't you find it hard at your age?"

"Norman said that fresh air and hard work never killed anyone."

Sammy emitted a sceptical snort. He wondered if Mickey spoke entirely in random phrases picked up on the pier. "Did he now? Is Norman your boss?"

Mickey shook his head. "Not any more. Not after the Observer Corps finished. Once we'd sorted Fucking Adolf out we didn't need to look for the bombers any more."

"Fucking Adolf! I like that. That's like something my grandad would have said."

"Was he in the war?"

"Both," Sammy replied. He was unsure how the conversation had turned, but it felt both natural and comforting to be able to relate a little of what he remembered about his grandfather. "He fought in the First World War, where he was gassed, which knackered his lungs, but he managed to hide that and joined the Home Guard during the Second World War and ended up with the Defence Medal for doing three years. He was a tough old bastard."

Mickey's spectacles winked and flashed in the gloom of the storeroom. "I've got my dad's medals from the first war. They're like rainbows, apart from his silver one with a stripy ribbon. He got that for being brave, but a sniper shot him in the throat and turned all the mud red."

"We have no idea, do we?" Sammy said, shaking his head. A thought occurred to him. "Hang on… you say your dad was in the *First* World War? And if he was killed that means you would have to have been born before 1918, so you must be at least ninety! Are you sure it wasn't the Second World War? I can't believe you're that old."

"As old as my tongue and a little older than my teeth."

"Yes, very good, but... " The comedian tried to think of another way of phrasing his question. "Your birthday. Can you remember the number on your cards?"

"It's time for you to go now," Mickey said. The sing-song timbre of his voice had altered, flattening out and becoming unusually business-like. "Time for the show."

Sammy glanced at his watch. "Shit, you're right. Well, it was good talking to you, Mickey, you take it easy, okay?"

The two men inched round the stacks of deckchairs and stepped back out onto the pier. Sammy began to move towards the door with the intention of swinging it shut for the deckchair attendant, but Mickey held up one hand and reached out for it himself.

"No, no, it has to be me," he explained. "Got to make sure it's all locked up safe and sound. All that wood and paint and stuff. It's a fire hazard, you see. I have to make sure the door is locked so nobody can get in and set it on fire." Mickey closed the hasp, re-attached the padlock and fastened it in place, then tugged at it to make sure it was securely locked. "There. All safe and sound." He dropped the bunch of keys back into his coat pocket and thrust out a hand. "Thank you for helping me, Mr Samuels."

"Don't mention it," Sammy replied, shaking the proffered hand, which he was astonished to find almost weightless, like gripping a model constructed out of tissue paper. "Any time."

Having checked his dressing room door was securely locked, Sammy scrabbled through the jumbled contents of a drawer, found the tin of barley sugar sweets and extracted the sealed plastic bag hidden under a layer of confectionery. Tapping out a quarter of the bag's contents, the comedian proceeded to shape the cocaine into two lines with one of his business cards, cut a length of drinking straw and snorted both lines, one for each nostril. A cold, tingling sensation expanded into his skull from some acute point behind his nose, and within seconds Sammy could feel his heart rate accelerate, his fingertips tingle. Thoughts and images and sensations cascaded through his mind, clamouring for pre-eminence until they merged, absorbed one into the other, a daunting fusion: the craving in Hannah Goodwin's eyes lit by the coruscation of an ocean aflame which was also the sudden extinguishing of sunlight erasing the lines in the palm of his hand as it was softly cupped by the fortune-teller whose gold rings branded their lies into his flesh but were pacified by the gossamer touch of Mickey Braithwaite who was not Mickey Braithwaite but his grandfather lying dead in the garden with birdshit on his face, that cream-and-black birthmark of humiliation so kindly assimilated by Mickey as though he possessed the capacity to atone for all the sin in the world, including the impenetrable violence of George Parr with which Sammy's bones ached in concord...

"Yes," the comedian said. He knew exactly what he had to do, and who would take the blame for his actions.

# Destiny's Alembic

Sammy found it difficult to contain the almost hysterical glee bubbling inside him as he lolled on the microphone stand that night, knowing that it would be the last time he stood on these boards and barked his sour jokes and observations at an audience he detested. But if the prospect of escape from this joyless existence made maintaining his customary deadpan delivery difficult, what made it even worse was the wonderfully gratifying and recurring mental image of Julian J Walker watching one of his key assets go up in flames without being able to do a damned thing about it. Sammy could not wait to turn up for his meeting tomorrow afternoon, look into that smug bastard's eye and point out the clause in his contract which stated that he could only be dismissed if EuroEnts as a company was brought into disrepute by his actions rather than any personal reputation. Then he could draw his attention to the smouldering wreck, the smoke from which would hopefully have permeated Julian's office, and by this time next week he would be sunning himself on the Costa Brava with some cute señorita's mouth round his cock.

His plan was simple, and its simplicity reassured him, not only of its likelihood of success but also its righteousness. What, for example, had been his chance encounter with Mickey Braithwaite if not a sign that destiny was on his side, guiding each cog in retribution's machine into place? How straightforward had it been to seek out the deckchair attendant earlier that afternoon, persuade him that he looked tired and offer to put away the deckchairs, pretend to have forgotten about the locked storeroom and then accept the bunch of keys needed, calming Mickey's reservations with a promise to return them the next day? And how hilariously ironic was it that he had found the crazy old fool locking the former fortune-teller's booth with that same bunch of keys, giving him not only access to the storeroom but also an ideal hiding place in which to wait for the pier to empty and be locked for the night? Who, in all honesty, would believe Mickey's story? Everyone knew he lived in his own little world; any explanation that included an act of kindness from Sammy Samuels would only reinforce that view, and provide the comedian with the perfect scapegoat.

With the show safely negotiated, Sammy returned to his dressing room, aware that it was important not to deviate from his normal routine. Fortunately most of the backstage staff had heard, or helped to disseminate, the gossip regarding his imminent meeting with Julian, allowing Sammy to be seen but not delayed. Once back in his room he collected together the few possessions he wanted to save and stuffed them into a rucksack, piling them on top of the green plastic petrol container he had purchased and filled at a garage thirty miles from the resort. His preparations complete, the comedian switched off the main light, sat down at his dressing table and lit a cigarette. The metallic click of his Zippo lighter, its brief flare reflected in the mirror's blackness, took on huge significance in his mind, like the opening bars in a symphony, where its recurring melodic theme is established. He flipped open the lighter again, flicked its flint wheel and brought the flame close to the side of his face, close enough to feel its heat. Sammy stared at his reflection, which seemed to him more like a few discrete patches of yellow skin separated by oozing shadows encroaching from the greater darkness surrounding him, as though he was being slowly absorbed by it. The lighter was getting hot, but he continued to stare, hoping to watch the last recognisable remnants of his face vanish.

"I'm a firestarter," he sang quietly to himself, "twisted firestarter... shit!" Sammy dropped the lighter and blew on his burned fingertips. "Shit shit shit." He retrieved the lighter, which had fortunately closed on impact with the floor. "Pull yourself together, you dickhead," he chided. "Don't set your fucking self on fire."

There was a peculiar sense of *deja vu* in actually performing the sequence of events he had mentally rehearsed so many times; closing his dressing room door, saying goodnight to Ivan to ensure the stage door manager had registered his leaving, walking down the pier as far as the booth and quickly unlocking it whilst making sure he was not observed, then slipping inside and locking the door behind him in case Ivan should try it in passing. Every phase of his plan had so far correlated perfectly with its imagined version, so much so that Samuels, safely shrouded in the booth's gloomy interior, afforded himself a few minutes of smug reflection on the decades which had passed since he had last been in this exact position.

The serendipity of his return to the booth, which he had always acknowledged was where his career began, struck Sammy as hilarious. It was like a hugely prolonged joke, over forty years in the telling, related by a most patient of narrators, a jester who understood the perversity of life and possessed the skill to bring the rambling anecdote of his existence full circle, finishing it with a suitably trenchant punchline. The joke had started the moment that con artist of a fortune-teller had snapped 'You should be on the stage', and would finish when he destroyed that stage, taking with it the theatre and pier which had become symbols of all his frustrations and disappointment. Only once they had been eradicated could he move on, cleansed in the flames he would soon ignite.

*Bet you didn't see this coming, did you* he thought, silently castigating the woman who had somehow conjured a living out of flattery and bullshit from this very booth. *You didn't see* anything *coming, did you, you just poisoned us all with your lies.* He held up his hand, palm facing out into the darkened booth. *It doesn't mean a thing, you stupid cow. Not a fucking thing. We're just here and then we're not, and that's all there is to it.*

Satisfied with his adjudication, the comedian pushed his rucksack into a corner, leaned against it and rested his head on the wall. Closing his eyes, Sammy took a deep breath; maybe, many years ago when he was young, when an impetuous Samuel Rosenberg had glimpsed the pier through the rain-blurred windscreen of his brother's Triumph TR4, when the wipers swept across the glass to reveal its steadfast form like a moment of clarity in a world of equivocation, when he opened the door as they stopped at a red light and ran off into the storm without even shutting the car door behind him because he wanted to cause the maximum inconvenience for his brother, maybe then, given the same circumstance, he would have sensed a lingering perfume in the booth's black air, or heard the echo of a cat's deep purr. Now, however, there was only silence and dust.

Not long after he heard footsteps approaching. Sammy pressed himself as tightly into the corner as he could, fighting down an impulse to burst out of the booth and give the stage door manager the fright of his life. The footsteps grew louder, until accompanying each one he felt a slight vibration carried through the pier's planking into his buttocks, then the vibrations receded, the footsteps heading towards the promenade.

"That's it, fuck off, Ivan," Sammy said silently. "I'm doing you a favour, anyway, sunshine. It's about time you retired."

He closed his eyes again. He was the only person left on the pier… the *last* person, in fact. Its history did not interest him, however, and his own memories of the structure consisted of little more than a parade of banalities, so Sammy felt no guilt or sense of impending loss regarding the pier's destruction.

Other piers had burnt down and were never rebuilt because, despite all the bleatings from civic societies and historians like that crazy fat bastard who had more or less accused him of planning to murder one of the town's whores, most people recognised them for the anachronisms they were. The resort was on its arse anyway. All the pier was good for now was to keep the rain off a quick blow-job, and there were plenty more places like that in the town.

Madame Kaminska! That was her name. How did these buried fragments worm their way to the surface? Yes, Madame Kaminska. He remembered her plump face and tiny eyes. What had happened to her? Sammy wondered. He'd never seen her again after the pier's centenary celebrations. He had found an agent, embarked on a punishing tour of working men's clubs, managed to grab a slot at Batley Variety Club, which in turn led to his appearance on the Royal Variety Show and a summer season at the resort, so by the time he returned to the pier the booth had become a fudge and toffee stall, and when he mentioned the fortune-teller the vacuous young girl behind the counter had simply shrugged.

"I bet you're dead," he whispered, his voice reverberating round the inside of the booth, "and I bet you never saw it coming. Well, Madame Kaminska," the comedian scoffed as a wave of tiredness washed over him and he settled his head into the soft padding of his rucksack, "wait 'til you see what's coming next."

Sammy started, woken by the sound of a siren on the prome-nade. For a moment he felt completely disorientated, baffled by the booth's unfamiliar gloom, but then he remembered why he was there; tonight at last the booth would fulfill its function as destiny's alembic.

He angled his watch to catch the pale light seeping in through a split in the boarding near his knee and noted with satisfaction that it was almost half-past two in the morning, the perfect time to execute his plan. Most of the clubs would have emptied by now, meaning there was less chance of anyone spotting the fire until it was already too well-established to be put out, yet still leaving him long enough to slip away into the night and be safely tucked up at home in time to blearily answer the phone and express his dismay at the news.

The pier was little more than a silhouette against the dark grey slabs of sea and sky. Sammy Samuels padded back down its silent old boards towards the rectangular mass of the theatre. He could hear the petrol sloshing around in the container slung over his shoulder, as though it too was excited at the prospect of such a profound ignition. As he walked he silently sang 'hi ho, hi ho, it's off to work I go,' energised by a feeling of impending release which came close to rapture.

Once shielded behind the theatre he switched on a small torch, sorted through the keys, unlocked the storeroom and swung open its door. Sammy's heart was beating faster now, his whole body quivering with excitement; this was how he used to feel before going on stage, so wonderfully alive, anticipating the laughter and applause he was about to create. And like then, he had to force himself to calm down, slow his breathing and clear his mind.

"Concentrate, Rosenberg," he reminded himself, "you've got work to do."

The storeroom was unchanged, with its geometrically perfect stacks of deckchairs creating a chest-high maze through which Sammy navigated, his path illuminated by the torch beam, until he reached the shelves loaded with paint tins and plastic bottles of turpentine. He wriggled out of the rucksack's straps and placed it on top of an adjacent pile of deckchairs, unfastened its drawstrings and lifted out the petrol container. It rocked gently as though encouraging the comedian, almost demonstrating to him what needed to be done. He then took out a bundle of old Hawaiian shirts; these would form the source of the fire, a choice that, notwithstanding its symbolic relevance, also possessed a degree of practicality, as Sammy reasoned that the shirts' polyester content would make them burn strongly. He manoeuvred a stack of deckchairs so that it was positioned directly beneath the paint and turpentine, then placed the shirts on top of the deckchairs, unscrewed the lid of the petrol can and poured its contents over the shirts, sloshing a little of the petrol so that it soaked into the stripy material of the chairs. With the heart of his fire thoroughly doused, Sammy then walked slowly round the storeroom, sprinkling petrol over each pile of deckchairs until the container was empty. He threw it away, its purpose fulfilled. The air was now thick with petrol fumes that stung his eyes and caught at the back of his throat, but at least the resulting blurred vision and metallic taste gave added impetus to his actions. The comedian hurried back to the pile of shirts, feeling in his pocket for his lighter as he wended his way through the deckchairs. Flipping open its metal cap, Sammy's thumb settled on the flint wheel, but then he hesitated. What if the petrol fumes in the storeroom ignited before he could light the fire? Had he inadvertently spilled some of the petrol on his clothes, which could seal his own fate as well as the pier's? He saw himself thrashing about amidst the blazing deckchairs before leaping from the end of the pier and plunging in a fiery arc into the black waters.

"Come on, don't bottle it now."

His thumb twitched on the milled flint wheel, there was the briefest of metallic scrapes, and a fat yellow flame sprang into being. Sammy stared at it, mesmerised by its purity. The flame was candid and yet scrupulously neutral, offering itself for good or bad without approbation or reproach for either. It could deliver protection from predator or cold, or equally destroy its wielder. The flame was nothing more than a tool; unlike the sea, whose vast coldness sensed the flame's heat and willed it to begin the pier's destruction, willed it with all its might, for its patience was at an end.

He had hoped the shirts would prove to be a good catalyst, but their dramatic combustion took even Sammy by surprise, causing him to jerk instinctively backwards to escape the ball of fire which seemed magically to appear the moment the lighter's flame touched a sleeve poking out of the pile.

"Shit a brick," he cursed as the corner of a deckchair jabbed him painfully in the small of his back, but the instant success of his first attempt at pyromania soothed the pain somewhat.

He watched as the pile of deckchairs under the blazing shirts began to smoulder and burn, then, satisfied that the fire was well-enough established to be left to its own devices, and also aware that the tins of paint and turpentine bottles would soon be either exploding or scattering burning liquid across the storeroom, he hoisted his rucksack onto his shoulder and turned towards the door, only to see it slam shut.

For a second Sammy frowned at the door. Had a gust of wind blown it shut? Or had lighting the fire created a sort of vacuum effect inside the storeroom?

"Who gives a shit?" he said, astounded by his own inertia. "Shift your arse!"

Sammy ran to the door and pushed, expecting it to swing back out into the night, into his new life, but when the palm of his hand hit the wooden panel it was met with firm resistance, sending a sharp jarring pain all the way up his arm and into his shoulder.

"What the fuck?" He pushed again, then with both hands, then with his shoulder and all his body weight. The door gave slightly, but Sammy could hear the padlock rattle in its hasp. He was locked in.

"Hey!" he shouted, slamming into the door. "Hey! Let me out! There's a fucking fire in here!" Silence, apart from the crackle and clamour of the flames. "Hey! I'm trapped in here! Somebody!"

The comedian took several steps backward, then charged at the door, but the joiners, under strict instructions to construct a sturdy barrier in order that valuable items could be safely stowed away in the room, had added cross-bracing and an inner layer of plywood. The door shuddered, stood firm. He tried again, and hurt his shoulder.

"Christ almighty," Sammy muttered. "What the fuck's going on? Help! Help!" He banged on the door with both fists. Smoke was beginning to fill the room. He banged on the door again, even though he knew it would do no good, that he had been deliberately locked in and that appealing to be released was probably what his captor most wanted to hear and was least likely to act on. Who had slammed shut this door? Julian. It had to be him, or more likely one of his henchmen. It was just the sort of trick he would pull; clear the pier to make way for his fairground rides, pin the arson on him and get rid of an awkward problem at the same time. And he had walked straight into the trap. But when Sammy inhaled to scream his name, if only to show that he had worked out who was behind the set-up, he breathed in a lungful of the smoke's acrid vapour and began to cough uncontrollably, his eyes watering as his body tried to expel the toxic gases being released by his Hawaiian shirts.

Convulsed by the needles pricking at his lungs, Sammy sank to his knees. The blurred flecks of light, cast out into the world so long ago by the lap dancing club's twirling glitterball and which, he now realised, had been waiting, biding their time just beyond the boundaries of his vision, began once again to flash across his eyes, only now they were not white but amber, taking up the colour of the flames in joyous brotherhood, and all at once Sammy thought of Amanda's crucifix, the gleaming silver man who nestled between her breasts, his arms outstretched in a gesture of complete candour. Or was it simply indifference?

The deckchairs were alight now, the smoke and heat adding to the glitterball's constellation. Sammy screwed shut his eyes, opened them again, blinked away tears, pulled his handkerchief from his trouser pocket and clamped it over his mouth, and then he noticed, half-hidden behind a pile of cardboard boxes at the back of the room, a door, an open door. How had he not noticed that? A part of him knew it was because the doorway had not been there before, that someone must have opened it, but even if, like a rat in a maze, he was being guided towards God alone knew what, at least it offered a respite from the heat and smoke. He ran towards it, pushed the boxes to one side and toppled through the doorway, slamming shut the door behind him. He leaned against it, panting, trembling, almost blind in the gloomy space after the flame-lit storeroom, but gradually his eyes adjusted, the white flecks fading once more, and he realised that he was beneath the stage. He could see the house lights shining through thin cracks between the boards, but why were they on? And then the boards creaked, relaying the unmistakable sound of footsteps crossing to centre-stage.

"Hey!" Sammy yelled. "Hey! Who's there? Who the fuck is that?"

He ran to the side, found a crude wooden staircase and charged up into the wings. Tucked away in the shadows was the control desk for the stage lighting, above which was a small monitor displaying a black-and-white image of the stage. On the screen Sammy could make out a figure, positioned centre-stage and facing out into the auditorium. He pushed the heavy black curtains to one side and ran out into the dazzling light, ready to tackle whoever it was trying to kill him, but to his amazement the stage was empty. Sammy, propelled by his own momentum, staggered to a halt at the same spot where he had seen the figure on the screen. Baffled by their sudden disappearance, the comedian glanced down at his feet and realised he was being ridiculous. How many hundreds of times had he stood on this stage? He knew every square foot of boarding, knew very well that there was no trapdoor, and yet still he looked, because there was no other way they could possibly have disappeared so quickly. He peered out into the theatre, squinting to minimise the glare from the row of spotlights shining directly at him. He brought up one hand and held it above his eyes. Was that someone moving in the shadows at the back of the auditorium?

Propelled into movement once more, and conscious that tendrils of smoke were beginning to seep out from vents set into the low wooden wall below the stage front, Samuels jumped down and ran up the centre aisle. A lifetime of heavy smoking was taking its toll on his breathing, but catching up with this elusive figure might mean the difference between escape and a horrific death, so Sammy ignored the stabbing pains in his chest and laboured up the slight incline, feet padding softly on the carpet, until he reached the main auditorium doors. Again, there was no one to be seen. He grabbed the door handles and pulled. They were locked. He ran across to the other doors, pulled again, already knowing what he would find.

"Fucking hell!" he raged, shaking the doors violently. "Come on, you bastards! Open!" Sammy vented all his fear and fury on the doors, pumping with both arms, even though he could feel that the security bars had been locked on the other side, that however hard he pulled it was a hopeless waste of energy, and all the time a devastating awareness was growing that whoever had devised this lethal snare had planned it down to the smallest detail, meaning he was unlikely to find a flaw in their process before either the smoke or the flames put an end to his search.

He shook the doors for over a minute until, arms aching and with cramp in his fingers, Sammy relinquished the door handles. In the ensuing silence he heard the sound of someone clapping. Whirling round, the comedian saw a white-haired figure sitting on the front row, staring up at the stage and applauding as though they were watching a performer take their bow. He recognised the tousled white hair instantly.

"You!"

Mickey Braithwaite shuffled round in his seat and waved. "Hello, Mr Samuels."

Sammy strode down to the front of the auditorium, keeping his eyes fixed on the deckchair attendant in case he attempted another one of his disappearing acts, marched up to him and grabbed the sleeve of his jacket. "Gotcha. Now get us out of here before the whole fucking lot comes down."

"I can't," Mickey said simply.

"What d'you mean, you *can't*? You're the one with the keys!"

"I gave them to you, Mr Samuels. Don't you remember?"

Sammy gripped Mickey's sleeve more tightly and leaned down towards him. "Don't play fucking dumb with me, sunshine, it won't wash. I left the *keys* in the *padlock* on the *outside* of the storeroom... the ones *you* must have used to lock me in, so get your fucking arse in gear and get us out of here. There's a bloody great fire in there now, in case you hadn't noticed."

The deckchair attendant glanced at the smoke now pouring out of the vents. "I threw them in the sea."

"*What?*"

"After I locked everywhere up and put the bars across I went to the ladies toilet and opened the window and threw them out. I heard them go splash."

"You fucking retard! How are we supposed to get out now?" Sammy glanced round the theatre, as though an explanation for such suicidal behaviour might be gleaned from its mute rows of seats, then looked back from their insensate cushions to a similar absence in Mickey's eyes. "This isn't... I can't believe you've done that... No, no, I take that back, I *can* believe you did that, I just can't figure out *why* you'd want to do it."

"It's time," Mickey replied, a note of profound regret in his voice. "Bella thought it was time when she saw the flames, but it wasn't, she only saw them because of you... because you touched her—"

"Hang on a minute." The comedian closed his eyes, unable to face the serenity shining out of the deckchair attendant's face, a serenity that could only mean the crazy old bastard was prepared to die. "Are you telling me that stupid bitch really *did* see the future? After all that bullshit she came out with?"

Mickey shrugged. "Perhaps it was a miracle, Mr Samuels, but I don't know why people wish for them because there's always something different hiding inside that isn't really what they wanted. It has to take something away as well."

Sammy let go of Mickey's sleeve and stood up. "I haven't got time to listen to your bollocks. You might not be bothered about burning to death in this bloody place but *I* am." He looked round. "There must be another way out of here."

"I don't think there is, Mr Samuels. I think I've locked them all up."

The smoke was getting denser, reducing visibility in the theatre and, as the walls and furthest rows of seats disappeared, it brought their dialogue into sharper focus, their converging fates illuminated by the spotlights in whose beams the smoke swirled and shifted in patterns anticipated years ago by the starlings.

Sammy pulled the deckchair attendant from his seat, and again the lightness of him was astonishing. "*Why*? What have I done to you? Why have you trapped me in here?"

"George lost everything," Mickey said by way of expla-nation, "so he didn't want to live any more, and you're the same. It's time."

"If you say 'it's time' once more I'll fucking swing for you. And who the fuck is George?"

"Didn't you listen to Mr Draper?"

"*Who*?"

"Mr Draper. He told you all about George, about when he strangled Hannah under the pier. It was in the olden days. Don't you remember?"

Sammy groaned. "Oh, Jesus, not him. What is it with the people in this town? Why are you all obsessed with something that happened a hundred years ago? So the guy strangled a tart and then strung himself up. So fucking what. Who gives a shit? It doesn't matter. It. Doesn't. Matter."

"Yes it *does*, Mr Samuels!" Mickey yelled, his voice shrill with a sudden vehemence, and then in one swift movement he writhed free of the comedian's grip, pushing him backwards with enough force to cause Sammy to tumble and bang his head on the arm of a chair. Mickey ran off towards the stage and vanished into the smoke.

Stunned by the sudden reversal of dominance, and winded by the fall, Sammy manoeuvred himself onto his hands and knees. The side of his head was pounding, and white flashes that beat in time with the pounding flickered across his vision. What was the matter with his lungs? They appeared to have shrivelled to tiny sacs, drawing in a hopelessly inadequate cupful of air with each breath, but when he tried to inhale more deeply the smoke snagged at his throat and made him cough violently. Levering himself upright on the arm of the chair, Sammy staggered in the direction he had seen the deckchair attendant disappear. He sensed that if he was to escape the fire then catching up with Mickey offered his only hope; surely not even he was either stupid or crazy enough to want to be burnt alive.

The smoke was slightly less thick in the narrow passageway that in one direction led to the stage door, in the other to the stairs. Sammy hesitated. Which way had Mickey gone? He could feel the heat of the fire through the concrete floor; it was making the linoleum blister and release an acrid smell that reminded him of the hot tar used by builders, which in turn prompted a memory from school when he had thrown a boy's PE pumps into a vat of gleaming black pitch being used to reseal the gym's flat roof... Kevin... Kevin... There was a bang upstairs. The comedian took the steps two at a time, ignoring the stabbing pains in his chest, and emerged onto the dressing room corridor just in time to see Mickey's legs climbing the final rungs of a ladder at the far end of the corridor, a ladder Sammy had never seen before, a ladder which allowed access to some sort of loft. And the reason no one had ever mentioned it, not in all his years on the pier, was because since the end of the war the room had, to all intents and purposes, ceased to exist.

He dashed along the corridor, too exhausted to shout, or even speak. Simply forcing his legs into motion took all his willpower, and when, with less than ten feet to go, Sammy watched the ladder begin to slide back up into the black rectangle of the trapdoor, its final rungs lingering just beyond his outstretched hand as though mocking his desperate lunge, and the trapdoor slammed shut above him, the comedian collapsed. A searing pain in his chest danced down his left arm, while the name of the boy whose pumps he had committed to the boiling tar echoed through his failing mind.

Ten feet above the prone comedian Mickey Braithwaite pushed the solid oak desk at which Taffy had once sat — fingers poised over the radio dials like a concert pianist about to begin — so that it rested on the trapdoor. Then, because Mickey was a thorough and diligent man, he piled the entire contents of the room on top of the desk, ensuring that the resulting heap was stable and would not fall away if anyone were to attempt to open the trapdoor from below.

Satisfied with this final execution of his duties, Mickey clambered out onto the flat section of roof where once he had watched the starlings plait together a vision of the future. He looked up, but the sky was obscured by plumes of smoke carrying glowing flecks of the pier away into the night. Mickey hesitated, disorientated by the smoke and the crackling fire. Was this the pier, or was it the smouldering remains of the Salvation Army building? Were the birds chittering and dancing beyond the grey clouds? Where had the protective wall of sandbags gone? Where were Mitch and Norman? Where was his steel helmet with OC painted on it?

"I'm coming," the deckchair attendant whispered.

He clambered onto the ledge at the end of which had once been attached a meteorological box. Mickey remembered the ledge, every inch of it, because Mitch had always sent him to check the thermometer and the air pressure, so the sheer drop to one side, all the way down to the black waves, did not worry him in the slightest. He scampered along the ledge, reached a sloping section of the theatre roof, slid down it, then walked across another flat section and climbed down the metal ladder fixed to the wall of the theatre. He reached the pier's decking just as one of the dressing room windows shattered, allowing a tongue of flame to curl out and up, as though the fire were tasting the outer skin of the theatre.

Without looking back Mickey Braithwaite headed off down the pier towards the resort. He knew he would be the last person to do so, and this made him very sad, but at the same time immensely proud. Was there anyone who had known the pier longer or more intimately than him, after all? They had both been well aware for a long time that this night was coming, long enough to find reconciliation, perhaps even joy, in its outcome, but this did not stop Mickey from weeping every step of his route back to the promenade, or prevent the gentlest of tremors from oscillating back and forth along the length of the pier, like the shiver of a resurgent memory. He heard the first sirens wailing along the promenade, but Mickey knew there was nothing the firemen could do now but contain the fire and prevent it spreading to the town, not when they found that someone had sabotaged the water pipes which led to the end of the pier. They would have to sacrifice the pier for the greater good, like the amputation of a limb in order to save the life of the patient. Mickey understood the necessity of this act; throughout his life, and particularly in wartime, he had witnessed how atrocities could not only be committed but also excused when prompted by a moral imperative. He was also aware that there was a cleansing quality to the fire, a rebalancing, a *symmetry* that resonated deep within him, and yet he could find no comfort in any of this knowledge. All the deckchair attendant could hope for was the reconciliation he sensed lay within an ending, no matter how brutal its cause.

More fire engines had arrived, a cordon had been established around the pier's entrance, and six hoses, illuminated by portable lighting rigs, played over the section of pier closest to the promenade, cooling and shielding it from the inferno which raged out on the water. Mickey stood at the railing with a growing crowd of bystanders, many of whom were either taking photographs or videoing the pier's destruction. His gaze never shifted from the flames, which were reflected in the thick lenses of his spectacles, consuming his vision. The *PIER THEATRE* sign tilted, then crashed down, swallowed in a pile of burning debris. Across the baroque sea he heard a series of off-key wails as the sun lounge's organ was consumed; it would serve, Mickey concluded, as a lament for the man he had lured into the theatre and condemned to death for his sure and certain absolution, the man whose body would now be little more than the blackened, twisted thing that had briefly stalked Bella's dreams. Sammy Samuels had needed to die in order to prevent history repeating itself, and by breaking this pattern also grant a long-awaited release to others still bound to the pier. Mickey knew that somehow, by hammer blow or other implement of creation, the pier had been imbued with a soul, and that it too was now liberated from the ocean's grasp, freed to ride the west wind for as long as it should wish to carry it.

His steady gaze was distracted by a small group of people standing on the beach. A man, a woman and a child, their details silhouetted and hidden by the fire, but Mickey could see the girl's wayward fair hair swaying gently in the breeze; it was also possible to discern that they were all holding hands. Mickey waved, and the girl waved back.

"We can go now," Mickey said.

# Murmuration

The blue-and-white police tape shivered in a strengthening wind. How meagre a demarcation it was, and yet no one crossed its boundary, no one questioned its authority, because they all knew what lay beyond the tape: the remains of two men, caged within the twisted skeleton of the pier. One a comedian, who had been blessed with the ability to create laughter and yet found precious little joy in life, the other a deckchair attendant whose astonishing vision had caused him so much inner turmoil and yet somehow still managed to find delight in almost everything. And as he leaned on the promenade railing, his hands grasping its cast iron with a vehemence that spoke of both love and a suspicion that relinquishing that grip would cause the railing, the promenade, perhaps the entire resort, to vanish, Colin Draper was forced to acknowledge his own part in this tragedy.

Why, for example, had he manipulated Mickey so recklessly, in effect carrying out a potentially disastrous psychological experiment in his obsessive search for the truth behind George and Hannah's deaths? And why had he been so stupid as to think that by pointing out the parallels between Sammy and George's actions he could have prevented anything? Samuels, like most people, regarded history as a completely separate world, whose influence on the present was negligible and whose inhabitants were nothing more than dust and echoes. It was only by careful study, the building of a detailed picture, an *archive,* from many sources, that these people could live again in all their vibrant, bumbling, hopeful, flawed richness. Then they could speak across the decades, or even centuries. Only then. Unless, like Mickey Braithwaite, you were not really of one age or another, but more a conduit linking several together, able to see further than most but denied understanding because its weight would prove unsupportable. And was that such a gift?

"It looks worse than it did on the telly."

Colin glanced to his left and saw a young couple standing at the railing. He had not heard them approach, and it was only when the girl spoke that their presence registered.

"How can it look worse?" The young man said incredulously. "It's a pile of scrap on a beach... it looks exactly the same."

"No, no, I don't mean like that." She paused, attempting to formulate the phrase which would best explain how she felt. "On the news it's just a story, isn't it? You know, like it could be a film or something, but when you see it right in front of you then you know it's for real."

"So you thought it was just a special effect before?"

She thumped his arm. "No, you wanker, it's just... different."

"A pile of scrap's a pile of scrap, Donna. The gippos'll have that away in no time."

"You really don't give a monkey's, do you? That comedian you like died in that fire, you know."

"Who?"

"Sammy Samuels."

"Shit! Did he?"

She sighed. "Weren't you watching?"

"Not really. Shit. Sammy Samuels? We went to see him on my stag weekend. He was fucking hilarious."

"And Mickey Braithwaite," Colin heard himself add. He did not want these two young people to leave the resort thinking that the fire had claimed only one victim.

The man turned to look at Colin. "Who was he, mate?"

"He looked after the deckchairs on the pier. He was very old. He'd worked on the pier since the war."

"They found his body then?"

Colin looked back to the knotted girders and spars which were all that remained of the theatre. "No, but he's missing. Everyone else who worked on the pier has been accounted for, but Mickey's gone. He must be somewhere in amongst all that."

The young woman grimaced. "That's horrible. Come on, Lee, I don't want to stop here if there's a body."

"Spoilsport. I want to watch the cops pull it out."

"He was a friend of mine," Colin said quietly, still looking out towards the theatre.

"Oh, sorry, mate, no offence." He gestured in the direction of the town with a tilt of his head to one side, raising his eyebrows to indicate to the girl that they should go. "Come on, it's three shots for a fiver before seven o'clock. See you later, mate. Sorry about your friend."

"Thank you. Have a nice evening."


The man and woman had only been gone for perhaps ten minutes when Colin heard a great chattering in the air above him. Looking up into the evening sky he saw a vast cloud of starlings pass overhead, low enough to be able to hear their numberless wings rustling like the pages of a book caught by the wind. The birds swooped over the still-smouldering remains of the theatre, arced up into the sky, their flimsy bodies shifting, now solid, now translucent, in a final elegiac pattern, and then they were gone.

# Acknowledgments

My thanks go to Mrs Evans, my English teacher at secondary school who went way beyond the call of duty marking and editing my first attempts at writing, to my parents for their patience and understanding during the years when I was busy collecting rejection letters, and to Lauren, Imogen, Tom and the team at Legend Press for all their encouragement and support.

COME VISIT US AT

WWW.LEGENDPRESS.CO.UK

FOLLOW US

@LEGEND_PRESS